I0664489

The Incomplete Man

Icki Iqbal

Copyright © 2012 Icki Iqbal
All rights reserved.

First published 1.12.2012
ISBN: 0-9570-2663-3
ISBN-13: 9780957026636

DDKM Publishing
Guadaleste, Sandy Way, Cobham, Surrey KT11 2EY
Telephone: 0044 1372 841881

The right of Muhammad Iqbal (a.k.a. Icki Iqbal) to be identified as the author of this work has been asserted in accordance with the Copyrights Design and Patents Act 1988.

Printed by CreateSpace

Dedication
To Zamin, Susie and the one and only Deena

Other books by the same author:

The Tebbit Test
Forthcoming titles:
Cobham Crime-Busters
Apocalypse Wow

Cambridge, Fame Bridge

Friday 20th February, 1976 is a day I will never forget.

It was the day of a debate organised by the Cambridge Union, the university's debating arm; the first in which I was a participant. I met two people who were to play leading roles in my life.

It was my second term and I had settled in well. The lectures were stimulating and I spent most of my spare time listening to debates. I studied and analysed each debater's approach and outcome. Now I had an opportunity to try out my theories.

It was a bitterly cold day. I had experienced cold weather in Lahore and Murree, but this was something else. A chill wind blew from Siberia making one gasp for breath. A new concept called the wind-chill factor made you feel colder than it really was. I also experienced snow for the first time. I had expected having to duck and weave to avoid slabs of ice. Instead I saw innocuous flakes descending at helical angles and settling on the ground as a white carpet.

A below average audience of perhaps forty was assembled. No doubt the weather played a part as the topic was one of considerable interest. There was a lot of chatter and pointing in the direction of the stage. The President of the Union, who chaired the meeting, called it to order.

'Good evening ladies and gentlemen. Thank you for braving the inclement weather to listen to today's debate. The proposition we are debating is, *Society progresses faster when self interest is the guiding principle behind every man's action*. Speaking for the motion is Nick Knights, reading classics at Kings; speaking against it is Majid Khan, reading mathematics at Trinity. Mr. Knights will begin the proceedings and speak for a maximum of fifteen minutes. Mr. Khan will then speak against it, for a similar length of time. I now call upon Nick Knights to state his case.'

Tall, willowy, wearing a beige suit and scarf, with a smile on his face that looked as if it was always there, Nick stood up. Scorning the microphone, he walked to the edge of the stage.

With the audience mesmerised by the prospect of him falling off it, he declaimed to them in short rapid sentences:

'Every man has a duty.

'The duty is to leave society richer than he found it.

'That's why I came to Cambridge.

'What? You may ask.

'For the good of mankind, I will say.

'How? You may ask.

'By becoming very successful myself, I say.

'I measure success in financial terms.

'I mean to become one of the richest persons in the UK.

'I've made a start by coming to Cambridge and by joining the Young Conservatives.

'Now you may think that the twin objectives are irreconcilable.

'Let me tell you something.

'They're not.

'If everyone maximises his wealth

'The shrewdest will accumulate enormous assets.

'Agreed

'But the less well off will progress in their slip-stream.

'There would be a greater concentration of wealth.

'Agreed.

'Doesn't matter.

'The poorer will be better off than they might otherwise have been.

'That is all that matters.

'Everything else is the politics of envy.'

So he carried on. As he spoke I feigned indifference and casually surveyed the audience. People probably thought that I was eying the female talent in view. Not true. I've never been interested in them. I was judging the audience's reaction to Nick's exposé. However I did notice one girl sitting in the front row who seemed to be staring at me. She was of medium height with golden brown hair, warm and friendly eyes, liquid and expressive. As we made eye contact, she smiled. I smiled back, a reflex action. She held her smile in acknowledgment. I quickly turned my face away from her and focussed again on what Nick was saying.

Soon it was my turn to speak.

I didn't want to be a distraction from the message. I therefore dressed to be sartorially invisible; neither smart nor scruffy.

I shunned histrionics and set out my case factually, in measured and, what I hoped were, authoritative tones. I looked at every member of the audience as if I was having a one-to-one chat with that person, a trick I learned from Brother Henderson at St Anthony's, the school where I studied in Lahore.

'Before we engage in the debate, we need to get our definition right.

'How should we measure the progress of a society?

'Is the aggregate accumulation of wealth the be all and end all?

'If it were, I'd vote for the motion.

'But what if another measure's more appropriate?

'Such as happiness or emotional contentment of society as a whole,

'Or social cohesion?

'Would you be so unequivocal?'

I paused for effect before continuing.

'Let me illustrate my point.'

Pause.

'Take the case of road traffic in my native city, Lahore. The roads carry less traffic than the roads in London but traffic jams are endemic. Why? Because self interest is the sole guiding force of every driver in Lahore. If they see the slightest gap in the traffic they will move to fill it,

'Even if it is not their right of way,

'Even if letting another car through could unblock the jam whilst them filling the gap would make matters worse.'

I paused to let the audience ponder the options before making their choice.

'I'm not going to direct you to vote for me. All I would say is that the way you vote indicates the type of person you are, what your priorities are.'

A show of hands showed a majority in my favour visually sufficient for the Chairman not to employ tellers for verification.

I was relieved rather than triumphant. Nick's hamming had left me more shaken than I cared to admit. When the results were announced, the audience clapped and surged forward to talk to the debaters. I gulped down the rest of the water in my glass and decided to go back to my room to reflect.

As I made to leave I was intercepted by the girl who'd been staring at me. I noticed that her golden hair came down below her shoulder blades. She shook my hand warmly and said:

'Hi, I'm Ellen Evan and I'm reading law at Newnham. You're doing maths I understand.'

'Yes,' I replied thinking what an odd name Ellen was. Did the registrar drop his aitches? Should she really be Helen? Maybe she's Helen Heaven.

'I liked your line of argument; seemed to come straight from the heart.'

'It did.'

'A mathematician with a social conscience?'

That seemed unnecessarily provocative and I responded by saying:

'We're not that rare.'

'I thought mathematicians were all logic and no feeling?'

I was being embarrassed by such clinical dissection within earshot of everyone. I mumbled:

'Doesn't stop you having a conscience.'

'Anyway, I knew you'd win the debate.'

'Why?' I asked her.

'Nick was all show and physical presence. You focussed on the issues.'

'All show eh?' said a voice from behind.

Both of us turned round and saw Nick Knights.

'How long have you been listening in?' she asked.

He didn't answer. Instead he said:

'You were staring at me when I was speaking.'

'I wasn't staring at you, I was staring at him,' she replied pointing to me.

'You fancy him over me?'

Before she could answer, he turned to me and said:

'You crafty devil. You manipulated the audience.'

'Isn't that what debating's all about?'

'I don't take kindly to losing.'

'Are you threatening me?'

'No, just warning you. And leave our girls alone.'

Ellen turned round and, one hand on hip waved one finger at him and said:

'You awful man.'

He went away leaving the two of us speechless. It was a minute or two before we recovered our poise. I looked at her without making eye-contact. She was making no effort to say good bye to me.

We walked to a coffee house. I shivered in the cold. She took off her shawl and draped it over me. She then put her arm around me which I initially resisted but gave in when I realised that she too needed to keep warm.

I bought coffee for both of us and sat down and waited for her to sit down. Observing all this, she said:

'Gentlemen usually let the ladies sit and serve them food and drink first.'

I told her that I knew that

'I know it's different in Pakistan,' she said.

'You've been to Pakistan?'

'No, but my parents know a lot about India; they grew up there. I imagine it's the same all over the sub-continent.'

She's been to India? Or was it just her parents? I was keen to find out but was too shy to ask. I suppose the onus was on me to keep the conversation going but I couldn't think of anything to say.

'Ask something,' she said.

Eventually I did:

'I noticed when the debate was about to start, everyone in the audience was pointing at us on the stage. What was that all about?'

'Don't you know?'

'No.'

'They were pointing at you. Everyone's noticed your striking resemblance to Tom Conti.'

'Who's he?'

'Don't you know anything? Haven't you heard of Glittering Prizes?'

'That stuff on the telly?'

'Yes, "that stuff" that BBC's broadcasting on Mondays about Cambridge students. Conti is the hero.'

I've never been able to handle unmerited praise, so I said nothing.

'What made you choose maths?' she asked.

'I like it.'

We talked for an hour; Ellen talking and I listening, mostly, with the occasional close-ended response thrown in. She bought a round of sandwiches for each of us. I insisted on paying but she would have none of it.

Looking outside we could see that heavy snow had settled on the streets and pavements. When we finished our sandwiches, she asked me if I would walk her to her Halls.

'Of course but I don't know the way.'

'I'll be with you silly.'

As we stepped out I realised that I was still wearing her shawl. I took it off and draped it around her.

'No, no, you keep it; you're shivering.'

'Can't do that, you'll shiver then. Let me get coats for both of us; my room's round the corner.'

'Are you inviting me into your room?'

I must have looked embarrassed as she gave me a hug and said:

'There are many ways to keep warm. Yes, let's do that.'

Once inside, Ellen was in no hurry to leave. She surveyed the large study-lounge and moved into the kitchen-diner. Her gaze moved from what I had inherited to the state it was currently in. It was a mess but luckily she didn't say anything. I quickly went into the bedroom and tidied up my bed and returned to the kitchen with my coat and a spare coat for her.

'Call this a room? You should see mine. This is an apartment.'

She was right. Trinity was the richest college in Cambridge.

'Come on, let's go before the snow returns,' I said.

'I could stay here.'

'No you can't, the Porter will kill me.'

'He needn't know.'

Seeing the panic in my eyes, she said:

'Perhaps not tonight, maybe the next time.'

I took her to her room, a fair distance in the snow. I didn't go in.

We didn't meet again over the weekend. I shut myself in my room. I had some serious thinking to do. I'd come to Cambridge to get a good maths degree and become an actuary. By way of diversion I was looking to develop my debating skills and, in the summer, watch a lot of cricket.

Girls didn't enter my thoughts. And here was Ellen making a beeline for me. Heaven knows why. Heaven knows what she sees in me. I should really fob her off but dammit, I was enjoying it. She was stirring emotions I didn't know were inside me. All weekend I wrestled with these thoughts. I was too shy to follow her up but unsure whether I wanted her to seek me out or not.

On Monday evening I went into the Common Room to watch Glittering Prizes. There was a fair crowd and Ellen was one of them. Everyone turned round when they saw me but Ellen came forward and hijacked me and we watched together.

'He's nothing like me,' I protested.

'Yes, he is. You're both wheat-complexioned and have thick black hair and are good enough to get into Cambridge.'

'Yes, but he's quite a bit taller than me and has a deep bass voice and his hair does not fall in clumps like mine; and he's good-looking. Girls obviously fancy him.'

'You're quite dishy too and you're not exactly a midget, what are you, five foot nine?'

She was at it again. So I said to her:

'Nobody's ever called me dishy. No girl's ever chased me.'

'I don't believe it.'

'It's true. Mind you I had no interest in them either.'

Can you imagine a worse rebuff than that? And yet it was one of many that the poor girl had to put up with in the following months One day she asked me:

'OK, you've no interest in girls. What other quirks do you have?'

'Don't know about quirks. I was good in maths and abstract ideas but didn't have much interest in people.'

'A typical mathematician, you mean?'

'Some people said I was autistic. It used to drive my Mum insane.'

'Anything else?'

'I have no sense of smell.'

'That's a big loss.'

'That's what Mum says but I don't see it that way. You can't miss what you've never had or remember having.'

Looking back, Ellen's patience with me was remarkable. I didn't deserve her and she deserved someone better than me. She was very open and talked about most things especially about how she felt about me. I was always nervous being seen with her. Part of the problem was that she was very tactile, always holding my hand or putting her arms around me and often kissing me. I ought to have been happier seeing her in my room but for the risk that she'd ask to spend the night there.

One day, possibly looking for a chink in my defensive armour, she made an intuitive deduction and asked:

'Do you have a sister?'

'No, I'm an only child.'

'You've never had a girlfriend have you?'

I didn't answer. She asked again. I still didn't answer. She then said:

'I suppose it's difficult to have a girlfriend in a segregated society. Did you go to a boys-only school?'

'St. Anthony's was boys-only but that didn't stop boys mixing with girls. Many had girlfriends.'

'So why are you ducking my question?'

That was a tough question to answer and I said so but she wouldn't give up.

'All it requires is one word, one syllable in fact.'

'Yes, but there's an assumption implicit in the answer.'

'Surely that depends on the answer?'

'No, there's an assumption either way.'

'Oh I give up, put me out of my misery.'

'If I say I've never had a girlfriend then that means you're not one; if I say I have then I'm assuming that you're my girlfriend but that would be presumptuous because I don't know how you feel about me.'

Ellen's face glowed as she stretched forward to bring me nearer to embrace me.

'You silly man, that makes two of us as you're my first boyfriend.'

Seeing the look of surprise on my face, she asked:

'What's the matter?'

'How can a girl as friendly and attractive as you not have had a boyfriend before?'

With a look that smacked of triumph, she said:

'You really are opening up today. First I am your girlfriend and now I'm pretty.'

'That doesn't answer the question.'

'Oh plenty of boys have shown interest in me and I've dated a few but you're the first one not to use flattery to get inside my knickers.'

By the end of the term Ellen had made me come out of my shell a little. I began to talk more freely about myself but still not about my feelings towards her.

It was when we broke up for Easter and she went home to Mold leaving me alone that I first realised that I needed her company.

When she returned for the next term, I met her during a break in lectures and took her past Emmanuel College to Parkers Piece. There we watched Cambridge hopefuls being put through their paces by the cricket coach.

'Do you play cricket?' she asked me.

'I've tried but I'm no good.'

Nick, dressed in immaculate creams, was batting with effortless grace.

'How can such a nasty man be so easy on the eye?' asked Ellen.

'He seems a natural ball player with good hand-eye coordination.'

Nick spotted us and came over after his batting session was over.

'You play cricket do you?' I asked.

'Not really, just having a net. Golf is my sport.'

'You seem to be good enough at cricket. Some people have all the luck.'

'You two still together? I thought I'd asked you to stay clear of our girls.'

'Who cares what you say, you pompous pig,' said Ellen.

'Ah, he's corrupted your language already?'

'I always use language appropriate to the listener.'

'Ah, a hussy with a tongue. You can keep her. You two deserve each other.'

Nick walked away, leaving a furious Ellen to have a go at me.

'What kind of man are you? Why do you let him insult you so much?'

'Why should I descend to his level?'

'But he was insulting me; shouldn't you be fighting my corner?'

'I'm no good at instant responses. Don't worry, we'll prevail.'

She might have been the one to make the first move but by the end of the first year, I seemed to seek Ellen out more often than she me. I always seemed to have more time to spare than her.

'How do you get away with studying so little?' she asked.

'Ah, that's the beauty of maths. It's all about concepts. Those who get it, find it straightforward; those who don't struggle endlessly.'

'With law you have to learn a whole universe of law and precedents, there are no short cuts.'

'What made you choose law as a career?'

'I haven't'

'But you're studying law?'

'With the aim of joining the police force.'

I was puzzled so she continued:

'I used to read Erle Stanley Gardner a lot, far more than Agatha Christie. We also had a school trip to the Chester law courts.'

'Did you live near Chester?'

'My parents live in Mold which is not that far from Chester. I studied at Queens in Chester. What was I saying? Yes, I went to the law courts where the trial of two men charged with armed robbery was taking place. Not much happened while I was there but I followed newspaper reports. They both got off as the police were found guilty of planting evidence. Two years later they were caught committing another robbery.'

'That made you interested in law?'

'I wanted to understand the legal process, how it struck a balance between being fair to the accused and protecting society. I wanted to study law and join the police. What do *you* plan to do after college?'

Study law and become a copper? I had trouble picturing her as one. I couldn't imagine brutal thugs taking any notice of her.

'You don't have to be a thug to deal with one,' she said reading my thoughts.

'How do you join the police?'

'I've got an interview in the summer holiday at their office in Hendon.'

I was thinking this over when she asked:

'Anyway, what'll *you* do after college?'

'Become an actuary and work for an insurance company.'

'What's that?'

'What's what, an actuary or an insurance company?'

'I know what insurance is, silly.'

'It's the profession that deals with the mathematics of uncertainty and risk.'

'I'm sorry I asked. Why did you choose it?'

'Uncertainty fascinates me.'

Ellen was quiet, probably wondering whether what I said was profoundly meta-physical or trite. Detecting her confusion, I said:

'Ever since I was a child I listened to my mother talking of God this and God that. He seemed a humourless autocrat hell-bent on meting out punishment. I couldn't bring myself to like such a self-centred individual. I couldn't even believe that such a guy existed.'

'What's that got to do with uncertainty?'

'I could ignore Him entirely and live the life I chose rather than one He dictated.'

'Why don't you?'

'What if I'm wrong? One way of dealing with uncertainty is to behave as if he existed. It's a form of insurance'

'I call it hedging your bets.'

'It is.'

'I don't understand why that drove you to become an actuary. Anyway, you could have picked a better industry. Only estate agents have a poorer image.'

'I know people think insurers turn down claims by relying on the small print. I'll do what I can to improve its image. Mind you I'll be doing financial analysis not looking at sales or claims.'

Ellen looked as if she was none the wiser, but let the matter rest.

I'm not sure why but at the end of the first year I was elected President of the Union. With that piece of good news I flew back to Lahore for the summer vacation. My parents, Daud and Fatima, were at the airport to receive me. Seeing them together I was reminded of the nursery rhyme about Jack Sprat and his wife. Mum still looked, to quote my irreverent friend Akbar, like a 'well-built six-footer who'd been flattened down to five feet. She was grossly overweight and waddled like a duck, all the time chewing *paan*, the stuffed betel leaf so popular with the older generation. People say that she stank as a result although I wouldn't know.

Dad, with his ramrod straight posture and handlebar moustache, looked every inch an active Brigadier, with the clout that goes with it, but was in fact retired. He whisked me through immigration and customs. His driver brought his air-conditioned car round and took us to our home in the cantonment area. This was an area developed by the British for their people to live in comparative comfort some distance from Lahore City where the locals lived.

Since independence the leafy St John's Park houses were taken over by the Government and let out to its civil servants and the military top brass. Dad occupied one from 1957 to 1972 when, in anticipation of retirement, he bought a smaller house in the same area. I travelled by bus from here to St Anthony's when I studied there.

Dad believed that life should not be too easy for a child and would not allow me to go by car; a view not shared by Mum, who would ask the driver to drop me at school whenever Dad was away.

Whether their contrasting styles made me a well-balanced person or a confused one is for others to say.

We entered the drive through the left-hand gate and the sweeping veranda, which ran along the front of the house, came into view. The old plantation chairs and floor-standing electric fan were still there. The faithful old cook was there to greet me. Chuffed at seeing his former charge return, he was getting ready to serve lunch, my favourite, lamb chop. After a quick shower I had lunch in the air-conditioned dining room, a redundant electric fan hanging from the tall ceiling on a long stem.

The baking summer heat confined me indoors and I only caught the tail end of the mango season. All my friends were back from their colleges.

It was strange that Akbar was a close friend as he was so unlike me, extroverted, good at sport modest at studies and fond of girls. It was widely rumoured that he had cheated in the A-level exams. He had won a place in an obscure US University in Stillwater, Oklahoma. Quite possibly he'd join the army and end up running the country.

Full of life and bonhomie, he came to visit me. Aside from boasting how good life in the US was, he was mainly interested in whether I was still on the sexual wagon.

'Are you still a misogynist?' he asked.

'I never was.'

'You've never gone after girls'

'Doesn't mean that I dislike them?'

'OK, I used the wrong big word. Are you still celibate?'

'Is that all you've learned in Stillwater, big words.'

'Aha, you're evading the question. You've got a girlfriend now have you?'

'You're wide of the mark.'

'You still haven't got a girlfriend?'

'I keep telling you, you're wide of the mark.'

'I get it; you've got a girlfriend but you're still a virgin.'

'You're jumping to a false conclusion from a dodgy beginning.'

'*You've* not changed, still talking in riddles. What dodgy beginning?'

'You asked if I was still celibate. That assumes I was celibate to begin with.'

'Oh come on, you've never known a woman in Lahore.'

'That's what you think.'

'You're playing on words. By knowing I mean had sex with.'

'Grow up Akbar. I can't believe that we were mates.'

That was the end of the conversation and we didn't meet again.

I had plenty of time at my disposal as life was very un-taxing. I'd only been away a year, nine months actually, but Lahore looked a different place. The comfortable lifestyle of the upper middle-classes living a cocooned existence in the Cantonment area seemed alien after the egalitarianism of university life. Lahore hadn't changed so maybe I had. I shunned company. Only twice did I go out, ostensibly to the bookshop but in reality to a public call box to phone Ellen. A worried Mum asked me:

'Are you unhappy at Cambridge?'

The question caught me by surprise but the answer was still 'No.'

'Why are you shutting out your friends and family?'

I shrugged my shoulders in denial.

'Oh yes you are ignoring us. Why?'

'Maths is difficult, Mum.'

'There you are. I told you not to waste time debating.'

'It's not a waste of time.'

'It is. You've got to change. Go talk to your Dad.'

'No.'

'Won't talk to your Dad?'

'No, I won't give up debating.'

'Why not?'

'I enjoy it, I'm good at it and I've just been elected President.'

'But you're no good at maths.'

'Leave it Mum.'

Later that evening Dad placated me, saying that Mum meant well. My problem was that she doted upon me, pampered me, fussed over me. I guess that as I was her only child, complications at the birth of my stillborn younger brother ensuring that, I kind of became her reason for living. Some would have found her overbearing but I had lapped it up.

Not any more. I began to find her intrusive and opinionated. She always wanted things her way.

I daren't admit it but I was missing Ellen. I missed her warmth, her tenderness and her affection. In many ways she was like Mum; obsessively tidy, fastidious about hygiene, devoted to me. She couldn't phone me as I had not given her my number. But she wrote regularly, twice a week, sometimes more often. Mum brought her letters round and had the irritating habit of hanging around to see me open it. I'd take the letter from her leave it on my desk and carry on doing whatever I was doing.

'Aren't you going to open it?'

'I'll get round to it. I'm busy.'

'Who's it from?'

'It's a boy from college.'

'A boy wouldn't write so often.'

'Mum, it's a boy from the debating club.'

'How do you know, you haven't opened it.'

'I recognise the handwriting.'

'But it's a girl's handwriting.'

'Wait till I tell him that.'

'You haven't got a girl in Cambridge have you?'

'No Mum.'

'Is that why you're so quiet? Are you missing her?'

'Stop it Mum. I don't have a girl.'

'Have you talked to your Dad about it?'

'No, stop it Mum.'

'You won't talk to your Dad.'

'I talk to him all the time. I don't have a girl. Stop it.'

'I understand. All the English boys have girls but you don't. Don't worry, as soon as you've got your degree we'll find you a good bride.'

'Stop it Mum, I don't want a girl.'

I was glad when it was time to return to Cambridge.

When I returned to Cambridge I was moved out of my first year apartment and given one that was in a quadrangle with rooms around the perimeter surrounding an inner courtyard. It looked very impressive and students craved for lodgings there but there was a snag. Bathroom and toilets were communal. I wasn't keen but I had to take what I was given. I wasn't expecting much post and didn't check until late afternoon after I had settled in, on my way to see Ellen. I was surprised to see a note from her asking me to meet her between 11 and 11.30 on that day in Trinity Lane. She'd be in a Land Rover.

It was too late as it was past three o'clock. So I went to Newnham to find her. Sure enough she was there.

'Where were you? My parents had come to see you.'

'I've only just seen your note.'

'I guessed. You know what parking's like in Cambridge. They had to go home but you have an invite to spend Christmas with us.'

She then asked:

'How was Lahore?'

I explained that it was hot and it was a dull place without her. Worse, I had to put up with Mum, whom I found increasingly irritating. She knew that as I'd told her in my letters. She wanted to know something more pertinent:

'Have you told her about me?'

'No, not yet.'

'Why not?'

'They expect me to be celibate.'

'You are celibate, so far.'

'You know what I mean.'

'No, I don't.'

'There's far less hassle if they think I don't have a girlfriend.'

'I see.'

She was dissatisfied with that answer so I said:

'Don't worry, it'll sort itself out.'

She looked at me suspiciously, 'You're not ashamed of our relationship are you?'

'Look, Mum's a force of nature. I don't know what she'd say. Like I said, it'll sort itself out.'

She wasn't convinced but I switched subjects.

'You haven't told me how you got on in Hendon in your police interview.'

'I passed,' she said, sparkle returning to her eyes, 'but it was a close run thing.'

'What happened?'

'The test is in two parts, physical and mental. I'd have failed the physical test if the minimum height had been five foot five instead of four. The mental test was a piece of cake. It's rare for them to take on a graduate so they'll place me in the CID wing after I'd first done the rounds. I have to wait to find out where I'll be placed.'

***

As the new President of the Cambridge Union, I read extensively about the achievements of my predecessors to see what traditions should be maintained and what new grounds I should break.

One day a first year student came to see me. Save for the fact that he had Semitic rather than Punjabi features (although I didn't then know what Semitic features were), he was very similar physically to me; about five foot nine or ten, with a heavy mop of black hair, lively eyes and slim build although he was a little heavier and his hair was light and wavy whilst mine fell in clumps. He spoke with a London accent.

'Majid Khan, I presume?' he asked.

'Correct.'

'I'm Ishtak Brownstein. I want to join the Union.'

'You're welcome.'

I introduced Ellen to him as my girlfriend, the first time I'd used that phrase. I asked Ishtak what his debating credentials were. He reeled off his record at school. He then asked how he should get started.

'Undergraduates are an argumentative and pedantic lot. You'll find them arguing in bars and coffee houses. That's where they get started. You should do the same,' I said.

I then explained how the Union could help. At this point we were joined by another fresher.

'I hope I'm not interrupting anything.'

He was an Indo-Asian, lighter-coloured, taller and more sturdily built, with eyes that seemed to bore right through you.

'I'm not sure, we may have just finished. Whom do you want to speak to?'

'You, I think. I'm Jalal Babar and I want to join the Union.'

'Come and join us.'

Jalal explained that he was from Rawalpindi, Pakistan. Like Ishtak he too excelled in school debates. He was attracted to the legal profession and wanted to become a barrister. He added:

'I'm an unorthodox Muslim, I mean I was born a Muslim but am a non-practicing one. I don't eat pork or drink alcohol but I don't insist on halal meat and don't observe Prayers.'

'What a lovely expression, "unorthodox Muslim". Well, I'm an unorthodox Jew,' said Ishtak. 'I don't eat pork but am not precious about kosher food. My mother was brought up in a convent and we've always celebrated Christmas.'

Ishtak and Jalal struck up a rapport and throughout the winter saw each other regularly. They always seemed to be arguing with each other. Some of these were on points of law covered in recent lectures.

More often they discussed the history of the Middle East and the common ground and differences between Jewish and Islamic faiths. They were incapable of having a mundane conversation without changing it into a debate. Their addiction to pranks provided a further bond between them.

One afternoon Ellen came to my room sobbing. I asked what happened and she said that she'd been made a fool of in public.

'Who did?'

'Ishtak and Jalal.'

It was several minutes before she calmed down enough to tell me what happened. Apparently Ishtak and Jalal spotted Ellen walking into Woolworths. They followed her into the shop and, with an authoritarian voice, Jalal said to her,

'OK, you've had your fun, let's go now.'

He took hold of her by her arm to lead her out, Ishtak lending him discreet support.

'Go where?' she asked.

Several heads turned to look at what was going on. Jalal turned to the store manager and said:

'It's alright, we've got her under control; we'll take her back.'

'What do you mean under control?' asked Ellen, struggling to free herself. 'There's nothing the matter with me.'

Jalal turned to the store manager and said:

'Denial; it's a common problem with schizophrenia. We've got several like her in Addenbrookes.'

'Leave me alone, I'm not schizophrenic; you're no medic, moron.'

Moments later Nick Knights who was busy going somewhere turned a corner and came fully into view. Ellen shouted:

'Help me Nick. Tell them who these imposters are.'

Nick looked at her and then looked at Ishtak and Jalal, and asked:

'What's the problem?'

Jalal said:

'She's a schizophrenic just escaped from Addenbrookes.'

Nick looked at her and said:

'So that's where she's from. I knew there was something wrong with her,' and walked off.

Jalal then turned to Ishtak:

'Come on let's take her back.'

He grabbed Ellen by the shoulder and Ishtak by her legs and, as she writhed and screamed, they carried her out horizontally.

The store manager provided additional support until they were out of the store premises. At that point, Jalal turned to her and said:

'Thank you we can manage from now on.'

He and Ishtak carried Ellen a further twenty yards and turned right, out of view from the store. They then put her down:

'Hope you enjoyed that, we did.'

She was hoarse by the time she finished telling me. It was the first time I had seen her lose her poise and she looked vulnerable but at the same time lovely. I comforted her and asked her what she wanted me to do to the two pranksters. She wanted them reported. And what about Nick? She wanted revenge but would bide her time. I said we'll talk it over in the morning. I took her to her room and stayed with her. I made her coffee, forgetting that she took no sugar. Rather than annoying her it put her in a better mood. She was used to my incompetence and felt comfortable with it. In a strange sort of way, I felt good. I was helping her out rather than the other way round.

By the evening she was beginning to see the funny side of it and was ready to forgive when Ishtak and Jalal came round to apologise; but not Nick, not that he bothered to come round.

Ellen had often talked about taking our relationship a stage further and making love. She was reluctant to go on the pill for fear of side-effects and I was too shy to go to a chemist. No would I let her go to one as people would deduce that we were an item.

'Don't be daft,' she said. 'They probably think we do it anyway.'

Still I wouldn't allow it. On this day when my comforting her had changed into something more passionate, she was frustrated at having to pull back from the brink.

'That's it,' she said. 'During the Christmas break, I'll see my GP and go on the pill.'

I took Ishtak and Jalal under my wing and taught them how to debate. Both had a scattergun approach releasing a volley of arguments in uncontrolled bursts. I encouraged them be more selective and have three or at most five key points. I talked of the importance of voice modulation and how and when to play to the gallery.

By the end of their first year both had become better debaters but voice projection remained a problem for Ishtak. Their styles were different; Ishtak was more cerebral whilst Jalal tended to be more histrionic.

The first formal debate in which they faced each other was a searing experience for Ishtak. The topic was, *'Decimalisation has been good for the economy.'* Ishtak, speaking for the motion presented a tightly argued case with masses of factual evidence in support. Jalal began his attack by saying,

'Ladies and gentlemen, I won't bore you with a load of facts which, for all you know, may be fiction.'

Ishtak immediately stood up, nostrils throbbing and dilated in anger, but was not allowed to speak as he'd had his say.

Nineteen seventy seven was a wet summer. One week when we had a dry spell, everyone basked in the sun, students, residents and college staff. Busy and bustling as ever were the tourists, American and Japanese mainly; the former concentrated on names in various honours boards to see if their surnames appeared on it; the latter were serial photographers and trophy collectors. A whole crowd of them had gathered outside King's College chapel when Jalal pulled out a gun and, to the sound of a pop, shouted,

'Die you bastard,'

Ishtak collapsed in a heap and blood flowed out of him in intermittent torrents.

There followed half an hour of chaos with the Japanese, in utter confusion running randomly and wailing in high pitched voice. Two students overwhelmed Jalal, which was easy as he was not resisting. Instead he smiled, 'It's a joke' and pointed to Ishtak who had got up and was removing his shirt and wearing another that he was carrying in a bag.

Their gag of using a water pistol and exploding ketchup bag didn't go down well with the authorities who were worried about its impact on the tourist trade. They were intent on expelling both and it took some determined pleading from their tutors, abject grovelling by Jalal and Ishtak and, a good word from me, to save them.

I took up the offer to spend Christmas at Ellen's parents' cattle farm in Mold in North Wales. Her father, Gareth, came in his Land Rover to pick us up. He greeted me with genuine affection and seemed to know a lot about me. He didn't seem to have any particular accent, certainly not a Welsh one. He looked quite tanned and was stockily built with brown wavy hair. He looked like a Welsh farmer who spends most of his time out in the sun. We talked all the way to Mold.

'What route are you taking,' I asked.

'It doesn't matter they're all equally bad. I told Ellen not to go to Cambridge, Oxford is much easier.'

'So which way are you going?'

'I'll find the M1 going north, catch the M62 somewhere near Hull, travel east and then drop down south on the M6.'

'That's sort of three sides of a rectangle instead of going straight down a diagonal.'

'Ah, but at least the three sides are there. There's no diagonal road and this way I get more time with you.'

'Shouldn't you be petitioning for one?'

'No use, not many people from Mold want to go to Cambridge.'

'So it's my fault is it?' asked Ellen.

'Yes, but if you hadn't, you wouldn't have met this young man.'

Four hours later, we left the M6 for M-something-or-the-other, still under construction, and then less busy A-roads and left those too for some dirt tracks. Eventually we reached a large house with several outbuildings. On the gate pillar was a wooden name plate carrying the words *Croeso Evan Plas*. Although it was dark I could read it as a little light shone on it. I couldn't however see very far. Gareth and Ellen, more familiar with the terrain walked towards the front door. Almost as if someone had shouted *Open sesame*, the door opened and the outside lights came on and suddenly everyone was visible. A middle-aged lady, darker than Ellen but otherwise very similar stood there with a smile that was Ellen's prototype. It was Glynis, her mum. She too had golden brown hair but it was short.

'I could hear the sound of the wheels on the shingled drive,' she said and then, upon seeing me, greeted me warmly and gave me an affectionate kiss on the cheek and said:

'Good to see you, I've heard a lot about you.'

'Not all bad I hope,' I said.

'On the contrary...'

'Stop it Mum, he neither praises nor takes praise.'

'Ah, I forgot that he was a mathematician,' said Glynis with a smile.

It was a large house made of stone rather than brick. The rooms were tall and difficult to keep warm. Certainly the hall was on the cold side of comfortable. We went into the lounge which had a hearty log fire.

'It's quite late,' said Glynis. 'Do you wish to freshen up and I'll serve dinner.'

'Ellen said that you grew up in India. Is there Indian blood in you?' I asked Glynis over dinner.

'Ah, you've noticed my dark skin. Yes, there is going back a few centuries.'

'Ellen said you are cattle farmers,' I said to Gareth.

'That's one way of describing it. Actually we're wholesale butchers. We have our own supply of cattle but we also buy them in.'

'Buy carcases in?'

'Oh no, we do the slaughtering. That's what our business is all about.'

'Where do you buy them from?'

'Mainly Ireland,' and seeing the incredulous look on my face he added, 'We buy live cattle but we import carcases. We have a slaughtering service in Ireland.'

'Must require a lot or organisation and control.'

'It was tough to begin with but the business is now a cash-cow, as business schools say,' said Gareth.

'Do you eat halal meat?' asked Glynis.

'I do,' I replied, 'but I don't only eat halal meat.'

'We specialise in halal and kosher meat.'

'What's the difference?'

'None really other than the words you utter when you send the animal to its doom.'

'Is that the only difference?'

'In terms of process yes, but Muslims, Asians really, eat mutton and rarely buy beef whereas Jews, English mainly, eat lamb and beef.'

'Are there many Jews in the North West?'

'There are conurbations in Manchester, Leeds and Liverpool.'

'And Muslims?'

'Oh there are far more Muslims in Lancashire, mostly around the old cotton mill towns. I do far more trade in halal meat than kosher.'

'He's not training to be a butcher,' said Glynis to Gareth.

'I'm curious,' I said. 'What made you go into this business and why are you acceptable to the more orthodox?'

'We're Jews and come from a family of butchers, or at least I do,' said Gareth.

'You do know we're Jews don't you? Hasn't Ellen told you?' asked Glynis

'She hasn't actually but that's probably because it never came up.'

'Does it worry you that Ellen's a Jew?'

'Not particularly.'

'Good to hear that. We're not particularly religious.'

'Me neither'

We sat talking late into the night. It was very cold but a log fire was burning and there was brandy, which I savoured for the first time and which kept my inside warm.

I stayed there for six weeks and had a really good time. I was shown the cattle farm (that was what they called it but actually it was largely sheep) which was thirty miles further into the heart of Wales. We went for walks and for drives. I didn't fancy the walks as it was very cold. North Wales is beautiful Ellen kept telling me.

Neither of us made any attempt to hide our closeness. We were sharing a single room anyway and her parents must have thought we were closer than we were. In fact we stayed celibate until well after Christmas. Ellen had gone to see her GP the day after we arrived but decided to wait until she'd had a full course before putting its efficacy to the test.

We returned to Cambridge late in January. As winter gave way to spring and blossoms appeared on plants and the cricket season commenced with the annual ritual of renewed hope, people noticed a change in me; 'thawed a little' according to my lecturer, became 'more normal' according to Ellen.

Certainly, something had happened and I can pinpoint fairly accurately when it did. Actuaries will tell you that just because one thing happens after another does not mean that there is a causal relationship between the two. So I won't jump to conclusions but I can at least get the chronology right.

The change happened whilst we were in Mold although it took me a little while to realise it. Looking back, it happened after the second time we made love.

The first time was a hit-and-miss affair between two novices. Akbar's taunts, which I won't repeat, paralysed me and it required all of Ellen's patience, and guiding hand, to help me through the mechanical process of love-making.

It was acutely embarrassing and disappointing for both of us. The following day, seeing our subdued demeanour, Glynis must have thought we'd had a row as she kept observing us waiting for tell-tale clues. So Ellen and I went out for a drive into the countryside.

She remarked, to no one in particular, how beautiful the Welsh countryside was. I noticed nothing.

We drove into Shrewsbury whose charms Ellen extolled but was lost on me. We came back in the evening and dined in the Star of Simla. I was hungry and went straight in but Ellen seemed to step back before entering.

Whatever the reason for that, we had a good meal. We analysed what happened the previous night. Perhaps sex wasn't all it was cracked up to be. Rather like the emperor's new clothes story everyone claims that the earth moved for them as that is what they were led to expect and they daren't admit that it was different for them.

'You're right,' said Ellen. 'Remember the film *The Last Picture Show*? That's exactly what Cybill Shepherd and Jeff Bridges did.'

'Dead right, they didn't even do it.'

'Hang on, if you fall off a horse what should you do?'

'Get right back on it?' I said confused by the change in subject.

'Come on let's have another go,' said Ellen.

That night we did. I will not attempt to describe it but when I woke up the following morning I had the twin sense of liberation and bonding. Liberation, from whatever it was that inhibited me in the past; bonding, in the sense that we felt in complete union with each other, physically and emotionally.

Whatever the cause, in the weeks that followed, I discovered a new sensation. I didn't know what to call it as I'd not experienced it before.

I said to Ellen that the flowers in the garden had a new vibrancy, it gave rise to a new sensation. It was a pleasant feeling.

'It's the Welsh air,' Ellen said. 'It disorientates mathematicians.'

'Your jokes are worse than mine,' I said.

She clearly didn't know what I was talking about but one day she had a thought.

'You haven't got your sense of smell back, have you?'

'Is that what it's called? How would I know?'

'I don't know but I guess that's what it is. If flowers are giving out a pleasing feeling then that's probably fragrance.'

'And you? Are you fragrant as well? You certainly are more pleasing today.'

'That's fragrance too but it's the new perfume, not me.'

'Very nice too. Yippeee I've got a sense of smell now.'

'There's only one way to be certain.'

That evening she took me back to the Star of Simla.

'Let's see if you notice any difference.'

As I opened the door I was overpowered and I recoiled back onto the street, into Ellen behind me, actually. It was like walking into a strong current.'

'Good, now you know the smell of garlic and garam masala,' said Ellen.

'Bloody hell is that what it is.'

'That's a pungent smell. You've definitely got your sense of smell back.'

Was this what love was all about? Akbar never mentioned the effect it had on your nostrils. To a person accused of being autistic and with no sense of smell, the earth may not have moved but it had certainly changed. To celebrate the event Ellen bought me an after shave and for herself, but for my benefit, a bottle of Chanel No. 5.

She hoped that more changes would come to make me a 'complete man.'

'So I was an incomplete man was I?'

'You were I'm afraid. I cannot lie.'

She didn't mind my being colour-blind in the orthodox sense of the term but it annoyed her that I didn't notice colour.

Who cared about colour? I had to come to terms with the sensuality of smell. I had to understand it first. What mechanism or chemical regulated it?

How can someone get the faculty if he doesn't have it? How do you lose it if you have it? Can I lose what I've just found? Surely someone in the science or medical faculty in Cambridge ought to know? I've got a year left in Cambridge so I have plenty of time. Let me enjoy the newly found faculty.

I was like a baby. Every day brought a new experience to savour. Fresh snow in the morning, cow pat on the field, freshly baked bread, stale stilton, falafel, a fairly frequent snack in the Evan household, Ellen in the morning, Ellen after a shower, exhaust fumes, log fire.

But how do I communicate my joy? I had to have the same vocabulary as the rest of society so that when I describe the smell of a particular slab of stilton as 'rancid' for example, people will understand precisely the smell I was describing. I asked Ellen to guide me. To my surprise I could detect a wider gradation of smell than she. All flowers had a pleasant fragrance to her. She did accept that a rose and a tulip had different fragrances but they were both pleasant. Her nose calibrated smell to the same degree of detail as mine now did, but her stock of adjectives was limited.

I saw more of Cambridge in the spring and summer. I went punting, went to Grantchester walked amongst the orchards. Although on the whole I was better off with the sense of smell restored there were disadvantages. Ishtak often smelt of falafel and Jalal of sweat. I moved from serial coffee-drinking to not liking its smell. My Maths tutor reeked of alcohol. I used to devour the free peanuts on offer in the pub but now I could smell traces of urine in them. But these were minor disadvantages. Rather like the long-case clock whose chimes at night you learn to ignore, I soon came to disregard body odour.

***

Early in the final year various employers came to Cambridge to entice promising students. I accepted the offer from Camelot Life, part of Camelot Insurance Group, one of UK's largest insurance companies. Although its head-office was in London, later on in the year it was shifting its administrative headquarters to Bristol. A juicy grant from the Regional Development Agency had played its part in tempting Dan Dawes, the Chief Executive who happened to be from the West Country.

Bristol was described to me as a fast-growing city close to the M4/M5 intersection providing ready access to both London and Mold. I liked the set-up. The city seemed big enough to satisfy a townie like me although I hadn't visited it.

Having sorted that out, I wanted to have at least one debate that people would never forget. I discussed several topics with Ellen. It had to be controversial for it to achieve enduring infamy. Some of the topics that we tossed around for consideration were:

Abortion should be made legal
Recreational drugs should be made legal
British monarchy should be banished
British monarchy should pass to the first born regardless of gender

We rejected all of them as, depending on the outcome of the debate, the Union would be branded 'left-wing' or 'right-wing' and become a distraction from the message. Then one day, listening to Ishtak and Jalal playing devil's advocates with each other gave me an idea.

I thought of a debate on the motion, *This House Believes that the Creation of the Modern State of Israel Was Unlawful.*

'I thought you wanted to be controversial?' asked Ishtak

'I do, and I want you to speak for the motion and Jalal to speak against it.'

'Why would we want to do that?'

'Look, doing it the other way round will prove nothing. This'll stir things up.'

'It'll do more than that. My lot will disown me. I won't do it.'

'This is a debating society. There is no better test of a person's debating skill than to be able to successfully argue a line he didn't believe in.'

'That's not what my lot would say.'

'Look at it this way. At present the two communities completely mistrust each other. Each is utterly convinced that they're in the right and the other wrong.'

'What else do you expect?'

'They can't both be right. If both of you play devil's advocate and do so cogently then both sides might see that the other has a point.'

'Yes, it might help open their eyes, but my Mum will be dreadfully upset. I'm not interested,' said Ishtak.

'Why don't you ask her?' I asked. I then turned to Jalal and said:

'You've not said anything.'

'Don't care about the PLO and other groups but threats of physical assaults would worry me. I'm a coward. Don't like the sight and smell of blood, my blood.'

Smell of blood? I wondered what that was like. I should go and talk to an expert about smell, but later.

'You're stupid. You'll have no peace if you say that. Does your Dad know about this?' I said to Jalal.

'No.'

'I thought so. Listen, I suggest you sound him out on my proposed debate. If he doesn't like it then I'll abandon it.'

Having kept quiet so far, Ellen now joined in.

'Are you crazy? All three of you will be assassination targets.'

'Don't say that. He'll say it's a price worth paying,' said Jalal.

'Well, I'm not paying it,' said Ishtak.

Ellen turned to me and said, 'They're sensible, not cowards.'

Exasperated by it all, I said:

'It's only a college debate, not a UN resolution. When did a college debate ever change the world?'

We argued for a while, three against one. In the end I said that if Ishtak's Mum and Jalal's Dad vetoed it, I'd abandon the idea.'

'What if one did and the other didn't?' asked Ellen.

'We'll still abandon it.'

That night Ishtak phoned his Mum and to his surprise, she encouraged him to participate in the debate. She reasoned that there was no way the motion would succeed. That being the case, he might as well use it as a test of his debating skills. That encouraged him and the following morning he said to me:

'Count me in.'

Jalal hadn't phoned his Dad but seeing Ishtak change his mind, he changed his.'

I looked at Ellen and asked:

'We have lift-off then?'

'I'm not happy about it. It's your show, you do what you want.'

Confused, I eventually abandoned the idea but Ishtak would have none of it.

'Are you mad? I've told Mum I'm doing it and I shall do it.'

'That's that then,' said Ellen.

Indeed it was. They set arguments aside and moved forward.'

I didn't have to publicise the event, just stick a notice in the Junior Common Room.

The Cambridge University Union

On Thursday 1ˢᵗ December 1977 at 7pm there will be a debate on the Motion:

"This House Believes that the Creation of the Modern State of Israel Was Unlawful"

Speaking for the motion: Ishtak Brownstein

Speaking against the motion: Jalal Babar

Moderator: Majid Khan

The first of December amounted to six week's notice. One morning I saw a student, walking to his lectures, when this item on the notice board caught his attention. Suddenly he stopped, probably thinking that Brownstein was a Jewish name. That student, a fresher, was the son of the Times' leading political commentator, he could sense a story here and he followed it up after the morning lectures.

He left a note in my pigeon-hole and eventually met me in a coffee house. No, the Notice hadn't got it wrong. Ishtak, a Jew, was speaking for the motion and Jalal a Muslim but not a Palestinian, against it.

'Both of them love a good argument and often try to argue a case they don't actually believe in.'

'But surely it is better for each side to argue from conviction?'

'What'll that prove? Nothing. This is not the United Nations. What we're proposing is far more challenging and newsworthy.'

'You bet it is. Can anyone attend, even non-students?'

'Yes, it's a free house.'

That evening he phoned his dad who got quite excited.

'This is a disaster waiting to happen. They'll both try to lose. The one who is worst at it will win. Come on, let's give it some publicity.'

He put a small news item in the Times. It was picked up by the entire world it seemed. The British, US and Middle Eastern media all gave notice of coming to witness and record the debate.

When the programme committee met again a week later it emerged that Ishtak had a letter from The Jewish Board of Deputies asking him to pull out or failing that to throw the debate.

'Are you changing your mind?' asked Jalal.

'Not bloody likely. I don't like being asked to throw the debate.'

'You'll be on your own. I'm backing out. I've had forceful letters from a number of Islamic organisations and a threatening one from the PLO.'

'Before you do that you'd better phone your Dad or write to him and find out his views,' I said.

Next day Jalal changed his mind.

'Did you speak to your Dad?' I asked him.

'Yes I did. He said, I'd shown courage to announce that I'd take part but will need greater courage to go through with it. But it was a worthwhile cause.'

'What cause?' asked Ishtak

'Bringing two blinkered communities together. So I thanked him for his support. It was just what I needed. Let's go for it.'

As the day approached, I was being hounded by the media practically on a daily basis, sometimes taking overseas calls in the middle of the night; at any rate taking flak from the Porter who had to field them. Concerned that the spotlight was on me rather than the debate I stood down as the moderator and persuaded Ellen to take over the role.

'So, you're putting me in the firing line?'

'No, it can still be my neck; I won't announce the change or reprint the posters.'

Ellen mulled over the options and decided to do it. This freed me to concentrate my energies on improving the debating skills of the two protagonists. The content had to be theirs but I could improve their delivery.

Through a cousin of Ishtak, I got in touch with a Voice Coach. She spent several hours with him and taught him the theory. The rest was down to practice.

Jalal's delivery was good and he had good presence. I had to make him tone down his natural desire to play to the gallery and to focus more on the content.

With the debate just a week away I knew that journalists from the Times, Telegraph, Mail, Guardian, and representatives of the embassies/High Commissions of the USA, UK, USSR, France, Germany, Egypt, Saudi Arabia, Syria, Jordan, Iraq' Lebanon, India and Pakistan as well as the United Nations would attend. Neither the Government of Israel nor the leadership of the PLO had said they would be sending a delegate, but they could still turn up.

As I'd said anyone could attend I had no idea how many would come in all. Eventually the day arrived.

Both friends prepared the way they would prepare for exams. Jalal was up all night revising one more time, thinking through all possible questions that might come up. Ishtak believed in keeping a clear head and spent the night watching two films, Exodus and Spartacus. The debate being at 7pm, they had the whole of the day to get through.

The railway station was busy as a steady stream of visitors arrived. Dignitaries arrived by car and had to deal with the usual problem in Cambridge, where to park.

Adding a shot of tension was the presence of security. They tried their best to be unobtrusive, but this was difficult as they were all in uniform. The seating in the auditorium was egalitarian, folding chairs made of metal for all. I sat in the back row unobtrusively observing the proceedings. The hall was filling up with a mixture of students and guests. It was easy to see which was which because of their age and gear. I noted that Nick, not a regular at debates, was attending. On stage was a table with three clear jugs filled with water and three glasses. Seated behind the desk were Ishtak, Ellen and Jalal.

'Good evening ladies and gentlemen,' began Ellen. 'Thank you for coming in such large numbers in many cases from very far, on a cold cold night. We hope that the quality of the debate will warm you up. The proposition we are debating is, *'This house believes that the creation of the modern state of Israel was unlawful.'* Speaking for the motion is Ishtak Brownstein, from King's; speaking against it is Jalal Babar, also from King's. Mr. Brownstein will begin the proceedings and speak for a maximum of fifteen minutes. Mr. Babar will then speak against it for a similar length of time. The debate will then be thrown open to the floor for half an hour. There will then be a show of hands. Tellers will then count the votes. There are 256 people in the audience. Please vote either for or against. You can abstain if you wish but please don't vote for both. Is that clear?'

A chorus of 'Yes' came back in response. Ellen then said,

'I now call upon Ishtak Brownstein to open the proceedings.'

'Good evening ladies and gentlemen, or should I say Shalom,' began Ishtak.

At this point the Times' political correspondent and his son entered the hall. The son spotted me. He came towards me and asked,

'Why aren't you on the stage?'

The entire audience turned back to watch what was happening.

That was the last thing I wanted, so I quickly disappeared, using a circuitous route, to the toilet in my Halls of Residence, where I locked myself in.

The following morning Ellen came round and said,

'You missed a fantastic evening. You should have sneaked back towards the end.'

'Who won?'

'It was a dead-heat and I refused to use my casting vote as a draw was fair.'

'What arguments did they use?'

'I'll get hold of their talks. Basically Ishtak said that the tribes of Israel had occupied the Promised Land for less than 5% of the biblical estimate of how long man had been on earth, so they had no legal claim on it. Jalal used the more emotive arguments of a persecuted race requiring a settled home and Europe wishing to atone for its past atrocities.'

'Exactly what I wanted to hear.'

'Its front page news in all the papers. Look,' she said showing copies of the Times, Telegraph, Guardian and Mail.

My face was splattered across newspaper pages. One particular photograph, which came to adorn my study, showed the two debaters flanking Ellen at the centre.

***

Ah yes, smell. The problem was getting up my nose. I'd been so busy with the debate that I hadn't followed it up. I now turned my attention to it. I got hold of a thesaurus but that was of limited help: fragrant, bouquet and aroma for good smell and stench, reek, stink for foul ones, odour and smell were neutral but generally used in a non-complimentary sense.

I observed what words people used in everyday speech and I also read a great variety of novelists. I noticed that people used analogies to achieve greater distinction between smells. 'She's as fragrant as a rose' might work when describing a girl but try using that to describe the smell of a rose. You get into tautological territory.

Ellen brought me back to earth saying:

'You're a mathematician not a linguist.'

'But precision of description is important to all,' I pleaded.

We were both right of course.

Rather than find someone in the medical or science faculty, I went to Heffers the academic bookshop, and spent an afternoon browsing. I learned that there are smell receptors in the upper part of the nasal cavity. How the brain decodes the chemical signals is not fully understood. Nor is the cause of loss of the sense of smell. Obviously if the receptors are damaged or non-existent that would be an explanation but my case was not mentioned. I then talked to the Dean of the medical faculty. He mentioned that a typical human can detect up to 10,000 different smells but would struggle to name them.

It looked as if I had better cherish my new found faculty and develop my own vocabulary.

***

The preparation for the debate and its aftermath, my obsession with understanding the sense of smell and the increasing amount of time I was spending with Ellen had its downside.

Having been on course for a first, I slipped badly in the third year to finish with a low second, what they call a 2:2. Ellen also slipped but still managed a 2:1. Ishtak and Jalal hosted a farewell dinner for us.

'You two are like brothers,' said Ellen. 'A year from now you'll leave Cambridge. Will you stay in touch?'

'With each other or you two?' asked Jalal.

'Well, each other first.'

'Well, I'll go back to Pakistan but we're committed to finding a solution to the Middle East problem so we'll stay in touch.'

'How about you two?' Ishtak asked Ellen and me.

'Our jobs may keep us physically separate but that's all,' said Ellen.

'Yes, we're inseparable,' I said.

'You'd have to be blind not to notice that. I meant, what's your take on the Middle East problem.'

'You know me, I'm apolitical. Yes, I'd like it solved and like you I think its best solved locally. But there are other trouble spots, my own sub-continent, the whole of Africa, the Balkans, Communism generally.'

'So you're ducking the issue.'

'No, I lack the dedication and duplicity necessary for politics. I'll stick to using the UK insurance industry as my canvas for bringing social justice.'

'You'd rather be a little fish in a little pond then?' taunted Jalal.

'Steady on, isn't it better to make the most of what you're good at? Isn't that the best thing to do rather than everyone trying to do the same thing whether they're good at it or not?'

'There speaks a woman in love. I was only winding him up.'

'We'll stay in touch though,' promised Ellen.

'So will we,' said Ishtak and Jalal in unison.

On our way back to our rooms we bumped into Nick. Nick turned to Ishtak and Jalal and said:

'It's been a pleasure knowing you both. Do stay in touch. Here's my parents' phone number which will do until I get my own place.'

He didn't say that to Ellen or me but I congratulated him on getting a first.

'I usually get what I set out to achieve,' he replied.

'What are you doing next?' I asked.

'Start work. I'm joining Camelot Life as a management trainee.'

'I'm joining them too as an actuarial trainee.'

'You got a 2:2 didn't you, is the offer still valid?'

'It was an unconditional offer. I guess our paths will cross again.'

'Well, who'd have thought,' he said offering his handshake. 'No doubt we'll see a lot of each other.'

And turning to Ellen, he said, 'And you too.'

Ellen and I spent a few precious days together in Mold before our careers took us our separate ways. She had just received her first sets of police uniform. She wore one pair and showed it to us. I must say, she looked quite fetching in it. Whether she thought the same I wouldn't know but she spent a lot of time in front of the mirror. I suspect it was more an expression of joy at the realisation of a dream than any narcissism. My only concern was that she looked so attractive that people might see her as an object of beauty rather than the face of authority.

We tested it out the very next day. We went for a drive in the direction of Shrewsbury, We were reluctant to go into the town as she was not on duty. We pulled up at a service station and went into the restaurant for a coffee. People turned to look at her but we couldn't establish why. So we were none the wiser.

When the day arrived we had a tearful parting.

'I'll miss you, you silly thing. I'll miss your corny humour, your company,' said Ellen.

'I'll miss you too but we'll be on the phone every day.'

'It won't be the same.'

How right she was. I'd miss stroking her long golden tresses, her twinkling eyes, her silken-smooth skin, the way she mothered me, her fragrance, yes her fragrance, her everything. I should've said all that. Instead, I said limply:

'You'd better go before traffic builds up,' pointing to Gareth who was waiting to take her to Hoylake. I then left for Bristol.

***

Ellen was placed in Hoylake police station on the Wirral peninsula, the tongue of land trapped between the mouth of the river Mersey and North Wales. She rented a room in West Kirby overlooking the Dee estuary. The location was pleasant. There were daily sightings of windsurfers. In the distance was Hilbre Island with its collection of rare living birds.

But after the bustle and stimulation of Cambridge it was a dull existence. Nothing much happened at work and even less when she was back in her bed-sit. There was no space for her books or CDs, which were in Mold. All she had was long chats with me. Her parents were only an hour's drive away in Mold and I at the most three hours away in Bristol. She couldn't afford a car so her parents and I visited her regularly.

She wanted to work with state-of-the- art technology and support but, having been to a police station for her initial interview, she had an idea what was in store for her. Nevertheless it was still a shock. One mechanical bell for a visitor to ring, if there was no one at the front desk. One spare room, which housed three policemen. It also doubled up as the interview room. One ancient Remington typewriter, whose keys were so stiff that they had to be struck really hard. One toilet, that had to be shared by all. A felt-and-cork notice board which carried information regarding rotas, cases going to court, etc. etc.

Her handler, the person responsible for supervising her training, was a kindly man in his fifties.

'So you want us to stop planting evidence?' he asked after hearing her reasons for joining the force.

'I never said you did.'

'These things happen. Not often, but they do; when we know that someone is guilty but is likely to get off.'

'Are you saying it's OK to bend the rules if the end justifies it?'

'Wait until you've been doing this job for ten years before forming a view. It may not change but it'll be based on experience.'

There were only half a dozen people at the station and Ellen was not just the only probationer, she was also the only female. Scouse humour, at the best at times, has a cutting edge but Ellen found that in the police-force this combined with a macho attitude to give razor-sharp sexist sarcasm. Without her handler's staying hand Ellen could well have been overwhelmed.

At the end of the second week I spent the weekend with her. Perhaps because it is a narrow peninsula, the temperature was equable. It seemed to rain a lot and a grey mist hung throughout. She had seemed very down in the dumps but brightened up on seeing me. She missed me as much as I missed her but she felt it more acutely because life in Hoylake was so dull. She said to me:

'I've had enough of this. Shall I resign and join Camelot's legal department?'

I tried to talk her out of it. I thought she might regret giving up on her lifelong ambition. Besides, things could change after probation. She was however insistent so I agreed to check with HR.

I did that when I got back to work only to find that legal department was in London. So I persuaded Ellen to stick where she was and made sure that we met every weekend.

Her job was boring. Mostly she was asked to patrol schools and fetes and go on the daytime beat in nearby shopping areas. All pretty routine, but in certain localities there was no respect for authority and the uniform seemed a liability; although Ellen didn't try exercising authority without the uniform. I suspect it would have been harder.

It was not always routine; there was the occasional drama. Once she accompanied the traffic police and they saw a lady-driver speeding on the M56, the motorway that runs along the length of the Wirral like a vein in the tongue and links up with the M6 which goes north from Birmingham towards Leeds. They gave chase but the lady accelerated further and linked up with M6 going north. They followed her, siren blazing and signalling her to stop. She did a further twenty miles before stopping, but only because she had run out of fuel. The car turned out to be stolen and she was given the routine caution:

'You're not obliged to say anything but if you do, everything you say will be taken down in writing, and may be used in evidence against you.'

Ellen got ready with a notepad, only to hear the car-thief say:

'Well in that case you'd better stop hitting me on the head with your truncheon?'

Ellen burst out laughing. The car-thief looked at her sternly and said:

'So you think it's funny to see your officer-friend hit me on the head?'

Streaks of fear snaked through her body as Ellen suddenly realised that she might have compromised a potential conviction. Her colleague was more relaxed.

'We'll let the court be the judge of your antics madam. We've got your blood alcohol reading.'

Back at the station Ellen was given a talking to by her handler not to fall into traps and to be professional throughout.

On another day when she was minding the front desk a middle-aged lady walked in and handed a small satchel.

'Where did you find it?' asked Ellen.

'I was walking from West Kirby towards Hoylake station when I heard a car coming at great speed. I looked round and there was an old Sierra being driven at speed. He slowed down when he saw me and the passenger threw this satchel out of the car towards me and said, *"Hey look after this. I'll be in touch to collect it. Phone me at the number on it."* They then sped away and I saw another car following them.'

'I see. Why have you come to us?'

'Well, I didn't know what to do. I looked in the satchel and there was a brown envelope and it felt as if it contained a bundle of notes. I'm scared it might be stolen and I don't want to get involved. It looks as if one lot is chasing the other for it.'

Ellen called in her handler's help and the matter was taken out of her hands. The bundle contained £50,000. It took them a year to trap the people involved.

One day a young man hobbled into the station and rang the bell. Ellen went to see him.

'The pavements are dangerous, do something about it.'

'Write to the local Council, we're the police.'

'I want you to record it. I've just tripped over a loose brick at the bottom of Stanley Road.'

'Any damage?'

'I've only twisted my bloody ankle, might have broken it. No, no damage.'

'You should get it seen to. Go to Arrowe Park Hospital and have it X-rayed.'

'Don't tell me what I have to do. Just record the complaint.'

'There's nothing to record. Arrowe Park will deal with it.'

'Do what I say, you tart.'

'That I will record, you swearing at a police officer.'

He leant forward and grabbed her by her shirt collar. Ellen range the bell with great force and her handler rushed out quickly.

'Leave her alone.'

An explanation followed. The handler recorded the meeting and warned him against threatening a police officer. He then explained to Ellen that this was a fairly common ruse to claim compensation.

On another occasion Ellen had to deal with an old lady in tears. Her son had bought her a brand new Mini and she had to go to the showroom in Liverpool to collect it.

As she drove it home, the car conked out at the mouth of the Birkenhead tunnel and she couldn't get it restarted. A young man seeing her in difficulty went up to her and said,

'I've had the same problem with my Mini. Shall I sort it out for you?'

The lady got out and he got in. After a moment's fiddling he got it to start and kept going, leaving the lady without her car.

That was the sum total of the interesting stuff in her two years that she told me about. She was glad when the probation was over. Early in 1981 she was given her first posting as a police officer based in Kilburn, North West London. She would henceforth be part of the Met. Together we scouted the area for accommodation and settled for a bedsit in Hoveden Road, Cricklewood. It was a Victorian detached house which had a lounge, reception room, breakfast room and kitchen downstairs and two double and two single bedrooms upstairs. Every room had been converted into a double or single bed-sit and the kitchen and toilets were shared. Early morning it was a bit like Waterloo station.

Ellen was not the first policewoman at the station; there was another in her thirties but she was plain-looking and behaved like a bloke, maybe as a defence mechanism.

The atmosphere was macho-male, the language coarse. She was in for a tough time, Ellen thought. We had long conversations on the phone every evening. Most weekends, I drove up to meet her, usually spending Saturday night with her sharing her bed, a single bed. On weekdays I would travel up by train and meet her at a pub in Paddington station, where we'd spend a couple of hours together. We never bothered to remember the pub's name. It was always 'the pub', an inadequately lit saloon with brown (or was it red?) sewn-on leather padding, coloured windows, stale beer and insipid pies. The place smelt of tobacco.

Practically the only thing going for it was that it was right there when I got off the train.

***

In October 1978 I joined Camelot Life. Nick Knights' taunts still ringing in my ears, I resolved to complete the actuarial exams quickly to regain lost ground.

It was a surprise to find that Bristol had none of Mold's pastoral beauty. In fact it had no defining character, or more precisely it had compromised its character. It used to be a city built on trade with the new colonies, in tobacco, cocoa and slaves; a city of grand buildings and alms houses, of the Elizabethan church, St Mary Redcliffe, and the Victorian Clifton Suspension Bridge and of lovely stone built houses. But these are interspersed with modern soulless buildings. The Regional Development Agency had been too successful in attracting financial services companies each relocating its staff to the city and surrounds. 'Immigration' brought a rich variety of accents. It was not uncommon to hear the impenetrable Bedminster accent, broad cockney, estuary English, guttural Welsh accent and Black country vowels all in the same supermarket. Four insurance companies had, or were about to relocate to Bristol and all had chosen to be at or near Broadmead: Sun Life, Clerical Medical, London Life and Phoenix. Camelot had chosen a site in Frenchay. When I got to know the city, I realized that it was a strange choice as the financial centre was where the other insurance companies had congregated. The grant must have been skewed in favour of Frenchay.

Practically all male staff, and quite a few female ones as well, had relocated from London the previous year when Diane Doors, a cheeky pun on the Chief Executive's wife's name, Camelot's brand new building in Bristol was built. So the office had the atmosphere of an immigrant community and the bulk of the conversation was sharing experiences looking for new plumbers, electricians and gardeners etc. the HR Department had a huge street-map of Bristol and surrounding areas showing which employee lived where. They wanted to prevent a repetition of the experience of one colleague, who had bought a house next door to his boss's.

Diane Doors was a curious building. It had huge double doors at the front, with an enormous rounded handle on each. The forecourt that preceded it had two five foot pillars hacked out of stone which surrounded a boulder embedded in which was a sword.

The overall impression was of a Druid place of worship; although the business end of the building was ultra-modern. Each floor, and there were eight of them, seemed a hundred yards long, perhaps that's an exaggeration but they were long.

Actuarial department was on the third floor. There was a toilet at each end, one for gents. Coffee vending machines were located at each end, near the toilets and a third one near the centre.

Lunch was in the canteen, referred to as the 'Dining Room' in a separate building nearby. I was to discover later that the eighth floor was the dining room for managers and directors.

After renting for a year I bought a small two-bedroom flat in Frampton Cottrell a small village to the north-east of Bristol, beyond the M4 and relatively close to the railway station.

In May 1979 I voted Conservative at the general election which swept Maggie Thatcher to power. Ellen teased me saying that I had sold out my social conscience but I felt that the country needed a Government.

By the summer of 1980 I had completed my exams and become an actuary. One of the first persons to congratulate me on qualifying as an actuary was Nick Knights. He phoned as soon as he read about it in an internal memo.

'You blighter, you made it.'

'Yes, the blighter made it.'

'I suppose I'll have to take you seriously now.'

'Not on my account, only if you have to.'

'Oh I must.'

The first task I then undertook was to look at how long pensioners lived. As Camelot was guaranteeing each of them an income for life, the longer they lived the less money Camelot made out of them. If they lived too long Camelot lost money. The analysis I carried out showed that one of them was one hundred and eight years old. Should Camelot grit its teeth and congratulate her; or was this evidence of fraud, some-one collecting pension when the pensioner was long dead? They didn't know and this was a concern. As a result Camelot introduced a certificate of existence, a form where the pensioner declares that he or she is still alive and signs (or places a thumb print) to that effect. Everyone over eighty had to sign it but the initial workload would be spread over five years. In order to keep the annuitants honest, there'd be random checks.

Around the time I became an actuary, Dan Dawes retired as Chief Executive. His replacement was Tim Fredricks, the Sales Director. Tim had made his name with a series of stunning business deals in the general insurance side of the business after some early success in life assurance. He made a rousing speech talking of a new era where merit and achievement mattered more than age and seniority. He also said that he'd asked HR to identify some high-flyers for fast-tracking.

A year later, he called me and fixed up a time for a chat. It was to be on a Monday morning. I travelled up on Friday night and stayed the weekend with Ellen. She'd been in her job for over a year. The work was very similar to those she carried out in Hoylake; perhaps a bit more fracas and drunkenness and a little less theft. But she didn't like the atmosphere and was impatient to join the CID. We talked a lot mostly about her. We didn't get round to wondering why I was called for a meeting. Bed-time was necessarily cosy as we had to share the single bed.

On Monday morning I went up to meet Tim Fredricks. It was my first visit to our head office, where the directors and certain functions such as the investment and legal departments work from. The office was in Bartholomew Lane behind the Royal Exchange and close to the Bank of England. Within Camelot the building was known as 'MewLane'.

MewLane was old-fashioned and suggested solidity, security and permanence, images that are appropriate for an insurance company. In his office, Tim looked the part. An old style desk and chair to work on, a mahogany bookshelf with glass doors behind him, a spare round table with four chairs for meetings and deep plush carpets; understated opulence.

'We've hand-picked four people to fast-track progress to higher ranks and you are one of them. You should have a rosy future but it is largely down to you,' said Tim.

'I'll do my best, Mr Fredricks,' I said, looking up to Tim, not because he was the boss but because, at six foot three, he was six inches taller.

We were both seated but as much of Tim's height was in his trunk, he seemed even taller. Tim's towering physical presence and booming voice commanded attention even in large gatherings.

'I respect clever people because I'm not clever myself. But I tell you something. Nothing beats hard work except good luck. It is more important than cleverness or connections.'

'I agree.'

'But always remember what Gary Player said.'

'I will, as soon as I've found out what he said.'

'Don't you know what he said?'

'No.'

'He said, "The harder I work, the luckier I get." Look at me, my father was a docker, who died young. I couldn't go to University and worked my way up starting at the bottom rung of sales. At each level I was the best and they had to promote me. Now, this year, I was promoted to Chief Executive.'

'I'll do my best.'

'Good. As a first step I suggest that you move out of your comfort zone of numbers and see how the company deals with people. I'm transferring you to the claims department where you'll be under the guidance of Phil Bunyan.'

I had met Phil once. He was a dapper pipe-smoking man in his early forties, pernickety, even fastidious in his work.

I was promoted to manager status, a change which entitled me to my own office, albeit with transparent walls, and a (shared) secretary. I moved out of the actuarial department where I'd enjoyed the company of other maths graduates and the use of the first desktop PC that Camelot had purchased. I joined the claims department which had neither and relied exclusively on paper files. It did, however, deal with real customers.

I was unhappy about a move away from financial analysis to claims but Ellen reminded me that I'd joined the insurance industry as it appealed to my social conscience. What could be better than to hand out money to grieving widows?

She was right of course. I resolved to use my time in the claims department to get closer to customers, to understand their needs and try to align Camelot's products and services to it.

So it was in a positive frame of mind that I went to my first day in the claims department.

Modern Methuselah?

Keen to show some initiative, I decided to personally carry out some of the random checks on pensioners who had completed and returned Certificates of Existence. I selected three names at random. One was Frank Butcher who lived in Barking, Essex; the second was Anne Smith, a lady aged one hundred and two living in Hartlepool; the third was Choudhry Karnail Singh, aged ninety-seven and living in Chandigarh, India.

I dealt with Frank Butcher first and was astonished to discover that Frank's annuity had commenced in 1925, nearly sixty years before. Nobody would surely reach one hundred and twenty, I thought to myself. I was sure that it was a fraud. So I examined his file and discovered that he was only eighty-two. How can that be? This was fraud quite possibly with the collusion of a member of staff.

I talked about it to nobody, keeping the coup to myself. Taking a day's holiday I went to London and then on the District Line to Barking. From there I took a cab to the address but asked the driver to drop me at a road nearby as I wanted to 'surprise an old friend.'

It was an unprepossessing terraced house in an unprepossessing street but both the road and the house were tidy. A clean white Ford Escort, probably ten years old, was parked outside the house. The owner clearly was house proud and diligent. When I rang the doorbell, after a delay an old lady answered.

'Good morning, does a Frank Butcher live here?'

'Yes he does. Who are you?'

'I'm from Camelot Life Insurance Company.'

'What's the matter? Has anything happened to our son John?'

'John Butcher the accountant?'

'Yes what about him?'

'He's your son?' I was more convinced than ever of a fraud.

'Of course he's my son. Come in, you're confusing me, talking in riddles.'

I took off my shoes and went inside the immaculate three bed-room house. They must have had a late breakfast as there was a smell of bacon in the hall.

'Now explain to me slowly, whom do you want to see, my husband Frank or my son John? John lives in his own house and Frank's just popped out for his daily pint at the Cock and Sparrow. He'll be back in half an hour. Would you like a cup of tea?'

'That would be nice thank you.'

She disappeared into the kitchen and returned ten minutes later with a tray carrying a cup of tea and a plate with three digestive biscuits.

'You've had a long life together as a retired couple.'

'Frank's been retired longer than we've been married.'

'Really? How did that come about?'

'When we first started going out together Frank was a very active person. He cycled everywhere, played good quality football. He had a trial with Leyton Orient but didn't follow it up. There was no money in football in them days and we wanted to get married.'

'Then something happened?'

'All of a sudden he became tired and, what's the word, listless. We thought nothing of it but then he started coughing and developed chest pains. We took him to the doctor and he diagnosed TB.'

'He caught TB in his twenties?'

'Yes, it shattered us. Mum put strong pressure on me to break off our relationship. I must say, Camelot were wonderful. They retired Frank on full pension at the age of 23.'

'You got married after that?'

'My God, what a palaver that was. Mum did everything to stop it happening. She said, "I can understand you marrying a sick person; I can just about understand you marrying a pensioner; but a pensioner with TB? Are you out of your mind?"'

'I suppose that made you even more determined?'

'I wasn't going to desert my Frank; not when he needed me most. No, we got married.'

'And you've lived happily ever since.'

'Frank was in a sanatorium for a year. When he came out we got married and he convalesced at home for another year. Not having to commute in the rush hour, his health recovered and he led an active life. Our son John is an employee of Camelot. He's approaching retirement now.'

As predicted Frank arrived in half an hour smelling of dry roasted peanuts. I had to think on my feet.

'Hello Frank I'm from Camelot Life. I've come to congratulate you. You hold the record for the longest period for which someone has received pension from Camelot. Fifty seven years. It's quite possibly a record for the whole of UK.'

'I should be thanking you for paying it for so long.'

'That's what we're here for.'

'I suppose I'll keep the record for ever. They've licked TB haven't they?'

'It'll be a long time before they beat that.'

'Hang on,' said his wife, 'Frank's not finished yet.'

I returned home chastened. I didn't disclose to anyone, other than Ellen, what I did with my holiday and resolved to be more careful with the next one I investigated which was Anne Smith.

I called up her file from the archives and read every page. In 1941 when she was fifty, a pension of £800 pa was settled on her, which must have been an exceptionally good pension then and to receive it from such a young age. What's more, it had grown to £5,243 pa which was more than the rise in cost of living. Reading further, I found that she was the ex-wife of a wealthy soap magnate and the pension was part of a divorce settlement.

Confident of my facts, I drove to Ellesmere Port. I went across the gleaming new Runcorn Bridge so reminiscent of the Harbour Bridge in Sydney. It seemed out of place, what with several industrial chimneys billowing out smoke. The smell was foul. Beyond Runcorn I arrived at a small village and, with some local help, found the address. The house was in what appeared to be a working class estate; not what I'd expected of the wife of a soap magnate, even an ex-wife. The house itself was better than those around it; a detached house surrounded by terraced ones. An old Jaguar, not the current design but the previous one, was parked in the drive. Unusually for the street, the house had a burglar alarm. Perhaps she'd fallen on hard times and the pension was a major source of her income.

When I rang the door bell, a lady answered.

'Can I speak to Mrs Smith please?'

'That's me.'

The lady looked too sprightly to be a nonagenarian. Whilst I was no judge of a woman's age she didn't look over sixty to me.

'Mrs A Smith?'

'That's still me. What do you want?'

'Mrs Anne Smith?'

'No, Angela Smith. There's no Anne Smith here. My mum was called that but she died ten years ago.'

'But this is her address, what are you doing here?'

'What's it got to do with you?'

'I'll tell you but you answer my question first.'

'I told you I'm her daughter. I inherited this house on her death and my husband and I moved in.'

'Well I'm from Camelot Life. I shall have to report you to the police for theft by falsely claiming that your mother was still alive.'

'What are you talking about?'

'We paid a pension to Anne Smith which should have ceased on her death. It has been falsely claimed by you after her death. You claimed that your mother was still alive.'

'I never said that. You send quarterly cheques made payable to A Smith. That's my name. I married a Roger Smith so that my married name didn't change from my maiden name. I thought the quarterly cheques were something my mum set up for me.'

'Nice try Mrs Smith. We'll let the courts decide on that one.'

The following day I mentioned my success and was commended by Phil who asked:

'Ellesmere Port? How did you put up with the smell from the industrial effluents?'

'You've been there have you?' I asked.

'I grew up in Merseyside. I'm a scouser.'

'Yes the stench was unbearable.'

'We used to avoid Ellesmere Port like the plague. My first girlfriend came from there and for years I thought all girls smelt the same.'

Angela Smith's case did not take long once it got to the courts. She pleaded guilty and was directed to return the pension falsely claimed with interest plus a further punitive fine of £25,000. A custodial sentence was not given.

***

One evening, I got back to my flat feeling quite tired after an uneventful but busy day. I poured myself a stiff drink, quickly drank it, poured another one and had a shower and settled down. I was going to grab something to eat out of the fridge before phoning Ellen when the doorbell rang.

I recognised him as a neighbour who lived across the road. We often waved to each other from our cars. We met once and he knew that I was in the insurance business.

'I wonder if you can give some advice on an insurance related matter?' he asked.

'I'll try,' I said and let him in.

'It's my 21year-old son. He drives a Morris Minor.'

'Is that the car with a massive floor-mounted gear lever?'

'That's the one.'

'He's been meaning to replace it but couldn't find any buyers. So he bought a new one and was on the point of scrapping the Minor when it got stolen. The police found it in Portishead, some twenty miles away and it had been completely burnt out.'

'That's not my area of expertise. Tell me the whole story and I'll check it out for you.'

'The insurer declined the claim.'

'Why?'

'He only has Third Party, Fire and Theft cover As the car was first stolen and then set fire to, they say that the loss is from Theft and Fire but the policy covers Fire and Theft.'

'That seems specious to me. I'll check it out for you.'

The next day I checked with Phil Bunyon. He had to take his pipe out of his mouth as he spluttered into laughter on hearing the story.

'Am I missing something?' I asked.

'They're trying it on. They're declining the claim because of some reason or the other but are not prepared to spell it out.'

'They might be thinking that his son set fire to a car he couldn't sell.'

'It happens all the time.'

I relayed that message and let him fight his own battle. He turned up again, a fortnight later.

'Did you sort out your son's claim?' I asked him.

'You were right, it was a try on. They came clean and said that they believed that Andrew had deliberately set fire to the car.'

'He didn't?'

'Of course not but how could he prove that he didn't? Nor could they prove that he did. We argued for ages then we settled for half the amount Andrew claimed.'

'We'd have done the same.'

'You insurance companies are short-changing honest customers.'

'Maybe, but it is a direct consequence of crooked customers short-changing us.'

'Nonsense.'

'Believe me, fiddling insurance claims is rampant, anything from overstating burglary loss to more sophisticated crimes.'

'Yes, yes.'

'So you agree with me?'

'Don't be daft. My family alone has suffered many times. Aside from Andrew's car we've had three claims turned down.'

'What were they?'

'Loss of camera whilst on holiday.'

'You said there were three claims?'

'Yes, they all related to the loss of cameras.'

'You mean we turned down the same claim three times?'

'Are you always this thick? Its three separate claims, for three separate losses.'

'This I've got to hear. What happened?'

'We go fishing a lot and each time a camera fell into the lake or river.'

'This happened three times?'

'Four times actually. The first time they paid up.'

'I'm not surprised that they turned down all subsequent claims.'

'They paid the smallest claim and turned other ones down. Do you think that's fair?'

'Why were the other claims larger?'

'Each time I lost a camera I bought a bigger and better one.'

'Well that's not how the insurer would have seen it. It sounds suspiciously like a fiddle. Most people would take care the next time, if their camera fell into the lake. Is it the same insurer who insured your son's jalopy?'

'Yes.'

'You're damn lucky they paid out what they did. We'd have black-listed you.'

I showed him the door.

***

My next visit was to Chandigarh, not far from Amritsar, in India. I decided to visit him over Christmas.

I asked Ellen if she fancied coming. She wanted to know why I was going.

'We've been paying a pension for yonks to a Choudhry Karnail Singh,' I said.

'Is it a big one?'

'It started off small but with the inflation of the past thirty years, it is worth £1200 every year.'

'Doesn't sound much, what's the problem?'

'It's not the size that's the problem although it's a princely sum if you live in a village in India. He's ninety-seven and not many Indians live that long.'

'Hang on, he retired thirty years ago, you said?'

'In 1950.'

'He must have worked for several years to get a pension. Were there Indians living in England in the thirties and forties?'

'Haven't heard of Queen Victoria's Indian paramour?'

'That's apocryphal.'

'Maybe, but there must've been an Indian on the premises, for the story to have legs.'

'Anyway, tell me about this chap.'

'He worked for the General Manager of a large chemical firm. We know he was illiterate. He was possibly a cook. That's as much as I know.'

'I get it, you suspect that someone else is claiming the pension and the real guy is dead. Give the guy a break. He might still be living.'

'If he is, great, that's what insurance is all about. But if he's not then its fraud.'

'But it'll cost you more to investigate it?'

'A fraud is a fraud. If unchecked it can spread like cancer.'

Luckily, Ellen had most of her year's holiday entitlement outstanding and she was able to have most of December off. I established that whilst Camelot wouldn't pay for her travel they wouldn't object to paying for a double room.

We set off for India in the first week of December. As we settled into our airline seats, Ellen asked:

'Why now, why didn't you check all these years?'

'Don't ask me why. We only introduced the certificate of existence form last year and Choudhry returned it only last month. Look, here it is.'

I took a document out of my briefcase and showed it to her.

Ellen studied it.

'It's not signed.'

'We accept thumbprints from the illiterate.'

Choudhry had clearly taken good care of it as the paper was still crisp and un-creased. Ellen sniffed it.

'He must have signed it in the kitchen. There's a faint smell of vinegar. Can't you smell it?'

'Of course I can but I didn't know it was the smell of vinegar.'

We flew to New Delhi and from there took a local flight to Chandigarh. It was not what Ellen expected. The temperature was distinctly chilly when we arrived in the evening. Most men were wearing sleeveless sweaters, some had draped a large shawl, almost a blanket across them and most ladies did the same. Chandigarh looked a new city, a sort of Indian Milton Keynes, except that there were plenty of pedestrians and rikshaws, unlike MK which pays homage to motorists alone. From Chandigarh airport we took a taxi to Choudhry's address which turned out to be on the outskirts of the city. We hired the taxi for a day so that we could return by it.

As we emerged from the taxi a pleasant fragrance (of jasmine, according to Ellen) was seeking to overpower the putrid smell of overflowing waste. The latter was winning. I commented on how foul India was compared to Pakistan but Ellen said she was not sure. Why? Because I had no sense of smell then but I do now. I felt foolish making a basic mistake like that.

I'd given no indication to Choudhry that I was coming. When I knocked on the door, a young boy in a white shirt and khakhi shorts, his hair tied in a bunch at the top but without a turban, came and asked in Punjabi, *'Kainoon chayeeday?* (Who do you want to see?)'

'Choudhry Karnail Singh.'

'Us naam da koi nahin yahan (no one by that name lives here.)'

'Hum un ko har mahina paisa bhejtay hain (But he does, we send him money every month).'

'Ithay baithoh (wait here)' replied the boy as he let us into what was the lounge and then disappeared.

The lounge was clean tidy and tastefully but sparsely furnished. The three out-side walls each had a window which was open revealing a grill, which given its narrow pores, must be to keep flies and insects out. Two planter's chairs took the pride of place on either side of a settee. A black and white television was in one corner and a radio next to it.

A glass cabinet set in a recess in the wall contained family photographs and ornamental chinaware. In the top right hand corner was a silver urn and a silver mug.

A middle-aged man came and, speaking in Punjabi said:

'My father's out?'

'That little boy said that nobody by the name of Karnail Singh lived here.'

'How many kids know their great-grandfather's name?'

'When will he be back?'

'Not for a few days. He's gone to Amritsar with a friend.'

'You're his son are you?'

'Yes, he's my father.'

'You're not at work? Are you relaxing?'

'No, I'm Toba Taik Singh.'

'Pardon?'

'I said my name is Toba Taik Singh.'

'According to our records, your father is ninety-seven.'

'Yes, he keeps himself mentally and physically fit.'

'Really? What does he do?'

'He walks to the library every day and back. It's a brisk two miles both ways. There he reads papers.'

'He can read can he?'

'Of course he can.'

'Then why does he use a thumb print rather than a signature?'

'His hand is not steady enough to reproduce the signature of ten-twenty years ago.'

I'd run out of questions to ask and looked at Ellen for inspiration but found none. I then said:

'We're here for another five days. When did you say your father's coming back?'

'I didn't. He goes for a week, sometime two. We only know when he's back.'

'We're keen to meet him. Let him know that I'll be back before I return to England.'

'OK.'

'Actually, I've never seen your father. I can't go back without seeing him but I might run out of time. Have you got a picture of him?'

'Not a very recent one. I've got one taken some ten years ago.'

He went across the room to the glass cabinet and took out a framed photograph and showed it. I studied it and showed it to Ellen.

'OK, we'll be off.'

We left. In the cab we talked softly so as not to be overheard by the driver.

'It's very strange,' said Ellen. 'Family ties are supposed to be stronger amongst Indians. Yet they allow a ninety-seven year old go away for days on end.'

'Not if he's already dead.'

Ignoring that remark, she asked, 'Did you notice a faint smell?'

'I did but I couldn't place it.'

'It was like formaldehyde but it can't be?'

'Why not?'

'You wouldn't find it in a house. It's the stuff they use in mortuaries.'

'You've been a copper too long.'

We went back to Chandigarh and from there flew to Amritsar and spent a few days there. I was keen that Ellen should try out basic Punjabi food, *aaloo-gobi* (dry potato and cauliflower curry), *saag-aloo* (dry spinach and potato curry) and, the piece de resistance, sheep's brains. She was game to try the first two and enjoyed both but balked at the last.

'Why are you squeamish? You eat sweetbreads don't you?'

'I don't actually.'

'What is sweetbread anyway? Is it testicle or udder?'

'Search me.'

'In that case it is definitely udder.'

'How did you work that one out?'

'I'm not likely to find testicles if I search you, am I?'

'Majid, sometimes you can be pathetic.'

On the second day we visited the Golden Temple, the holy place of the Sikhs. Ellen was struck by the peaceful way a vast array of people were purifying themselves and praying. Whilst many were praying, a few were preying. Unaware of that she went and enjoyed the free meal provided, basic but wholesome fare. When we were ready to leave both of us found that our shoes had been stolen. As we made our way out the soles of our bare feet couldn't bear to make contact with the tar-road in the hot-mid-day sun. Yes December nights are cold but the midday sun is hot. Ellen remembered a nature program which showed snakes in the Sahara. As they moved across the sand at great speed they looked like a triple-w, www, thereby keeping the point of contact with the ground to a minimum.

As soon as I saw a passing taxi, I hailed it and asked the driver to take us to the nearest shoe shop where we purchased two pairs of cheap flip-flops.

That evening she said, 'We must go back soon. I'm running out of holidays.'

Eventually, a week later, we flew back to Chandigarh and from the airport gave Toba Taik Singh a call. 'Has your father called? I can be back at your place tomorrow.'

'Where have you been? I've been trying to contact you.'

'Why? What's up?'

'My father came back a day after you left and was looking forward to meeting you.'

'I can be there tomorrow evening.'

'That'll be too late. He's going again tomorrow morning.'

'Again?'

'Yes. A friend of his went on a trip to the Himalayas. He tripped and broke his leg, not a nice thing when you're over eighty. Dad's gone to look after him.'

'A ninety-seven year old, looking after someone fifteen years younger? Doesn't he have friends or family?'

'He does but they're all in the United States. But don't worry about Dad. He's strong as an ox and it is such adventures that keep him that way.'

'OK, if I can't see him, I can't see him. Give him my regards.'

'I will. Next time you come let us know in advance.'

I said to Ellen, 'Let's surprise Toba.'

We got into a taxi and went straight to his house. Toba was speechless when he saw us. He mumbled something about his father being out. I said we'd wait. Toba sat us down in the lounge and said he'd fish his father out of next door. I heard him ask his grandson to stand guard while he was away.

He returned ten minutes later with a very old man, with a curvature of the spine, who was almost bent double.

'This is my father.'

'He looks hardly able to look after himself. How was he going to look after an eighty –year-old with a broken leg?'

'Oh, he's very fit.'

'But he looks nothing like you father's picture.'

As he spoke, Ellen went to the glass cabinet and opened it to get the framed photograph to refresh her memory.

As she opened the door of the cabinet and took the photograph, she stepped back and said:

'Look, it's the same funny smell. It appears to be coming from the silver mug.'

Toba rushed to grab the photograph. I moved quickly to follow him and got hold of the mug. Toba dropped the photograph and went for the same mug. A tussle ensued as neither was prepared to let go. We knocked over the silver urn scattering a cloud of ash. Toba let go of the mug wailing, 'That's my father's ashes you're scattering'.

Meanwhile the release of his grip on the mug sent it and me crashing in the other direction with a splash of liquid. Out popped a pale object.

It was a thumb.

A Meeting of Managers

Compared to her Spartan existence as a copper, Ellen must regard the lifestyle of an actuary as opulent. She certainly found the idiosyncrasies of our perks quaint. We had a surreal conversation on one occasion when she came to spend a weekend with me.

'You seem unusually glad to see me,' she said.

'I'm always glad to see you,'

'No, you seem unusually cheerful.'

'Oh that must be because I've been promoted.'

'Congratulations. What are you now?'

'Still the same as before.'

'You're talking in riddles again.'

'Don't ask me to explain the HR reward system. We have fifteen grades, starting from two and going to.'

'Let me guess, sixteen.'

'Yes. Grades thirteen to sixteen are departmental managers.'

'What's beyond sixteen?'

'You enter the stratosphere, you become an Executive'

'And then?'

'Most people don't get beyond sixteen but a very lucky few go beyond Executive and become Directors.'

'Sounds very scientific. Pay goes up likewise?'

'Yes but they overlap. Someone who's been ages on grade thirteen can earn more than someone who's just been promoted to grade fourteen.'

'So why are you cheerful?'

'I've been promoted to fourteen. I owe it to the pickled thumb.'

'Congratulations. More money?'

'No, but I get wall-to-wall carpet in my room.' When she looked askance at me, I added:

'When I was promoted to manager last year, I was only a grade thirteen and that didn't entitle me to wall-to-wall carpet. They built my office on an area that already had wall-to-wall carpet. So they came and took away twelve inches of carpet right round the inside of my office.'

'That's sheer waste.'

'No, they're quite clever. They use carpet tiles and they simply removed one row of tiles right round the office and now, on promotion, put them back.'

'Who was it that said the devil finds work for idle hands?'

***

Camelot held a conference every year to which all managers were invited. It gave the sales managers the chance to get to know the admin managers. It also enabled the directors to assess the emerging talent. Wives and partners were invited. Kate Spencer, the Company Secretary was the sole female manager. In her early forties, she had risen through the ranks, after taking the law exams by correspondence course. Some say that she was Tim's token female presence in the Boardroom as well as the management group; others that she was an honorary bloke. Certainly she had a stern exterior and a bulldog face.

This year, 1982, the conference was held in Coventry during the month of April. It wasn't clear why Tim selected Coventry, a drab city, UK's Detroit. In the days when Britain had a thriving but fragmented automobile industry, it churned out motor cars but not any more. Today the only thing the city can boast of is a highly regarded university, which is called the University of Warwick. The conference was to last three days and two nights.

The location didn't matter to the delegates as they'd be spending all their time in a hotel. Their partners had special programmes; visits to Warwick Castle, Broadway (in Worcestershire, not New York) and the Cotswolds.

All four on the fast-track programme, Nick Knights, Bruce Herrington, John Michael and I, were attending; all bar John Michael for the first time. Being five years older, John Michael had made it to manager status a year earlier than the rest of us three.

On the opening day, during a coffee break, I met Nick and Bruce. Nick, as ever, was immaculately turned out. This was his third year in life insurance sales department and he'd made some eye-catching sales.

Bruce, six inches shorter at five foot eight, more or less my height, was untidy in the extreme. His suit had not been pressed for weeks. He was very precise in his speech but delivered it in a thick Glaswegian accent. He'd so far worked in the Finance Department. John Michael, whom I met later, was different. He was not really an insurance man having chosen to make a career in investments.

He was known to everyone as 'JM'

The delegates had several learning sessions leavened by entertainment and bonding sessions. The high point was right at the start. Tim Fredricks, gave a stirring speech developing a grand vision for the future.

Another highlight was the lunch on the second day in honour of the Sales Director who was shortly to retire. Tim organised it in great secrecy. The only people in the know were Phil Bunyon who was in charge of that year's conference, and three other people who were integral to a stunt he had organised.

On the second day one of the lighter sessions was led by Tim. Perhaps in recognition of serious matters being discussed in a light hearted atmosphere, he wore a pink shirt without a tie inside a pin-striped suit. He set out one Aunt Sally after another, and invited people's views on them. One such was the assertion that men waste too much time playing golf. I was inclined to agree and so did John Michael.

'Why do you say to that JM?' asked Tim.

'It's a crass waste of time. All you want to know about a company or its management can be obtained by studying their balance sheet.'

'Nonsense,' said Nick. 'Golf helps you establish rapport with brokers and clients.'

'But does it win you any business?' I asked.

'As a matter of fact it does. I established a rapport with a broker with strong connections in the farming community. He was finding it difficult to break the stranglehold of National Farmers Union with its own insurance company. I was able to recommend a health insurance policy which replaces lost income in the event of long term illness.'

'That was you was it?' asked Tim.

'Yes Sir. Looks like we're cornering the market.'

'Great stuff Nick. Does it matter who wins at golf?' asked Tim.

'Not really so long as the contest is close, but a decent handicap is good for your image.'

'I agree,' said Tim. 'I always encouraged my salesmen to play golf to a good standard. But if their handicap fell below ten then I used to fire them.'

I asked why.

'If they're that good, they're spending too much time on the golf course,' said Nick.

'Boom boom,' said Tim. 'Competitive sport helps you develop negotiation skills.'

'How do you do that?' asked Clem Hill, Camelot's Actuary, the man who was the favourite to become the next Chief Executive until Tim pipped him to the post.

'Well, take cricket as an example. As a spinner you learn to trade runs for wickets. As a batsman you're watchful when the bowler is in command but cash in when he tires.'

'That's tactics, not negotiation,' I said.

'Same difference.'

'Sport teaches you that winning is all,' said Tim

'and coming second is no good,' said Nick, almost completing Tim's sentence.

'At the same time you learn to take defeat in your stride. Salesmen learn this all the time,' said Tim, regaining control.

'Also the concept of the professional foul has analogies in business,' said Nick.

'You mean you can cheat if you can get away with it?' I asked.

'You do live in a queer world,' said Nick.

'I live in a queer world?'

'Let's stop fighting each other,' said Tim. 'It's the same for both sides in a game. It's a bit like driving at 75mph in a 70 mile limit area. Certain types of behaviour are accepted, others are taboo and win instant red cards.'

'No matter how good you've been, you start each match with a clean slate. Every football match starts nil-nil; every batsman starts his innings on nought,' said Nick.

'Starting a new year with a clean slate again. I hadn't thought of that,' said Tim.'

'You also learn to do as much of your fouls and retaliations off-the-ball,' added Nick.

My dubious look prompted Tim to ask, 'OK, saintly actuary, what does your profession teach you? How does it equip you for success in business?'

'I'm not sure that it does. Not in the way you're thinking. However it does teach you that the future is uncertain and teaches you to respect the odds.'

'OK, give me an example.'

I thought for a while, then I decided to try out an old trick.

'OK, there are thirty of us in this room, give or take. I'll offer odds of two to one that at least two of us will have the same birthday. Let me explain. I'll bet ten pounds with whoever accepts the bet. If no two people share a birthday then he wins my tenner but if they do he owes me twenty.'

Both Clem and JM winked at me as if to say, 'I know your game'.

Bruce said, 'You're out of your mind Majid. There are three hundred and sixty five days in a year and there are only thirty of us here.'

'I'll put my money where my mouth is.'

'OK, then. You're on,' said Bruce.

'Me too,' said Tim, Nick and, before I knew it everyone in the room bar Clem and JM.

'No, that's too much. I'd be staking £300; that's too much.'

'You can't back out now.'

I was extremely reluctant to stake £300 but Clem looked at JM and when he nodded, said:

'You can lay off a third each with JM and me.'

'OK. Can each of you write down in a slip of paper the day and month of your birthday and put it on this table.' The process took five minutes. I studied them and said after a while, 'I've won folks. We've got two people born on 13th of June'

'That's me,' said Tim.

'And me,' said Phil.

'Well, I'll be blowed,' said Bruce. 'How did you work it out?'

'It's down to probability theory and some messy calculations on a spreadsheet. Basically the odds are about even if you have two dozen randomly selected people. With more people the odds are better. So the bet I offered was loaded in my favour.'

'That's insider dealing then. You should be banned,' said Tim.

'Insider dealing? How did you work that one out?'

'If you had a better handle on the odds than the rest of us, that's insider dealing isn't it?'

'I had no more information than the rest of you. My analysis was better. That's skill, not insider dealing.'

'He's right,' said Clem.

Tim turned to Clem and tried to bait him. 'So that's what you actuaries are. You are bookies' clerks and you load the odds in your favour.'

'There are plenty of companies around so we'd lose business if we're too cautious.'

'Yay, yay.'

'Actually, using a sporting analogy, I'd like to think of us as umpires whose job is to ensure fair play. We learn which of you batsmen walk and which of you don't; which of you footballers engage in professional cheating etc. I've learned a lot from this session.'

At dinner Ellen and I shared a table with Nick and his girlfriend Phyllis, a leggy blonde; JM, Bruce and their wives. Ellen was very cold towards Nick. It started when Nick said:

'You two are suited to each other.'

'What do you mean by that?' she asked immediately

'You two complement each other.'

'In what way?' she asked, probably expecting a back-handed compliment.

'You've got to admit, he's a bit dry. You make him human by adding warmth.'

'That's how durable relationships are built. Something in common as glue, and the rest complementary to extend the scope of the individual.'

'Rather like intersecting Venn diagrams,' I said.

'See what I mean? Some people never change,' said Nick. 'Once a nerd always a nerd.'

'What have you and Phyllis got in common?' asked Ellen.

'Still searching,' said Nick. 'I'll let you know when I find out.'

'We act as punch-bags to each other,' said Phyllis.

Phyllis seemed a match for him. She spoke non-stop on anything and everything. Nick then turned round and said:

'Waiter, can you bring a bottle of your best claret.'

Whilst the waiter went to do as he was told, Phyllis said:

'Steady, you've not set a price limit.'

'I'm neither an accountant nor an actuary. I don't count my pennies.'

'Are you mad?'

'No, ecstatic. I've been promoted to the next grade. The fastest promotion in Camelot's history, I'm told.'

'So has Majid,' said Ellen.

'Aren't there fifteen grades of indoor manager?' Nick asked Majid.

'Yes.'

'There are only seven sales grades.'

'So?' I asked.

'My moving up one grade is twice as valuable as you moving up one.'

'Only if the end points of the two sets are the same and grades are evenly spaced,' I replied.

'Well, everyone knows that the Sales Director earns more than the Actuary,' retorted Nick.

'What is it about you men, always competing?' asked Phyllis.

'Did you get more money?' he asked me, ignoring Phyllis.

'No he didn't,' said Ellen.

'But I got wall-to-wall carpet. How about you, did you get a rise?' I asked.

'Not immediately but I'll get higher commission on future sales.'

'Jam tomorrow, eh?'

'I also get a better company car.'

'Which one?'

'Cavalier CD.'

'I thought you already had a Cavalier?'

'Yes, but this one is a Cavalier CD with leather upholstery and stereo.'

The waiter came round with two bottles of claret for Nick to choose from. I can't remember the vintage but both bottles cost over £300.'

'What?' exclaimed Nick. 'That's extortion.'

'You did ask for the best, Sir.'

'Yes, the best, not the most expensive.'

'Comes to the same thing, Sir.'

'Get out of it. Anyway, these guys tell me that I've nothing to celebrate. Cancel the order.'

Phyllis burst out laughing.

'What are you grinning at?' asked Nick.

'Isn't it all a bit OTT, offices with or without wall-to-wall carpet, cars with different trims. Can't they simplify things?' asked Phyllis.

'It's quite clever,' said JM. 'It enables them to keep pay down.'

'You're not exactly badly paid,' said Ellen.

'I work in investments and I could double my salary elsewhere.'

'What's keeping you here?' asked Phyllis.

'It's not about me. We're talking about Camelot creating minor but visible differences between grades more valued than their worth.'

'I don't regard your pay as low, not compared to a policeman.'

'That's different. You pay comes out of people's taxation,' said Nick.

'And yours comes out of premiums people pay on policies,' replied Ellen.

'Hold it,' I said. 'We're not going to solve this by debate. Let's change the subject.'

They didn't have to. It was time for speeches. Tim made a witty after dinner speech. He extolled the company's performance and thanked all staff. He hoped that anyone who was courageous enough to sample the bottled pickle on their table did check to make sure that it wasn't a thumb.

He then thanked the wives and partners for the support they gave their spouses.

Nick was asked to respond on behalf of the attendees, which he did with great panache. Unexpectedly he thanked partners or, specifically one partner:

'Tim has thanked all wives and partners for their support and it is my job to thank the company on behalf of the attendees but if I may, I'd like to single out Majid Khan's partner, Ellen Evan as an example of help they can provide. We're all aware of the 'pickled thumb' fraud that Majid uncovered. Few know that it was Ellen's nose that sniffed it out.'

That evening, in the bar, everyone was on good behaviour when the wives were present.

But when they'd gone, heavy drinking brought out candour and aggression. The discussion drifted from women to company cars to sport.

Ted Leary, the head of HR, studied psychology at college and his questions were always loaded, or so people feared. He asked, 'Is it possible for a guy to form a deep friendship with a girl without sex entering into the equation?'

Nick said 'No'

I said that in certain circumstances you could.

Bruce said, 'I agree. I do have a deep friendship with one girl which is completely platonic.'

'I don't believe you,' said Ted.

'It's true.'

'What's the bond between the two of you?'

'She's my twin sister.'

'Boom boom, I rest my case,' said Ted.

'What nonsense you talk, Ted,' said Tim. 'I have deep and completely platonic friendships with several girls, well with two, no three.'

'As deep as with your closest male friend?'

'No,' said Tim. He then added, 'This is silly. 'Let's change the subject. This is a management conference, let's talk about work. We're an insurance company but we sell a lot of investment products. Where should our focus be, insurance or investments?'

Nick was off the mark first saying, 'Why do we have to make a choice? People need both, we'll offer both. We can focus on what makes most money but that will change from time to time.'

I took the opposite view, 'You can't be all things to all men. Insurance is something only an insurance company can provide so we should concentrate on that.'

'Two of the most successful UK firms in recent times are Marks and Spencer and Tesco,' said Nick. 'Do they confine themselves so narrowly?'

'They're retailers. They don't have to tool up for every passing fancy.'

'I'm with Nick on that,' said Tim.

And, finally, the surprise at lunch. When everyone had sat down with their buffet lunch, Tim, who was sitting next to Desmond, must have given a pre-arranged signal to Phil who was waiting by the door.

As soon as he got it Phil nodded in the direction of the corridor where I was waiting. I picked up a bugle from behind the curtain and started playing the Trumpet Voluntary on it. Moments later JM emerged from the end of the corridor pulling at a lead, followed by a pantomime horse with a completely naked woman in her forties astride it, singing or rather, shouting

Desmond, Desmond, living in denial
There's more to life than mere survival
Come into the arms of Lady Godiva
Enjoy to the full your love life's revival

Tim had quietly moved out of the chair next to Desmond, ostensibly to see what was going on. Godiva was having trouble staying on the horse as the front end of the horse was noticeably higher than its rear. She constantly pulled herself forward holding tight to the horse's neck.

As she got close to the top table the head came off in her hand. She threw it to me and tried hard not to fall backwards off the horse. Over-zealousness led to the horse's back being broken and the cloth draped over it folding inwards into a v-shape. Godiva was trapped between the front and rear of the horse. With some difficulty I dismantled the horse, taking care not to touch Godiva's body. Nick emerged from the front of the horse and Bruce from the rear. I collected the steady stream of bread-rolls that had been disgorged from the horse's tail.

Godiva sat down in the chair that Tim had vacated and ate from the untouched plate he had filled. She sat with utter nonchalance making conversation with Desmond as if it was the done thing to eat in the altogether. All the other managers found it extremely embarrassing as they did not know where to look. Not everyone thought the stunt was in good taste; no mention was made of it to the wives when they returned from Broadway.

In the bar that evening I said, 'I'm glad I declined to be part of the horse. It must've been dark in there.'

'Your card is marked mate. No one turns down Tim,' said Nick who then added:

'It was dark but manageable until the tart slid and then pulled herself back up.'

When the conference ended and people were making their way back to the car park, JM came up to me and asked, 'Why are you rotting in the claims department? Come and join me in the investment department.'

'I was told it was good for the soul, stop me being a nerd.'

'Oh come on, you'll vegetate.'

'I'll move somewhere else in a couple of years as part of the fast track programme.'

'I'm on it too but I'll not leave investment department.'

'Broaden your experience, don't ossify.'

'No chance of that. You're the one who should worry.'

'No, I'll learn all about claims management as quickly as possible, two or three years maximum and then I'll move back.'

That was a challenge I'd set myself and stuck to.

On our way back Ellen observed that Nick could certainly lay on the charm when he wanted to. She was also struck by the old fashioned politeness of the people at the conference, in striking contrast to the boorish behaviour at her police station.

Nick as a competitor was tough to evaluate as we were not running the same race. He was in his natural habitat, sales whilst I was out of mine. I'd better return to financial forecasting quickly.

The rest of the year was fairly uneventful, Ellen and I got on with our jobs and met regularly. This is not to say that life was dull. Claims management always throws up fascinating surprises. Some of these are set out in the next and later chapters. I have chosen ones that are relevant to the story of this book.

Stalking the Dead

The pickled thumb affair gave me enormous publicity not just within Camelot but in the media too. Phil Bunyan, slightly miffed at a junior gathering all the attention, decided to throw me in at the deep end. He gave me what seemed an innocuous case but was far from it. He pulled out a file, slid it across his desk to me.

'What is it?' I asked.

'Diljeet Singh died last December in a remote village in Punjab in India just before his life insurance policy expired.'

I thumbed through the file. Aside from information collected at the time the policy was taken out, there was a letter from the broker notifying Diljeet's death and a copy of the death certificate.

'Do you think that the death might have occurred after the policy expired?' I asked.

'We should check that out. Also, the cause of death is shown on the death certificate as asphyxiation. I've not come across that before. It certainly deserves investigation but keep an open mind while you do so.'

'Wait a minute. He's a Sikh, they go for cremation, don't they? Yes, a funeral pyre. Is that what they meant by asphyxiation?'

'You only cremate dead people and a death certificate is usually obtained first. In the past eighteen months, the UK insurance industry has had a spate of similar claims.'

He showed a table compiled by the Association of British Insurers, the trade body. It had eight policies spread over eight insurance companies, with the insured's names missing.

'Eight is a spate is it?'

'It is when they're all relatively young Asians. We don't have too many such clients.'

I noted that Camelot Life wasn't on the list. Phil explained that the list was compiled last week. The Diljeet case only arrived yesterday.

'So there are nine in all. So you *are* suggesting fraud aren't you?'

'You're the actuary, what are the chances of it being a coincidence?'

That sounded like a trick question so I played safe:

'No idea, I haven't examined the evidence.'

'Let me give you a few clues. All eight claims were on policies taken out by owners of modest businesses which were going through difficult times. They were all introduced by the same broker. Cannily, he spread his business around a number of insurance companies. There may have been good reasons for that but it does help to avoid suspicion.'

'Is all that true of Diljeet as well?'

'That's for you to find out but, yes, it was placed by the same broker.'

I looked through the file again. It was a straightforward life assurance policy with the proceeds payable to the widow. It wasn't written in trust or anything fancy like that. Nor was it taken out by a company that Diljeet owned.'

'Nothing here to suggest that this is premeditated fraud.'

'Well it's very unusual not to write the policy in trust. Diljeet is either guileless or wily.'

'Meaning?'

'He might have intended collecting the cash and doing a bunk. Easier to do that when there are no trustees to stop you.'

I looked at the table again and said, 'I see that the first two such claims have been settled.'

'Yes, neither insurer suspected anything untoward. It was a casual conversation between their claims managers that made them suspicious. It turned out that the two policyholders were married to each other and their death certificates are now known to be forgeries.'

'Are they trying to recover the amount they paid?'

'They'll find it hard. The couple have sold their Wembley house and returned to India. That's how we know that they're still alive.'

'Has someone talked to the broker who arranged these policies?'

'Not sure.'

'They're all Asians, are they?'

'The ones we're aware of are. There may be others. That's a matter for the police.'

'So the police are involved?'

'Yes, the trade body has alerted Scotland Yard. The detective handling it is Detective Stanley.' He won't know about Diljeet yet.

'What do we do next?'

'It's your case. You follow it up. Begin by contacting Leicester police.'

I looked at him for clarification.

'That's where Diljeet lived. Go on, no time to waste.'

I returned to my desk. A colleague, who sat nearby, sensed that I was unsure of what to do next He suggested a cautious approach.

'If you find that it is a legit case then you'll have egg on your face if you haven't shown tact.'

'Are you suggesting that we pay up?'

'No, just proceed with caution; don't imply that they're trying it on. Come on let's go to the police station.'

'What, in Leicester?'

'No, here.'

The sergeant on duty at the police station was helpful. He put them in touch with Bill Sparling of Leicester and we talked on the phone. Bill had no knowledge of this case.

'Of course we follow up suspicious deaths but someone needs to tell us. Now that you've done that we'll follow it up and let you know.'

Next day, Bill phoned to say that he'd met Diljeet's widow who confirmed her husband's death and showed him the death certificate. She hadn't suspected foul play and saw no reason to report it.

'How did she explain asphyxiation?'

'She didn't know what the term meant and thought it was a medical condition. She says he died in his sleep. She knew, she was in the same bed. He'd covered his head with a pillow to ward off mosquitoes.'

'Sounds unlikely.'

'It does, doesn't it? But the Indian police ought to have taken an interest in it if it was suspicious. I intend to get in touch with them.'

'If they don't pursue, it will you?'

'We don't have the resources or budget to travel to India.'

I considered what to do next. Better to consult Ellen, whom I was due to meet that evening. After work I travelled up to London to our usual rendezvous, the pub at Paddington railway station.

Ellen was already there when I arrived.

'You're still in your business suit,' she said reproachfully.

'I didn't have time to go back and change.'

'But you must make time for that.'

'Oh come on luv, we've been here before. You don't judge a book by its cover.'

'But they do. The first thing that grabs your attention is the cover and the title. The content matters most but you have to get a look in first.'

'OK, OK, I'll make the time to change in the future.'

'Why not buy another suit?'

'Waste of money. Anyway, I want to talk to you about a death claim.'

It was a while before I got Ellen to focus on what I was saying rather than what I was wearing but eventually she got there. I summarised the issues. She confirmed that police budgets were under severe pressure.

'Couldn't Bill make a special case? Asphyxiation sounds pretty suspicious.'

'He wouldn't succeed; not if the widow isn't complaining and the Indians aren't interested either.'

'The alternative is to pay the claim. I'm reluctant to do that, not on my first case.'

'There is another alternative. Camelot could hire a private investigator.'

'That'll cost money.'

'See, you're in the same boat as the police.'

A week later, Bill Sparling phoned to say that Indian police didn't suspect any foul play. So I approached Phil but instead of giving advice he asked me what I'd do.

'Someone should go to India to investigate the death. Not sure whether it'll be cost-effective though?' I said.

'What's your concern?'

'If there's a death certificate and the Indian police don't wish to contest it, the odds are that we'd pay up. If we send someone to India to investigate, then that will cost, I don't know, but with hotels and air fares, a few thousand quid.

Even if it's as low as £2,000, as the amount of insurance under the policy is only £100,000 we'd need a better than one in fifty chance of us discovering that the claim is fraudulent for it to be worthwhile.'

'You can't reduce everything to numbers you know. It's not as simple as that. I attended a meeting yesterday called by the trade body. We believe that this type of fraud is likely to increase. It's not organised crime, more copy-cat crime.'

'I don't understand.'

'A lot of Asians came here in the fifties and sixties as economic migrants. They worked hard, saved money and built houses back home. They also got settled in England.'

'I know that.'

'Then in the past five years many have lost their jobs or businesses. Two houses to maintain and no income, things got hard. One person fakes a death claim and others follow suit. That's the hypothesis but we must test it out. If true it's a perfect victimless crime and could become a major problem for insurers.'

'If you look at it like that the odds change.'

'You must go to India and establish the facts. It's handy that you understand the local language and culture.'

'Oh no, not me. I'm the wrong guy.'

'I know you grew up in Pakistan but isn't the Punjabi culture and language the same in both countries?'

'Up to a point, but surely English is all you need to deal with these matters?'

'But there'll be many who don't speak English. Anyway you can't be worse than the rest of us here.'

I had deep reservations. I knew what I could do and what I couldn't do. I was an actuary, a mathematician, a number cruncher. People tell me that I had little empathy for people issues. Nor did I have the necessary forensic skills. I didn't know what to look for, or how to extract information that people were withholding.

'OK, but I'm still the wrong man. I'm trained to do sums; I'd be no good as a sleuth.'

'You can't pick and choose what you take on you know.'

'I'm not being difficult or anything. I have a head for figures not a nose for funny smells.'

'Your choice but if you turn this down I'll want you out of my department.'

In my three years at Camelot, I'd learnt a few things about the insurance business. Like the judiciary it relied heavily upon precedent.

If something new cropped up, it was thoroughly researched and all pros and cons evaluated before a course of action was agreed, implemented and documented as precedent for the future. That was how the actuaries, the heartbeat of the business, worked.

The same applied to claims and the approach taken on the Diljeet Singh case could well become a precedent for the future.

Despite my reservations this was a great opportunity. But it was also a great opportunity to make a fool of myself. The odds were higher for the latter.

Even if the odds were the same, humiliation would carry a greater stigma than the kudos of success. I really oughtn't to go. But then again the ignominy of being sent back to actuarial was far worse.

Events in the real world seem far more complex than in my mathematical models. I decided to ask Ellen to come with me. Her presence ought to help.

'OK I'll do it,' I said to Phil. 'Diljeet Singh is a Punjabi name and his people will speak Hindi or Punjabi; I'm fluent in Hindi and can follow Punjabi, though I can't speak it.'

'Good man. We have a local contact, recommended to us by the British High Commission. Detective Oliver Stanley of Scotland Yard is co-ordinating everything from this end. You should get in touch with him and travel together to India. But remember, he's very status conscious. You must refer to him as Detective Stanley, not as Oliver or even as Mr Stanley.'

Early next morning I telephoned Dad and shared my concerns about the assignment I'd been bounced into accepting. He's someone who values discipline and manliness above all other attributes so I expected him to regard this as more worthwhile than building mathematical models. He didn't say so. Instead he warned me to be careful as I had 'a lot to learn about people'.

'Are you asking me to turn this down?'

'No, not at all. This could be the making of you, if you're up to it.'

I then had a long chat with Ellen and she took a similar line but said it more directly.

'I don't think you'd be up to it but you ought to take it.'

'Why am I not up to it?'

'You're hopeless at reading people's motives and emotions.'

'That's your opinion.'

'It's true.'

'OK, tell me then why I ought to take it up?'

'Here's a chance for your social conscience. If he's a crook nail him; if he's not help his widow.'

'You have a way of making the unwelcome palatable. Tell you what? Would you like to come with me?'

She was keen provided she could obtain leave.

Detective Stanley was unhelpful. He didn't want outside interference in police matters nor did he want any help. However when I said that I was required to go and investigate anyway, he relented.

'I don't want you ruining our investigations by asking the wrong sort of questions. You can come with me so long as you recognise that I'm in charge.'

I accepted that so long as Ellen could come with me. Detective Stanley was reluctant so I played my trump card.

'She's a policewoman.'

'In that case she's definitely not coming. I don't want her interfering in my patch.'

So I played my second trump card and said that in that case the two of us would go on our own. He liked that even less so we reached a compromise. She could come so long as she said nothing and did not report back to her superiors. Although I did not check with Ellen, I accepted that.

When I did check with Ellen I found that she had considerable difficulty obtaining leave. A junior policewoman had no right to make such requests. She had to fit her holidays around others'. Eventually repeated pleading led to a special concession with a warning 'You'll have to pay for this favour'.

I met Detective Stanley again as we waited to board a British Airways plane to Bombay and introduced Ellen to him. He was quite unlike any of the detective stereotypes I was familiar with from books and television. He could easily have been mistaken for a civil servant with grey hair, pinstripe suit and tie. I'd arranged for the three of us to sit together on the plane. I asked him, in a soft voice:

'I know these are police matters. Are you able to tell me anything about the two deaths known to be forgeries? Is there any connection with the Diljeet Singh case?'

'They're through the same broker. Our problem is the lack of central control of cremations. Cremation in India is carried out outdoors. The body is placed on a funeral pyre made of dry fast burning wood interspersed with sweet smelling sandalwood.'

'Aren't there official rules and procedures?

'Oh there are, but Indians are like the Italians and Greeks. Rules are there to apportion blame if things go wrong; they're not there to be followed. This is especially so in the villages. A cremation could take place in the back garden, and often does, and is reported after the event, if at all.'

'But they have to die before they're cremated. Surely a qualified doctor certifies that the man is dead.'

'They do, but that's not the real issue.'

'What is, then?'

'You can be certain that the person being cremated was dead. But you can't be sure that the he's the person you think he is.'

I had a thought:

'Hang on, were they all cremations?

'No, two were Muslims and one a Parsi They bring their own challenges. Parsis leave their corpse on a tower for kites to feed off, Muslims bury theirs.'

'What's the problem with either? Surely they have to be pronounced dead first? I get it, we can't be sure who's been buried or fed to the kites.'

'Muslim custom is to bury their dead within a day, preferably on the same day. It's only in cities that there's a post mortem, and then only if there are grounds for suspicion.'

'What about the Parsi case?'

'Polly Mehr-Homji. He's the one I'm really interested in. Diljeet is small fry. Polly came from a well-to-do Bombay family. He branched out on his own setting up business in Slough. He expanded too fast, borrowed too much and the business went belly up.'

'And then he died?'

'It doesn't concern you.'

'Of course it doesn't. I'll shut up.'

'That makes two of us,' said Ellen.

It was getting late and for the rest of the journey the three of us caught some low quality sleep. On landing in Bombay it was mayhem in the aisles. We held back and let the rest rush through.

Seeing Ellen's discomfort, Detective Stanley said:

'Yes, it's hotter than usual. Even the locals are sweating.'

When we'd been through customs and come out at the other end, an Indian came forward and talked with Detective Stanley as if they knew each other.

Detective Stanley looked round for an empty table to sit around and have a quiet chat. The airport was full of people and there was hardly a spare chair, never mind a whole table. In the end we huddled in a corner and tried to keep our voices down. Detective Stanley then introduced Arun Shastri to me. Arun stared at me unblinkingly, so that in the end I had to look away. Ellen asked:

'Hey mister, what are you staring at?'

He ignored the challenge and continued to stare at me.

'You're not English, are you?'

'I'm British,' I said.

'But you were originally Indian, no?'

'I'm originally from Pakistan.'

'Can you speak Hindi?' asked Arun.

I nodded.

'Can you speak Punjabi?'

'I can't really speak it but I can follow it. Why do you ask?'

'I'm thinking how you can help us.'

'I'm here to find out what really happened.'

'So you're not here to help?'

'Shall we visit Diljeet's family tomorrow?' asked Detective Stanley quickly.

'Yes, it's all arranged. I went to their house and arranged it. His grandfather burst into tears. They can't get over his suicide.'

'You're not meant to set it up.'

'Don't you want to meet them?'

'Yes, but I don't want to tell them in advance. Still, what's done is done.'

I then asked:

'Suicide? Who's talking of suicide? The death certificate said that he died of asphyxiation.'

'Both. He lit a funeral pyre and jumped into it.'

'That sounds like Suttee, where widows jump into the funeral pyre of their husbands,' said Detective Stanley.

Ellen intervened to say, 'I read about Suttee. The widows didn't jump, they were forcibly pushed screaming into the pyre by their husbands' families. They did it to make sure that the husband's property didn't pass to the widow.'

'Let's not start a fight. Suttee was banned a long time ago, in the nineteenth century. But she has a point. People don't voluntarily jump into fire. I don't buy the suicide story.'

'I agree, it doesn't sound very plausible. Why would he commit suicide anyway?' asked Detective Stanley.

'He was very depressed, according to his grandfather. Business problems, I think.'

'Why didn't someone stop him from jumping into the pyre?'

'He lit the pyre in the middle of the night.'

'But he must have collected a lot of wood to assemble it. Surely someone must have noticed?' I asked.

'I guess that's one reason he probably went to Nangapur, to his ancestral home. There are fewer people there.'

'How do we know that it was his body that got cremated and that he cremated himself?'

'You doubt it? The local authorities don't. They issued Diljeet's death certificate with asphyxiation as the cause of death. That's what you wanted, wasn't it?'

'My priority is to establish the facts. If the fact is that he's dead then I need a death certificate showing the cause of death.'

'Now that we're here, I'd like to see it for myself,' I said.

'But these people don't speak English.'

'I'll speak to them in Hindi.'

'Their Hindi is not good.'

'OK, I'll try to speak in Punjabi.'

'But your Pakistani Punjabi is different to Sikh's Punjabi.'

This irritated Detective Stanley but I said it was OK, and that I'd go without Arun.

'OK, let's go to Amritsar then,' said Arun quickly. 'You wait here and I'll go and get the air tickets.'

When Arun left, I turned to Detective Stanley and asked, 'Are you sure that he's on your side?'

'He's on the side that pays him most. That has been us in the past. Not sure this time.'

Arun came back to say, 'I can't get four tickets for later this evening. I can only get one. So I've booked you into a hotel in Bombay and bought tickets for tomorrow. I'll use the single ticket to go on ahead myself. I'll see you in Amritsar.'

'Why don't you stay with us and travel together?'

'I was going to but then I thought if I went ahead of you I could sort out the accommodation for you.'

'That's very helpful,' I said.

Arun took them to the taxi rank and hailed one for them. The light was quite bright, much the same as in Lahore but much brighter than Bristol. The same comparison could be made about the general level of noise.

The hotel we stayed that night in was the Taj by the Gateway of India overlooking the Arabian Sea. It was a good hotel but really all we wanted was a cool shower and bed. The following morning, on our way back to Bombay airport, Ellen asked me:

'Won't suicide help you? Nobody should profit from his crime and all that?'

'That's true but, as you know, suicide isn't a crime any more.'

Arun was there at Amritsar airport to receive us when we arrived the following evening. Looking a little tired and haggard, he took us to our hotel. Arun phoned Diljeet's grandfather. When the call was answered, he spoke in Punjabi. I listened carefully.

Arun reported that Diljeet's grandfather asked us to come along at nine the following morning. I nodded to corroborate the story.

The following day we went to meet Balbir Singh, Diljeet's grandfather, at his house on the outskirts of Amritsar. Arun had hired a taxi for the whole day. Balbir was a small man with a flowing salt and pepper beard and a warm smile. A servant came with a tray of tea and sweetmeats.

Balbir was very affectionate but behind the smile there appeared to be sadness. He talked of how heart-broken he was at Diljeet's suicide. 'Sikh people are very brave. They fight to the end. Diljeet's suicide brings shame to the family. He must've been under tremendous pressure.'

I maintained that people wouldn't jump into a blazing fire. Their nerve would fail. They would choose other forms of suicide. Balbir said that Diljeet's nerve clearly didn't. I was adamant but with great patience Balbir held his line. Sikh people were brave and didn't fear death. Later, when Detective Stanley had popped into the toilet, Balbir said to me in a mixture of Hindi/Punjabi,

'*Putra, tu hamare khilaf kyun khada hai. Hamra saaath do. Ham such boltai hain. Agar jhoot bhi ho to kya bura, choti si baat haiy. Goronse lootne main kya bura. Sadyon tak inhone hamen choda hai.*'

I was considering how to respond but abandoned it when I saw Arun watching me intently. Meanwhile Ellen sidled up to me and whispered, 'What's that all about?'

'Do you know what the cheeky devil said to me in Hindi/Punjabi? "*Son, why do you doubt us? You should be on our side. We're speaking the truth; even if we weren't, what's the harm in stealing pennies from the English? They've been robbing us for centuries.*"'

Having reached stalemate, Detective Stanley decided to visit the ancestral home in Nangapur, the scene of the alleged suicide. Six in a taxi was a squeeze in the hot weather but we kept going.

It took three hours to reach a dilapidated farm house set in a two-acre field. It was the time of day when dusk was about to yield to night and all sorts of insects were flying past their ears, mouths and eyes. Crickets were making a din rubbing their legs together and frogs were croaking.

Ellen was astonished at the number of stars in the sky. Balbir showed the spot where the cremation had taken place. The scorched earth was the only evidence of it. I asked:

'Where did he jump into the pyre from?'

'From the top of a tree, I'm told. How do I know? I wasn't there,' said Balbir.

'I see no tree in the vicinity.'

'The fire ate it.'

'A tree strong enough to support his weight while he jumps off it was burned down?'

'That's what fire does. Nobody asked it to avoid the tree did they?'

The following day Arun took them to the office of the Registrar of Births and Deaths to obtain another copy of the death certificate. Detective Stanley said he'd seen enough. I drew him to one side and whispered,

'You've seen enough? The whole set up stinks. I'm sure Balbir is an imposter. What feedback can you give when you get back?'

'Son, this is small fish. It might be fraudulent. We haven't got conclusive evidence either way but you're only talking of a hundred grand of insurance company money.'

'So you're leaving me in the lurch.'

'No, I'm leaving you in charge of the insurance investigation, as you always were. The police investigation is closed.'

I went back to Arun and said, 'I'm not convinced that Diljeet is dead but there's no more I can ask for the moment. Tell Balbir that we won't pay the insurance amount.'

With that Ellen and I left. We flew to New Delhi that evening and stayed in a three star hotel, as this time Camelot was not going to pick up the cost. It was a mistake as it was run down and not very clean. We ate sparingly that night avoiding meat altogether and sticking to boiled water for fluids. Next morning we set off by coach to Agra to see the Taj Mahal. I said to Ellen:

'You can soon tick off one of your dreams.'

'I can't wait. For years I've fantasised about my prince building a Taj Mahal in my memory. Now it won't live up to its reputation. Most things don't.'

'Well, we're nearly there now. Look, over there.'

She leant over me to look out of the window. For the next three hours I couldn't get a word out of her.

She watched agape, every single brick from every possible aspect, often going back to remind herself, at the same time listening intently to the guide. Marble from Rajasthan, architect from Iran, not Persia, she noted; local manual labour, skilled artisans from abroad. What planning, what dedication. She was clearly smitten.

On the coach journey back, she was silent probably reflecting on the last thing the guide said. The king was imprisoned by his son and never saw the completed Taj. I decided it was best to give her space. Gradually, as she went over the day, her thoughts appeared to have turned to the Taj itself as she said to me:

'It's so beautiful, and all for the love of a woman.'

I looked at her. She seemed to be in a state of trance. I didn't respond other than to nod my head. Ellen turned round and winsomely asked:

'Will you build one for me?'

'Its symmetry is impressive but where did the money come from?'

'What do you mean? He was the king wasn't he?'

'But it's the nation's money he was wasting.'

'Oh Majid, call this waste? One of the seven wonders of the world?'

An hour later, we needed to get back to the coach which was about to leave but she was still gazing at the Taj.

'Can we at least have a photograph taken?' she asked.

We posed in front of the Taj Mahal and had a snap taken.

When I got back to my desk, Phil called me to his office for a debriefing. I expressed concern at the way the investigation had gone.

'I don't think we've got to the bottom of this. I'm sure Arun's in the pay of Diljeet's family.'

'How could they possibly know him?'

'Don't know, maybe he approached them.'

'Anyway, what are your grounds for suspicion?'

'The idea of jumping onto a funeral pyre seemed a bit far-fetched. Also, I think the grandfather's an impostor. He actually said that I ought to be on his side.'

'No use complaining to me here. You should've done something about it when you were out there.'

'Detective Stanley only let me go with him if he ran the show. He said this case was small beer and he was devoting more time to another case which had more at stake.'

'Next time stand your ground.'

'Will there be a next time?'

'Who can say? Now, what do you want to do with the death claim? Pay up, ask for more evidence or decline,' asked Phil.

'We can't pay up whilst there is doubt in our minds.'

'With the other two options you have to give valid reasons for your decision.'

'Can't we say that we don't believe he's dead?'

'Whoever you're casting aspersions on won't like it.'

'So what? The onus is on the claimant to prove that he or she has a valid claim.'

That is what I chose to do.

I waited for the flak.

***

Two months passed without anything memorable happening. Ellen, who had come down to Bristol for a long weekend, expressed surprise at Diljeet's widow not chasing up for the insurance money.

'She's no widow and she knows that we know that,' I replied.

'Even if it was a try on, I'd have expected them to go through the motions.'

'No point worrying about it.'

She looked at me and said:

'You're not dealing with a mathematical problem. You're dealing with real people making claims.'

'A problem's a problem.'

'No, you need to understand human psychology. Just as we coppers need to.'

'You may, I don't. I can rely on you for that.'

She was about to respond but didn't when she saw me smiling.

We drove to Durdham Downs and went for a stroll. Although it was late evening and very windy, several intrepid climbers were getting ready to descend down the sheer rock face that drops down to Portway, the road that links up with M5. Ellen looked at them and sighed,

'Stupid people.'

'Brave or foolhardy, perhaps. Why stupid.'

'They're risking their lives with no concern for others.'

'Why should they, they're no danger to others.'

'Their families, silly. They must be somebody's children or parents.'

'But they're not risking their lives.'

'Haven't you seen how steep the fall is?'

'It's only risky if you misjudge your own skill level. Most of them are experienced climbers and know exactly what they should attempt.'

'Its dicey whichever way you look at it.'

'It's a matter of definition.'

'Where's this leading?'

'When we talk of risk we really mean undue risk. Otherwise there's risk in everything. We just took a risk by crossing that busy little road.'

'OK, finish what you're trying to say.'

'What you need to do is to calibrate the intrinsic risk in going down that rock face against your own capabilities.'

'You mean, see if you can manage it.'

I thought about it for a moment and said, 'I guess that's the layman's way of putting it.'

'I'm sorry I asked. You actuaries take a simple thing and complicate it to confuse us.'

'That's a nice one coming from a lawyer. Legal documents I've seen are dense and impenetrable. Why don't you believe in punctuations?'

'I'm a policewoman not a lawyer.'

By now we had reached the pub, The Case is Altered. We wanted to have a swift half, but the pub was very noisy and we turned back.

'When are you going to move in with me?' I asked.

Ellen didn't respond so I asked again and she replied:

'You know very well that there are no vacancies in the Bristol police force.'

'You can't move here, I can't move to London. Do we just carry on as usual?'

Neither of us was happy with a life of intermittent contact but both were unsure how to change it. In the end we set ourselves a target. Within three years one or both of us would move so that we could live together.

I said we should look for a larger flat, now that I was earning a healthy salary.

'OK, I'll help you find one if you promise to keep it clean and tidy. '

Back at the flat we unfolded an A3-sized map of Bristol. There are some nice villages both north and south of the city within commuting distance. However they were all ruled out as easy access to Bristol railway station was important.

Ellen came back on three weekends to help me select a flat.

We visited several firms of estate agents and saw a number of flats. Eventually we settled for a first-floor three-bedroom flat in Downleaze in Stoke Bishop.

It was the conversion of a large Edwardian house with tall rooms and solid brick walls. It was on the wrong side of the city. The office was in Frenchay but I didn't fancy living in East Bristol.

Ellen and I agreed on the overall layout. The large front room would be the lounge diner. The master bedroom would be kitted out as if we were living together; a double bed and a double wardrobe. The second bedroom was designated as the guest bedroom.

The third bedroom, which was quite small, had a single bed and was going to be a sin bin. This was Ellen's idea having read in a women's magazine that every relationship needed an escape valve for it to be durable. The idea was that if we quarrelled, then the originator of the quarrel would have to move into the sin bin. I did wonder whether we'd quarrel about who started the quarrel but chose not to ask, in case that started a quarrel. We'd not quarrelled yet and I wanted it to stay that way.

Although not a quarrel we disagreed on how to furnish the flat. I was content with functional furniture and indeed was going to put up chipboard shelves in the lounge to store my books. She wanted something more pleasing to the eye and more durable. In the end we compromised. Instead of buying a large bookcase we agreed to use a local carpenter to put up mahogany shelves in the recess between chimneys in the lounge-diner. Ellen chose some reproduction furniture from a shop in the High Street and settees and matching curtains from a department store.

One item where I wanted to spend more was the cooker hood. I wanted a powerful and deep one as I fancied cooking curry from time to time. I didn't want the smell of garlic to infuse the flat.

I need not have worried about the total cost; Ellen was quite savvy.

***

I received a letter from a Leicester firm of solicitors acting on behalf of Diljeet Singh's widow saying, 'Pay up or we'll take you to court.'

I gave Detective Stanley a call to find out the current state of play.

'Ah the insurance frauds. We've had a breakthrough. Can't talk about it but we've got evidence from someone who wants to turn himself in.'

'Is it Arun?'

'What's Arun got to do with it?'

'He's the Indian we met when we went out there.'

'Oh you're not still thinking of the Sikh suicide, are you?'

'What else?'

'No, I was talking about the Mehr-Homji case. What's your problem? You've got a death certificate haven't you?'

'But we haven't established, to my satisfaction, that he did die.'

'I can see that you're still wet behind your ears. In life you have to learn to prioritise. I can't chase everything. The Singh case has no wider ramifications. Anyway you insurance companies can afford it.'

I wondered whether to approach the broker involved but didn't know his name and I was reluctant to ask Phil. Instead I asked his secretary for the files on the correspondence with the trade body. I quickly reviewed it and gave it back to her.

Hanuman Shastri of Satyem Insurance brokers, Ealing Road, Wembley. 'Shastri, eh?' I muttered to myself.

I thought of confronting him but decided that that was not within my remit. I was not a copper. Maybe I should stir up Bill Sparling Yes, that's what I'd do.

I caught a train to Leicester and then a cab to the main police station. There I met Bill. The sight of him didn't fill me with optimism. He had a kindly and warm smile but looked close to retirement. 'Not likely to stir himself,' I thought.

'I'm interested in the Diljeet Singh case.'

'Who might you be?'

'Oh, I'm from Camelot Life Insurance Company. I went to India with Detective Stanley to follow up the death claim.'

'Oh that was you was it?' asked Bill.

'I felt that we were taken for a ride.'

'Not what Detective Stanley said. He came back with the death certificate. The file is closed'

I sensed that I was on my own. Was I wasting my time? Should I pay up? Would that be a precedent I'd live to regret? Perhaps I should give it one last go?

But how could I prove that Diljeet was still alive? A sighting would help but how and where? If he was still alive where would he be?

In India? If he was he'd take steps to sell his house and his wife would join him. In the meantime the family would be in limbo. There was no evidence of this. Alternatively, no it's unthinkable.

Alternatively he was still in the UK either in some other city or, if he's foolhardy, in his own house. With Diljeet's solicitor on the phone every day, I consulted Phil.

'We've no option but to pay. We'd be on very dodgy ground if we declined a case where the police accepts that the client is dead.'

'It stinks.'

'Well, you had your chance and you didn't take it.'

I settled the claim but was far from happy and resolved not to 'close the file' in my mind.

On the Beat

I phoned Ellen that evening to tell her that I had failed in the Diljeet case. I expected a sympathetic ear. Instead, I found her bursting to tell me her own experience.

'You'll never guess what happened today.'

'What?'

'A colleague and I were observing two men acting suspiciously. Eventually one took a crate from the boot of his car and gave it to the other. The other person yanked off the lid, took a packet out, opened it with a knife and dipped the tip of his knife in it and took it to his nose to smell it.'

'Cannabis was it?'

'That's what I thought. We confronted and arrested them.'

'Well done. Is this a first for you?'

'It is but an unfortunate one. It wasn't cannabis at all; it was garam masala.'

'Isn't it a different colour altogether.'

'We couldn't see what it was from a distance.'

'Why were they acting suspiciously?'

'It was stolen property.'

'Still it could've been worse. It could've been cannabis and you could've left it thinking it was garam masala.'

'You know they call me Paki-lover at the station because of you? Now they're taunting me saying, *"Fancy a Paki-lover not recognising garam masala."*'

'I'm sorry. Am I a problem for you?'

'I'm not giving you up if that's what you mean.'

Some time after that she was promoted to night-time beat duties. Her patch was near Earl's Court tube station. I was worried that she might be attacked by drunks but she wasn't afraid.

'I've only been doing it for a fortnight but already I've come across a cross-section of societies I don't normally see.'

'You mean the tarts and kerb-crawlers you find in that area.'

'Don't be a cynic, there's plenty of what you may call normal people with problems.'

'Such as?'

'I met a Fijian lady yesterday. One of nature's unlucky ones, her first husband used to beat her up. She eventually abandoned him and took her baby son with her. She was befriended by another no-gooder. She moved in with him but he was an alcoholic and used to physically abuse her baby.

She couldn't find work with a baby to look after and he never gave her any money. Eventually she had to cash her savings, which was a £25 premium bond. You'll never guess, the following week her number came up and she would have won a thousand had she not cashed it.'

'She wants social services not the police.'

'I don't know why I bother to talk to you, you're all heart.'

'It's not that I don't care, I'm looking at the best use of resources.'

'For your information, that's whom I directed her to but she needed someone to listen and that's what I did.'

'You really are all heart.'

***

Christmas was approaching and Ellen and I planned to travel together to her parents' farm in Mold. On Christmas Eve I woke up to find the road covered in snow. I'd heard stories of Bristol roads being chaotic in snow but I'd not witnessed it before.

I wanted to get in to work and clear up a backlog of claims before the office shut at lunchtime. It would have been nice if those cheques had reached the clients before Christmas. That will not now happen but at least they could leave my desk.

My car was covered with snow and I had to clear the drive before I could get it out. I didn't get very far, as the wheels struggled to get traction on the road. After struggling for half an hour and seeing many cars abandoned on the road, I decided to do the same thing and walked to work. It took me ninety minutes. As soon I got to my desk I phoned Ellen and said it was not a very good idea to come to my flat. We discussed whether she should go alone to Mold and I would join her later; or whatever. In the end we agreed that she would come off the motorway service station near Bristol and I would wait for her there.

The warmth of the greeting in Mold made us forget the weather.

'That was a lovely Christmas card you sent us, Glynis said to me.

'What does it say?' asked Ellen.

Glynis took the card from the mantelpiece. It was of the three wise men. Ellen opened it and saw in my handwriting, the words:

Merry Christmas
From one heathen to another.

One of many reasons why Gareth and I got on so famously was that we shared the belief that our own religion was in no way superior (or inferior) to the others. It was what each of us was born into. Both ate pork or at any rate didn't avoid eating it.'So we're heathens are we?' asked Ellen.

'In a Christian country, yes we are. The rules are made by the majority, think of the bias against us left-handers.'

'Or by the victors, although that's often the same thing,' said Gareth.

We sat in the lounge with an open fire to keep us warm.

'I've had a good year, learned a lot about insurance claims,' I said.

'Saved Camelot some money I understand,' said Gareth,

'Not always.'

'How long will you work on claims?' asked Gareth.

'I'll get out once there's nothing more to learn. Perhaps another couple of years, at the most.'

'Yes, get back to what you're best at.'

Ellen then asked him:

'How is Nick getting on?'

'Our paths don't cross as we're at the opposite ends of the spectrum. He deals with sales and I with claims. I guess he's doing quite well. He's that sort of guy.'

Gareth then turned to Ellen and said:

'How about you, how are you getting on?'

'You don't actually learn a lot by going on the beat but the experience is useful. I'd be glad to get out of it.'

'You're not quitting?' I asked.

'No silly, you'd be the first to know if I was. I just don't like the atmosphere at the station. I can't wait to move into forensic CID work.'

'If she stays there much longer she'll become anti-men or at least anti-policemen.'

'How soon can you get a move? You've had less than two years in your present post,' said Gareth.

'Not sure.'

Glynis, who was busy in the kitchen returned to the lounge and asked:

'How long have you two been together?'

The question was posed to me but it was Ellen who gave the answer:

'Since February 1976.'

'That's nearly seven years, and the relationship seems strong,' said Gareth.

'Rock solid,' I said, adding 'Isn't it?' as I looked at Ellen. She nodded.

'Isn't it time Ellen met your parents?'

'We'd like to meet them too,' added Glynis.

'We can go to Lahore,' said Gareth.

'No that would be a disaster. I'll see what I can do. They're thinking of coming over next year.'

'That would be great,' said Gareth.

'It *could* be great. I'll have to play it by the ear. Mum can be a handful.'

'You've said that before,' said Ellen. 'You can't put it off for ever.'

'Leave it to me.'

A Force of Nature

I was enjoying learning about claims. Yes, really. Ellen and I were making the best of our semi-detached existence. We missed each other during the week but boy we made up for it during weekends. There was only one dark cloud on the horizon. Mum and Dad were coming over to see me. As an antidote I'd organised a break for us.

We planned to spend a week retracing St Paul's journey from Antioch to Rome. We knew that this journey was an amalgam of several journeys. Nevertheless we enjoyed it very much.

'Amazing man, Paul,' said Ellen afterwards, 'Christianity should really be called Paulianity.'

'You know Paul was out to exterminate Christians in Damascus when he had his famous conversion? Exactly the same thing happened to Omar who was on his way to kill the Prophet Muhammad. What changed him was the spellbinding beauty of Quraanic poetry that he heard being recited.'

'Who's Omar?'

'The second Caliph, the best.'

'Makes you wonder.'

'Wonder what?'

'Whether the scribes who wrote the scriptures, copied from each other,' said Ellen.

'What's the harm in borrowing valid concepts? Knowledge is built upon knowledge, that's how science progresses.'

'No faith will admit to building upon other faiths. Each claims to be unique.'

'That's where you're wrong. My lot have a quite clever take on that. Islamic lore has it that Jesus and all the Old Testament prophets from Adam to Moses were precursors of Muhammad, preaching essentially the same religion. All the Prophets have a place in the Quraan, including one, Zalqarnain, who's not in the Bible. Muslim scholars think he might be Alexander the Great.'

'Alexander a Prophet?'

'Yeah , I know, probably the prophet of doom.'

'By the way, you do know that Jesus was a Jew, don't you?' asked Ellen.

'Only on his mother's side.'

'Ha ha, very funny.'

'Actually I don't see why monotheism is superior to polytheism. Certainly there are some towering intellects who were Hindus or Greeks or Romans and there are some idiotic narrow minded Muslim clerics. I know whose views I'd rather accept.'

When we got to Rome it wasn't the Vatican City that interested me. I wanted to see locations used in films; the scene where Gregory Peck's arm was bitten off in *Roman Holiday*, the fountain by the Spanish Steps that featured in *Three Coins in A Fountain*, Anita Ekberg's famous scene in *8 ½* , the location shots of *I Claudius* etc. But yes we also did the Vatican City, the Coliseum and the Sistine Chapel.

On the way back I said:

'That was fun, now back to grim reality.'

Ellen gave me a quizzical look.

'Mum—We've still not discussed how to deal with my parents' visit in September. Mum's going to pester me to get married. I know it.'

'Have you told them that I'm your girlfriend?'

'Well, that depends.'

'On what?'

'On what you mean by the term girlfriend.'

'You know perfectly well what I mean by it. Do they know about me?'

'No.'

'So how are you going to introduce me?'

'I wasn't going to.'

'I see.' She paused but then went on. 'If you want to marry someone you haven't seen, that's down to you. What do I care?'

'It's not like that. Dad's pretty liberal and would be quite happy if I came up with a suitable girl. Mum's different.'

'Maybe, but we've got to meet some time.'

'It's a question of finding the right time.'

'The longer you leave it, the harder it'll be.'

'You don't understand. She's a force of nature. She's got a vile temper.'

'Are you scared of her?'

'Me, scared of Mum? Ha ha. Her temper falls as quickly as it rises. No, I'm not scared of her.'

'So that's it. There'll never be a right time. I might as well cut my losses.'

'Don't be like that Ellen. Her heart's in the right place. She thinks about what she says but usually after she's said it. For all her huffing and puffing she usually falls in line. Of course she'll have her opinions. "Does she come from a good family? Is she nice? Is she pretty? Can she cook?" You score on all those points.'

'So why don't you introduce me formally?'

'It's not that simple.'

'Let's hear it.'

'She wouldn't want to give people an excuse to gossip. Sex before marriage is a big 'No No'. The other big 'No No' is marrying out of faith. If I introduce you there'll be pressure to marry you and then to convert you. If I pretend to be unattached she'll force a girl on me.'

'I'm happy to tell her that we're OK as we are when we meet.'

'Oh, you can't meet her.'

'Why not?'

Here we go again, I thought.

'I told you, she'd insist on us getting married.'

'Leave it to me to talk her round to my way of thinking.'

'No, I can't risk you failing.'

'OK, why don't we tell her that we'll get married and be done with it?'

'Oh, no that'll be too much of a shock for her. We need to break the news gently.'

That killed the conversation. For a while neither of us said anything. Then Ellen said:

'Is marriage not on the cards? Am I wasting my time?'

I made several attempts to answer that without saying anything.

'Don't bother. I get the message,' said Ellen.

***

I left the office later than I'd planned to and had to drive rapidly on the M4, knowing that I'd be late. The problem was the need to make a detour to Southall to buy *paan* and a spittoon. *Paan* was Mum's addiction, a heady mixture of spices and what looked like chalk and tobacco leaf, wrapped in betel leaf. She was a chain-chewer and I dreaded her kiss that left a stain. Still it was better than her temper without *paan*.

I reached Heathrow airport an hour after they were due to land. Luckily they were detained for almost the same length of time when subjected to a random check as they walked through the 'Nothing to Declare' channel. Mum had brought plenty of snacks for me and some of them were examined carefully in case they were a conduit for drugs. I arrived moments before a tall ramrod-straight man in a suit and a short substantial woman in a sari, walked out of the Exit door.

The traditional Asian greeting made me realise that the sense of smell was a mixed blessing. Mum really stank of *paan*. When I recoiled she reacted:

'What's the matter, I'm not good enough for you?'

'No, Mum, I don't want to overstay in the car park and pay more.'

I took them to the Short Stay car park but I'd forgotten which floor I'd left my car in. I used the lift to take them to the top floor and went right round and then, lugging the heavy luggage down the stairs, went one floor down and repeated the process. Mum was getting increasingly agitated as she waddled behind us.

'Can't find your car? Has it been stolen?'

'No, Mum it was here five minutes ago.'

'Five minutes? I thought you'd been waiting an hour?'

'You know what I mean.'

'I don't. Have you been waiting an hour?'

'I had to go to a shop to buy *paan* and a spittoon for you, Mum. You can't get them in Bristol.'

'I've brought my own *paan*.'

They carried on searching for the car, prompting Fatima to say:

'I've been reading about it in Pakistan Times, London is a hot-spot for crime.'

'Come on Mum, sitting in Pakistan you call London a hot-spot for crime? It's one of the safest cities in the world?'

'OK, then, where's your car? You do have a car don't you?'

'Yes Mum. I've just forgotten where I left it. Ah there it is,' I said as I saw my Austin Princess, which I'd taken the trouble to clean and polish. Dad sat comfortably in the back seat, Mum with difficulty in the front. She draped the seat belt across her.

'No, belt yourself Mum.'

'I can't breathe when I'm being strangled.'

'It's the law of the land, Mum.'

'Only if you're caught. You're a safe driver aren't you? Aren't you?'

'I am, but even safe drivers can have accidents. It only takes one lunatic.'

'Fatima, do as the boy says.'

'No one ever listens to me. I'm only a mum.'

Eventually we drove off. When we arrived at a roundabout, noticing that all the traffic was coming from the right and none from the other direction, she shouted, 'Come on, go right.'

'I can't it's a roundabout. I can only go clockwise.'

'I know, the same rule applies in Pakistan but don't worry, there's no one watching.'

'Mum, let me do the driving. Would you rather sit in the back?'

'You mean you'd like me to shut up? No thanks.'

Once we were out of the Heathrow complex and on to the M4, Fatima commenced a monologue with occasional punctuations from Dad and me,

'You know Akbar, your class mate from St Anthony's? He has two children now. Twins. He writes every week without fail to his mother.'

'Have you seen his letters?' I said, turning my head to look at her. The car swerved slightly and there was a loud horn from the car in the middle lane.

'Watch out,' shouted Mum. 'I thought you could drive.'

'I'm sorry, Mum. What were we saying? Yes, have you seen Akbar's letters?'

'No, but his mother won't lie.'

'I bet she won't'

'Don't be sarcastic.'

'I mean how many people write letters these days when it's so cheap to phone. I phone you every week don't I?'

'But letters can be read over and over again.' Then after a five minutes pause, 'You know who he married? Nina, a good local girl.'

'I'm glad for them.'

'How can you drive? The sun is blinding me. I can't see a thing.'

'That's quite common here.'

As we drove past Reading with much of the journey still to be travelled, I said, 'I can't talk any more, Mum. The next fifty miles, as we go past an air-force base, is an accident hot spot. Drivers can't talk and traffic police observe them from helicopters using powerful telescopic lens.'

'What nonsense.'

'Seriously, a friend of mine was caught talking and banned for three months.'

'You're trying to shut your Mum up.'

'I can't talk, Mum.'

'Listen to what the boy says,' said Dad.

For ten minutes no one spoke then Mum stretched forward to reach her handbag. She took out a small box from which she selected a pre-prepared *paan*. As she was about to put it in her mouth, I said,

'Mum I hope you won't spit in the car.'

She ignored that as she started chewing the *paan*.

'Mum, did you hear me. I hope you don't spit in the car.'

She signalled with her hand to say that she wasn't allowed to speak.

'You don't have to answer, just don't spit in the car.'

As they approached the Bath exit I said, 'Right we're out of the range of the helicopters. You can talk now.'

'What makes you think I'll spit in your car? I'll open the window and spit out if I have to.'

'Mum, it'll splash back on to the side of the car and possibly inside it as well.'

'Son, she's just winding you up. She'll wait until we get to your flat.'

She grunted, 'Huh' as if to say, 'What do you take me for.' She then said:

'I didn't see any helicopters. You were just trying to shut me up. What has the world come to, no respect for your elders? Anyway I would never spit in your car. If I had to, I'd ask you to pull up at the next, what do you call it?'

'Service station.'

Eventually we were off the motorway and, half an hour later, were in my flat. I showed them round the flat and left them to shower and change. I put the spittoon in the bedroom, my bedroom which I was making available to them by moving into the spare room.

As we sat down for lunch that I'd prepared in advance, Mum asked:

'The room we're staying in, is it the guest bedroom?'

'No, it's mine actually.'

'Do you have a girlfriend then?'

'Why?'

'Why have you got a double bed then?'

'Married couples, such as you and Dad, sometimes come to stay with me. So I needed a double bed and I put it in the largest bedroom in the house, which happens to be my bedroom. I move into the spare room when couples stay with me.'

'Leave the boy alone,' said Dad.

They sat down to eat. Before taking her first morsel, Mum asked, 'Is this meat halal?'

'Yes Mum.'

'Is there a halal butcher nearby?'

'Not nearby, a few miles away. But I buy mine in bulk from a wholesale butcher in Wales.'

'Does he deliver?'

'No, I go and collect.'

'It's not necessary to be fussy about halal meat, son. There are more important things in life,' said Dad.

'There you go again, always teaching him the wrong things.'

'Mum, if you carry on like this. I'll go back to work.'

'Who wants my opinion? I'm only a mother. Don't call me Mum again.'

I was in for that ancient form of maternal torture, the silent treatment where your mother behaves as if you weren't in the room. Eventually it was Dad who said to her:

'We're only here for a few days. Stop acting like a child.'

I apologised to her for being rude and peace reigned for a while. We spent the rest of the day touring Bristol and the rest of the week touring the Cotswold and Somerset. Dad had a childhood fascination for the Arthurian legend and we spent much time discussing the case for Glastonbury. I felt reasonably in control of the situation and was hopeful that their stay would remain peaceful.

On the sixth day, whilst Mum was having a shower, Dad said to me, 'Son, you really must be careful when you make your bedroom available to guests.'

'Why?'

'Your mother found this under a pile of underwear in your drawer,' he said, brandishing a packet of condoms.

'Oh.'

'Is that all you have to say? Your mother is beside herself with worry. It's no longer whether you have a girlfriend. She now thinks that you're a promiscuous lecher.'

'Oh'

'What do I tell her?'

'I'm thinking, Dad. You know what Mum's like.'

'Yes I do. I got it in the neck too for not bringing you up properly. Tell me, you do have a girlfriend, don't you?'

'Yes, the same girl I've known since Cambridge. Her name is Ellen. She lives and works in London. I am monogamous but because I'm not married Mum'll think it's sinful. Pious Muslims have many wives, but that's allowed. What sort of logic is that?'

'Don't blaspheme and don't compare yourself with practices of fourteen hundred years ago. I'm relieved that you've got a steady girlfriend. Your mother needn't know about it. I'll ask you who stayed in your bedroom before us and you say that it was a young married couple. She can draw her own conclusion.'

'Thanks, Dad. Her parents are very keen to meet you two but I guess now's not the right time.'

'No, it isn't. Not when you have a contraceptive to explain. When do you plan to get married?'

'We've not thought about it. We're happy as we are.'

'Now that won't go down well. We'll be back again in a couple of years. You must sort yourselves out by then and then tell your Mum. Is that clear?'

'I'll ask Ellen.'

'Is that clear?'

'It is but I must ask Ellen.'

'You can do that but you must marry. Let's leave that to one side, are things going OK at work?'

'Yes. You know I'm on the fast track programme. Tim Fredricks our Chief Executive has taken me out of the world of numbers and formulae to one of people.'

'That's a high risk strategy. You'll either soar or sink, staying afloat will not be on.'

'But you encouraged me to do it.'

'Yes, I did but keep your eyes and ears open.'

'I'm doing OK so far.'

'Good. Everyone wants to get to the top of the pyramid but higher you go the fewer the positions. The race doesn't always go to the fastest or the best. You need guile as well as talent.'

'What are you talking about?' asked Mum who had come out of the shower.

'Oh, just man talk,' said Dad.

I excused myself saying I had to phone work and made a quick call to Nick Knights. I asked him to drop in with his 'wife' Phyllis and briefed him on what was required of him. As Phyllis was un-contactable, Nick came with my secretary Louise. They came shortly after lunch. I introduced them to my parents.

'Please meet two of my closest friends, Nick Knights and his wife Louise. They live in London but have taken two weeks' holiday touring the West Country. In fact they stayed with me and only moved out when you came.'

'Oh I'm very sorry,' said Mum. 'If we'd known we'd have come later. You must've left in a hurry. Are you sure you didn't leave anything behind?'

'Nothing that I can't replace by going to the chemist,' said Nick.

Later that day Mum said 'Son, it is unnatural to stay single for too long. Let me find you a bride.'

'Isn't it time you accepted that I'm a grown up adult?'

'Son, to me you're still a child and you will remain a child until you become a father. For that you must get married.'

'I'll marry when I'm ready.'

'What are you waiting for?'

'I've got a lot on, a career to build. I don't want distractions.'

'I call that a draw, would you agree?' asked Dad.

'You're useless. Can't you see it's a defeat for us and a loss for him?'

'Perhaps I should call it stalemate. Come on. It's time to go back to Lahore'

***

I took Mum and Dad to Heathrow and stayed with them until they had checked in and said good bye as they went into the 'Passengers Only' area. I then decided to pay Ellen a visit. I'd not been in touch whilst my parents were in the country and was aching to see her again. I didn't know how she would receive me but there was no point delaying the confrontation.

I drove to her flat in Hoveden Road in Cricklewood and reached there around eight o'clock. Hoveden Road is a row of large Edwardian houses, mostly used as bed-sits. As most tenants have a beat-up old car, the street afforded little spare parking space for visitors. I had to park in an adjacent road some hundred yards away.

As I walked towards her flat I had a sudden attack of cold feet. What if she threw me out? I hadn't got my defences lined up. I slowed down and thought for a while and began to wonder whether it was such a good idea seeing her that night.

I thought about it but couldn't think of a better idea. But I was scared of the downside and suddenly courage deserted me.

I needed a drink, hoping that it would stiffen my resolve. I'd driven past a pub just round the corner so I walked there and ordered a pint of Guinness, downed it, ordered another and downed that almost as quickly and ordered a third.

'Steady on,' said the barman. 'What's the hurry? We don't close for another couple of hours.'

I drank the third pint more slowly and set off to see Ellen. I lingered at the front door for a while before I realised that I could wait no more. I rang the door bell. One of the ground-floor tenants opened the door for him. I rushed upstairs unsteadily and knocked on Ellen's door.

'Who's there?'

'Me, Majid.'

There was no response but a few seconds later Ellen opened the door.

'Can I come in?'

'If you must.'

'Yes, I must,' I said as I pushed past her and went straight to the toilet to relieve myself.

'I'm sorry darling, I had three pints inside me.'

I moved forward to kiss her but she offered only her cheek, the right cheek.

'I'm sorry, I've been busy the last two weeks.'

'Is Mummy happy with her boy?'

'Don't be like that. I'm not Mummy's boy.'

'Then what are you?'

'Oh come on. If only you'd seen the grilling she gave me.'

'How could I, you didn't want me there.'

'Let's not make a mountain out of a molehill.'

'Your Mum *is* a mountain, I don't have to make her one.'

'That's a cheap remark. What's her fatness got to do with anything?'

'Why is me wanting to meet your parents a molehill?'

'You don't understand. We don't want to get married yet; she can't contemplate us living in sin. How can I reconcile the two?'

'And you think living a lie is the best way?'

'I know my parents best and I've got to find the best way of not losing either you or them.'

'You're not man enough to stand up for yourself; you'd better leave.'

'Oh come on, luv, its gone ten o'clock and I've had too much to drink. Can't we sleep on it?'

'Not in my flat you can't. You'd better leave.'

'What, now?'

'Leave.'

Reluctantly I left. I tripped downstairs and walked to my car. I'd forgotten which side-street I'd left it in and it took me half an hour to find it. I got in sat down, turned the key and started the engine.

What am I doing? I can't drive to Bristol now, not in the state I'm in.

I briefly thought of finding a hotel but no that was too much trouble. Instead I slept in the car. Luckily I kept a blanket in the boot. So I lay in the back seat, covered myself from head to toe with the blanket and was soon fast asleep.

I woke up confused by a sense of motion. I was unsure where I was. Eyes still closed, I tried to work that out. I'd seen Mum and Dad off, had a row with Ellen… slept in my car. Blimey what's going on, the car's moving. I removed the blanket from my face and saw a young man, possibly in his twenties, driving the car.

'What are you doing in my car?'

A startled driver turned round, taking the steering with him.

'Watch out, you're going to crash my car,' I shouted while trying as quickly as I could, to control the steering wheel from the back seat. The ensuing tussle only made matters worse as the car zigzagged from the fast lane to the slow lane, to the sounds of horns and screeching tyres as other motorists tried to get out of the way. I eventually let go and the car thief brought the car to a halt.

'Ghost, I see a ghost,' he shouted as, badly shaken, he got out of the car and ran off along the hard shoulder and eventually down the slope into neighbouring fields. One of the other motorists must have phoned the police as a panda car arrived within half an hour. Still trembling, I looked at my watch. It was three in the morning.

'Where am I officer?'

'On the M4, Sir.'

'How did I get here?'

'You tell me, Sir.'

'I don't know.'

'I see. In that case, would you like to breathe in this equipment?'

'Look, I'm not drunk.'

'Let me be the judge of that, Sir.'

'I mean, I did drink last night, three pints, but I didn't drive.'

'So the car drove itself, did it? What is it, Chitty Chitty Bang Bang?'

The policeman laughed at his own joke. Then suddenly he pulled himself up and said, 'Come on, don't waste police time.'

'You can check with my girl-friend. We had a row and she threw me out. I slept in my car in Cricklewood, London. When I was asleep the car got hi-jacked.'

'You expect me to believe that?'

'Look, if I was making it up I'd have thought of something more plausible.'

'We'll worry about that later. Can you breathe into this?'

I did as I was told. I was over the limit but not by much. I was taken to the Reading police station to spend the night in a cell. I pleaded that I needed a lawyer, but. was told that I was not being charged, yet anyway.

'But I still demand to see my lawyer.'

'OK, what's his name?'

'It's a she, Ellen Evan of 8 Hoveden Road, London NW2.'

'OK, you call her?'

'No, could you call her?'

'OK.'

The policeman disappeared to make a call but came back ten minutes later to say:

'Are you taking the Michael out of me?'

'What have I done?'

'Ellen Evan is a policewoman.'

'But she's also a trained lawyer.'

'But she can't act for you.'

'Not in a formal sense but she can advise me.'

'She can't and she won't.'

'Have you asked her?'

'Yes. And if you ask me I'd just sleep. You're not being charged, just being kept here for your own safety. You can go home tomorrow, if you can prove your story.'

The following morning I was discharged.

'You believe me then?'

We picked up a vagrant who was wandering in the fields not far from where you were picked up by us. He fitted your description of the car thief.

***

It was noon before I returned to my flat in Bristol. I had to hire a cab to take me to the spot on the M4 where my car had been left on the hard shoulder. All my thoughts were now focussed on Ellen. It was most unlike her, compassionate by nature, to decline to help when I was in custody. She must be really angry and it was up to me to bring her round. What's more I'd better be quick.

Unsure of winning a war of words, I decided to write her a letter. I took my time over it and made it brief:

Darling

I got it horribly wrong and for that I apologise. I'm not going to tell you how much you mean to me. If you don't know that by now, you never will. But is it such a crime to be sensitive to the feelings of my parents?

88

I talked to Dad and told him how long we've been together. He was OK. We agreed that it was time I told Mum. If I'd told him in advance he'd have prepared the ground and we could have done it this time. That was what you wanted but I foolishly didn't listen to you.

Dad promised to come again in a couple of years and we will then introduce you to her. He'll be in the doghouse as she will guess that he knew before her. That's what fathers are there for. Although I didn't tell him this, we can then announce that we intend to get married. She will first try to stop it and when she fails, try to have it straightaway. I'll say, we'll marry in a couple of years. So 1987 is the goal.

Is that OK?

I'll call you in two days by which time you'd have got this.

I re-read the letter but decided not to send it. It didn't say much about me if I couldn't thrash out the differences face to face or at least by conversation; or perhaps it said it all. I'd phone her in a day or two.

I phoned her in the evening but got no response. I tried again the following day, Saturday, in the morning; again no response. Perhaps she's at work, I thought keeping more negative thoughts at bay.

Two weeks passed without any news from her. Our quarrel was in danger of becoming public knowledge as the year's management conference was only a fortnight away and it looked as if Ellen wouldn't attend.

She'd been looking forward to it but she gave me no reply to voice-mail messages I'd left her. There was always the chance that she'd turn up at the conference without telling me. So I told the conference organisers nothing and thought I'd sort it out on the day.

As I drove to the conference I realised that there was no way Ellen could just turn up as she didn't know which hotel it was being held in. But it was too late as the organisers had laid out seating plans as if she would be there.

Never Knowingly Oversold

When it was announced that the management conference of 1983 was to be held in Nottingham, a city not far from Leicester, my mind went back to Diljeet Singh. I decided to make a surprise visit to his address, after the conference was over. It was over a year since the claim was settled. Assuming that he was alive, he might have become complacent.

Tim began the conference by saying that he had an important announcement to make but would make it at the end of conference to prevent it overshadowing the rest of the conference. That left us on tenterhooks. A clue was two gentlemen sitting in the front row but as none of us recognised them it was a pretty useless clue.

The conference followed a familiar pattern but there was no Lady Godiva this time. Instead during a coffee break Tim called the 'high-flyers' together for a chat.

'You first, Majid, how're you getting on?

I told him that I was learning a lot about claims. I also mentioned the dodgy death which I'd not given up on and will follow up after the conference.

'The smart thing would have been to sort it out before the conference so that you could boast about that too,' said Tim.

Nick was more positive.

'I moved into general insurance sales six months ago. Very exciting. I won a couple of very large contracts, The London Black Cabs and NatWest Bank.'

'What?'

'It's the insurance of the cabs and the employers' liability of the bank.'

'How did you win it?'

'I play golf with the broker.'

'That won it for you?'

'That, and arm-twisting of the Pricing Actuary.

Bruce was more self-effacing. He'd got a good grounding in the Finance and had recently moved into branch administration.

JM, on the other hand was resisting a move out of the investment department, preferring to be a specialist rather than a 'Jack-of-all-trades.'

Everyone was waiting for the announcement on the final day and Tim spoke as follows:

'Ladies and gentlemen, we had a good 1982 and 1983 has started well. Our success is down to the hard work you all have put in. However, one year we may work just as hard but get little or no business. That's the risk we take by dealing exclusively through brokers.

'We have therefore decided to set up a sales force that approaches customers direct, cutting out the middleman. I have recruited Archie Balaskas to take charge of this development. Archie will now explain our approach in more detail.'

A man in his mid-forties stood up from the front row, and walked up to the podium, preceded and followed by cigar smoke. He was taller than me but not by much, corpulent but not obese, practically bald, a lock of straw-coloured hair carefully arranged from left to right to cover as much of the dome as possible. He walked to the podium a sheaf of papers in one hand a glass of clear liquid, which looked like water but was gin, in the other. When he got there, he placed the papers on the lectern with the glass of gin on its left. He then took the cigar from his mouth, put it out and placed it on the lectern to the right of the papers. He lowered his glasses from the bridge of his nose to its tip, looked at the audience and looked at his nose, cleared his throat and commenced speaking.

'Hello everyone. You'll have guessed from my accent that I'm from the West Country. My name is A C Balaskas. The Balaskas came from my Greek grandfather who opened a kebab shop in Clifton. It didn't work out so he shifted to Bedminster, where he did good trade. A C stands for Archibald Christofides.'

Archie relit his cigar, took a puff and, after a sip of the clear liquid, said: 'Tim has already told you why I'm here. Competition for brokers' business is driving profits downwards. If you sell direct to the public, a good salesman can persuade his customer to buy even if the product is expensive. We can then make a decent profit.'

Nick was the first on his feet with a question which turned out to be an observation.

'I can see that this is the right strategic choice for us as a company. It makes the job of those of us who deal with brokers harder but that's life.'

'Thank you,' said Archie.

There was a pause and after a while Tim returned to the podium and asked:

'Any other questions?'

JM asked if a strategy that relied upon exploiting customer ignorance was sustainable.

'Nobody's exploiting anyone. We won't sell a product that the customer does not need,' said Archie.

'If we put the price up we'll lose broker business, possibly all of it,' I said.

'There's a risk of that.'

'Doesn't that kill the idea?'

'They've thought of it,' said Tim. 'The plan is to have two prices. A cheaper product sold through brokers and a dearer product direct.'

'That'll cause confusion.'

'We'll set up a separate company, a subsidiary of Camelot, to sell direct to the public. That'll get over your problem,' said Tim.

'What are you going to call it?' I asked.

'Merlin Life. We've registered the name,' said Archie.

Unfortunately I had a fit of giggles, prompting Archie to ask:

'What's funny?'

'I've got just the right slogan for Merlin Life.'

'Oh yeah, what is it?'

'Never knowingly oversold.'

Spontaneous laughter echoed round the hall and just as suddenly died down when Tim said:

'Why is everyone so negative? If broker business were to decline, we'd be grateful if Archie and his team made a success of Merlin.'

'Thank you for your support,' said Archie. 'Let me say here and now, if we make a success of this venture, then the credit should go to Tim. It was his idea and he's been quite single-minded and supportive.'

'What's the next step?' I asked.

'I need a team of four to lead the sales, product development, finance and administration departments. In fact I've already recruited the Sales Director. He's Jeff Hamilton-Jones and he's here today.'

Jeff then made a short speech.

'My job is to recruit and manage the sales-force. We'll operate from different premises. We will not pinch your brokers' clients, so we'll bring genuine new business. These salesmen will be paid only commission, no basic salary or company cars. My job is to motivate them to stay with us and produce business.'

That evening at dinner, Ellen and I were to sit at the same table as Nick and Phyllis Knights and John and Jane Michael, Bruce and Heather Herrington, the same seating plan as the previous year. But of course there was no Ellen. The wives and partners, back from their trip to the New Forest, Phyllis was the first to ask where Ellen was. I explained that she couldn't take time off.

Phyllis is quite sharp. She noticed that the usual male bonhomie was absent.

'Come on, something has happened. Is somebody going to tell me?' she asked.

'We've done a U-turn?'

'What U-turn?'

'For years we've criticised direct sales companies as being leaches fleecing poor customers.'

'There you go mixing metaphors again,' said Phyllis.

'And there you go stepping in before I finish.'

'Are you going to tell me what it's all about?'

'If you let me.'

Taking Phyllis's silence to mean consent, he carried on:

'We're setting up a direct sales-force.'

'You mean knocking at doors?'

'Sort of. We've told brokers we'll never do that. Now we have to tell them that we've changed tack.'

'That'll make your job harder?'

'Not half.'

Having kept silent so far, I said:

'There's something wrong with the idea that if you cut out the middleman then the customer gets a dearer product not a cheaper one.'

'Quite,' said JM. 'It beggars belief.'

'I'm not sure that I should believe anything you say,' said Nick to me.

'What have I said?'

'I tried your trick of betting that two people in a group will have a common birthday.'

'No, the odds are even if there were two dozen in a randomly selected group.'

'I tried it in my golf club when there were forty-one but it didn't work.'

'With forty-one the odds are much better than evens but its still not a dead-cert. Even favourites get beat you know.'

'So why do you bet?'

'You make sure that the odds you are offered are such that a win is worthwhile.'

'Come on boys,' said Phyllis.

The food arrived and the conversation moved away to more mundane subjects. Then suddenly Nick asked me whether either Ellen or I had heard from Ishtak or Jalal. I said we hadn't other than Christmas and New Year cards. Nick had kept in touch with both.

'Jalal seems fed up with the influx of Taliban refugees from Afghanistan,' he said.

'Yes the Americans armed them to fight the Soviets but then abandoned them when there was a change of strategy.'

We had to stop as the professional after dinner speaker we had engaged stood up to do his piece. He made a number of witty and topical observations. Although from his stock repertoire, he'd taken the trouble to get some background about Camelot and had woven them in. There were jokes at the expense of Tim, direct salesmen and Archie. Everyone found it funny.

Everyone, except Tim and Archie.

Later we had ballroom dancing and unattached people hung around in the bar. I was having a quiet drink when Jeff Hamilton-Jones joined me.

'You're an actuary, I believe. What are you doing handling claims?'

'Broadening my experience. I'll move on.'

'Do you want to join us? We're creating our own management team.'

'Are you looking for a gatekeeper?'

'No, that's me. Direct selling is a lonely job. If you don't sell you don't earn. You're lucky if you make one sale out of ten so you're facing rejection most of the time. So the temptation to cut corners or commit fraud is always there.'

'So what do you do?'

'I give them tender love and care but if they cross the line, I cold-bloodedly cull them. A sort of iron fist in a velvet glove.'

'Rather you than me. What are you offering me?'

'I want you to take hold of the product side of things and design attractive but profitable products.'

'At present I have an upward career path that's quite attractive. If I join you I'll have a narrower path.'

'But you'll earn a lot more. We'll increase your salary by a quarter. In addition you'll get attractive share options. In five years you'll make substantial amounts of money.'

'Shares in Camelot?'

'No shares in Merlin.'

'How will you price it?'

'That's to be decided. Perhaps we'll float it on the stockmarket.'

I said I'd think it over. I thought I'd wait before saying 'No'.

It took Archie a further three months to fill the positions. One of them was an actuary called Wayne Furlong.

***

Once the conference was over I took a cab and asked the driver to drop me at the top of Leamington Spa Road. From there I walked casually along it. There were enough Asians about for me to walk unnoticed. When I approached house number 117, I casually observed it. I didn't see anyone but there was a Ford Escort parked in the drive and the litter bin looked overfull. Somebody was definitely living there.'

I went to the police station to see Bill Sparling.

'I have a hunch that Diljeet Singh is still alive.'

'When will you learn to give up, the guy's dead.'

'His house is occupied and it wouldn't surprise me if he was living there.'

'That's not possible. His death was notified to us and, I'm sure, to his friends and neighbours. I'm also sure that his bank account's been frozen.'

'Don't bank on it. Not all Asians mix with their neighbours and, when it comes to defrauding an insurance company, the community would not rat on its own. I seem to recall that it was us that notified you.'

'What about the DSS and NI records and PAYE? Death was notified to us and the DSS will find out'

'Are the Police and the DSS really joined up? Remember, he ran his own business.'

'No they're not joined up,' conceded Bill.

'There you are. Also he could be an illegal immigrant and not on the DSS system.'

'We can soon establish that.' He disappeared for about half an hour. He came back and said:

'Address, 117 Leamington Spa Road, Leicester?'

'That's him.'

'Well according to the system he's still alive. NI contributions have been paid regularly. No notification of death or request for the Death Grant.'

I let Bill digest his discovery.

'Hasn't Detective Stanley talked to you about other similar cases?'

'No, he operates on a need to know basis.'

'Well, let me tell you, the broker is Hanuman Shastri of Satyem Insurance Brokers, Ealing Road, Wembley. He's arranged similar policies for a number of Asian clients; many of them have died in similar circumstances.' He showed Bill the list and said it was about time someone interrogated Hanuman Shastri.

The table was an eye opener to old Bill, 'Leave it with me. I'll have a word with the Wembley Police. Hanuman has a few questions to answer. But first we need to deal with Diljeet. Let me round up a few officers and pay him a visit. Come with us.'

Two unmarked cars containing four plain-clothed police officers plus me, travelled towards Leamington Spa Road. That road being a thoroughfare with double yellow lines, they parked in a side road. One policeman walked towards the front of the house and took up position two houses away. Half an hour later a call came from him on the mobile saying that a Sikh answering to Diljeet's description had just come out and emptied the contents of his kitchen bin into the large bin outside the house.

I was asked to stay in the car whilst the four policemen moved in, two going to the back to cover escape through there.

Diljeet didn't resist arrest. When they examined his passport they found that he was in the UK at the time of his alleged death. He had no visa; as a British citizen he would have needed one. However he was in India at the time the claim was submitted via Hanuman. He had returned to the UK to complete the sale of his house, using the same solicitor who had sent a terse reminder to Camelot.

Diljeet was charged with conspiracy to defraud Camelot. There were a lot of procedural discussions and the selection of the jury took a few days. Although required to be in attendance, I was called only for a week. How wasteful of resources? The trial lasted three months. Diljeet was found guilty and sentenced to three years in prison. Hanuman Shastri was also arrested and brought to trial the charge being conspiracy to defraud insurance companies. His business was closed down by the DTI and he was barred from holding the directorship of any financial services company. The trial lasted six months and upon being found guilty, he too was sentenced to three years in prison. The solicitor who had submitted the death claim knowing that Diljeet was alive was struck off.

* * *

There was nothing if not variety in the work of the claims department. The next interesting one was the first of its kind that I'd seen. A farmer had put in a claim under his permanent health insurance policy because a back injury was preventing him from working. I got the file out to see what precisely the farmer had bought. The policy promised to pay £2,000 per month after four weeks' disability and for as long as he remained disabled. If he was a lifelong farmer, good for nothing else and he was not actually doing anything else then he had a valid claim. But if he was a farm owner he might be capable of doing administrative type jobs. I talked to Phil about it. His unhelpful comment was:

'We should never have accepted the business in the first place.'

'That's a bit like saying, if you want to go to Edinburgh, you wouldn't start from Bristol. We are where we are.'

'Don't give me smart-Alec comments. You remember Nick Knights talking at the last management conference about how he sold health insurance to farmers.'

'What's wrong with that?'

'Their work is seasonal with nothing to do in the winter months. One farmer sensed an opportunity to generate income by putting in a claim under his policy. That was last year. This year there have been several copy-cat claims.'

'They may try that but they have to prove that they're disabled first.'

'Back injuries are notoriously difficult to disprove. Let's see how you get on.'

I did some research. The customer lived in Kent, sometimes known as the Hop County, sometimes the Garden of England. It was now November, the harvesting would be over. Perhaps Phil was right. There was only one way to find out; pay the customer an unannounced visit.

The best way to make sure that he was in when I turned up was to see him in the morning, perhaps at nine or ten. Sittingbourne was a long way from Bristol so I had to set off at five in the morning. I arrived at a quarter to ten and drove up to the gate. I chose not to drive up the shingled drive. Instead I walked up it, a clipboard with some blank sheets of paper and a Parker ballpoint in my hand. I rang the door bell and scribbled some notes on the sheet of paper. The door was opened by a man wearing a blue boiler suit with the air of someone who was being distracted from doing something important. I went to shake hands as he said 'Hello' but found that my own hands were occupied. I tried to put the clipboard under my armpit but in the process dropped the ballpoint. 'Oops,' I said as the man in the boiler suit stooped to pick it up.

Having recovered my poise, and pen, I said:

'Sorry about that. I was trying to do some paperwork while waiting. Are you Mr Mick Berry?'

'Who's asking?'

'I'm Majid Khan from Camelot Life Insurance Company. Are you Mick Berry?'

'I might be, why do you want to know?

'I wanted to discuss the claim you've recently submitted under your permanent health insurance policy.'

'Oh that, do come in,' he replied clutching his back.'

I was led into the study where Mick pulled up a chair for him and cleared some coats and jumper off a second chair and sat down gingerly.

'Ah, your back's hurting, I see. Can you tell me how it started?'

'We'd harvested our apple crop and put them in boxes. I was in a hurry. I tried to pick up three boxes in one go and my back went. I couldn't move for half an hour.'

'Did you call an ambulance?'

'No. I could barely move and there was no one else there. I was there for an hour before my wife turned up. Gradually she took me back to our house'

'That's awful. Were you able to sleep that night?'

'You're kidding. I was propped on a chair. I couldn't take my clothes off. I daren't lie down in case I couldn't get up again.'

'When did you get better?'

'The pain eased to just bearable after a couple of days but it's remained there since."

'Until now you mean? I mean you're better now aren't you?'

'What do you mean I'm better now? I wouldn't have put in a claim if I was, would I? You insurance companies are all the same, to the fore when collecting premiums but backward when it comes to paying claims.'

'That's unfair. I set off at five in the morning to approve this claim but I need to be satisfied that you're disabled.'

'What do you think? I can hardly bend. All my farming chores are neglected.'

'Are you sure? You had no problem in bending to pick up my ballpoint at your doorstep. You showed no reaction to that spontaneous act either.'

It was clear from the expression on Mick's face that I had caught him completely by surprise. There was panic in his eyes. After a long gap, perhaps thirty seconds, he said:

'Well, that was an exception. I must have been in remission.'

'I don't know about remission, what we've got here is fabrication and what I'm looking for is retraction.'

'Don't play with words Mister. Are you calling me a liar?'

'All I'm saying is that if you go by the definition in the policy, you're not disabled so this claim will not succeed.'

Mick got up briskly, walked towards and opened the front door and said:

'Get out, stop wasting my time.'

'And you stop wasting mine.'

Horseplay?

I was settling down to listen to Wagner. I'd never really come to grips with him; occasional good melody between long boring bits is someone's apt description of the Ring cycle. I received advice on how to appreciate him from an unexpected quarter. I'd met Robert Plinth, one of Archie Balaskas's salesmen operating from Cardiff branch, at a corporate hospitality event. Robert said that Wagner demanded undivided attention as every bar of music had a purpose.

'Read Ernest Newman's *Wagner Nights* and read about each opera as you listen to it.'

So I bought the book and was going to make a start. I needed a diversion to settle my concerns but I couldn't settle down. Three months had passed since I went to Ellen's place drunk but I'd still not heard from her. I was sitting alone in my flat, feeling sorry for myself. And wondering what she was playing at. Would she ever forgive me? Christmas was two days away and it distressed me that she would not be with me. Christmas in Mold had become an established routine. What should I do this time? Go anyway and confront her in her parents' house? I hadn't talked to Gareth and Glynis for a while either. Have I alienated them too? I poured myself a drink and was beginning to contemplate unwelcome thoughts when the phone rang. It was Gareth asking me to go immediately to see Ellen. He was going there himself.

'What's happened?'

'Her colleagues have been harassing her. She's in a bad way.'

'What happened?'

'No time, let's get moving.'

'I want to speak to her first.'

'No, no phone calls. Talk face-to-face, she needs a hug and a cuddle.'

'Don't like the sound of this. Why didn't she phone me?'

'You're wasting time. GO, you can get there sooner than me.'

Perplexed but heeding the advice, I decided that at this time of the evening it was quicker to drive. I sped off as fast as the law would allow and sometimes faster.

My mind was racing. What could it be?

She'd been having a hard time with all the banter. Banter? Taunts, more like. What is it that caused her to phone her Dad and not me? Oh my God, she's not been raped has she? By a policeman? Policemen?

Unpleasant thoughts were racing through my mind as I sped past the Chippenham exit. All tensed up, my foot was coming down hard on the pedal. I was jolted by the sound of horns from the adjacent lane into which I'd been straying as the car meandered. When I realised this, I overcorrected the steering and the car instead of going straight did a U-turn and, cutting across two lanes, ended up on the hard shoulder. Luckily there was no damage as traffic was light. I was badly shaken and it took over half an hour to get back on the road again. When I reached the bed-sit and rang the door-bell Ellen opened the door. She was dishevelled and her eyes were red but, most strikingly, her lovely long golden tresses had gone. It looked as if someone had attacked it randomly with a pair of scissors.

'Who's done that? What happened?'

She collapsed in my arms and started sobbing.

'What happened?'

Instead of replying, she took me to her room. Gareth and Glynis were there.

'I can't show my face in the Station again.'

'Why?'

'We'd just finished our Christmas party and everyone had gone home except the night shift, me and three others. They'd had had too much to drink. They decided to, what was it they said? "You Paki-lover, we'll show you what you're missing"'

I grimaced and asked, 'What did they do?'

'They groped me, kissed me. I fought with all my strength but they were too powerful. They lifted me and lay me on a desk and.'

Overwhelmed, she stopped and sobbed.

'What did they do to you?'

Ellen continued to sob.

'Did they rape you?'

Wiping tears but still sobbing she said:

'They could have, but first they cut my hair short.'

'Cut short? Look what a mess they made of it.'

'Let her finish,' said Gareth.

'Luckily the bell at the front desk rang. Someone had come into the Station and needed dealing with.'

I was shocked and said:

'It's a disgrace. I'll go round and sort them out tomorrow, no, I'll go now.'

'That wouldn't be very clever,' said Gareth.

I was taken aback. I looked at Gareth and said,

'I can't just do nothing?'

'I've already complained to the sergeant,' said Ellen. 'The official line is that it was just pre-Christmas horseplay, nothing more.'

'Horseplay? We'll let the law, and I don't mean the Police, decide that. I'll hire a lawyer to take them on.'

'Think it through, think it through rationally,' said Gareth.

'I have; they need to be punished.'

'She was taunted as a Paki-lover. The story will run and run in the tabloids. It's got a racist angle, a sexist angle, comedians will make material out of it. You may win the case but her reputation would be ruined.'

'So I do nothing?'

'If you go for confrontation Ellen's career in the forces will be finished and you'll be famous for all the wrong reasons.'

'Leave it Dad, Majid and I need to discuss it.'

'OK, we'll go,' said Gareth. 'You two talk it through.'

Before he could go I had a thought:

'Hang on, we should have the evidence on the CCTV.'

'No, the sergeant had it switched off before the Christmas party. He didn't want to waste community money filming festivities. Nothing sinister in that, its common practice.'

'You're not driving back to Mold this late at night?' I asked.

'No, we'll pull up somewhere for the night.'

After the furious discussion, once Gareth and Glynis had gone there was silence which was broken when at last Ellen spoke.

'I didn't know how you'd take it. That's why I phoned Dad.'

I hugged and kissed her. I stroked her hair and said, 'You've done nothing wrong. You were right to phone your Dad. He's better at handling such things.'

'No, I was proud of the way you reacted. It showed that you cared. I was afraid that you'd react the way Dad reacted.'

'Of course I care about you. But your Dad is right. We should focus on what's best for you rather than be obsessed with revenge.'

I then added, 'But we're not going to let the bastards get away with it.'

Ellen did not respond. She was looking at herself in the mirror. I went up to her and stroked her hair and put my arms round her and squeezed her breast gently.

'First things first, we must go to the hairdresser and ask her to give you a new hairstyle.'

'But I must tidy it up first. I can't go outside like this. You should've seen the looks I got on the train. I look like someone out of a concentration camp.'

'You do actually. Can I help tidy it up?'

'I doubt it. What you can do is to go to Marks & Spencer in Edgware Road and buy me a hat. No, you might buy the wrong one. We'll go together tomorrow morning. It's Christmas Eve.'

'OK. You're going for an interim style aren't you?'

'What do you mean?'

'You will grow your hair long again? You're defined by your long golden tresses. I can't imagine you without it.'

'I don't know how long it will take; a year? Two years? Somehow long hair doesn't fit a policewoman's image.'

'Oh Ellen, don't give up your tresses; don't stop being Goldilocks.'

'How did you know I was Goldilocks?'

'I didn't. It just seemed an appropriate name.'

'That was what all the girls at my school called me. OK darling, just to please you I'll grow it long again. You may have to wait a while.'

I prepared to sleep on the settee which doubles up as an emergency bed just in case Ellen was averse to physical contact. She would have none of it and we slept together.

Ellen slept soundly but I lay awake for quite a while. In the dark I couldn't see her but the image of her head shorn of hair kept recurring as were images of the humiliation she'd undergone. When I woke up in the morning there was enough light to see her lying there peaceful and motionless, the body utterly relaxed and limp. To think that we'd not spoken to each other for three months. I'd have to broach the subject soon, can't ignore it. But I didn't want to rush it in case she thought that I was ignoring her present problems.

Eventually, it was Ellen who confronted the elephant in the room over breakfast.

'Go on, then; aren't you going to tell me all about your Mum and Dad's visit?'

I did.

She burst out laughing on hearing that Mum had found condoms in the drawer.

'Good job, I didn't meet her. You'd have had trouble wriggling out of it then.'

'Would've been fun watching her realise that we'd been sleeping together.'

'It was sporting of Nick to help you out.'

'He's friendly enough socially.'

'Now tell me, how did you come to have condoms in your possession?'

This was a difficult one to answer given my past reluctance to go to a chemist. I could tell her the truth but would she believe me? Maybe not but I had to tell her.

'I bought it a week before the parents came but forgot to properly hide it.'

'But why did you buy it? You'd always refused to go to a chemist?'

'It took a great deal of courage, I tell you. I thought it wasn't fair you going on the pill seeing as you're concerned about its side-effects. It was going to be my peace offering to you.'

With a stern face as she asked:

'You've not got a new girlfriend, have you?'

'Don't be daft. Who can possibly replace you?'

'Three months is a long time. Hang on a second, you bought it before your parents got here. What's going on?'

'I knew I'd be in trouble for not introducing you to them so I bought it as a peace offering when we came back from our holiday retracing St Paul's journey.'

'A likely story.'

'Darling, you've got to believe me. I do stupid things and maybe this was stupid, but I don't do lies. You know that by now, surely?'

'I'm used to the pill now, so let's forget it. Now tell me, how did you come to be in Reading police station?'

I gave her the full story. Ellen, all attentive, her face a picture of concern but occasionally bursting into peals of laughter said at the end:

'You didn't seriously think that I, a policewoman, could assist you, did you?'

'I don't see why not? I was only asking you to confirm facts, not a legal defence.'

Ellen didn't respond but continued to listen and I went on:

'Actually, I was playing the sympathy card. I was hoping that your anger would melt.'

'What, by waking me up at four in the morning?'

'I'm sorry, I got it wrong again.'

'Come here, if you had one more brain cell you'd be an amoeba.'

In moments like these I suspect that it's my follies that she finds endearing. Anyway she said cheerfully:

'We must do this more often.'

'Do what?'

'Quarrel.'

'How can you say that? It was horrible.'

'I agree but wasn't it fun making up?'

I had not yet shown her the letter I had written but not sent to her. I wondered whether to commit myself to getting married in 1987. I wasn't against it but if for some reason that turned out to be impractical, it would be marginally better not to have made that commitment. In the end an urge to tell the truth prevailed. Luckily it was still in my briefcase.

'I forgot to show you the grovelling letter I wrote but didn't send.'

Ellen read it and, tears streaming down her face, embraced me.

'We must quarrel more often.'

She then asked me what happened at the management conference.

'Phyllis was asking after you and so was Nick.'

'What did you say to them?'

'I said you couldn't get time off work.'

'So, you can tell lies.'

She'd got me there. I had no answer to give. She said white lies are what good relationships are built upon.

She then asked how I was getting on compared to the other high flyers.

'This is a marathon, not a sprint and anyway, it's not my opinion that matters.'

'I know but I'd still like to hear it.'

'But we're not all running the same race.'

'Is this another one of your corny jokes?'

'No. Not everyone wants to be the Chief Executive.'

'This is getting a bit obtuse. Leave that for the minute. How are the others getting on?'

'Nick's clearly going for the top job, never misses an opportunity to impress Tim.'

'And Bruce?'

'I don't know, seems content to do a good job hoping that rewards will follow.'

'And you?'

'Me?'

'Yes, you.'

'I'm not sure. I guess I'm a bit like Bruce. I wouldn't say that I'm over-ambitious.'

'No?'

'You know me better than that?'

'But you hate coming second?'

'That's different.'

'Why is it different?'

'I hate losing; that's not the same thing as obsession with winning.'

'Especially losing to Nick?'

'Especially to that toe-rag.'

'So, if Nick's going for the top job, then you want it too?'

'You're putting me in a corner. I became an actuary to do financial analysis and my ambition was to be the Actuary of Camelot. I had no desire to be its Chief Executive.'

'Why not?'

'Actuaries don't make good leaders. A leader has to lead his troops with no self-doubt. Sometimes he'll lead them into the Valley of Death. So he needs good advisers. Actuaries are plagued by doubt. They know there is no right answer or course of action.'

'So who'll make a good leader?'

'Tim's a good leader, potentially. He just needs to listen a little more. He beat Clem to the top job. Clem is not a good leader but he's a good adviser and devil's advocate.'

'You're not telling me that Nick would make a good leader and you a good No. 2'

'Sadly yes.'

'I noticed that you used the past tense when you said you had no desire to be Chief Executive. Is that what Nick's done to you?'

. 'Yes, I won't let that toe-rag beat me.'

I should have known better than to argue with a lawyer. I shouldn't have fallen into her trap. Mind you it wasn't exactly a trap. Circumstances have forced me to run the wrong race.

It was time to go to the hairdresser. More in hope than expectation, we went together, Ellen covering her head with a scarf.

I had tidied up her hair with a pair of scissors. Luckily there was a cancellation. The hairdresser, a Caribbean girl looked at Ellen's head and said:

'Jeez, who cut your hair?'

'A trainee hairdresser cut it for free.'

'Free? She pay you for making a mess like that.'

'I know that's why I've come to you.'

'Who's your normal hairdresser?'

'She got married and moved to Abergevenny.'

'Abba what?'

'It's a place in Wales.'

When she came out of the hairdressers, she looked more like Lulu than herself. Afterwards we decided to return to normal life which, this being Christmas Eve, meant going to Mold.

Along the way we examined all options open to her. If we chose to lodge a complaint, the lawyer in Ellen could see challenges. Evidence or proof would be the problem. No CCTV. There was no rape or attempted rape. She might have been saved by the bell but that is neither here nor there. The only thing that she suffered was hair loss.

However, carrying on as if nothing happened would only encourage the bastards to misbehave further. Even if she was transferred elsewhere she'd be taunted. She could leave the force but why give up on her lifelong ambition?

So we decided that she should launch a formal complaint and that I would join her. Gareth and Glynis were wary but went along with it if the fall-back position was to leave the force.

On the day after Boxing Day we returned to London and went to the Kilburn police station. There we lodged a complaint against the three policemen.

'This is a pretty serious charge,' said the sergeant

'It's a pretty serious offence,' I said.

'You must expect them to defend themselves vigorously.'

'We'll let the facts be the judge.'

'Are you sure you want to expose yourself to the glare of publicity?' he said to Ellen.

'I'll have to put up with it, if I have to.'

'If we go through the formal process they'd be suspended on full pay. The press will find out. You'll have stiff cross examination. They will pry into your personal life.'

He rambled on, jumbling up his points.

'What's the alternative?' I asked.

'We could ask the three men whether they would accept a reprimand that will be placed on their file. If they agree they're tacitly admitting guilt.'

'What do I gain from it?'

'You escape prurient cross-examination.'

'Not enough.'

'Please think it over. Have you ever witnessed a rape or sexual assault trial? It doesn't matter whether the man is guilty or not the girl is put though the mincer. Her sex life is pored over and she is made to look a harlot who's asked for it.'

'No thanks to your officers, this is luckily not a rape case. They can dig as much as like, Ellen is pure.'

'Are you sure about that? You only have her word for it.'

'How dare you?'

'I'm only pointing out the down side.'

'Anyway, what option does she have? If she doesn't complain people would say that she asked for it.'

'OK, let me call the guys in, at least Byrne and Stein. Whitbread's on leave.'

He telephoned and asked them to come in Stein came in first followed by Byrne. Both did a double take when they saw Ellen and then me.

'Well guys, Evan here, your colleague, has levelled a serious charge against you.'

'What charge?'

'Physical assault. She says you cut her hair off and engaged in physical assault.'

'When?'

'On the evening of the 22nd.'

'22nd of what?'

'December'

'You mean yesterday?'

'Cut out the sarcasm, you know pretty well what you did and when,' I said.

'No need for anger. We're police officers and we deal in facts.'

'What are the facts then?' I asked.

'There was no physical assault. As part of her training we were showing her what a physical assault looks like so that she may recognise it if she comes across a case on her beat. OK there was some horseplay but she was a willing participant.'

'What a load of nonsense,' said an angry Ellen.

'That's enough you may go now,' said the sergeant to Byrne and Stein.

'You're not going to let her get away with it?' asked Stein.

'I said go,' he bellowed.

He waited for his anger to die down and then turned round and, with a smile on his face, said to us:

'See what you're up against?'

'I can see it but quite frankly I don't trust you. Anyway what are you proposing?' I asked.

'If I get them to tacitly admit guilt and also arrange a transfer for Ellen, would that be OK?'

'What guilt will they admit to?' Ellen asked.

'That will be a matter for negotiation.'

'Don't like the sound of that,' I said

'There are two sides to every story. They have their rights too.'

'Before we get bogged down in that, will their admission be placed on their files as a black mark?' asked Ellen.

'That will kill their promotion prospects for good.'

'As it should.'

'But that means that they won't accept it. Having nothing to lose they'll go for all out character assassination.'

'You leave us no choice but to fight the case. I'll talk to Kate Spencer, our in house lawyer and ask her to act for Ellen,' I said.

We returned to Ellen's bedsit. This was going to be tough. Was a career in the forces worthwhile? I wondered. That evening the doorbell and Ellen answered it.

'Majid, come here quick,' she shouted.

I quickly ran to the front door and saw a large person, with a granite-like face that made him look more like a villain. He had a demonic expression on his face that was, frankly, frightening.

He stayed at the doorstep but spoke loudly,

'If you bring false charge against us, I'll make life hell for you and your Paki-lover.'

'You disgusting man, he has a name and he's a man not an uncouth animal like you?'

'What did you say?' he said grabbing her by the blouse collar.'

'Leave her alone. I can assure you we don't have to bring false charges against you. True ones will do,' I said.

I had worked out by now that he must be Whitbread, the policeman who was on leave when we went to lodge a complaint.

The general commotion brought one of the other residents to the front door and Whitbread left. I had to go back to Bristol later that day. I asked Ellen to take a couple of days off.

Next day I talked to Kate. The same arguments were reversed. Kate said that the legal system was loaded in favour of men and Ellen should be prepared for some flak. In the end we decided that Kate would draft a formal charge which would be served upon the miscreants but actually delivered to the sergeant. He would strive, might and main, to avoid his station being engulfed in a scandal. It was then a question of driving a hard bargain.

The process took three weeks during which Ellen was on sick leave but in the end a compromise was reached. The miscreants were reprimanded for an unspecified offence and Ellen was transferred to the Earl's Court station with a promise of a move within a year into CID work.

I left for Bristol the following day, our relationship back on course. I bought myself a bunch of roses from the local florist and put them in a jug on the dining table. Its fragrance was a constant reminder of the gift of smell which she had given me. Actually a rose was not the most appropriate flower. It was too priggish. A marigold or sunflower was more appropriate to her sunny and friendly nature.

Within three months Ellen had got her wish and she was doing CID work.

Torching the Stock

The start of 1984 was overshadowed by Ellen's ordeal and her reluctance to show her face, or rather, hair, in public. It was March and her move to CID that brought a measure of serenity in her life.

Camelot Life's fast-track management development programme had its first casualty. JM resigned to join a firm of investment analysts. Ted Leary had wanted him to spend a year in the customer services department which JM didn't fancy. I had a lot of time for JM and we agreed to stay in touch.

I like to think that three years in life insurance claims, which I completed in the summer, had hardened me and made me more street-smart. I felt that the experiment of taking me out of the world of numbers to one of people had been a success. Now I wanted to return to the world of financial forecasting, the natural habitat of actuaries.

The request was denied and I was chided for lacking ambition. Instead, I was transferred to the claims department of Camelot General, the sister company that did general insurance. General insurance is the collective term for the insurance of goods and chattels, car, house, business etc. I moved into a new office, which was identical to my previous one but one floor up and directly above. On the first morning, when I went to get my second cup of coffee, I visited the toilet which was next door to the vending machine. I realised that something was not quite right. There were two dispensers on the wall; one for aspirin and the other, sanitary towels. I saw no urinals. I realised what had happened. I was one floor up from before. As toilet gender alternated between floors, I was in the Ladies. The doors to the cubicles didn't come down to the floor, there was an eighteen inch gap. I could see that they were all empty. I was on my own.

I was about to make a hasty retreat when I heard the voices of two girls coming from the buffer room that separates the toilet from the office area. I panicked and dashed into a cubicle, shut its door and sat down on the toilet seat with the lid down.

The girls were just having a natter and it suddenly occurred to me that my shoes, which would be visible from underneath the door, would give the game away.

My thighs started to ache from having to hold my feet eighteen inches off the ground whilst the girls rabbited on. A third girl joined in and I couldn't recognise any of the voices.

They were saying which of the Camelot blokes they'd most like to bed and which they'd like least. Nick Knights was clearly a favourite; he had the looks. Tim also scored well; he had the money. To my horror, the worst three were all actuaries or actuarial students. I daren't wait to find out which of the two categories I would come in. So I got up cleared my throat and, as the girls turned around startled, I opened the cubicle door, said 'Excuse me,' and walked out.

***

The first few weeks dealing with general insurance claims made me wonder if people were basically dishonest. There was a lot of petty fraud such as overstatement of loss on burglary; so common that it was allowed for in the pricing; in effect the honest subsidised the crooked.

One Saturday I set off for an evening meeting with Ellen. As I drove on the M4 my mind was on the imminent management development course that HR was organising. Many promising careers had foundered at such courses. I'd have to be on guard. My thoughts were interrupted by a roadblock which forced me to get off at the next exit and use the A4, as did every other driver who was on the M4. I made painful progress afterwards and I braced myself for further delays when I heard the siren of fire engines and had to make way. When I continued the journey I saw smoke billowing into the sky. I was able to get back on to the M4 at the next exit and was only an hour late. Ellen was not in her flat. She'd left a note pinned to her door saying,

'Sorry, called away on urgent business. Couldn't phone you'd left home. I'll give you a call late tonight, if you decide to go home. I'm on duty tomorrow.'

I lingered for half an hour and then drove back home, stopping at a service station for a sandwich. I reached home at 8pm and half an hour later Ellen phoned.

'I'm sorry, there was a fire in an industrial warehouse in Slough.'

'Slough? That's not your patch?'

'No, it's the next one due West. They were short of staff.'

'I saw the smoke. But why you and not the fire brigade?'

'Oh, they got there first. We're involved because of suspected arson.'

I thought no more about it until on the following morning, Sunday, the manager of Slough branch, Bruce Herrington, phoned to say, 'Two big claims are on the cards. Fire has destroyed the entire warehouse stock of two of our biggest clients. The loss on each could top a million.'

'Who are these clients?'

'One is the Roaring Forties, makers of ladies clothes, for the premium end of the mass-market and the other Mehr Enterprises, an ethnic beer to pickles manufacturers, whose pickles and condiments warehouse was burned down.'

As was usual practice in such cases, on Monday morning I phoned Ken Steiger, an independent loss-assessor to review the damage caused by the fire. We met later that afternoon in the Slough branch.

'The critical question is the cause of the fire. Was it arson? Was the fire started by the policyholder or at his instigation? Or was it something else? We won't pay if the fire was started by the policyholder or at his behest. If that is not the case, we'd estimate the size of the damage." said Ken.

'Arson I understand but why would someone want to set fire to his own possessions?'

'It happens all the time. Whether you buy clothes in or make them yourself you'd plan to sell it at four times the cost price. That means that the cost price is one-quarter or 25% of the shop price. At the end of the season you maybe left with a lot of unsold stock. You then have a choice: you can try to shift it in a grand sale at a 70% discount, making next to no money on it; or you set fire to it and haggle with the insurance company and settle for a value of say 60%. You'll have to pay say 10% to the gang that torches your stock so you shift your warehouse stock for 50% of the railing price, i.e. double the cost price.'

'You're telling me that they make more money by setting fire to their stock?'

'Five times as much as from shifting it in an end-of-season sale'

'I can understand that for clothes but surely not pickles and condiments and why was the beer mountain left untouched?'

'That's easy, you can't set fire to liquid. Pickles can suffer the same problem as clothing. If one brand gains dominance then others remain unsold.'

'Why can't the gangs be caught?'

'Proving it is the problem but we have a go every time.'

'Count me in when you have a go?'

'I don't get involved in it and I recommend you don't either. These are really nasty people and you could well end up in a lump of concrete.'

I phoned Ellen that evening. She confirmed that arson by the owners was suspected. It followed a familiar pattern. Mehr Enterprises was owned by Polly Mehr-Homji, the guy Detective Stanley was so determined to prove alive.

'Well, I'd never. Is he alive then?'

'I don't know but his business has suffered through neglect.'

'Do you think you'll catch them?'

'Even if we do, we'd lack evidence that'll hold up in a court of law.'

'Are you suggesting that we pay up even if we suspect fraud?'

'That's what I'm saying, unofficially. Officially, it's up to you; I have no view.'

'I'm not going to let them get away with it; not on my watch.'

'You don't understand. Even tough-as-nails coppers won't take them on alone.'

'So I just chicken out do I?'

'No, you follow the advice of the police and the loss assessor; they're the experts.'

'I'll think about it,'

I had no intention of giving in to thugs, whatever others might say. Next day I spent some time trying to work out how to decline the claim. I couldn't say that the claim was fraudulent as I didn't have concrete proof. In the end I drafted a brief letter but didn't post it allowing myself some thinking time. The letter said:

We remain unconvinced that the fire was not started deliberately by the insured.

Not terribly good English, what with the use of double negatives but it was the best I could manage. But before I left the office, Louise my secretary buzzed me to say that there was a policewoman waiting downstairs for me. Intrigued, I popped down and saw Ellen waiting. She was in uniform and was carrying a bag.

'Sorry darling, I wanted to see you urgently.'

'OK, what's up?'

'I'll tell you in a minute. Can I go to the Ladies first?'

When she emerged from it she was no longer in uniform but in skirt and blouse with a marigold in her jacket pocket.

'I'm here not as a policewoman but as your girlfriend. Can you promise me that you won't contest this claim?'

'And let the thugs win?'

'You can stop them winning but you'll lose your life. Is that a fair bargain?'

'Someone's got to make a stand.'

'What about me? I'll be the innocent victim if I lose you.'

That made me think. I can't put my interest ahead of the company's but I'll be blowed if I was going to put the company ahead of the love of my life.

'Point taken,' I said.

I took her to my office. Together we redrafted the letter settling the claim but adding a coda stating that should it subsequently be proven to be fraud the amount paid should be refunded with interest.

We went back and spent the night in my flat. Ellen celebrated as if she'd found someone she thought she'd lost. I was smothered in hugs and kisses; yes and that too.

Nick Steals a March

I had done a year in general insurance claims and was back in the life insurance company. I was moved to the new business and marketing side of things, taking over from Nick Knights. Nick moved to Manchester to become the regional sales manager for the North West region. He had transformed the marketing department and created an enormous impression. I sought his advice.

'All I hear in marketing, since taking over from you is about the F-Plan. Do you have any advice to give me on how to build successful products?'

'I've got a big piece of business going through right now. Listen to what the brokers want. They're your real customers.'

'I tried that but all they ask for is more commission and the cheapest price.'

'Ah that's because they know that you're an actuary and they think you're a soft touch. A canny guy like me knows how to ask questions. Keep trying.'

That was an unhelpful remark. I joined the Institute of Marketing and got hold of the standard textbook by Kotler. I found his concepts revealing. It was nothing like Nick's approach of 'me too' product development. Kotler said, 'Put the customer first, find out what he needs, deliver it efficiently. If you then get the pricing right, everyone would be happy'. I could see that that *might* be true for a tangible product such as a car or a Michael Jackson concert. Was it true for an intangible product such an insurance policy, where you collect money now in return for a promise whose delivery was sometime well into the future? I was not sure. All I could say was that whilst delivering the customer what he needs might not guarantee success, it can do no harm. The opposite can do untold harm.

***

I had to temporarily shelve these issues as the two-day management development course had arrived. I'll have to pit myself against my rivals.

They say that it is not like that but deep down you know it will be. The participants were Nick, currently the regional sales manager for the North West, Bruce, currently the manager of Slough branch, Kate Spencer, Clem Hill, the actuary of Camelot and Shane Barnes, the managing director of Camelot's Australian business. Ted Leary from HR also took part, partly as a mole but also as he too was highly regarded. And of course there was me.

All of us were regarded as 'high-flyers', people with great potential. The exception was Clem Hill who had already risen, in effect to his limit having fairly recently been beaten to the top job. He was denied that position for a perceived lack of negotiation skills. This course addressed that failing.

The eighth person was to have been John Michael. When he resigned a replacement had to be found. 'Tiger' Lilley, a friend of Tim Fredricks stepped in.

Ellen wanted to accompany me. However the rules of the course demanded that the participants should be cocooned in a world of their own. A monastic existence may or may not improve business performance but the rules forbade interaction with people outside the participants. Ellen wasn't happy as she quite fancied spending time with me in the Lake Districts where she spent a lot of childhood holidays. I promised to make it up to up to her with a special holiday, free of insurance talk. .

The course was led by Derek Rowan, an earthy South African, six feet two inches of well toned flesh covered by sun-drenched skin. He met the eight delegates at dinner and afterwards he outlined the programme.

'The first exercise on this course is about negotiating skills; the second about team-building. They are the two most important skills in business, Afterwards you can reflect upon where you can improve. Please make the most of this course. And finally, there will also be a talk on the competencies required in a successful team.

'All that is for tomorrow. In the meantime bond.'

In the bar there was guarded banter. Nick was full of beans and very proud of a new product he'd designed which was called F-Plan, short for Freedom Plan.

'Freedom from what?' I asked.

'Freedom to take your accrued pension rights when you leave employment.'

'You mean transfer it to your new employer?'

'You can hold on to the policy until you retire and the pension is started?'

'Can't you do that anyway?'

'Not always, the pensions red-tape is unbelievable.'

'I shall watch its progress with interest.'

Next morning, Derek introduced the negotiation game,.

'You are in the motor trade. Four of you, Majid, Bruce, Tiger and Kate are dealers; the other four, Nick, Shane, Ted and Clem are customers.

'The selections are purely random. Each dealer has a Porsche to sell, which costs £10,000 to manufacture and has a recommended list price of £20,000.

'Here are the rules of the game. You don't have to take them down. They're all on flip-chart.

'Each dealer must sell his car and each customer must buy one; fail to do that and you're out of the game. Dealers must display their showroom price for all to see. No dealer knows the price bid by a customer to another dealer. A customer is allowed only four bids spread over four rounds. The dealer who gets the highest price and the customer the cheapest price are the winners.'

'It sounds like a game of poker,' I said.

'Remember,' said Derek, 'Customers are allowed only one bid per round. They have to decide which of the four cars to bid for and how much to bid. From a dealer's perspective, if someone bids less than the price he had advertised should he accept it or wait for the next round?'

Derek paused but got no reaction, so he carried on.

'OK, the first round starts now. Come on dealers, set your opening prices.'

They did. Derek input those into his computer and put them on the flip chart.

Round 1				
Dealer	Majid	Bruce	Tiger	Kate
Car offered at	£20,000	£20,000	£20,000	£20,000

'Come on customers you have half an hour to put in your bids,' urged Derek. They did and Derek input that into his computer which spewed out the results within a minute or so. Derek put them on the flip chart.

Round 1				
Dealer	Majid	Bruce	Tiger	Kate
Car offered at	£20,000	£20,000	£20,000	£20,000
Car sold?	x	x	x	x

Everyone was feeling their way. I had received two bids; £17,000 and £15,000, both below my offer price. I should have really accepted the higher of the two but I wanted to see how the game would develop. The rules were driven by logic rather than emotion and I backed myself to prevail.

After lunch, Derek proceeded to the team-building computer game. Four teams of two were formed, I was paired with Nick. An Indian jungle infested with man-eating tigers was simulated. The aim of the game was to capture and kill tigers to extract parts which were in great demand from the Chinese for their alleged medicinal and aphrodisiacal properties. The team that makes the most money wins.

Nick and I got together to map out our approach. We agreed that there were three distinct tasks; catching and killing the tiger, extracting the necessary parts and selling them to the Chinese. We couldn't agree on how the job should be allocated. Nick argued that he was the better than me at all three and should therefore do the lot; but his solo effort should be recognised. I said that who was better remained to be proved; that was the purpose of the course.

In the end we agreed to take turns. Nick would go out first to hunt and kill whilst I would remain back at the ranch ready to skin and extract the parts when the catch has been made. We would then swap round. Each had his own PC and whilst Nick went into the jungle on his, I sat at mine and tried to see if I could crack the logic behind the computer game. Such insight would enable us to 'beat the system' but the code was protected.

I then tried to think through the sale to the Chinese. There were various ways that could be done. They could enter into a forward contract to deliver a fixed number of material for an attractive price; but then they'd have to deliver. Otherwise the price you got was dependent upon supply and demand at the time of delivery. Should we sabotage the competition? If so, how?

Suddenly, there was a commotion. A roaring tiger burst into view into the simulated building that I was in. It had been lassoed and leapt towards me, its teeth bared and front paws aloft. I saw Nick being dragged into the room, holding on to the other end of the lassoo. When he saw me, he let go of the lassoo and said:

'Right you kill this tiger and I'll go and catch the next one.'

Nick was off quicker than you could say, 'Coward'. I felt the hot breath of the tiger around my neck. I was terrified and in sheer panic I pressed the abort button on the computer. Nothing happened. I tried again and just when I felt a sharp prick on my neck the computer switched off.

Badly shaken, I found myself in a room with a bank of PCs with no sight of a jungle or tiger. A period of recrimination followed, each blaming the other. We decided to have another go but the computer wouldn't let us.

That evening before dinner Derek reviewed the results.

'I hope you've learned something about yourselves this afternoon.'

'Yes, this game is unreal,' I said.

'No, the game's OK. What we've got here is bunch of individualists with strong egos. None of you is a team player apart from Kate. The worst pairing was of Majid and Nick.'

'I'm surprised,' said Nick. 'Our skills are complementary surely?'

'Maybe,' said Derek, 'but ego can get in the way.'

After coffee we returned to the negotiations game. Each dealer had to submit the price at which they would offer their car in Round 2. Derek put it on the flip chart and then input it into the computer. Next morning the customers made their bids and the results, produced by the computer were reviewed by Derek. 'Ha ha, we're slow learners, are we?' pointing to the flip chart:

	Round 2			
Dealer	Majid	Bruce	Tiger	Kate
Car offered at	£17,000	£17,000	£16,000	£14,000
Car sold?	x	x	x	√
Winner				Clem
Winning price				£15,500

Disaster. Clem however managed to buy. Clever guy. He must have reckoned that as Kate had the lowest offered price, everyone will bid for it. He prevailed by offering more.

After dinner the remaining dealers submitted their Round 3 prices to the computer and the following morning the remaining customers put their bids in.

This was turning into a humiliation. Undercut again, mine was the only unsold car. Shane had managed to buy a car relatively cheap.

Round 3			
Dealer	Majid	Bruce	Tiger
Car offered at	£16,000	£15,000	£14,000
Car sold?	x	√	√
Winner		Ted	Shane
Winning price		£15,000	£14,500

Only one round left and, only one customer, Nick. He had offered me £15,500 but I had turned it down. One of us had been very foolish.

Shane had done well.

The golf course beckoned for most of the participants. Not for me. I was sweating over how to deal with the next round. Nick was more carefree and enjoyed a round of golf; well, pitch and putt, actually.

Could I turn defeat into victory and get the highest price after all?

Round 4	
Dealer	Majid
Car offered at	£20,000
Car sold?	√
Winner	Nick
Price sold at	£10,000

I'd forgotten that although Nick *had* to buy, I *had* to sell as well.

Nick was declared the winning customer as he paid only £10,000; Kate was the winning dealer having got £15,500.

'Bad luck,' commiserated Shane. 'What tactic did you follow?'

'It's called suck it and see. How about you?'

'Didn't go for the jackpot, took what was available. Mind you, not sure what it proves with Kate winning. She wasn't even trying.'

'That's what all losers say,' taunted Shane. 'She's a canny old Sheila.'

Shocking Fatima

It was Christmas 1984 and we were at Ellen's parents' farm. I wanted to discuss my parents' visit next year.

'Do you want the good news or the bad news?' I asked.

'It's like that is it? OK, let's have the good news first,' said Gareth.

'Mum and Dad are visiting next year.'

'Great. What's the bad news?'

'Mum said that she won't go back without obtaining my consent to marriage.'

'Did she now?' asked Glynis.

'Why is that bad news? Don't you want to get married?'

'We do,' I said, looking at Ellen, 'but not just yet. We want to wait until we're both living together.'

'Does she have someone in mind?' asked Gareth.

'I wouldn't put it past her but Dad is likely to over-rule her.'

'I thought your Mum wore the trousers in your family?'

'She speaks most but Dad's the unobtrusive boss.'

'I see,' said Glynis.

'It's about time I introduced Ellen to Mum. She's got to find out some time.'

'What about your Dad?'

'I told him the last time he was here and he was thrilled. I should have listened to Ellen and come clean to Mum too but I chickened out.'

'You think Mum can handle it now?'

'It's damned difficult. Mum is unforgiving if you lie to her but she's so demanding you sometimes have to lie for a quiet life. But you can't lie for ever.'

'Are you sure? You may be forced to choose between her and me,' said Ellen.

'I'm not sure and I might chicken out.'

Ellen didn't reply so I said, speaking to Glynis and Gareth, 'I know you feel that it's about time you met them.

'Was your Dad happy about keeping a secret from his wife?'

'I don't think he was, but everything is relative. He knew that she would have exploded if I'd sprung this news on her last time.'

'Why do you think it would be any better this time?'

'It won't really. I should've listened to Ellen. But at least I can stop it getting worse.'

'Any way, you should clear it with him.'

'Oh he phoned me last week and said that I'd better come clean when we meet again. He didn't want to live a lie. That's why he doesn't want to speak to any of you three before Mum's in the loop.'

***

Ellen and I took a complete break from the world of insurance and the impending visit of my parents. We booked a week's beach holiday in Acapulco in February.

As we boarded the aircraft and walked through the Business Class section to our Economy seats I saw Tim Fredricks, Archie Balaskas and Jeff Hamilton-Jones, all wearing florid maroon Merlin Life ties. We walked past three other similar ties before they reached our seats, which were in the first row behind the Business Class seats. As I paused before opening the overhead locker I looked around and saw many similar ties and also some women wearing cravats in the same florid maroon. I didn't recognise any of the faces.

'Something's going on. There are a lot of direct salesmen here.'

More and more people went down the aisle past me. Then a couple came along to occupy seats on the last row of the Business Class. I recognised him. He was Robert Plinth, the direct salesman who was a Wagnerian.

'Hello, Robert, what's going on? Why are so many from Merlin here?' I asked.

'Don't you know? It's the sales convention. Aren't you going to the same place?'

'No such luck. We're paying for our holiday.'

'This is no freebie mate. It's reward for success. There are learning sessions too.'

'Yea, yea.'

'Who's we, by the way?'

'My girlfriend Ellen and I.'

I turned round and introduced Ellen. Robert greeted her and then said:

'This is Stella, Stella Gainsborough, our branch secretary, who's accompanying me.'

'Is that allowed?'

'I don't know but it should be. Without her I wouldn't be here. It's not as if I'm married. I'm going through a divorce.'

'I'm sorry, I wasn't being nosey.'

'Actually, I want to have a word with you. Business has been great but I've got a problem that needs dealing with.'

'Phone me when we get back. I'm on holiday.'

'It'll only take an hour.'

'I'm on holiday with my girl-friend.'

'OK, I'll give you a call.'

We sat down and fastened our seat belts for take off. Ellen whispered to me,

'You *were* nosey.'

'No, I wasn't. I recognised her and I knew she was the secretary and that's not allowed.'

'But he said he's going through a divorce. Surely you can bring a partner in?'

'He didn't say she was his partner. Anyway even if she was, partners aren't allowed?'

'So you're a prude then?'

'You know I'm not. Rules are there to be obeyed. I didn't make them.'

Ellen was not amused.

After a while I got up to go to the toilet and passed Jeff who was returning from it.

'Fancy bumping into you,' said Jeff.

'Yes, I booked Acapulco to have a break from insurance.'

'Chance would be a fine thing.'

'Tell me, why are some of your salesmen travelling Business Class and not others.'

'The top three travel Business Class, the rest go Economy.'

'Doesn't that devalue the achievement of the rest?'

'No, it motivates them to try harder next year.'

'Does that work?'

'Believe me it does. That's why wives are invited so that they may egg their spouses on next year.'

'How cynical can you get?'

'It's a free world. They can choose to coast.'

'When we arrived in Acapulco, we went our separate ways, the Merlin Life lot being looked after by one travel agent, and us two by another.

We checked into the hotel, freshened up and went down to the outdoor bar for a drink. I surveyed the scene and said to Ellen,

'Jeff Hamilton-Jones and his wife are there with Tim.'

Ellen very gradually turned her head and in a rakish and feminine way observed without appearing to be looking. She saw Jeff advance towards them and say, 'Come and join us.'

Tim came across and said, 'Yes, do join us.'

'You must excuse us,' I said. 'I'm trying to get away from insurance and spend some time with Ellen.'

'You prefer to be anti-social? Suit yourself.'

We got ourselves a place to sit and a waiter came round to take the order for drinks. Both of us went for tequila and sat quietly sipping it and noting the rapidly increasing number of people in the hotel. One chap came round and said hello to us in an American accent.

'Howde guys, can I interest you in some life insurance?'

'No thanks,' I said.

'You think you don't need life insurance?'

'No'

'You've got to be kidding; everyone needs life insurance.'

'What I said was *I* don't need life insurance.'

'That's where you're wrong; *everyone* needs life insurance.'

'Not if you already have enough.'

'Nobody has enough.'

'I work in life insurance, please leave us alone.'

'Work in life insurance eh? If I showed you a cheaper way, would you be interested?'

'No.'

'Tell me how you sell life insurance. How do you create a demand?'

'I don't.'

'I tell you what I do. I back the hearse up the drive and let the wife smell the flowers. Guaranteed to put the fear of God in her.'

'I told you I'm not interested.'

'What's the matter with you English? You can't all be in insurance?'

'You'll find that they're having a sales convention.'

'No kidding. So are we. Secure & Prosperous Life is the biggest direct selling company in the US We're having our sales convention here.'

'How many of you are here?'

'Only the top thousand. Nice to meet you. Bye.'

***

Later that year, Ellen came down to Bristol in readiness for the imminent visit of Mum and Dad, her tryst with destiny. She took great care on how I dressed. All photographs she'd seen of Dad had him wearing a blazer so she wanted me to wear one. The snag was that she had eliminated blazers from my wardrobe so she had to go with me to buy one. Time was short as I had to get to London to pick them up. Out went the dark brown shirt I was about to wear and in came a lighter coloured shirt. Out went the jeans in favour of a casual pair of trousers. Out went the hush-puppies, in case Mum knew that they were made from pig-leather.

'What are you doing to me?'

'I'm dressing you how an Asian mother expects a well-dressed young man to dress.'

'How would you know?'

'I'm a woman. I've got eyes.'

Suitably attired, I went to meet them. The journey back to Bristol was more pleasant than last time. Mum was less strident and I was careful to manage her mood ahead of the fateful meeting with Ellen.

Mum asked:

'What happened to the shut-up zone?'

'Oh, they've sorted it out,' I said.

When we reached my flat, waiting for us at the front door was a well dressed girl of medium height with a friendly smile. Mum looked at her then looked at me then looked at her again and looked at Dad. I could see her mind whirring thinking, 'Who's this woman? She's too well dressed to be the cleaner or the housekeeper.' I shut the front door of the building and went upstairs to my flat. Eventually when we entered the flat, she blurted out:

'Isn't somebody going to introduce me?'

'Mum, meet someone very special to me. This is Ellen, Ellen Evan whom I first met when we were both at Cambridge.'

She continued to gape alternately at Ellen and me. She then said, 'Ellen Ellen Evan? What kind of name is that?'

'Ellen Evan, not Ellen Ellen Evan, it's a Welsh name. Mum you know the famous debate I organised at Cambridge? Ellen chaired it.'

She didn't respond immediately but then suddenly she said:

'You mean you've been together for ten years.'

'Yes Mum, we're committed to each other.'

'So you've been lying to me all these years.'

'With the best of motives, Mum.'

I might as well have been reciting the Magna Carta, Mum wasn't really listening. She suddenly turned round and, looking at Dad, asked me:

'When did your father find out about this?'

'Just now.'

'I don't believe it. He must have known.'

'No, he's found out just now.'

She looked at her husband with deep scepticism and said to me, keeping her eyes on Dad's face:

'Why isn't he shocked then? Why isn't he saying anything?'

'I'm silent because you're so much more eloquent my dear.'

Again, she wasn't listening. She'd made her mind up as could be guessed from the deeply suspicious look she was continuing to give Dad.

She then turned to Ellen and asked her, 'Are you a Christian?'

'No Mum, she's a Jew.'

'A Jew, a Yehudi?'

'Yes Mum. Isn't that nice? The Quraan regards them as People of the Book. They eat kosher meat, which is the same as halal meat and their men are circumcised.'

'Nobody in our family has ever met a Jew and I don't think my friends have either.'

'But I'm family Mum and I've met plenty of Jews. They're perfectly normal; a lot like you actually.'

'Don't be funny. I don't know how our family and friends will take it, you marrying a Jew. Nobody likes Israel. Their treatment of Palestinians is inhuman.'

'Forget politics Mum. You have to consider each person on their merits. Ellen is a wonderful person. I see so much of you in her that you're bound to get on. Hang on, did you say "marrying a Jew"? We're not getting married.'

Fatima stared at me utterly bewildered. Were she an actress, she'd be a ham although she would resent the suggestion that a Muslim could be a ham. Everything about her was exaggerated. He mouth wasn't the only communication medium; she used her hands, arms and above all eyes.

'You're not getting married? So what are you telling me? Are you saying that you're living together as man and wife but are not married?'

'No, we're not living together. Ellen works in London and has a flat there. I live here. But we're an item.'

Poor Mum was on the point of losing it. She turned to her husband.

'This is getting worse by the minute. What's this boy saying? They're not getting married, they're not living together. What are they doing? What's he trying to say?'

'Do you remember that shortly after Majid was born I went to Los Angeles for a twelve month course? We weren't actually living together because you were in Lahore and I was in Los Angeles. But in the sense that we were one unit people would have understood it had we said that we were living together. It's the same with these two. Because of their jobs they have to live apart but they're in other respects living together.'

'So you did know about this,' she said reproachfully.

'I'm only interpreting what he was saying.'

'We're an item is how they describe it here.'

'Just now your dad said the two of you were one unit, now you're saying you're an item. Which is it?'

'Either will do. Agony aunts call it something else; they call it cohabiting.'

'My God, that sounds terrible this cohabiting thing. Don't use that word in front of my friends.'

'I was going to ask you. How do you want to deal with your friends?'

'I wasn't going to tell anyone that my son was marrying a Jew. But hearing it all, frankly I'd rather say that than suggest that my son was cohabiting.'

'You can't say we're marrying when we're not.'

'You're living as man and wife, aren't you?'

'That's just the point, we're not. I live here, Ellen in London.'

'I wasn't born yesterday you know. You've known each other for years and years. Don't tell me you don't do it?'

'I think we should call a halt to this subject,' said Dad. 'I could do with a drink.'

'Tea or coffee?' asked Ellen quickly, trying to change the subject. Having established that tea was preferred she went into the kitchen and organised it and some snacks. Dad and Mum freshened up, Mum still grumbling to herself. The four of them sat drinking in silence. Ellen then said,

'My parents, Gareth and Glynis, would like to meet you.'

'Do they know about you two?'

'Yes,' I replied.

Mum sat in silence, no doubt thinking that she was the only one kept in the dark. Before she made an issue of it, Dad asked:

'Are they in London?'

'No, they live in Mold.'

'Where's that?'

'In North Wales.'

'Are they near you?'

'No we're in Bristol but yes, compared to distances in Pakistan, it is near.'

'What do they do?' asked Mum.

'They have the largest wholesale kosher and halal meat business in the North West. They own large tracts of North Wales and Shropshire.'

'You mean they own it all?'

'Yes they do,' said Ellen.

'All of the business not all of North Wales and Shropshire,' I said.

As she digested this information the tension gradually receded from her face and was replaced by a smile.

'Welcome to our family, Ellen dear. I look forward to meeting your parents.'

'What are they like?' she asked me.

'They're great people.'

'When did you first meet them?'

'Eight years ago. I usually spend Christmas with them.'

'So your mother was the last person to be told.'

'OK I made a mistake but you know now. Can we forget about it?'

'Don't be too hard on the boy. He did what he thought was best. Anyway, when can we meet them?' asked Dad.

'They're waiting to see you, hopefully tomorrow,' replied Ellen

Mum didn't respond. She carried the baleful look of someone who feels manipulated, someone who likes to be in control but is not. But it didn't last. Soon she threw herself into preparation for meeting Ellen's parents. She wanted suitable gifts for them. A frantic search in Bristol's department stores showed up nothing that caught her fancy. In the end she settled for the fall-back position of giving the gifts she'd brought from Lahore; a very heavy onyx paper-weight, a shawl, and a ladies waistcoat with tiny mirror-glass circles sewn into it.

The next day, the four of us piled into my car and, the spittoon safely in the boot, set off. It was raining heavily but Mum was in a cheerful mood. She said to Ellen:

'My dear, I'm really looking forward to meeting your parents. I will use my best English when speaking to them.'

'Oh no,' I said.

Mum gave me a baleful look.

We set forth along the M4 and left it for the M5 and then M6 and left that for less busy A-roads and left that too for some dirt tracks. The heavy rain and poor visibility made driving difficult. Eventually we got there. I drove in and got out to ring the door bell. I didn't need to, as Gareth and Glynis came out to receive us.

'We are lucky to be here. It was literally raining cats and dogs all the way,' said Mum.

It was lunch-time and after a short exchange of pleasantries we went into the dining room. Mum was quiet but busy noting everything.

'I was interested to see that you wash hands before sitting down to eat. It's an Eastern custom and I thought the English didn't do it,' said Mum.

'We're Welsh not English. Well, I'll let you into a secret, we're not Welsh really. We're Indian, from Cochin' said Gareth.

'What?'

'Yes there were sizeable Jewish communities in port cities such as Bombay, Calcutta, Karachi and Cochin. Our ancestors settled down where the ship took them. They were traders.

'Is there still a large community in Cochin?' asked Dad.

'I'm not in touch but I guess a few hundred.'

'Persecution?'

'Oh no, Jews, Christians, Muslims and Hindus lived in perfect harmony. I was a kosher butcher but most of my clients migrated to Israel when that country was formed. By 1952, my market had dried up. So I moved too but to England. I lived in Manchester before moving to Mold. Ellen was born here.'

'Actually Glynis looks Indian but you less so,' said Dad.

'She's descended from Yemeni Jews who came around 800 AD and I from European Jews who fled from the Inquisition six or seven centuries later.'

Mum, who'd been silent got up to leave the room.

'We're not boring you, my dear?' asked Dad.

'You are but I'll be back.'

An anxious Glynis followed her into the hall and came back after a while.

'Is Fatima alright?' asked Dad.

'Oh she's spitting out the debris of her *paan* into the spittoon to take a fresh one.'

I asked Gareth:

'You say you're not Welsh but Gareth Evan doesn't strike me as the name of an Indian Jew.'

'That's why I chose it. I changed my name from Abraham Ashkinazy when I settled in the UK.'

'What about Glynis, was she always Glynis?'

'She was Hannah.'

They had soup as the first course which was followed by a rack of lamb. Mum asked if it was halal and Glynis replied, 'Yours is halal but mine is kosher.'

'What's the difference?'

'None, apart from the words that are chanted. By uttering both we make sure that the meat is both halal and kosher.'

They finished dinner and the men retired to the lounge whilst Mum followed Glynis and Ellen into the kitchen. Dad resumed conversation by asking Gareth,

'You must have been very young when you emigrated from India.'

'1952, I was twenty-four and newly married.'

'Did you like Indian music? Did you like Mohammad Rafi?' I asked.

'Rafi was just beginning then. He had one or two hits. The singing star of the thirties and forties was K L Saigal, such pathos did he bring to his singing that you felt that he was singing from the heart.'

'Yes he was great, but Rafi was better.'

'Was?'

'He died in 1980.'

Mum, rejoining the discussion, said:

'OK, you men, enough of showing off your general knowledge. Majid, this is no time for discussing music. It's your future we should be talking about. Glynis, what do you think about your daughter marrying a Muslim?'

'Or even not marrying a Muslim,' added Dad.

'What nonsense are you talking?' asked Mum.

'They are showing no signs of wanting to get married, are they?'

Glynis intervened to say, 'Just like Gareth. He too hijacks conversations. Had they decided to get married we'd have been delighted. They've chosen to live together and, although I wouldn't do it myself, if that's what they want, it's OK with us.'

'You really don't mind Ellen being with a Muslim?'

Suddenly Mum turned to me and said:

'I forgot to mention about your friend Akbar. The hand that rocked his cradle kicked the bucket.'

'What are you on about?'

'You mathematicians don't understand good English. His mother died.'

'Oh I am sorry.'

Nobody knew what to say next. After a while Glynis spoke:

'We really don't mind what persuasion Majid is, we like him. What about you, do you mind him marrying a Jew?'

Mum, more used to asking questions than answering them was taken aback. She dithered and then said:

'I mind their living together and will probably tell my friends that Majid has got married.'

'To a Jew?'

'Every lining has a silver cloud. As she'll in due course become a Muslim. I wasn't going to say anything but if pressed I'd say she was a Muslim. I'll call her Deena.'

Startled, I sprang from my chair and said:

'We may or may not get married but I'm certainly not going to ask her to convert to Islam.'

'Son, I know that but you must let me deal with my problems my way.'

'But you must think through the consequences.'

'What consequences? Why do you use big words I don't understand?'

'What'll you tell your friends if we do decide to get married, if you've told them I'm already married?'

'She'll say that you've committed bigamy with the same woman,' said Dad.

'Big game? What big game?' As everyone broke into laughter, 'Everything's a joke to you.'

As the evening receded and nightfall came Mum thawed. Gone was the militant mother, instead she was a diplomat as she turned on her charm on Ellen. 'My dear, I regard you as my daughter-in-law but I don't know much about you. I know its Majid's fault but can we put that right?'

'Of course. What do you want to know?'

'Everything; I want to know everything.'

'You know things about me that even I didn't know until today. Dad never told me of my Indian roots.'

'Tell me why you keep your hair short? Girls should have long hair.'

'She did have lovely long golden tresses. She cut it off as an experiment. She's growing it back now.'

'Good. Girls should look like girls.'

'That's rude Mum,' I said.

'I'm not talking to you, I'm talking to her. What did you study in Cambridge?'

'Law.'

'How did you get into Cambridge?'

'I applied and got the necessary grades.'

'As simple as that? My Majid had to work very hard to get a place.'

'They interviewed me and offered me a place subject to my getting three A levels at grade A and I got them.'

'What made you choose law?'

Ellen explained and Mum seemed content as she went quiet. Then, just as I was thinking it was time for bed, she was off again.

'Is your flat in London a comfortable one?'

'It's OK.'

'You mean it's not comfortable? Is it not as good as Majid's flat in Bristol?'

'Mum, policemen don't get paid much and London is much more expensive than Bristol. So Ellen rents an affordable flat.'

'Rents?'

'Yes rents. She doesn't work for a generous insurance company.'

'But you should live together in a single house and share your income.'

'You want us to live together?'

'Of course you'll have to get married first.'

'All in good time, I'm sure,' said Glynis.

'But you should help her Majid. You earn good money.'

'He does help me,' said Ellen. 'We have a joint bank account into which both our salaries go.'

'So you're practically married then?'

Dad didn't like where this could lead and quickly steered the conversation away.

'Fatima has asked Ellen about her background. Do you want to know about Majid or has he told you everything?'

'No, he's never talked about his childhood.'

'Don't you start, Dad.'

Come on son, Gareth and Glynis are family now,' said Dad who then turned and spoke to them:

'We're proud of what Majid has achieved but we couldn't have predicted it. When he was in primary school he was the best in class but the next best kid lined up the entire class against him. Majid so lost his nerve that he refused to go back to school. I had to take him out of the school. Even today he relies heavily on reassurance from his peers.'

'I've not noticed it,' said Ellen.

'It's good to hear it. Maybe the English do not play office politics. He wouldn't last two minutes in Lahore.'

'Thank you Dad.'

'You're all pretty fair-skinned. You must come from Aryan stock,' asked Gareth.

'I wouldn't see we were fair skinned, more wheat coloured. Our ancestors came from Kazhakastan on the silk route and settled in Gujerat; not the Gujerat which is now in India but the city of that name in Punjab. A century ago my grandfather moved to Lahore. We live in a nice part of Lahore and Majid went to St Anthony's, the best school in Lahore.'

It was getting late and Dad was surreptitiously looking at his watch when Mum got second, no third wind. 'Tell me, I've heard a lot about the debate my son organized at Cambridge but nobody's bothered to explain to me what it was about. Ellen my dear, can you tell me about it?'

'That's no problem,' said Ellen. 'Every single aspect of that episode is vivid in my mind. Do you want to hear it?'

'Yes, my dear,'

'How long have you got?'

'We don't go back for a few days yet.'

'Majid was a key member of the Cambridge Union, the debating society. In his second year, he was approached by a fresher.'

'What's a fresher?'

'First-year student. His name was Ishtak Brownstein, an interesting character. His ancestors were German Jews.'

'You mean Ishtak isn't a Jew himself?'

'Oh yes he is. I was just explaining that he was of German stock.'

'Fatima, if you keep interrupting we could be here all year,' said Daud.

Fatima was stung and an eerie silence prevailed as each waited for the other to make the first move. Eventually, Ellen asked, 'Shall I carry on?'

'Yes please,' said a chastened Fatima.

'Ishtak wanted to join the debating society. Then another fresher came along. His name was Jalal Baber and he too wanted to join. He was from Rawalpindi, Pakistan. Like Ishtak he too was studying law. He was the son of a Palestinian who had settled in Pakistan.'

'This could take all day,' I said. 'Come on, its way past Mum's bedtime. She turns into a witch after midnight.'

'What's a witch?' asked Mum.

'A *chudail*.'

'*Hayey Allah,* my son insulting me in front of my future daughter-in-law.'

'Don't worry, I'll tell you the rest later,' said Ellen.

Both Ellen and I had to return to work the following day but Mum and Dad stayed another week in Mold and were taken to the airport by Gareth and Glynis.

Ellen Prospers

Ellen was looking quite attractive again. Her hair, whilst not as long as before was now of shoulder length. Not yet Goldilocks but more Julie Christie than Lulu. She was quite busy at work and found it interesting. She would talk about her work, which was still based in Earl's Court, without giving any specifics away. It seemed to me that a lot of it was about tracking suspected drug dealers from the Caribbean and South America. A connected issue was money laundering. A constant complaint was the lack of coordination between the police stations dotted around the country. Information was held on paper cards and it was nigh on impossible to collate them quickly.

There was one interesting case she was involved in that she couldn't keep from me. Why? Because, Camelot had insured the premises. A year previously, Nick had sold a comprehensive insurance package to a new firm based near Earl's Court called *Mazboot Aur Mahfooz,* which sounded like two brothers but was a private firm that offered safety deposit facilities to private individuals. Each box which could only be opened by the simultaneous use of two keys, one held by the firm and the other by the individual. No questions were asked about its contents. The owners didn't wish to know but they obviously knew the identity of each key-holder. One person could have several boxes so long as he paid the rent on each.

The police kept a watchful eye wary that 'no questions asked' might be a magnet for illegal money.

One night, the premises were burgled. The security men were bound up and blindfolded, every security box opened by destroying their locks and the entire contents stolen. The police suspected the proprietor but he was a mysterious Middle Eastern gentleman who couldn't be traced despite the valiant efforts of Ellen and her colleagues.

Camelot had a potentially crippling claim on its hands. I was no longer working in the claims department but I came to hear of it. I asked what made them think that the proprietor was from the Middle East. I asked this because the name of the firm are three Urdu words meaning Strong and Secure. But nobody knew. There was an internal inquiry within Camelot as to how we came to insure premises without having an idea of the amount being insured. It turned out that Nick had put pressure on the pricing actuary. That was by the by, we had issued a contract and now had to settle the claim. We approached the manager of the company for a list of names and addresses of the box-holders. He said that he didn't have such a list as the clients wanted assurance of anonymity. So long as they came along with a matching key the could open their box.

So a press release was issued saying that if anyone had suffered a loss, Camelot would pay provided that they could provide satisfactory proof of loss.

No one came forward. Indeed at the time of writing this book, no one has yet come forward. Ellen said that it must all have been black money.

Nick made a great virtue of this, saying that he knew from the beginning that if there was a claim, we wouldn't have to pay it.

At least I was glad for Ellen as she was at last enjoying her work.

But it didn't last. You know how a man can live without food for days on end but when he starts eating, there's no stopping him. The more she worked on forensic work the more she enjoyed it. She'd enjoy it even more if MI5 didn't keep hoovering up all the more interesting cases.

She started putting out feelers for a move to MI5. Meanwhile, frustrated at the lack of coordination between various police forces she did a paper recommending a centralised database on the computer. The paper was welcomed by the police hierarchy, partly because it was well argued but also because it was an idea whose time had come.

The paper came to the attention of MI5 and led to an interview. They were impressed but there were no vacancies and cost pressures were a constraint. Ellen's heart sank but not for long. An operative was due to retire on 1st of April 1988 and Ellen was offered a post from that date. It was a wait of nearly two years, but she didn't mind.

The snag was that the job was based in London with no prospect of a move to Bristol. That disappointed both of us but did not alter our view that she should take the job

***

Once, when I was spending a weekend with her, Ellen had a visitor. Ishtak Brownstein.

'What've you been up to? Haven't seen you for ages,' I asked him.

'Not since Cambridge. I did see Ellen a couple of years ago but not you. Been busy, building my legal practice.'

'Not conveyancing?'

'Yes actually. I've got a portfolio of clients who've purchased holiday homes in Israel.'

'Doing well?'

'Yes. I'm opening up a branch in Tel Aviv to service these clients. In due course I plan to build a successful local practice.'

'But based in London?'

'No, the plan is to migrate to Israel. The medium term goal is to enter politics there.'

'You'd be giving up a certain life for an uncertain one,' said Ellen. 'Are you sure you're doing the right thing?'

'Duty calls,' he said

'What duty?'

'Well, I owe it to my grandmother. She sent my mother to a convent to be brought up as a Catholic to escape the Nazis. She sent my mother's twin brother elsewhere, my mother knows not where. My immediate challenge is to locate him and my gran. Are they still alive and if so where?'

'Why should you enter Israeli politics?'

'Nothing would please my gran more.'

'That's not enough in itself. Do you see it as a vocation or a job?'

'Jalal and I used to talk about bringing lasting peace.'

'You used to say that the Yanks and the Brits must be kept out of it,' I recalled.

'That's still my view but we'll see how things go.'

'Are you still in touch with Jalal?'

'I was until last year. He's not replied to my last two letters. It'll be difficult to maintain contact when I move to Israel so I do hope he responds soon.

He then asked me how I was getting on and how Nick was. I was surprised that he remembered Nick but apparently Nick is in touch with Jalal.

Ishtak then turned to Ellen and said:

'It was you that I came to see and I've been talking to this scoundrel. How are you?'

'I'm still working for the police but move to MI5 next April. Later that month we're getting married.'

'Fantastic. What took you so long?'

'We were waiting for both of to be in the same place at the same time. In the end we stopped waiting.'

'MI5 eh? Our paths might cross again.'

***

I asked Gareth and Glynis what they thought of my parents. On the whole they had formed a favourable impression. Glynis thought that Mum was the heartbeat of the family but Dad was the quiet boss.

'Where are you two on the question of marriage?'

'Ellen's been quite busy so we haven't discussed it since my parents' visit. We had previously thought of getting married in 1987.'

'That's just over a year away. You've kept it quiet?' said Glynis.

'We'd have to live together so one of us will have to change jobs and move; not easy.'

'Not easy at all,' said Ellen. 'I've at last got the job I wanted and wouldn't want to leave.'

'So, I'll have to move.'

After further discussion we decided to pencil in, but not ink, 1987.

We discussed visiting Australia to see the Ashes Tests next winter. I fancied watching an Ashes Test or two but wasn't convinced that the cricket would be of high quality as the Aussies were a poor side. Still a thumping is a thumping. Ellen was game to try anything once but her parents declined. So the two of us decided to set aside three weeks holiday and intended to see the Adelaide and the Boxing Day Tests.

The Wheel Turns

By the summer of 1986, I had not done actuarial work for six years. I had in effect burned my bridges; rather they were burned for me. From now on I had to compete on skills I had acquired in the last six years, rather than those innate in me. It's like asking a novelist to become an actor.

At least I was no longer dealing with claims fraud. Other types of fraud awaited me. They took up a lot of my time; just as well as Ellen was immersed in her new role and seeing me less and less.

***

Ellen and I decided to spend a weekend in Bath. The city is only a few miles from Bristol but we'd never explored it.

Schizophrenic is the word that comes to mind when I think of Bath. Its town planners were caught between retaining its Roman roots and modernising it. We wandered aimlessly past the hot baths, the Nash terraces and, like a magnet, got drawn to a pub. We ordered a pint and a bite to eat. We were having an argument, nothing of any great consequence. There was only one other person in the bar; a man, possibly in his sixties, thick-set rather than fat, with an unlined face and an easy smile, a man at peace with himself. He couldn't help hearing the tail end of an argument between us, the pub being so quiet.

'Doesn't sound like a normal quarrel,' he said with a smile.

'What do you expect? He's an actuary,' said Ellen.

'Did you say he's an actuary?'

'Yes, I am. Hello, I'm Majid Khan.'

'Do you work for an insurance company?'

'Yes, Camelot Life.'

'Do you now? It's a small world. I am Daniel Drinkwater. My financial adviser has got some smashing products but it's from a company called Merlin Life.'

'It *is* a small world. Merlin is a subsidiary of Camelot. What's his name?'

'Robert Plinth.'

'I've met Robert, seems a good guy.'

'You're telling me. He's got some smashing products. Through him I've invested £50,000 in the Capital Redemption Fund and £25,000 in a Merlin Bond.'

'What's the Capital Redemption Fund?' I asked, not sure that I was hearing right.

'You mean you don't know about it?'

'There's no such thing. Are you sure we're talking of the same person?'

'Robert did say that it was a rare and exclusive product that only a select few people were allowed to invest in.'

'Our Robert Plinth wouldn't say anything like that. He can only sell Merlin Life products and Capital Thingammyjig isn't one of them.'

'I promise you, he sells it and a damn good product it is too. Guaranteed 12% tax free income each year. Where else can you get that sort of return? No need to declare it to the taxman either.'

'I'll need to talk to Robert.'

'It's a damn good product and I'm so happy with it that I recommended my son to invest £10,000 in it but Robert, having initially said yes, changed his position and said the product is withdrawn.'

'And?'

'Well, I want my son to be able to invest in it as he had committed himself before the product was withdrawn.'

'I'll look into this and get back to you.'

I was alarmed. It sounded as if Robert was selling an unauthorised product. Since he is one of Merlin's salesmen they are responsible for his conduct. Fine, censure, ignominy, they all loomed and the good name of the parent company Camelot would be dragged into it.

The first thing I did was to phone Jeff Hamilton-Jones. Jeff was away in Hawaii making the arrangements for the second sales convention of Merlin Life. I then got in touch with the Internal Auditor, the in-house watchdog.

'Ah, Robert Plinth, he's been on our radar for a while,' said he.

'Really? Why?'

'Oh nothing specific. Jeff asked us to routinely investigate all salesmen who have a sudden surge in sales. Usually it's because all the hard work suddenly falls into place and everything clicks but sometimes it points to fraud.'

'Which is it in Robert's case?'

'He was the first salesmen Jeff took on and has been with us three years. He's had moderate success, just beating his targets until last year when his production level suddenly trebled. He became the top salesman of the year, his commission earnings for the year topping a quarter of a million.'

'Yes, but was it kosher or was it fraud?'

'He acquired a flamboyance that he did not have before. Last Christmas he bought every person who processed his business an expensive bottle of champagne and a large turkey. The branch looked like Fortnum and Masons.'

'You're still not answering the question; maybe you can't. You'd better do a formal investigation into his business.'

I went home still not believing that someone who loved cricket was capable of dishonesty. But that very evening I had a call from Robert.

'Majid, I need help and I need it urgently. Can I talk to you this evening?'

'Yes, I wanted to talk to you too. Can we meet in the office tomorrow?'

'No, this is private. Can I see you at home?'

'Come along.'

Robert arrived in an hour and seemed inhibited by the presence of Ellen.

'She's my girlfriend and I have no secrets from her.'

'That's OK when you're sharing your own secrets but I don't want her hearing mine. She's a copper isn't she?'

'I'll pretend I didn't hear that,' said Ellen getting up from the seat she was sitting on. 'Strictly speaking that should put me on alert.' She then turned to me and said:

'I'm off for a stroll. Is half an hour enough?'

'I hope so.'

Once she had left the room Robert began by saying:

'Can I rely on your confidence?"

'If you've done something unlawful or criminal I'll insist on you reporting it; or I'll do it myself.'

Robert hesitated before saying:

'Then I'll have to keep it to myself but I desperately need a second opinion.'

'Shouldn't you be speaking to Jeff Hamilton-Jones?'

'I can't.'

After thinking about it, I said:

'OK, unless what you've done might lead to trouble for Camelot, in which case I'd report you, I'll ask you to confess but I shan't report you myself.'

'Last year I got fed up of my sales production hitting a plateau and decided that I needed an inducement. I asked the marketing guys to give me a product that guaranteed an income of 12%. I knew I could sell it but they couldn't do it.'

'I'm not surprised.'

'But the customers wanted it. Isn't that what marketing's about?'

'Not if you end up losing money hand over fist.'

'So I did it myself. I called it the Capital Redemption Fund. I offered 12% return tax free for ten years and demanded a minimum premium of £10,000.'

'You're out of your mind.'

'It was so popular that I started rationing it. They could put £10,000 in it provided they put a similar amount in a Merlin Bond. The Merlin Bond did so badly last year that they started calling it the Bogus Bond and the other the Redemption Bond.'

'What did you do with all the money you received?

'Stuck it in a bank account.'

'How did you pay the 12% interest when you can only earn 4-5% on deposits?'

'Money was coming in all the time so I used some of the new monies to pay interest on the prior years' sales.'

'That's robbing Peter to pay Paul. The accounting can become extremely complex. How did you keep up?'

'This is it. I had a nice little spreadsheet going but it got out of control as soon as sales mushroomed. I'm having a steady stream of "Where's my 12%?" type of complaints and a stampede of people wanting to invest more.'

'Where's all the money?'

'Some of it's been spent; Ferrari, villa in Barbados etc and the rest is in my bank account. Money is not the problem as sales are so good. It's the paperwork that's the problem. I've lost track of who has put in what.'

'Money *is* the problem. The product is not viable. What you've done is run a Ponzi scheme or a chain letter. Everyone is happy except those at the bottom.'

'Can't you help me with the paperwork as a favour? I taught you how to appreciate Wagner. This could be how you pay back?'

'You're kidding. What you've done is both illegal and criminal. You'd better go to a police station and confess. I'll have to tell Jeff and the regulators tomorrow morning.'

'Oh no, I'm stuffed.'

'You certainly are.'

'If you report me I will say that I wouldn't have got into such a mess if you had helped me out.'

That remark stunned me and I asked:

'What do you mean by that? Our paths never cross?'

'On the airplane to Acapulco, I wanted to have a word with you but you declined.'

'You must be sinking as you're clutching at straws.'

As soon as Robert Plinth had gone, I tried to phone Archie but didn't have his home number. I then phoned Kate Spencer and Tim Fredricks. Tim went ballistic. 'How many customers are involved?'

'Don't know.'

'How much is it going to cost us in compensation?'

'Don't know'

'How big a fine are we likely to suffer?'

'Don't know.'

'What do you know?'

'I know that we'd better tell the regulators and get a story ready for the press.'

'You got us into this mess, you'd better get us out of it.'

Tim's tendency to shoot the messenger was too well known for me to react to that last remark. By the morning Tim had cooled down and was able to dispassionately review the press release drafted by Kate with my input:

> *Camelot Life has reported to the police the unauthorised conduct of a salesman attached to its subsidiary Merlin Life. He was selling an unlicensed and entirely fictitious product offering a highly attractive return that the market will not support. As a result he sold substantial volumes of business and has a large number of happy customers. However the terms offered are so good that he was going to run out of money and leave behind an even larger number of unhappy customers. All this is nothing to do with Camelot Life or Merlin Life and purchasers of the product should have known that the terms were too good to be true. However the salesman made extensive use of our notepaper. We will therefore make good any loss suffered by any client of the salesman.*

Tim approved the text. He wanted to know why Archie and Jeff were not involved and I explained. A task force was set up to scope the damage and deal with it. I took it to be my duty to lead (taking my cue from Tim's 'you got us into this mess...' diatribe). Archie Balaskas, in the absence of Jeff Hamilton-Jones, was asked to have a complete list of all people who were Robert's customers. He had to work with Bruce Herrington, now back in a senior accountancy role, to determine what each had been sold and what benefits had been paid. It took them a while to do this as they needed access to Robert Plinth's computer which was in the police's possession.

They established, to everyone's relief, that monies destined to purchase a Merlin Life product reached Merlin and there were no discrepancies. As to the Capital Redemption Fund, a total of £25m was destined for it. A total of £1.5m was due to be paid out as interest but only £0.9m had been. The amount remaining in the bank account was £21m.

Thus there was a shortfall of £4.6m. Merlin offered to give everyone their money back plus accrued income which would have cost them around £7m.

Some customers were insisting that the contract they purchased i.e. paying 12% p.a. for ten years be honoured. Merlin argued that the contract was unenforceable as Robert had no authority to conclude such a contract.

If Camelot lost the total compensation cost could top £25m. To recover some of the loss we bankrupted Plinth. That did not yield as much as at first thought. His opulence was funded on credit.

A week later I had a call from Jeff thanking me for managing the crisis caused by Plinth. Jeff would carry out a thorough investigation to make sure that this was not being replicated by other salesmen. I said the Internal Audit was already doing that.

'Why did he do it?' I asked. 'He was earning an adequate living.'

'Divorce is one of our tried and tested levers but it backfired.'

'What do you mean?'

'Archie and I have observed that all good salesmen plateau when they reach an income level that gives them their material aspirations. It is helpful if he then falls for a branch bimbo. The marriage breaks up and he has two families to support.'

'That's callous and cynical.'

'We don't encourage it; if it happens then it has beneficial side effects.'

'You are a callous bastard.'

'Mind your language. Anyway Stella is hardly a bimbo.'

'Whatever.'

'It's a great shame. We've had three great years. We're way ahead of targets and on course to cash our share options in 1988.'

'The loss on this will hit you I suppose.'

'I'd be more worried if the Directors lost faith in us. Luckily Tim's been very supportive.'

***

Nick phoned me one day and said, 'Can you give Henry Shilling a call?'

'Who's he?'

'He's an independent intermediary from Macclesfield who gives my region a fair amount of business. He wants to speak to someone "in a position of authority" as he wanted to get 'the best possible deal for a VIP, and I mean VIP, client.'

'Why me?'

'He was talking of a billion pounds if not more, which is outside my limit.'

'I'm not surprised. It'll probably have to go to the Board for approval.'

'Can you at least talk to him?'

'OK, I'll give him a call.'

'Better still, I'll arrange a meeting between the two of you.'

We met in Nick's office. Henry was a weedy little man wearing an old blazer and grey trousers, a pipe in his mouth, like someone out of a low-budget detective film, the villain not the detective. Perhaps it was my prejudice but I was wary. He said:

'Through a friend of mine I have access to the Sultan of Brunei. Do you know him?'

'Who, your friend or the Sultan of Brunei?'

'The Sultan.'

'No.'

'But you must know that he's the wealthiest man in the world.'

'I can quite believe it. I know he's quite wealthy.'

'Yes, he's the wealthiest. Isn't Brunei the world's biggest oil producer,' asked Nick.

'I don't think they're that big, Saudi Arabia is bigger. The difference is that in Brunei's case it is the Sultan not the country that owns most of it.'

'Anyway, he needs to finance his South American business,' said Henry. 'He'll place $1billion with Camelot for ten years if you can guarantee an interest rate of 10% pa.'

'You mean US dollars? We deal at the retail end with ordinary people. A £100,000 investment is a big case for us. We're not geared to handle sums as large as a billion.'

'But surely you're not going to turn it down?' asked Nick.

'But we're not geared up for it. He should go to the corporate banking arm of a bank.'

'But he doesn't want to go to them. He has his own reasons,' said Henry.

'But if we were to offer him 10% we would need to be able to find an investment that gives us slightly more or we'll be out of money.'

'That's your job. You're an actuary aren't you?' said Nick.

'An actuary not a magician. There's no dollar investment that will pay more than 4.5% pa for ten years.'

'You can get it on sterling bonds,' said Henry.

'But then you're taking a huge currency risk. I'm not prepared to do that.'

'You can hedge the currency risk, can't you?' asked Nick.

'I could but then the rate would come down to 4.5%.'

'Look, you've got to find a way,' said Henry to Nick. 'If we land this it'll be the making of both of us. I'm even prepared to slash my commission to ¼%.'

'That'll still give you £2.5 million. But I still can't do it. I'm sorry,' I said.

'I'll get back to my client,' said a despondent Henry as he took his leave.

Nick rounded on me and said:

'I'm very disappointed. I'd hoped that you'd take a commercial view of the opportunity.'

'Isn't it commercial to look at the downside before you leap?'

'You should be looking to get round it. I can't tell you how much this piece of business would mean to this region. It would transform it from a middle ranking region to the top one in the country.'

'And I'm sure it would do your career prospects no end of good. But think of what would happen if the business turned out to be rotten?'

'Don't try to justify it. You're just trying to undermine me.'

I didn't rise to the bait. The following day Henry came back.

'My contact has talked to the Sultan. He's prepared to hedge the currency risk.'

'But then the effective rate will drop from 10% to 4.5%. It's not worth it.'

'Majid, you've got to believe me. He's got whiz-kid currency dealers.'

'They're dealing with other whiz-kids so their skills cancel out.'

'Look all I need is a letter from Camelot, on your notepaper, saying that if a sum of $1 billion is invested with you for ten years, you will guarantee interest rate of 10% pa for ten years on its sterling equivalent The sterling equivalent of the initial investment will be returned at the end of ten years.'

'That's more feasible. I'll get back to you.'

As soon as he'd rung off, I phoned Kate Spencer. She had a warning:

'Whether the sums add up is something you have to decide. My concern is money laundering. If the Sultan of Brunei wanted to do this why would he go to an insurance broker in Macclesfield?'

'That thought did occur to me.'

'And why would he trust an anonymous middleman to act for him? Why not go to a bank to set it up for him?'

'You think it could be drugs money or illegal arms money?'

'Well, ill-gotten in some way.'

Next I talked to Camelot's investment department for some advice. They amended the proposed letter to say that the terms are conditional on $1 billion of cleared funds being placed by electronic transfer this afternoon.'

'I can mention that but I'm inclined to give it a miss. Kate thinks it is probably ill gotten money.'

'No, try it. Kate might be right but I have another theory. What they are asking of you is a kind of letter of credit. They'd take it to a US bank and borrow $1 billion on the strength of it.'

'What, you mean, and they'll then scoot?'

'Yes. But with my wording it won't work. If we don't offer our guarantee without cleared funds, the bank won't release those funds to be placed with us.'

I got back to Henry Shilling and said, 'We're in business. Subject to a small amendment to the proposed letter, I'm prepared to sign and release it.'

'That's great. I'll get back to them.'

That was the last I heard of it.

***

It was autumn already and I was having misgivings about my proposed trip to Australia to watch the Ashes tests in the winter of 1986/87. Since their historic win in 1985 the wheels had come off the England bus. Gower's sense of humour backfired on him. The irony inherent in his statement, 'I bet they're quaking in their boots,' was lost on the prickly Richards. He made sure that England was thrashed five-nil. Gower lost the captaincy to Gatting and England had a poor summer under him as well. Should we cancel the trip, I wondered. The more pragmatic Ellen reminded me that however bad England might be, the Aussies were worse. So we decided to go.

Early in November, Tim Fredricks phoned me and asked whether I was interested in a short assignment in Australia. I was taken aback.

'What is it?'

'You know we have a branch there. It was never very big. Now two local firms are so dominant that small players are being squeezed out. We'd like to sell. Our local MD, Shane Barnes is leading the hunt for a buyer. His background is sales not finance. Someone needs to look at the terms being offered.'

'I met Shane a couple of years ago at a management development course. You're asking him to work himself out of a job?'

'Yes, unless the buyer wants him. He'll get a good payoff from us if they don't. So he'll be OK. If you can go over the numbers it would be a great help.'

'I've got a lot on my plate at the moment that I would like to see to completion. Besides, much of this month is booked as holiday.'

'My spies tell me that you'll be holidaying in Australia?'

'That's right, I'm booked to see a couple of the Test matches.'

'Look Majid, this is only a suggestion but don't forget who's making it. It is vital not just to Camelot but also to our country to extract the best possible terms when we exit Australia.'

I didn't respond immediately so Tim asked:

That's it then? You'll put pleasure before duty?'

'Actually there is a gap in my schedule,' I said looking at my diary. I'm due in Adelaide on 10th of December and there's a Test match from 12th to 16th. The next Test match in Melbourne doesn't start until Boxing Day, so there's nine days in between. Is that sufficient? I need to clear it with my girlfriend first.'

***

We arrived in Adelaide on the 10th December. We were in a party of twelve who arrived on the same flight. When we checked into our hotel, there was a message waiting for me from Shane Barnes. 'Welcome to Australia. Look forward to seeing you again next week.'

After all the anticipation, the Adelaide Test was a bore. On a perfect batting pitch England piled on a lot of runs, Australia almost as much. The one person who could have done something out of the ordinary, Botham, was not playing.

From Adelaide we flew to Melbourne and took a cab straight to Camelot's Australian head office. I was still in travel clothes but reckoned that Aussies would be informal. Waiting for me in Shane Barnes' office were Kate Spencer, who had flown over to assist on legal matters and Will Coode, Shane's Australian lawyer, all immaculately dressed.

'How much do you know?' asked Shane.

'Very little,' said Kate.

'Less than that,' I said.

'The most important point is that Camelot does not have an Australian subsidiary to deal with its Australian business. It had set up a branch through which Camelot obtains business in Australia. The strength of the UK company stands behind the Australian policies,' said Will.

'What does it mean in practice?' I asked.

'You cannot exit Australia by selling a subsidiary. All you can do is lay off the liability by reinsuring it all with an Australian company,' said Will.

'Sounds like a technicality as far as the customer is concerned,' I said.

'From the customers' point of view nothing will change. Their contract with Camelot will remain. So we don't have to tell them although we probably will,' said Will.

'OK, where are we then? How can I help? I'm only available until Christmas.'

'The total Australian business represents funds of A$200million. We're prepared to make a further A$25million available as additional security for the customers. In return for making A$225million available, the purchaser would have to take over all of the liabilities relating to our Australian business,' said Shane.

'Why are we making an additional A$25million available?'

'These customers benefited from the financial strength of Camelot. A$25million is their proportion of the available security funds,' said Shane.

'What's in it for a buyer?'

'They get to keep all of the profits emerging from the business. A fair part of the additional security of A$25million should become available when the last policyholder goes off the books. That's what I've been told,' said Shane.

'Has anyone expressed any interest?'

'Four have. The two big players have both offered to take it off our hands at no cost. Their argument is that they're shielding us from further losses. The last year we made a profit was as long ago as 1976.'

'OK, what about the other two?'

'They are both private equity groups. One, the Southern Cross Investors offered $2million up front plus one-quarter of any emerging profits; the other the Sword of Truth Group offered a cleaner transaction with the payment of A$10million up front.'

'That suggests that we should go with the Sword of Truth, right?'

'That's my view but Tim doesn't take my word for it. Like him, I'm a salesman. That's where you come in.'

'Well, if we've been making losses since 1977, what makes these guys think they can make money out of it?'

'They believe that they can run a slicker operation.'

'We can all run other people's businesses better than they can. How good are they at running their own life insurance business?'

'Sword of Truth does not have a life insurance company. It has applied for a licence. Southern Cross does have a life company but I haven't studied their performance.'

'We really must study Southern Cross's performance. What information have you collected about them?'

'None but isn't this over the top. Look at what they're offering.'

'Never mind, let's look at Sword of Truth who appear to offer the better deal. Licence is one thing, competence another. What expertise do they have?'

'They're offering a higher price because they need the business badly. Their plan is to appoint me as the Chief Executive and we will offer jobs to key members of our staff.'

'We? Whose side are you on?'

'I'll ignore that remark.'

'OK what's the background to the Sword of Truth?'

'They're owned by Ben Shmeuli and Ariel Cohen, two South African citizens who've been resident in Melbourne for the past ten years. Their interests range from hospitals, hotels and media, to insurance.'

'Do they own the group outright?'

'There are no other shareholders but they have a huge bank debt.'

I wanted to meet them but there was a snag. Both of them had gone to South Africa for Christmas and wouldn't be back until the New Year. I couldn't even talk to them as they were un-contactable. Shane had found that out the previous day.

'I can't go any further without seeing them.'

'Tim only asked you to comment on the financial side of things. I take care of the business side,' replied Shane.

'Financials do not just refer to the size of the numbers but the quality of the credit. Can they be trusted? I'm not suggesting anything but, as Will said, the customers' contract remains with us.'

'If you're not suggesting anything, what are you really saying?'

'We're talking of a book of business on which we've not made money for ten years. Our principal competitors don't think they will either and yet two organisations who don't really know the business think that they can. Anyone would be worried.'

'With respect, those are business issues and that's what I'm paid to do. Remember, I beat you at the negotiation exercise.'

'Well in that case I'll go back to cricket.'

The meeting ended and Kate and I left together. We were staying at the same hotel so we shared a cab. We agreed to meet in the foyer at eight o'clock for dinner together.

When Kate turned up at the appointed hour, she met Ellen for the first time since the Coventry conference. We went to a surf'n'turf restaurant nearby. We exchanged pleasantries until the waiter had come to take the order and bring drinks. I then brought Ellen up to speed on what had happened during the day.

'I don't like it. There's a clear conflict of interest if the South Africans have offered Shane a job.'

'Does it matter if the overall deal is better from our point of view?' asked Kate.

'Perhaps not, but I still think we should check out the South Africans.'

'There's no harm in that,' said Kate.

'I think it is essential,' said Ellen.

'Right, I'll give Tim a call.'

I did it later that night before going to bed. Tim thanked me and asked me to enjoy the rest of my holiday.

I did. With Ellen I had a Christmas barbecue in the hotel. We had a surprise visitor as Shane Barnes turned up with his girlfriend. He'd split from his wife and was not welcome at the family home, not on Christmas Day.

'Are you two married?' he asked us.

'No. Mind you, Bruce Herrington, an accountant colleague said that it was better to be married as there are better tax breaks for married couples.'

'That's what an accountant might think. My wife's a lawyer and she's taking me to the cleaners because I've taken up with lovely Clare,' said Shane looking lovingly at his girlfriend.

'So the accountant is pro-marriage but the lawyer is against it, if he wants to play the field. What does the actuary think?' asked Ellen.

'Me?'

'Yes.'

'Seeing as you're not married, you must share the lawyer's view?' said Shane.

'Watch it, Ellen's a lawyer,' I said. 'You know, I'd never given it much thought, but come to think of it, why not have both?'

'Why?'

'You can tell your wife you're with your mistress and your mistress that you're with your wife. That way you can stay longer in the office and work.'

Seeing the baleful look on Ellen's face I immediately said, 'Except of course if you have Ellen, then you need nobody else.'

'One day your corny jokes will be the death of you.'

The Boxing Day Test ended in three days with a first day's batting collapse dooming the home side to defeat. It meant that England retained the Ashes and I had two extra days with Ellen.

We enjoyed Melbourne. Architecturally, it appeared not to have changed much since the days of not Bradman but Trumper. The cuisine was more varied and the quality of seafood exceptional. The term fresh took on a new meaning. As we flew back Ellen said:

'You're doing OK at Camelot aren't you?'

'How do you mean?'

'You've come a long way in six years. I mean Tim's asking you to check out his Aussie company. He must trust your judgment.'

'More likely, he's sizing me up.'

'Why are you always so pessimistic?'

'No, I mustn't complain. They've given me a good overview of all activities.'

'All?'

'Well, nearly all; still haven't done investments.'

'Good, that gives you something to look forward to.'

'We'll see.'

'Shane said you're being groomed to succeed Tim'

'There's four of us, no three, JM's gone; but they could look beyond us. It's really too far ahead.'

'But you're ahead of the other two aren't you?'

'It's a marathon not a sprint and it's being in front at the finish that counts.'

'I do wish you'd be a bit more positive otherwise you'd be overtaken by the more outgoing Nick.'

'I know, I know. The thing is, everything's going too well. Something's bound to go wrong.'

***

Ted Leary, the head of HR dropped in as I sat in my office and handed me a letter. I'd been promoted to be the head of marketing.

'I should have given you the letter before the year-end but Tim was away and he needed to sign off your new salary.'

I was inwardly ecstatic. I was now a member of the Executive, one rung below Director. I'd have a slightly bigger office, deep pile carpet and a BMW or Mercedes rather than a Ford or Leyland. My salary would be an astronomic £40,000 and I would be granted share options. I seem to have sneaked ahead of Nick.

That evening I phoned Ellen as well as Mum and Dad to give them the good news. I told Ellen:

'I'll suggest to Tim that as marketing is a key corporate function, it was best if it was based in London, close to the directors. He'll probably say that they chose Bristol on cost grounds. If so I'll suggest that at least I should be near him.'

Ellen didn't say anything but it was the silence of concurrence.

'I'll have to choose my moment.'

'Why what's the problem?'

'If he says no, then I'll have blown it and the only way we can be together would be to leave Camelot.'

'I told you, I'm in no hurry to get married. We've got to be practical.'

'Even a romantic like you?'

'Particularly me.'

We discussed the issue at length. I would now be more marketable so I would put out feelers with head hunters and wait for developments. In the meantime I'd try to excel in the job as that would increase my marketability. And, at the appropriate time ask Tim for a transfer to London.

On that basis, we decided to put a date for the wedding, a date we'd stick to even if the job situation did not resolve itself by then. We'd hold it in Mold and settled upon a date in the spring of 1988, say the first of May.

Yes, Yes, Yes, the Answer's Yes, What's the Question?

Camelot was doing well in 1987. The external environment was exceptionally congenial. Britain had a strong stable government. Individual aspiration had replaced envy. Greed was good. The stock-market boomed, house prices were going up and up, people felt richer and spent more, often on credit. So many business opportunities were presenting themselves that, unusually, the question Tim Fredricks had to consider was which ones to reject rather than the opposite. He was a great believer in the biblical theory of feast and famine. When the good times come, cash in as lean times will follow. He retained a firm of consultants to advise him on how to maximise the opportunities.

A key recommendation of theirs was to move into estate agency business with a target of one thousand estate agents by the end of 1990. The logic was straightforward.

The first major financial decision that most people make is buying their first house. There is scope for selling them an endowment to repay the mortgage. Two companies, Holborn Bars and Monarch Insurance had taken a strategic decision to significantly increase the commission they paid on the sale of an endowment policy as long as they could have an exclusive tie and got all the endowment business. They found it difficult to enforce the exclusivity without buying the estate agent. So they went on a buying spree.

Tim wanted Camelot to join the queue of potential buyers.

Another recommendation was to go aggressively for personal pensions business to take advantage of the Government's campaign to 'unlock people's pensions'. Millions of people were in good pension schemes where the pension was based upon the salary at the date of retirement. Maggie Thatcher, a convert to Keith Joseph's philosophy of private ownership, had achieved popular success by privatising council houses. She now turned her attention to company pensions and promised to put in incentives to encourage people already in pension schemes to opt out and set up a private personal pensions. The change was due to come into effect in the summer of 1988.

Pensions experts who had an involvement in company pension schemes which were in danger of being cannibalised were warning of a disaster waiting to happen. They were met with the classic Mandy Rice-Davies remark, 'They would wouldn't they?' The truth of that remark masked the truth in the experts' concerns. The media predicted a bonanza for insurers and Tim wanted to make sure that Camelot got more than its due share of it.

Whilst these strategic recommendations were vital, the consultants retained by Tim were adamant that the necessary environment must be created to achieve success. They believed that it was essential to empower people at the coal face; 'they are closest to the customers and should make all the key decisions'. 'Power to the People' was the catchphrase.

Tim sought the Board's approval of the recommended approach.

Approval was given.

In a memorable speech, given at the year's management conference, delayed until September, he announced the new strategy. We listened intently. He began by saying that it was not really a new strategy, merely a logical extension of the strategy he began by launching a direct sales-force. That has been very successful. Archie will talk about it shortly. What the Board has done is to agree a framework for further growth. No business proposition was off limits so long as it met the profit target. Equally, if a business did not meet those targets then Camelot would pull out of it. He cited as an example the planned exit from Australia. The sale of the branch business to the Sword of Truth group would go ahead as soon as regulatory clearance was obtained.

If a business met the profit targets but there was insufficient capital to chase them, they'd get more capital. If there was a shortage of expertise, they'd buy it in. If there were insufficient resources in Customer Services, they'd recruit them in. No more excuses, no more barriers to success. The Board has a new slogan,

Yes, Yes, Yes, the Answer's Yes, What's the Question?

Spontaneous applause greeted the announcement. Tim invited questions. Ever the contrary person, I said:

'Mr Fredricks. I have a few questions of detail. May I ask them now or should I write to you?'

'Go ahead, let everyone hear it,' he said cheerfully.

'Any new venture carries a risk of failure; so each venture needs careful tending. If all of us go out hunting, who will mind the shop?'

'Are you making a speech or do you have a point to make?' asked a more serious Tim.

'You're placing a number of large bets using borrowed money. It is very unlikely that they'd all come off. If half of them didn't the effect could be catastrophic.'

'Success is an attitude of mind. If you start thinking about failure you will fail.'

'I'm not suggesting that the fear of failure should overwhelm us. All I'm asking whether it is wise to place all the bets at the same time. Let's do them one after the other.'

'You're reverting to type,' was Tim's withering remark. 'I thought we'd saved you by taking you out of the actuarial department.'

'Please hear me out. Take personal pensions. We're moving into uncharted territory, encouraging people to move from company pension scheme where the employer bears all the risk to one where the individual carries it himself. We need to study the issues carefully or we may have to bear the consequences.'

'If you don't like the heat, get out of the kitchen.'

'Take estate agencies. We know nothing about the housing market? Can we control?'

The chairman, Sir Alfred Lyttleton, intervened to say:

'Majid, you're in a unique position to prove yourself wrong as we want you to lead it.'

'Or,' added Tim, 'if you don't have the bottle, let me know and we'll find someone who does.'

'I had to bring my concerns to your attention. That's my duty but you are the bosses. I will implement your wishes. Did you say you want me to run the estate agency business?'

'Yes.'

With that I sat down.

After that, Archie's presentation was an anti-climax. As Merlin was a separate company, none of the audience could relate to the success story he was proudly announcing. I did note that they continued to beat plan and expected to float next year.

After the presentation ended and people were dispersing Nick Knights shouted out, 'party pooper'. I wasn't best pleased not least because I felt the same.

At the end of the month JM, now a highly respected insurance analyst made the same points under the provocative title, '*Gambling addict places long odds serial bets with borrowed funds.*'

In fact it was no consolation at all. The first I heard of it was when Tim phoned me and threatened to fire me for sending negative copy to the analyst. It was untrue and I denied it vigorously but he wouldn't accept it. In the end what saved me was that whilst I might have had the motive to leak my concerns to the press, the opportunity wasn't there. Tim had gone straight from the staff meeting to the meeting with the analysts. There JM had asked some of the questions he later developed into an article.

Camelot's sales performance in 1987 showed a 30% increase on the previous year. North-West, Nick's patch, did even better showing 50% growth. With the increasing emphasis on performance related pay, staff got record bonuses. I got 30% of basic salary plus some share options.

Nick, Bruce and I were promoted to head up, respectively, sales, finance and marketing/business development starting in January 1988. As we reported direct to Tim Fredricks, we might in another company be directors with a seat on the Board.

Of Mice And Men

When we assembled for Christmas, Ellen and I knew that our lives would change shortly. I would be running an estate agency business, Ellen would be joining MI5 and we'd be getting married. 30th of April 1988, our special day was getting nearer. A slot had been booked with the registrar. Ellen had kept her parents informed but I had yet to tell mine.

We discussed this over Christmas lunch.

'Why aren't you telling your parents?' asked Glynis.

'It looks as if we'd have to continue to live apart. Mum would never understand.'

'Even if she doesn't, you can't keep it from her. It ought to be the biggest day of her life.'

She was right of course but something held me back. Perhaps it was the fear of Mum's capacity for creating a drama out of everything. Even if Ellen had been Muslim, the right sort of Muslim, there would be tantrums as she'd be losing her son to another woman.

Still, she had a right to know and be there. I'll tell her. Not today, perhaps tomorrow or the day after.

Seeing me silent, Ellen sidled up to me and asked:

'What are you thinking of? Me?'

'Mum, actually.'

'Mum?'

'She's losing a son.'

'No she's not, she's gaining me.'

'Whatever. I guess I'll have to tell her about the wedding.'

'Good, shall I fetch the phone?'

I thought for a while and said:

'Not today. Let's not spoil Christmas, I'll tell her tomorrow.'

'I'm sure that's the right thing to do, telling her. Don't leave it.'

She looked wistfully towards the window and added,

'Mum wants me to wear the dress she got married in. '

'Gosh that was thirty-odd years ago. Was it the dress her Mum got married in too?'

'No silly, it's hers.'

'Still, you'll look like Miss Havisham. Are you sure it's the right size?'

'Let's have a look.'

'You're serious about this?'

Ellen had gone. She returned a quarter of an hour later with her Mum. She was carrying a dress wrapped in paper and reeking of naphthalene balls. She un-wrapped it and out came a cream coloured brocade dress. It was so faded that both Glynis and Ellen said:

'No, this won't do.'

Just then the phone rang. It was Dad wishing everyone Merry Christmas, followed by Mum. They spoke to the entire family including me.

'Have you any news for me?' Mum asked.

'Not at the moment.'

Afterwards Ellen chided me saying:

'You can't avoid it for ever you know.'

Glynis, ever practical, said:

'You'd both need wedding clothes and rings for the wedding. Why don't you go to Manchester or London for Boxing Day sales?'

So the next day we went to Manchester and spent the day traipsing around jewellers and Kendalls, the Department Store. My suit was no problem but we couldn't find a ring or her wedding dress. So we went to London the next day. We found a ring but not the wedding dress. Ellen decided to have one made by a tailor Glynis knew.

When we met again, late in January, I had an idea which I put to Ellen:

'Let's bring our wedding forward a day, let us make it 29ᵗʰ April.'

'Why?'

'It'll be a double landmark, as that's the date the Financial Services Act comes into force.'

'So?'

'Just as my life will change for ever, so will the insurance industry.'

'You're all heart aren't you?'

'But there's one difference.'

'Go on, I can see a corny joke coming.'

'I'll welcome my loss of independence but the industry will feel shackled.'

'Stop digging…. Hang on, what day of the week is it?'

She fished out her diary and said:

'29ᵗʰ April is a Friday .'

'Shall we settle for the Friday?'

'Friday it is.'

'Right, I'll get in touch with the Registrar and you get in touch with your parents.'

The following day Ellen reminded me to phone Mum. I dithered, saying that I'd do that later. I took her to Wells, an unspoilt cathedral city south of Bristol. We visited Wells Cathedral and looked in awe at its sheer grandeur.

'I wonder if they permit weddings in the Cathedral?'

'Why?' she asked.

'We could get married here.'

'A Muslim and a Jew getting married in a Cathedral?'

'Can't get more ecumenical than that, can you?'

'I like it; shall I find out?'

'There must be some technical reason why it's not feasible? Like, registry office weddings can only take place in locations designated for that purpose and cathedrals aren't one of those.'

'Or that only Christian weddings can be conducted in churches and cathedrals.'

'Just as well. Can you imagine what my Mum will go through if she found out?'

We strolled outside and then stopped to have scones and clotted cream in one of the nearby cafes. We then drove to the Cheddar gorge. Ellen wanted to leave after lunch to beat the traffic on the M4 back to London but I persuaded her to stay on until 8pm, arguing that there'd be less traffic then than at 4pm.

After she'd gone I had long chats on the phone with Bruce and Nick. Not long afterwards my phone rang,

'Thank God you've come off the phone. I've been trying for ages. I am, never mind who I am, it's your girlfriend; she's been car-jacked.'

'My God, where? Is she alright? Who're you?'

'I'm just a motorist who saw it all. It was at the Chippenham motorway service station in the car park.'

'What was she doing there?'

'Don't know but as she was getting out of the car, a man appeared from nowhere and brutally dragged her out of the car. He got in himself and proceeded to drive off.'

'So she lost her car but is she OK?'

'She was badly shaken but got up straightaway and made for the boot and opened it and took out a briefcase. The car-thief reversed and felled her. Luckily she was not run over. Seeing that he was spotted by me, the car-thief drove off. It all happened so quickly that I hardly had time to react. I got out to see if she was OK. She was in great pain. I think she'd broken her leg. I phoned the police and called for an ambulance to take her to the Bristol Royal Infirmary. She gave me your number. I've been trying all this time.'

I took down his number and then washed my face, had a glass of water and drove to Bristol Royal Infirmary. Ellen was heavily sedated. She did not show much warmth but did recognise me. I spoke to the sister-in-charge. No operation was necessary. They would reset her leg and put it in a plaster cast. She'll be in plaster for three months and it could take her a year before she walked with her old fluency.

I visited her again in the morning but she was asleep. Having been assured by the sister that there was nothing I could do, that Ellen was in safe hands, I asked her if I could go to work. The answer was yes.

So I went back to my office but the first thing I did was to phone the police to ascertain the whereabouts of Ellen's car. It took me a while to get through to the right person and when I did, to convince them that I was Ellen's boyfriend. I eventually established that the car was still missing.

I visited Ellen every morning before going to work and again in the evening. I struggled to cope with the increased load at work. In-spite of that my main concern was Ellen's well being, and the imminence of our wedding. Will that have to be postponed? Just as well I hadn't got round to telling Mum.

***

Ellen left Bristol Royal Infirmary after three weeks and convalesced in my flat. Glynis, who had travelled every day from Mold to keep her company, wanted a break.

I therefore took a few days off to help Ellen settle in the flat. She was very unhappy with life.

'I'll never make it to our wedding.'

'I'll help you get better but if it takes too long then it doesn't matter. We can rearrange the wedding date.'

It was also clear that she wouldn't be able to join MI5 on 1st April. I phoned on her behalf and received the assurance that they'd wait for her.

I devoted a lot of time in the following weeks helping her to walk; before I went to work, during the lunch break and in the evening, returning early from work. Initially I walked her inside the flat, encouraging her to trust her damaged leg. Going down and particularly up the stairs was the biggest challenge. Luckily the entire flat was on a single floor, the first. Once she was comfortable negotiating the stairs, I decided to drive her to local common, some four hundred yards away. It offered many possibilities for a walk. You could make it as long or as short as you wanted.

That was the theory and I talked her into giving it a try. Reluctantly she came down and got into my car. When we got to the common, she refused to get out so we went back.

One day the police phoned to say that her car had been recovered. It was a wreck having been driven into a tree in Edgbaston. Would she please come to identify it? No she wouldn't. I said if it was a write-off what was the point? The point was that if it could not be confirmed to be Ellen's car the insurance company wouldn't pay out. I said I'd take care of that as I worked for the company that insured her car.

That weekend Gareth and Glynis paid a visit. They too tried to persuade her to walk. This time, with three people to comfort her, she agreed to go. Once again she refused to get out of the car when we got to the common.

'What's the matter?' asked Gareth.

'It's dark.'

'So what?'

Ellen didn't answer. Perplexed, I asked, 'so what?'

'I won't see a black man coming.' All of a sudden she ducked as if she was avoiding a missile. I turned round and all I could see was a harmless-looking man, an Afro-Caribbean, walking aimlessly in their general direction.

'What's it this time?' I asked.

'Can you see the man who's walking towards us? He looks like the person who mugged me. Is he the same person?'

'Can't say, but probably not. There must be a million such men in the UK, most of them decent. You must know that from your work.'

We went back to the flat and changed the topic of conversation to take her mind off whatever was worrying her.

I asked Gareth whether Ellen was in the right frame of mind to get married. He thought not and urged a postponement. Gareth and Glynis went back home the next day.

Days and weeks passed marked by repetitiveness of the routine; repetitive but not monotonous. Having been looked after all my life, first by Mum and then by Ellen, I found it strangely therapeutic caring for Ellen. For the first time I realised how much effort goes into leading normal lives. As Mum used to say, things don't just happen, somebody has to make them happen.

Quite often Nick Knights and his wife Phyllis would come to either to assist or to relieve me. It was Phyllis who persuaded Ellen that the wedding be postponed and when Ellen suggested that to me, I agreed.

After three months her plaster came off and regular exercise and walks enabled her to walk without a pronounced limp. I increased the length of the walk, once walking two miles and, most daring of all, took her to Easton to see Bristol Rovers. Rovers was a modest club with limited aspirations. The greatest sportsman on its books in its entire history was in fact a cricketer, Wally Hammond. But it wasn't a game of football that I was introducing her to. It was a raucous crowd of perhaps fifteen thousand with plenty of black faces. To begin with Ellen clutched my arm tight, much as a child might its mother when confronted by strangers. Once the game got going the excitement of goals and misses got her absorbed. She was happier than she'd been for a long time. She became a regular visitor; sometimes with me sometimes with Nick and sometimes with both of us. This encouraged both of us to believe that she was fit to resume work. Ellen got in touch with her new boss in MI5.

'We've missed you and can't wait to have you join us. We're just waiting for a medical report from your GP,' was the warm response with which she was received. Three weeks later, having received a medical report, they called for a psychiatrist's report. This upset her but I said it was pointless arguing with them. So she went for the tests, which lasted two days. She received a letter from her boss-to-be asking her to come in for a chat, alone.

She was told that the psychiatrists report said that she was afraid of black people. If that were true he'd have to withdraw the offer of employment. However he assumed that the psychiatrist had made a mistake and it was the dark she was afraid of. Was he right?

It took Ellen a few minutes to realise that he was looking to overturn the report. As soon as she realised that, she quickly said that was indeed the case.

'Right, why don't you start in six weeks?'

So it was that she at last joined the MI5 on 1St September 1988, she became a 'spy' I stressed repeatedly to her that she should not reveal her fear of black people as that could lead to instant dismissal.

She stayed in her Earl's Court flat so I stayed with her in London until she found a new flat. It meant that I had to leave at crack of dawn for Bristol on most days. We looked for an affordable flat, accessible from her place of work and mindful of her phobia. The latter was a severe limitation and in the end we settled for Knightsbridge but recognised that the flat would be pokey. She bought a flat in Montpelier Place, not far from Harrods using the bonus I'd received the previous year as deposit. I used the remainder of the bonus to buy her a second-hand three series BMW automatic.

One day, not long after she became a 'spy' I said, if things had gone according to plan we'd have been married six months. Should we fix another date?

'Not yet,' said Ellen. 'Not until I've settled down in my new job.'

That wasn't the answer I was expecting but perhaps was a wise approach. Both of us were learning too many new tricks to be able to do justice to marriage.

Camelot Estates

By January 1988 a new company was set up called Camelot Estates to buy and own estate agencies. Tim appointed me as its first Chief Executive. He did it with a mixture of motivation and warning:

'I'm giving you the chance to prove me right. Rewards will be plenty if you do. If *you're* right then you'll have worked yourself out of a job. Best of luck.'

He made it sound as if I lose both ways. I did wonder whether I was being set up for a fall. I took up the challenge, but only after checking with Ellen as it put paid to any chances of relocating to London.

I wanted to appoint Nick as the Sales Director and Bruce as the Finance Director. Ellen was fiercely opposed to both but particularly Nick.

'How can you trust him after how he's behaved in the past?'

'I know I can't rely on him but he's very capable. I'd rather he was working for me than against me.'

'He may do both.'

'It's easier to watch him when he's near me. Anyway he's streets better than the other candidates.'

'OK but watch him.'

So I approached both. Nick was asked to focus on targeting estate agencies Camelot wanted to buy and then negotiating with them; Bruce was asked to develop a financial model to determine what price to offer and to get the money together to buy. Both were initially reluctant to accept the job offered as it would imply that I was senior to them. They were placated by Tim who assured them that for all three of us this was in addition to our main jobs.

I moved the team out of DD to an old Georgian house in a less fashionable part of the town opposite the maternity wing of Bristol Royal Infirmary.

I now had a job with a spending power of over £100m as compared to the budget of £3m in the marketing department of Camelot Life. However I had exchanged an opulent office, which I still kept for the day-job, for a Spartan one. The security was of the Heath Robinson type. I shared my office with my secretary.

There were no dining facilities; you had to pop out for a sandwich. The heating probably failed the Health and Safety requirements. The parsimony was self-imposed as an example to estate agencies we were seeking to buy.

Neil Hawke, who also lived in Stoke Bishop, was the sole owner of an up-market agency in Whiteladies Road, Bristol's premier road. I invited him and his wife for drinks one Saturday afternoon when Ellen was staying with me. I also invited Nick and Bruce and their spouses.

'I've never seen you before,' said Neil to Ellen.

'We've been together for twelve years, ever since we met at Cambridge. But he works in Bristol and my job is in London.'

'That's tough.'

'We're in touch every day and meet at weekends.'

'I suppose it keeps the relationship fresh.'

'You bet.'

'What do you do?'

'I'm a Civil Servant.'

I looked at her and was about to say that I thought she was a policewoman when I was interrupted by Ellen.

'Changing subjects,' she said, 'Majid bought this flat five years ago. What's the market like for three bedroom detached houses in this area? He's toying with the idea of moving out of this flat into a house.'

'Prices are likely to rise. Many people want to buy but not many houses are coming on to the market.'

'That's bad news for you isn't it? No transactions, no income,' I asked.

'I'd heard that estate agents are not taking on new instructions. It's a distraction when there are so many suitors looking to buy them,' said Bruce chipping in before Neil could answer me.

'There's some truth in that,' admitted Neil.

'Have you been approached?' I asked.

'Yes, but not very aggressively. They're trying to sign up all the big networks before turning to smaller agencies.'

'You mean to say if they really wanted you they'd come with a better offer?'

'I think they're not really geared up to buying small agencies. So they offered me a ridiculously low price.'

'You don't have to answer this but it would be useful if you gave an indicative figure. You see we too might enter the market.'

'They offered to pay an amount equal to the net assets plus last year's profit.'

'Actually that's not as derisory as you think,' said Bruce. 'That's the standard basis for valuing a brokerage.'

'You won't get very far with that.'

'No, that's the standard approach,' said Bruce.

'You've got two big companies slugging it out. The effect is to push the price up.'

'Of course, but often the reality is different from the rumours.'

'Well, take the network Wilberforce and Wilberforce, not that big, only ten branches, it went for net assets plus five times last year's profit.'

'That is ridiculous. Anyway, how do you know it is true?' asked Bruce

'Oh it's true alright. My brother is a shareholder. Your problem is that you're looking at it from the wrong end. Don't think of what it's worth to the estate agent, think of what it's worth to you.'

'That'll give a much higher figure but the difference is the result of our effort. Why should we pay you for it?' I asked.

'You're not going to go very far in life with that attitude.'

'What do you mean?'

'Come on Majid,' said Neil. 'Your competitors are doing it.'

I shrugged my shoulders prompting Neil to add, 'If you're serious about entering this business I suggest that you try to understand the culture and ethos of the business. Start by understanding the shorthand used by estate agents when describing property.'

'Such as?'

'Has development potential means it is run down

'Easily maintained gardens means there isn't one

'The view alone is worth £10,000 means the rest of the house isn't worth much more

'Ideal for the busy individual means it is pokey

'A haven of peace and tranquillity means miles from anywhere

'Requires some attention means it is uninhabitable.'

***

Ellen's accident happened around this time and she became number one priority when she returned from hospital.

All I could do with my commitment to Camelot was to manage the reduced time efficiently and rely more and more on others.

I told investment banks that I was in the market to buy estate agencies and if they knew of any on the market I'd like to know. Weeks passed, nothing happened. The team badly needed a transaction to cut their teeth. It didn't matter if they made a loss on it. They would learn from it.

'How are you getting on with buying estate agencies?' asked Gareth when we were walking Ellen on Bristol common.

'Drawn a blank so far. People are quoting silly prices, and buyers are giving in.'

'Not surprising; to the estate agent this is their once in a lifetime opportunity to make a pile. They'll always be better prepared than you and not above making false or misleading statements.'

'I'll watch out.'

'Go to an auction, any auction and see for yourself. A kind of bidding frenzy can overwhelm even sensible people. If Camelot is competing with one or two other companies, then the same can happen.'

'Yes, it's happening now. I'm too rational to fall into that trap. But of course I end up not winning any.'

I was quite taken in by Gareth's advice and went to an auction of cricketing memorabilia. There was a bidding frenzy for a rare 1916 Wisden. I came away unsure whether I was unfit for this job or a safe pair of hands.

We carried on as normal. Nick approached Ruaridh Royston of Royston, Royston & Royston, a firm of estate agents with one hundred branches in Middlesex, Essex and the northern fringes of London. It was owned by three brothers, Ruaridh, Roland and Roger. They were often referred to as the 3R's, perhaps indicative of the lack of formal education amongst the brothers. Nick got short shrift. 'We value our independence. We're not for sale.'

We then decided to go back to Neil Hawke. Nick offered five times last year's profit. 'No thank you, I prefer my independence,' was the reply. Neil in fact used the opportunity to negotiate an increase in commission to one and half times the normal rate.

Next we approached Peel & Co the only network in Bristol not already signed up by our competitors. Again they wanted ten times last year's profit. Again no deal and we ended up having to concede a similar increase in commission.

***

Tim Fredricks rang and asked me how long have I've had responsibility for Camelot Estates. He knew jolly well that it was getting on for a year.

'You've still not acquired the first estate agency. How long do you expect me to wait? I'll be the laughing stock of the city.'

'We're working flat out; we've made offers to over fifty firms but we've been unable to do a deal.'

'What's the problem?'

'Holborn Bars and Monarch have started a bidding war. I can't match them and still make money.'

'Are you telling me that they're doing silly deals?'

'No, I'm not saying that. All I'm saying is that on their terms we can't make any money.'

'I see, everyone else has got it wrong, you're the only one who's got it right.'

'Yes, that happens. It is called the herd instinct. That's what drives markets.'

'You're the one who's wrong.'

'What do you want me to do?'

'I give you six months. If you don't have a hundred estate agents on our books by then you'll be fired.'

'OK. I assume that you're not worried about making money?'

'Don't be sarcastic. These are strategic investments. It doesn't matter if we lose money in the short term. It'll all come out in the wash.'

'OK, shall I take that as my mandate?'

'Nothing's changed; and one other thing: Don't try to save money by not using an investment bank. That is false economy. I've asked Tracy Pitt of Coppersmith Leonard to get in touch with you.'

Later that evening I had a call from Tracy Pitt's secretary and an appointment was fixed for the following day. When Tracy turned up for the meeting I was surprised to find a 6' 5" tall man being ushered in to his room. Where's Tracy?' I asked.

'You're looking at him.'

'I'm sorry, shouldn't you be a woman?'

'Most people think so but I promise you, I'm a man.'

'Bet you had trouble at school.'

'Not really, not for long anyway. Being the tallest, and the biggest, I beat up any bugger who tried to get smart with me.'

'I dare say it prepared you well for your career as an investment banker.'

'Yes and don't you forget it.'

'Let me introduce you to my colleagues Nick Knights and Bruce Herrington.'

'You seem to have a sticking point on price. How do you calculate it? Do you have a formula?' asked Tracy.

'The price we offer depends upon our estimate of how profitable the business is,' I replied.

'How do you determine that?'

'We make the best estimate of housing sales and the commission income that would generate. We make assumptions regarding other income such as survey fees, management of rental property etc. We total all of them to estimate the annual income of the business.'

'OK'

'We then make our best estimate of the annual expense of the estate agency we're targeting. We deduct this amount from the estimated income and get an estimate of the profit for the year. That was what we originally offered. Now we're multiplying it by five.'

'OK that's clear enough. What do you include in your estimate of annual expense?' asked Tracy.

'We look at the expense budget in their Operational Plan but adjust it for additional costs that a properly run company would incur.'

'What do you mean by that?'

'Their system for monitoring sales practices is of the anecdotal variety and accounting systems are practically non existent. You have to factor in the cost of each.'

'That's where you're wrong. Those are shareholder costs and should not be allowed to enter the expense base of the target company,' said Tracy.

'I don't agree with that.'

'Not relevant. Your competitors do it.'

Bruce and I eyed each other incredulously.

'Not that old canard again,' I said.

'Yes, it's called the real world.'

'Go on, what next? I suppose you'll massage the income side of things?'

'You're obviously wet behind the ears but yes, what income other than estate agents' fees do you take into account?'

'Only those that I've told you about.'

'What about the commission on the endowments they sell?'

'But, we're paying that to them. It's our money. Why should we then pay to buy it back?' I asked.

'But once you pay it, it's their income and it's their income you're valuing.'

'So if I trebled their commission so that we make a loss on the endowment, we'd be putting an even higher value on the estate agency, so we lose twice.'

'Tim's made it clear that these are strategic investments and is prepared to suffer an initial loss. Besides, if you hadn't been so tardy you could have bought some of the agencies at a much lower price. Now the bidding war is red hot,' replied Tracy.

'OK, its my fault, but hear me out. Why don't we pretend that we're trebling the commission and so inflate the valuation of the estate agency? That way we get to buy the agency but don't actually lose money on the endowment.'

'That's deception.'

'Who am I deceiving? Nobody. In fact why go through this charade. Just find out what the competition is offering and offer a thousand quid more,' I said.

'And how do we find out what the opposition is offering?'

'By bribing someone in the know; darn sight cheaper than trebling the commission.'

'I can't do that; it's dishonest,' replied Tracy.

'Oh, I see,' I said, unable to keep up with a banker's business morality. Eventually I said:

'OK, we'll do it your way. Bruce has been taking notes. We'll inflate income as far as we can; we'll emasculate expenses as far as we can. Is that all?'

'That'll give you an idea of the profit for a year. Be prepared to go up to ten times that figure.

***

My head was still reeling when I answered Ellen's call that evening.

'It's good to hear your voice,' I said. 'I haven't heard from you for ages. How's everything?'

'It's only a fortnight since we last spoke. I've been quite busy actually, getting up to speed on various live issues.'

'Really? What are they?'

'You know I can't talk about any of them. I've settled into my new way of life. I'm less afraid of the dark. So long as I live in Knightsbridge I'm OK. The flat is pokey but a bed and a desk is all I need. How are you getting on with Camelot Estates?'

'I don't think I'm cut out for it. I'm circumcised.'

'Are you out of your mind?'

'It's true. You must be a complete prick to buy an estate agency today.'

'What happened?'

'Crazy people they want me to buy estate agencies at a loss using phoney figures.'

'Does Tim know about this?'

'He's the one who wants it this way.'

'Make sure it doesn't rebound on you.'

'Have no fear. Bruce has been taking the minutes.'

'Why don't you stick to your guns?'

'Because they'll fire me; I'll be remembered as a failure. Better to play the game by their rules and then resign.'

Proof that I wasn't completely insane came when JM's latest circular landed on my desk. I read it with much amusement. He was expressing relief at Camelot's failure to sign up any estate agencies.

'I am confused.' said he. 'Either they are playing a deep game, talking up the prices of estate agencies without actually buying them; making sure that Holborn Bars and Monarch suffer the loss; or they're incompetent at buying. If it's the former let's salute Tim or Majid, I'm not sure which; if it's the latter, may they long be incompetent.'

I wondered how Tim would take it.

***

It was over a year since Nick was rebuffed by Royston, Royston & Royston. They were now the largest firms of estate agents still remaining independent. Nick and I were looking for a fresh excuse for re-establishing contact.

Unexpectedly, out of the blue as it were, Ruaridh Royston phoned me for a chat. We arranged a meeting.

When Ruaridh came to Bristol to meet me, I saw a tallish man with an imposing presence. He was fleshy without being fat; the kind of man who appears slim when standing up with his jacket buttoned but then has to unbutton it to sit down. He had a deep voice with a delicious inflection that commanded attention.

'I see that you're still independent. What have you been up to?' I asked.

'We've been improving our house.'

'I beg your pardon?'

'How do you say it? We've been tidying up our business.'

'I get it. You've been putting your house in order.'

'That's it.'

'People normally do that before they sell. Is that what you've come to tell us?'

'Holborn Bars and Monarch kept coming to us each time with never to be repeated higher offers. I said to my brother Roger, we should cash in our chips. He said we'd only do this once so we'd better make sure we get the best deal. So we spent a year improving our internal controls and sales techniques and cut costs. We've increased the proportion of endowment mortgages to 88%.'

'Great.'

Ruaridh paused at this point to drink his coffee. Perhaps he expected me to say something but I didn't; he was waiting for the punch-line.

'What are you waiting for?' asked Ruaridh, 'here's your chance. Gazump them and we are yours.'

'Have you got audited figures?'

'Yes. I should add that the best deal is not just about price but also what role you envisage for us.'

I said, 'Before we talk numbers can I say a bit about ourselves, to get to know each other better.' I then gave my background.

'Well, like you my bothers and I are foreign too. We're from Ireland. We went to no fancy college. We're from the farming community. However I've been a wheeler dealer for as long as I remember. I buy things for ten punts and sell them for twenty. I know that's only ten per cent but I made an adequate living. I then came over to England and got into estate agency business.'

He gave some background about his brothers. He then produced some figures for income and expenses and went through their rationale.

The total income forecast for 1989 was £15m and the total expenses £10m. The major part of the income was commission on the sale of houses. Though not as large, the commission paid by the insurance company on the sale of its endowment was significant. As it was marginal income it was pure profit.

At this time a phone call came through for Ruaridh on my line.

'What now?' asked Ruaridh. Shrugging his shoulders, he then said to me, 'I'm sorry about this. Only my secretary and Roger know that I'm here with you. It might be important.'

Bruce, Nick and I got into a huddle in one corner and started having a discussion,

'What do you think? Shall I make an indicative offer?' I asked looking at Nick but he was straining every sinew to listen to what Tim was saying. I therefore turned to Bruce.

'Yes, provided we make it clear that it is subject to verification of the numbers supplied,' replied Bruce.

'They're talking of an annual profit of £5m shall we offer a multiple of five, say £25m?'

'Going by what Tracy said we should be prepared to go up to £50m. Should we offer that and be done with or see if we can get away with a lower figure?'

I sat down. You're not telling me that this lot are worth £50m? It's a joke.'

'Well, others are doing it,' said Bruce.

'Isn't profit the small difference between two large numbers?' I asked Bruce.

'It is.'

'If the income has been overstated by 10% and the expenses understated by 10%, both within the bounds of forecasting error, then the profit halves.'

'Deadright. A 20% discrepancy would eliminate the profit altogether.'

At this point Nick rejoined the conversation to say:

'I've been eavesdropping on Ruaridh. It was hard as he kept his voice down but I think he was talking to his brother about an offer for the 3R's. I think it was from Holborn Bars but I'm not sure. He ended by saying "go for £40m in cash or £50m, half in cash and half in shares."'

'Then we should offer £50m in cash,' said Bruce.

'He's trying it on. I bet there was no one at the other end,' I said.

'There definitely was someone at the other end,' said Nick.

I said, 'Even if there was, I don't have the authority to make a final offer.'

'Why not'

'Well, for a start I don't know whether we have the necessary cash to make an all cash offer. My instructions are to liaise with Tracy.'

'Surely you can make an offer but not commit yourself on whether it would be cash or shares or a bit of each?'

At this point Ruaridh came off the phone and, with a jaunty air, walked towards them and said, 'Sorry about that, chaps. I guessed that it was something important as I'd asked not to be disturbed,'

'Everything OK?'

'Of course. Why shouldn't it be?'

'Look Ruaridh,' I said. 'We're very keen to make an offer but I need to talk to my Chief Executive to clarify a few things. I'm thinking of an offer in the region of £25m, possibly more. Am I in the right ball park?'

'No you're not I'm afraid. You're an entire pitch behind?'

'How do you mean?'

'Someone's prepared to offer double that.'

'Subject to due diligence, no doubt.'

'Of course. But my point is that you've got to beat it.'

'OK tell me, what will secure the deal?'

'£55m in cash or £50m in cash with no due diligence.'

'That's rubbish,' I said. 'Most of your profit comes from the commission on the endowments. If we buy you you'll be selling our endowments. It's crazy to pay money to buy what comes from us in the first place.'

'OK, it's your call. We'll go back to the other offer on the table.'

After the Roystons had gone, Nick tore into me. 'You're never going to make a purchase the way you're going.'

'Do you really want me to authorise silly prices; they're not even silly, they're ridiculous.'

'I thought Tim had said to you that these were strategic purchases?'

'That's consultancy-speak to justify the unjustifiable.'

'Can I quote you on that?'

'No.'

'Majid, we don't make the rules of the game. We either play by the rules or get off the pitch. If you don't play by the rules then I'm off.'

'Off where?'

'Back to Camelot Life.'

I looked to see how serious he was but Nick didn't give anything away. So I asked:

'Are you threatening me?'

'I have no wish to be associated with a failure.'

'You know we're being set up. That phone call was a pretty juvenile trick.'

'I heard what I heard.'

That evening Ellen phoned me for a chat. What she got was a torrent of complaints about how silly the market had become and the cheek of Ruaridh to try a juvenile trick and expect me to fall for it. Ellen listened sympathetically but didn't say anything.

Next morning we went up to London to have a chat with Tracy. I explained the position and added:

'It's a crazy price they're asking, we'll never ever make any money on it.'

In response, Nick said:

'I think we should stop pussyfooting around and make our mind up. Do we want this business or not? If we do we have to pay the market rate.'

'Well said,' said Tracy. 'That is what Tim wants; to buy our way into this business.'

I had lost and decided to go with the flow. Together we agreed to offer £45m in cash or £50m, half in cash and half in Camelot shares, both subject to due diligence. I then phoned Ruaridh and said we'd go across to the 3R's head office in Chelmsford. We got there in the afternoon and I put the alternative offers to them. Yet again they were interrupted by a phone call. Again Ruaridh took it but this time in the other room. He talked in a soft voice so there was no prospect of overhearing him.

Ruaridh returned and apologised and sat in silence. Eventually he said, 'OK then.'

'You've not responded to our offer.'

'Oh that, thank you for coming all the way here to see me. It must have been a pig of a journey. I'm afraid we've had a better offer and I'll close the deal later this afternoon.'

Tracy looked at me and then turned to Ruaridh and said, 'OK we'll offer £52m cash or £57m half in cash and half in shares.'

'What about due diligence?'

'What about it? We assume that you carried out your spring cleaning with due diligence,' said Tracy.

'What role do you envisage for me and my brothers?'

'3R's will be a subsidiary of Camelot Estates. The three of you, who are its directors, will remain so. We shall not interfere in the day to day running of the business. However, as we have or will have paid good money to buy them, we will have certain requirements that each of them shall have to comply with.' I made sure I said this before Tracy said something anodyne.

'Such as?'

'We want to make sure that we get an adequate return on our investment. So the first requirement is accurate reporting of the financial performance of the business. That is most important. If we don't get an accurate picture of how the business is doing then we're shooting blind-folded.'

'Surely it is performance compared to the target that you really want to know?'

'It is but the figures have to be reliable in the first place.'

'Is that it?'

'No there will be others. I'm not sure which business has a poorer image, estate agencies or insurance companies but the two combined will have a serious image problem. So we'll be monitoring the level of customer complaints. In due course there'll be other issues.'

Ruaridh got up and went to shake hands of first me then Nick, Bruce and Tracy, 'Gentlemen, we have a deal. We accept your £52m cash offer. My lawyers have produced a draft Heads of Agreement. Sign it today and we're in business.' He took a document out of his drawer and crossed out 'Holborn Bars' and wrote in 'Camelot' and gave it to me.

'I'll get back to you,' I said.

'One other thing. My brothers and I expect to be Directors of Camelot Estates.'

'We want to appoint to the Board three or four additional directors from the estate agencies we own. In fact I'd like you, as the Managing Director of 3R's to join the Board. We can't have all three of you on the Board.'

'That's not acceptable. We've always done things together.'

'Not always surely?'

'Yes, we hunt as a pack.'

'I'm sure you'll find that there are things you do on your own.'

'No, I'm telling you, we do everything together.'

'You don't share wives, for example, surely?'

'No, but we married three sisters.'

'You amaze me.'

'We Irish are an amazing lot.'

Nothing could top that.

I passed the draft Heads of Agreement to Kate Spencer for a quick review before I signed it. I then saw Tim Fredricks. It was a few months since I last saw him and I was shocked. He was under immense pressure to deliver on his wonderful campaign slogan, **Yes, Yes, Yes, the Answer is Yes, What is the Question?**, but I hadn't realised that it had taken a toll on his health. He looked listless and wan. He perked up marginally on hearing of the 3R's deal, even managing a weak smile.

'Well done. Use the same blueprint for other purchases and make sure you reach the goals set.'

'It's not yet a done deal. They're threatening to pull out unless all three brothers get a seat on the Camelot Estates Board.'

'That's an easy one.'

'Not really. That'll give them three votes out of seven, enabling them to hold us to ransom if they get one other director to side with them. It could also create similar demands from other firms we buy and then the Board will become unwieldy.'

'But if you don't sign up 3R's pretty soon we'll have to wind up Camelot Estates.'

'So you suggest that I give in?'

'It's a no-brainer.'

So it was that I gave in. I then went to Kate to check on the Heads of Agreement. She said there were a few changes necessary and she will get back after she'd agreed them with the vendors.

. That evening Bruce and Nick visited me in my flat.

'You're going to have fun managing this lot. They're used to their independence,' said Nick.

'These guys are probably better than others we'll have to deal with,' said Bruce.

'Do you believe his story about the three brothers marrying three sisters?' asked Majid.

'I don't see why he would make that up. He didn't say they were their own sisters,' said Bruce.

'Do you think it's a Catholic thing, the family being important and all that?' asked Majid.

'Maybe. Family *is* important to them.'

'So it is to us Asians but we don't often see three brothers marrying three sisters.'

Ruaridh was on the phone to me, early next morning. 'I've talked to my brothers. Can you put all three of us on the Camelot Estates Board?'

'I can't do that it'll be top heavy with 3R's people. Our plan is to have at least 500 agents of which 3R's represent one hundred. It'll upset all the others.'

'Well in that case have none of us on your Board.'

'OK, if that's what you want.'

'You may think you're calling my bluff but remember this. We Irish don't take kindly to taxation without representation.'

I didn't respond and the meeting ended.

Fortified by this success, I asked Nick to once more approach Helena Peel, the owner of Peel & Co. They were still independent but were not wedded to it. Nick thought that they were quite shrewd and were trying to guess when the market will peak. Unlike the 3R's, this lot had not undergone a spring clean and their figures were unreliable. Bruce had looked at last year's accounts which showed a profit of £100,000 so he offered ten times that i.e. a million pounds. The offer was accepted. Suddenly Camelot Estates owned two firms, 3R's around London's northern periphery and one in Bristol; or, as the press release said, 'Camelot now has one-hundred and one estate agency branches around the country. Helena joined the Camelot Estates Board.

Events My Dear, Events

They say that only women can multi-task. Maybe I'm a woman but I've always been able to do so. I have the ability, when working on a particular task, to shut out everything else. Without that I would not have survived 1988 and 1989. Looking back, I'm amazed that I came through it, scathed perhaps but at least I survived.

Just think of it. First there was Ellen's accident and coping with her working for MI5. Then there was Tim's *Yes, Yes, Yes, the Answer's Yes, What's the Question?* and its ill-conceived off-spring, 'Power to the People' which brought a string of half-baked ideas for Marketing department to evaluate. One of these, Camelot Estates, was taking up a lot of time. But perhaps the biggest problem was the need to deal with a changing business landscape. And just to further complicate matters there was a new demon stalking the insurance industry, AIDS.

It was early 1988 before I realised that the changes being introduced by the Financial Services Act placed marketing at the epicentre of the organisation making me a very powerful person. Although this was good for the ego, it represented a serious problem. Why? Because the rest of my management colleagues weren't aware of this power shift. Worse, the estate agency arm was a cuckoo chick leaving little time for my day-job, marketing. Although I had a good team to hold the fort, this was a perilous state of affairs. As I sometimes did when faced with a problem, I talked to myself or rather my alter ego, Percy:

'Let me understand this. You have more power than the company thinks they've given you. Right?' asked Percy.

'Right.'

'So if you tried to exercise those powers your colleagues might thwart you, right?'

'Right.'

'But if you don't and things go wrong, it'll be your fault and you'll get it in the neck from the regulators, right?'

'Right.'

'You'd better do something about it then.'

'The real problem is that Chief Executives such as Tim have had their freedom severely shackled. The regulators now call the tune.'

'Right, you'd better tell Tim.'

'What? with his tendency to shoot the messenger? No thanks.'

'Don't say I didn't warn you.'

Percy had a point. It was either my neck or Tim's. My mind went back to I Claudius, the television series. Claudius' wife, a nymphomaniac, was bringing Rome into disrepute and someone had to tell Claudius. But he was blindly in love with her and liable to have anyone who spoke ill of her, killed. In the end they got an old prostitute, a confidante of Claudius, to tell him. Who could perform a similar role? The only person I could think of was Kate. I thought about calling her but before that I thought through the issues in further detail.

There were so many significant changes in the business environment in the UK that perhaps it was time to adopt the teachings of Kotler. 'Put the customer first, find out what he needs, deliver it efficiently and everyone's happy.'

But, what about the intermediary? OK, we can try to understand his needs as well. But there was an added complexity that Kotler didn't address. Gifted as he was, Kotler wasn't clairvoyant. He couldn't foresee that the Financial Services Act in the UK would stipulate that the person making a sale must give 'best advice.' In no other industry as far as I was aware, was there a requirement that, in effect, you should sell the cheapest product. I was unsure whether the regulators fully appreciated what genie they had let out of the bottle. No doubt they will determine with hindsight what they meant by the term 'best advice' and no doubt many companies would pay the price for not having come to the same conclusion ahead of the regulators. Archie was setting Tim up for a fall.

The more I thought about it the more concerned I became. The insurance industry faced its biggest challenge since the forties. Far sighted leadership was needed to deal with them but the industry might be let down by its leaders. Tim was not unique.

Whilst these thoughts were exercising my mind, Kate Spencer dropped in for a chat.

She had three concerns: her workload, the cavalier attitude of management, both of which I concurred with, and her own ability to be an effective Compliance Manager.

'Come on, Kate, the legal aspects are well within your capabilities. Are you afraid of having to police senior people?'

'No, a lot of the requirements are very mathematical. I don't even know the difference between a billion and a million.'

'So what, sometimes I can't remember the difference between a billion and a billion.'

'Don't be daft.'

'No, seriously, American billion is different to English billion. It has only nine zeroes, the English one has twelve. What were we talking about?'

'My ability to be Compliance Officer given that I'm non-numerate'

'That's complete nonsense. Where do you need numeracy?'

'To understand illustrations you make of what a policy can provide for example; or in assessing whether one product is preferable to another.'

'Look, these are easy things. Just insist that marketing obtain a formal sign off from me confirming that we've complied with the rules.'

'That'll be very helpful.'

'Any concern, just give me a call and I'll help you out. No one else needs to know.'

Visibly relieved, she thanked me.

'That's that sorted. Don't you think the Board is a little too relaxed about the new environment? I don't think they appreciate the sea change this Act represents.'

'I agree with that.'

'I think we should join forces and issue a list of guidelines, some relating to the sales process and one for my marketing team to take note of. We can also circulate them to the Board to make the directors aware of the issues. Change has to come from the top. We can issue a series of such documents.'

'I'm a little uncomfortable confronting management. Why don't we issue the circulars under the generic title, *Marketing and Compliance Circular,* but under your name?' said Kate.

'I don't mind so long as you approve the content.'

'Agreed. Let's plan to issue the first two Circulars early in March.'

I agreed but was conscious that I had to find time for these whilst caring for Ellen. Late in March, I issued the inaugural *Marketing & Compliance Circular*: After a page setting the scene, it set out the first two rules:

Rule No. 1: If the same product is available at more than one price, your own salesmen must offer the cheapest price to its customers.

Rule No. 2: The product must be suitable to the customer's requirements and affordable by him. A rule of thumb for affordability is that, in the case of a mortgage the total monthly cost outlay must not exceed 25% of take home pay.

I was surprised at the relative lack of response. After a fortnight, I phoned Nick and Bruce to check if they'd read it. They had, but the timetable to get the company ready both in terms of system changes and training was so tight that they couldn't afford to challenge the basis. They had to comply first and then have a posthumous debate.

The Financial Services Act was largely about selling practices. In due course the regulators will come and see if their guidelines have been adhered to. Rules 1 and 2 were key. Both Kate and I felt that it was unwise to let the sales department produce information regarding sales volume. If selling practices were ever challenged, it would be better that the sales data was produced by a department that would not be judged by it. It should be either marketing or finance. Nick did not agree. 'Why fix what aint broke? It's not as if we're not busy.'

Nick won.

There was another issue. I realised that it was no longer possible to look at Camelot and Merlin in separate silos. Even though I wasn't responsible for it, I'd have to take an interest in Merlin's business. I started to have meetings with Wayne Furlong and explored the approach taken by the Merlin team. Archie didn't like it and complained to Tim about interference. Tim asked me to leave Merlin alone. 'Forget the regulators, I have shareholders to look after.' A battle for the future, I guess.

***

At least one (small) distraction had been dealt with. An internal memorandum from Tim confirmed that the sale of the Australian business to the Sword of Truth Group had been completed.

***

First of July 1988 was the culmination of a three year campaign by the Government to 'unlock people's pensions'.

Millions of people were in good pension schemes where the pension is based upon the salary at the date of retirement. The problem of finding the necessary resources to finance these pensions was a matter for the employer, with the trustees as the intermediary. Roughly one-half of these were in the public sector and the remainder in the private sector.

The pensions industry argued strongly that exchanging a product where the employer took the inflation and investment risk for one where the individual bore those risks could lead to grief. But the urge to privatise everything was unstoppable. Legislation had been enacted in 1986 to come into force in 1988. Camelot entered the race for a share of this business. I made another unsuccessful attempt to persuade the Board to defer the launch of the product until they were ready.

My team then played a key role in designing the new personal pensions product and devising a questionnaire to make sure that it was financially appropriate to come out of the company pension.

Marketing and Compliance Circular

Rule No. 3: Public sector employees who are entitled to join or are already in a defined benefit pension scheme that is underwritten by the Government and to which the employer contributes should not be switched into an Camelot Personal Pension.

Rule No. 4: Individuals who were in a public sector pension scheme but are no longer so, may consider switching their accrued pension rights in the public sector scheme into an Camelot Personal Pension if Camelot considers it to be advantageous to do so.

These were issued early in June. Salesmen were given the barest minimum of training. There was no system of checking that the guidelines were being adhered to. In the Power to the People regime, trust was the watchword.

***

I yearned for regular contact with Ellen. In her new job she was busy getting to know the job, the people and procedures, protocol and obligations. The last of these began to irritate me. I visited her every weekend and often during the week as well. She was a source of comfort and guidance as I grappled with the world of estate agencies.

It took me a while to realise that she was talking less and less about herself and especially her work.

As 1988 drew to a close I was ready for a break. I'd never been so mentally tired.

***

As we entered 1989 with management in a buoyant mood, I couldn't concentrate. Whichever way I looked I saw black clouds. I looked in my in-tray for some light relief. Instead I saw an item marked by Louise as a 'complaint, potentially serious'. It came from Russell Flint, the manager of the Leeds Branch. After reading his memo, I phoned him.

'Can you do something about the actuaries in the pensions department? They're stopping me from writing business.' implored Russell.

'What type of business?'

'It's about a redundant mineworker who has no faith in Black Gold's management. He wants to take his pension away from their pension scheme into one of our personal pensions.'

'There's usually a test to see if it's in his interests to do so.'

'Yes, his numbers have been put through the system. You know that it is based upon the traffic light system. Green is OK, red is No. It came out amber and still they rejected it.'

'That's a sensibly cautious approach but I'll check it out for you.'

I did just that and I discovered a can of worms. In the past few months the pensions department had accepted forty such cases and had forgotten to check that it was right to switch out. They therefore decided to be overcautious and in the future regard amber as red. So I went back to the Leeds branch and said that it was not in the customer's interest to switch his pension.

'But he's determined to switch. He has no faith in his employer.'

'But the pension scheme is a separate entity run by its trustees safe from the employer.'

'But one of the trustees is from the employer.'

'Whatever he says, we won't accept the business.'

'You're denying me the right to earn a living. If you don't accept his business there are plenty of other companies that will.'

'That's down to them.'

'You haven't heard the last of this. I'll write to Tim Fredricks.'

He was wrong. After a month I phoned Russell to ask how he got on with Tim.

'Oh, he asked me to see him and hauled in the pensions actuary and reviewed the facts. He directed the pensions actuary to do one of two things: either use more optimistic assumptions so that more of the cases came out green and fewer amber or red; or let amber cases through. He chose the latter.

'"Who'll tell Majid?" I asked him and he said it was nothing to do with you.'

***

A new phenomenon had hit society and the insurance industry was in the front line: AIDS. The highly publicised deaths of Rock Hudson and Liberace led people to believe that these were symptoms of the excesses of the entertainment industry. Because all reported incidents related to gay people and the disease could only be transmitted by the exchange of bodily fluids, most people believed that the disease was containable to a small section of the population. God was punishing gay people for being unnatural.

However the medical and the actuarial professions and the insurance industry knew that the problem was far more serious. Firstly the gay community was much larger than people suspected it to be. Secondly gay people tended to be far more promiscuous so that it was quite likely that before long a high proportion of gay people would get AIDS. What made it worse was that many gay people were in fact bisexual so that there was a high risk of transmission to the hetero-sexual community.

The insurance industry decided to take a consistent approach and convened a meeting involving a mixture of actuaries (to assess the financial impact) and marketing men (to assess the commercial consequences). I attended in a marketing rather than actuarial capacity.

'Let's consider first how we deal with the impact of AIDS on our existing business,' said the representative of the Association of British Insurers who was chairing the meeting.

'That's straightforward in principle. So long as there had been no non-disclosure at the time the policy was taken out, the customer is covered and we will pay if he dies as a result of AIDS,' said the actuary of Holborn Bars.

'What would amount to non-disclosure?' I asked.

'Off-hand I cannot think of any. This disease was unknown until very recently. We didn't ask searching questions because we didn't foresee this disease. We may for future cases ask questions regarding lifestyle and sexual orientation which some of our policyholders might fail if asked today, but the point is we did not deem it necessary to ask then.'

'So that's it then? We do nothing?'

'Not quite. We may have to honour any claims but such claims are going to be more frequent and possibly for a higher amount. We have to assess the amount and set aside resources to meet them.'

.OK, what about new customers?'

'That's trickier,' I said. I've been discussing this with my counterparts in other companies. The questions we want to ask about sexual habits will upset a majority of the clients whose lifestyle does not expose them to the risk. Another problem is that a key question is about monogamy/promiscuity. Where a husband and wife are jointly taking out insurance it may be that one is promiscuous but the other not; the former is unlikely to give a truthful answer.'

'But then you can have him for non-disclosure'

'Yes, but we'd rather screen them out than decline claims when they arise. Imagine the newspaper headlines. *"Widow discovers that her late husband was gay AND that the heartless insurance company won't pay the death claim"'*

'So what's the solution?'

'An imperfect one. Ask if they are in a long-term relationship with a single person. If they are not, then ask them to complete detailed lifestyle questionnaires. If on the other hand they are in a long-term relationship, even if it is with a person of the same sex, then they would only be required to fill in the questionnaire if the sum insured is greater than a high threshold.'

'That will neither completely protect us nor avoid a public outcry against intrusion into privacy.'

'But it is the best compromise we can come up with.'

In the end the proposals were adopted by the industry. I reported back to our management. I was unprepared for the reaction of Tim.

'You had no right to bind Camelot to a course of action without clearing it with me.'

'I'm sorry I thought people were aware of the direction the debate was taking. Also, it is the ABI that is seeking consensus not me.'

'There is no objective evidence that homosexuality is the cause of AIDS. This is out and out queer-bashing and I don't think we should be a party to it.'

'I thought there was plenty of evidence particularly in the US, Canada and Sweden that the spread of AIDS was caused largely by homosexual promiscuity.'

'But that's not the same as saying that homosexuality is the cause of it. We don't know what the origin of the disease was.'

'You're absolutely right but we are businessmen not scientists. We are less concerned about the cause than whether a potential policyholder is likely to contract it and all the evidence is that you're more likely to come into contact with it if you're a promiscuous homosexual or are in relationship with one who is.'

'I'll ask the Board to consider its position on this debate.'

'That's your prerogative but if you go contrary to ABI's guidelines we may have to leave the ABI. You also run the risk of being swamped with all the gay business.'

The Board was consulted but the other directors did not want to march out of step with the ABI.

Two months later we received an angry letter, 'How dare you suggest that we are a homosexual couple? John is my son.'

What had happened was that a proposal was received for a sum insured of £100,000 on the lives of two men. The system automatically sent out lifestyle questionnaires for completion. In fact a father was helping his son buy a house by guaranteeing his mortgage so the bank wanted both lives to be insured.

Such oddities kept recurring over the following months.

**

'Boy I'm glad to see the back of 1989,' I said to Gareth. 'I'm totally drained. I knew how wide-ranging my responsibilities were but I hadn't expected problems on all fronts at the same time.'

'Do you lack adequate support?' asked Gareth.

'It's not that. Ours is a slow-moving industry where change is implemented after much thought. Suddenly a whole range of new opportunities have arisen and it's forced us to embrace change with inadequate preparation.'

'Why chase all the opportunities rather than some?' asked Gareth.

'Because if we don't our competitors will.'

'That's no reason for abandoning your standards,' said Gareth.

'I think you're preaching to the converted,' said Ellen. 'He made that case but he lost.'

'The problem is that if things go wrong in his patch then he'd still be blamed for it.'

'He knows that too Dad; he's just had an unjust reprimand.'

'OK, OK, I'll mind my own business.'

'My business is your business. I rely heavily on the advice of both you and Ellen but it's not always possible to do anything about it.'

That night I said to Ellen,

'We haven't set a date yet for our postponed wedding.'

'You're dead right but I'm so busy learning new things that I don't think it would be fair on you. You're doing too much for me already.'

'I'm pretty busy learning new things myself but I hate life without goals. Can't we set a tentative date so that we know where we are?'

'Shall we say mid –ninety-one?'
'Mid-ninety-one.'

***

Tim sent me a faxed copy of a letter he'd received from the Black Gold pension scheme:

Dear Mr Fredricks
Your own salesmen and several brokers are encouraging new employees not to join our pension scheme but instead to take out a Camelot Personal Pension. Unless this practice is ended immediately I will have little option but to inform the regulators and your firm will have to face the consequences.
There are several reasons why a switch to your Personal Pension is not in the employee's financial interest, the two principal ones being:
1. He loses the benefit of the employers contributions
2. He loses the benefit of the Government's guarantee that the scheme will honour its promise

It was followed by Tim's reply:
I would ask you to retract your letter of ….
Whilst I accept that there may in the past have been isolated cases of salesmen overstepping the mark I resent the implied slur that we are encouraging your employees to act against their own best interests. I ask you to withdraw your allegation or suffer the consequences.

I read both and immediately phoned Tim and said, 'I wouldn't send this letter out.'

'Too bad, it's already gone. What's the problem?'

'There is some substance to what he says.'

I then related what we had found out when a broker had complained. Tim listened and said,

'That's precisely my point. An isolated incident but we've put it right.'

'But it wasn't an isolated incident, it was a systemic failure and we couldn't undo what had been done. Instead we decided to be particularly harsh on future cases.'

'Go away Majid, I'm not going to argue with you. You're a pedant.'

'I'm not. This is a complex subject. The latest complaint is not about encouraging people to leave the Black Gold pension scheme but of discouraging them from joining in the first place.'

Tim ignored that remark

***

Christmas of 1990 was again spent in Mold but this time there was no Ellen.

She was on some confidential mission which meant working over Christmas. Neither I nor her parents knew what it was but they knew it involved an overseas trip as she'd asked Glynis to post her passport to her.

I began to wonder if it was a wise thing I did when I encouraged her to join the secret service. An Iron Curtain seems to have descended between us. Actually that's a bad analogy. It's more like human skin, permeable only in one direction. Is it good to be so immersed in her work that she forgets even her loved ones; or has she forged a new alliance? For the first time doubt crept in. I decided to give her a call when she was back in the New Year.

The Sword of Truth

While management were busy coming to terms with the changing landscape, I personally had to come terms with a shock. .The year (1988) was drawing to a close when I received a confidential internal memo from Kate Spencer addressed to all senior management. It related to the business of Camelot's Australian branch, which had been sold to the Sword of Truth Group. Ben Shmeuli and Ariel Cohen, the two directors and sole owners of the company had disappeared and so had the funds of A\$225million which had been transferred by Camelot to the Group in return for it taking over its Australian liabilities. Shane Barnes, formerly the Managing Director of Camelot's Australian branch was also missing. The theft was discovered six months earlier. At the request of the Australian police complete confidentiality was enforced. It now looks as if the money has gone to South America.

Kate Spencer said that the legal position was that 'We cannot avoid our obligation to our policyholders. We didn't sell on the business, we had simply laid it off. As far as the customers are concerned we're still their insurer'.

Christmas was again spent with the Evan family. My mind kept going back to the theft of Australian funds. Did Tim follow up his phone call? Ellen placated me by saying that I'd done all the right things.

Dad kept up his recent practice of phoning on Christmas day. After he'd spoken to Gareth and Glynis, Glynis spoke to Mum who then spoke with me.

'How's my dear son and how is that dear girl, Helen?'

'Ellen Mum, not Helen She's fine too. She's now an important member of the British Secret Service, MI5.'

She must have been stunned as there was no reply for the best part of a minute.'

'She's only changed jobs Mum.

'What, you're friendly with a British spy?'

'Shh! Nobody should know about it.'

I could hear her say to Dad 'My son's friendly with a spy and he's worried that I'll tell people about it.'

'No, not that. Nobody knows that she works for MI5.'

'Why didn't you tell me before?'

'Because I knew how you would react. She had no choice Mum. After her car accident, she lost her job with the police and this was the best we could find for her.'

'When are you men going to stop treating me like a second class citizen?'

'When you stop panicking.'

***

The Board of Camelot asked its Audit Committee to look at the circumstances surrounding the sale of Camelot Life's Australian business, following the latest report from the police. Ben Shmeuli, Ariel Cohen and Shane Barnes were all in Venezuela but attempts to extradite them were continuing to be thwarted. I was summoned for an interview.

I went to the meeting unaccompanied. Waiting for me were Bill Ashford, a director of Camelot who was the Chairman of the Audit Committee, as well as two independent members of the Committee, Ted MacAfee and Ernie Absolom. Ted Leary from HR sat in as an observer. Bill Ashford began by explaining that they were seeking clarification of my involvement in the sale of the Australian business. I said I welcomed the opportunity to explain all the facts.

. 'You were asked to review the proposed sale of our Australian business when you were in Australia,' began Bill Ashford.

'I was going to Australia on holiday and Tim Fredricks asked me to review the terms being offered by all the potential purchasers. It is not what I normally do and I only had at most three days available. I said I'd do what I could. In the event I spent perhaps three hours, no more.'

'Brevity of involvement is no excuse. Did Shane Barnes give you the background to the Sword of Truth Group?'

'He did after I specifically asked him about it. I asked Shane about conflict of interest. I wondered how they expected to make money when we couldn't and asked to see the owners of the business.'

'You knew that the owners were Ben Shmeuli and Ariel Cohen.'

'Yes, those were the names given to me by Shane.'

'Why did you not check them out?'

'I wanted to but was told that they were abroad until after the Christmas break. I then phoned Tim, expressed my concerns and said the owners must be checked out.'

'Do you have evidence of any of these?'

'Kate Spencer will confirm what I said at the meeting as she was there. Tim Fredricks will confirm that I phoned him.'

'Did you not make any notes at the time?' asked Ted MacAfee.

'No, I didn't. Don't forget I was on holiday.'

The meeting ended, but a week later I was called again. 'Kate Spencer confirms your version of the meeting but Tim Fredricks has no recollection of a phone call from you. He says he would without doubt have acted upon it if you had said what you say you said.'

'What can I say? My recollection is vivid.'

'So it's your word against his?'

'It would seem so. Shall I speak with him?'

'That won't be necessary.'

There being no further questions, I left.

***

A few weeks later, I received a note from HR saying, 'The Audit Committee has reviewed your role in the sale of our Australian business. It felt that your conduct fell short of the standards expected of a person in your position. You did not put your concerns in writing and therefore failed to alert us to the severity of the fraud risk. Whilst the error was not serious enough to merit a dismissal we have decided to place it as a blot in your record and it will be held against you when future promotion prospects are considered. In taking this step we were mindful of the fact that this was not an isolated incident. You declined Robert Plinth help when he asked for it.'

I was stunned. I didn't know how to respond but decided against a knee-jerk action. Instead I travelled up to London and met Ellen in the Paddington pub and briefed her.

'Bloody Teflon Tim, it seems that your Dad was right.'

'I didn't see it coming. I was prepared for flak on the estate agency front but not this one.

After initial anger we discussed objectively the options open to me. The conclusion was that to appeal against the ruling was not going to be helpful.

Unless Tim changed his story, I had no new information to cause the verdict to be reviewed. If I appealed and lost it would be worse than not having appealed. If I won the stigma would still be there.

Did the punishment fit the crime? What I did was something of a favour whilst on holiday; it was no part of my daily job. But that line of defence had been tried and they'd come up with the old canard, 'Senior management never switch off, even when on holiday.'

Reference to Robert Plinth was harsh but having that expunged would achieve nothing as that was a minor issue.

Although I've never been over-ambitious, the thought of losing out to Nick was hurtful. My career had hit a roadblock, leaving a clear path for him.

. The best course of action was to excel in the present job and use it as a springboard to move elsewhere. Mind you I'd been saying that for a while now. The problem was my punishing work schedule which left little time for myself.

I had a mental picture of an ass with a carrot tied to his forehead dangling in front of him.

Taken To The Cleaners

As if I wasn't busy enough, in the summer of 1988 at the height of the landscape changing, I had a call from Tim. He wanted to discuss Merlin. I went up to London intending to tell him the problems posed by new regulations. But Tim was busy and had no time to listen, only to tell me what he wanted.

'It was always our intention to float Merlin Life on the stockmarket in 1989. That's the best way to determine what it is worth. It will also enable us to establish the worth of the share options granted to the management and sales-force of Merlin.'

'What do you want me to do?'

'We're trying to estimate what Merlin might be worth. Clem Hill is doing the necessary calculations and Wayne Furlong is reviewing them. I'd like you to have a look as a disinterested observer.'

'Won't I be duplicating Wayne's work?'

'He's got substantial share options and is therefore not unbiased. I'm assuming that you bring no baggage of bias of your own.'

So I met up with Wayne and Clem. I began by asking details of the share options. I was staggered to find that as much as a quarter (25%) of the company's share capital would be in their hands once the options were exercised; split equally between Merlin management and sales-force. Management's 12.5% was shared, 5% to Archie, 2.5% to Jeff and the remaining 5% split equally among the four executive management. The remaining 12.5% was allocated to the sales-force in proportion to the business generated.

Clem had valued the share in two parts. First he valued the worth of the business already on the books, value in the bag as it were. In practice such profits would depend upon how long they stayed on the books so the value was still subjective. Depending upon the assumptions made the value ranged from £8m to £28m.

The second component was the value to be placed upon business that will be written in the future. This was subjective and lay in the realms of conjecture or, to use a technical expression, it was a 'finger in the air' job.

You have to estimate the number of salesmen Merlin would have each year, their productivity, the cost of recruiting them (some might need golden hellos) and future production expenses. This gave a value ranging from £15m to £150m. Thus the total value ranged from £23m to £178m. (Archie's share ranged from £1.15m to £8.9m). Within this range, Wayne was inclined to value the company at around £150m, Clem at £40m.

I had no quarrel with the approach taken with the first component and would have settled for a value of £15m. However I had three serious reservations about the second. First, the margins were bound to be squeezed and therefore future business was likely to be less profitable than before. Secondly I thought that under the new regulatory regime salesmen would find life tough and therefore the forecast growth in numbers was optimistic. Thirdly, if 12.5% of the profits generated goes to the salesman as share options, then that should be regarded as a cost. With all these uncertainties I felt that the value should be cut further back as a sort of 'credibility' adjustment. My total value of the business was no more than £20-25m.

Wayne thought I was being pessimistic in the extreme.

'Nonsense, you are assuming that you'd land six with every throw of the dice,' I replied.

Wayne conceded that perhaps he'd gone over the top but believed that the business was worth at least £100m. I disagreed.

That was the end of the matter, for the moment, that is. The following day I had a call from Tim's secretary asking me to be available for a meeting later that day. When I arrived for the meeting I found Sir Alfred, the Chairman, Archie, Jeff and Wayne also present.

'I hear that you're taking pessimism to the extreme in valuing Merlin?' asked Tim.

'I did what I thought a rational investor would do.'

'A rational investor wouldn't assume the worst in every case,' said Tim.

'But they won't assume that good days will last for ever.'

Archie stood up, picked up his file and pipe as if preparing to leave and said to Tim:

'What do you expect? He's been trying to undermine you ever since *Yes, Yes, Yes, the Answer's Yes, What's the Question?* strategy was revealed.'

'Why would putting a sensible value on Merlin undermine Tim?' I asked.

Archie looked at Sir Alfred as if to say, 'Do I have to deal with this idiot?' and said 'Tim has publicly put his weight behind Merlin Life and you know he'd look silly if it generated the sort of puny values you suggest.'

'That's too Machiavellian for me. Anyway, wouldn't he look sillier if he paid you a fancy price and then found that the reality was much lower?'

'I don't have to waste my time listening to a kid, who thinks he knows it all.'

'What does it matter what I say? When you float next year the market will decide. Don't take my word for it just wait and see.'

Archie ignored me and walked out, followed by Jeff and Wayne. However, Tim asked me to stay behind.

'You're not covering yourself with glory. You seem out of step with not just Archie but also Clem. We'll take your advice and not consult you next year but wait for the market's verdict.'

***

I heard no more for a year and I was beginning to wonder what Archie Balaskas was up to. They'd had an exceptional 1988, and 1989, so far, had been better. They had said they'd float in 1989 and it seemed the right time to do so. Yet I'd not heard anything. Then towards the end of 1989 I, as head of marketing, was asked to issue a press release:

Tim Fredricks is pleased to announce that Camelot Life has bought out the share options owned by the sales management and salesmen of Merlin Life. Together they own 25% of Merlin Life's equity capital and Camelot paid £37.5m for it, valuing Merlin Life at £150m. This is a tremendous achievement over a period of five years. The value of £150m was arrived at by the Directors after receiving independent actuarial advice. On some assumptions the value could be thrice that amount.

I was gobsmacked. They'd clearly extrapolated the exceptional sales growth of 1988/89 well into the future and disregarded my note of caution. I did a quick calculation. Archie would make £7.5m by selling his shares, Jeff half-that sum whilst the salesmen collectively will make nearly £19m.

Believe me these were substantial sums in those days. It was a daylight heist. I sensed that Archie must have played 'Tim's idea was a success' card, but why did the independent actuary fall for it? I found out who he was and challenged him.

'Don't you start,' he replied angrily. 'I nearly issued a public statement dissociating myself from the press release's contents.'

'You mean you didn't support the value?'

'Don't be daft. They wanted to float but needed some guidance as to where to pitch the share price. I gather you were unhelpful last year. So they consulted me, but my valuation, though higher than yours, was in the same ball park.'

'Well you should have complained against using your name in vain.'

'I did but your lawyer, Kate Spencer, said that their statement was chronologically correct. They arrived at a value *after* I'd given them independent advice. They didn't say that their value bore any resemblance to mine.'

'What sort of charlatans am I working for?'

'Pass.'

'I suppose that's why they didn't float. The market might have more sense than Tim.'

'Yes, but overpaying Archie and his team is tantamount to defrauding the shareholders of Camelot.'

'Why don't you publicise it?' I asked.

'I've got to earn a living.'

'You know it's the inertia of decent people such as you that lets crooks get away with murder.'

'I wouldn't call Tim a crook.'

'If he cuts corners to make Camelot look good for personal gain then he's a crook.'

'Why don't you tell him?' he asked.

'I've got to earn a living too.'

'I think we'd better stop this conversation.'

Herding Cats

Managing Camelot Estates, a large and disparate organisation, was a challenge. I decided that my focus should be on rationalising and managing the firms we had already acquired. I gave Nick total control of signing new ones. Bruce was looking at harmonising working practices and reporting systems. I reckon that Nick had the easiest job of us three given that money was no object under the *Yes, Yes, Yes, the Answer's Yes, What's the Question?* strategy.

I divided the UK into four regions London and South East, South West, Midlands and North West. Each Region had a Managing Director respectively, Ruaridh Royston, Helena Peel, Paul Postlethwaite and Magnus Droitwich. These Regional Managing Directors were appointed to the Board of Camelot Estates:

The first Board meeting of Camelot Estates after the Board membership was expanded didn't last long. Tim's first question was 'Are housing sales up?'

Ruaridh said that the 3R's sales last month were 15% up on the previous year. Helena Peel said that Peel & Co.'s sales last month were 7% up on the previous month but she did not have a ready comparison with last year's performance.'

'Can you produce that for next month's Board?'

'No I can't. We shred each year's statistics as soon as we enter a new year.'

'That's insane. We can learn a lot from history,' I said.

'Not as much as we can learn from instinct, intuition and studying future trends.'

'I'm not going to argue with you Helena, we rely heavily on them. We'll have to have a common approach.'

'And what's that approach?' asked Ruaridh.

'I'll come to that in a minute, let's move on,' I said. 'How do you measure sales? When do you regard a house as being sold so that we may take credit for estate agent's fees?'

'As soon as the contracts are exchanged,' said Ruaridh

'We do it when the offer is accepted,' said Helena.

'What happens if the sale falls through?'

'Then we reverse the transaction.'

'But someone may make an offer on three houses but exchange only on one'

'Yes, it'll all come out in the wash.'

'If everyone did that then we'd be seriously overstating the market.'

'Maybe.'

'OK' I said, trying my best to hide a sense of panic, 'when you report sales for say the month of January, what is the cut off point?'

'Why, the 31st January of course,' said Ruaridh.

'We compile our stats on a weekly basis so we report sales to the end of the last Saturday of January, said Helena.

'So some months you get four weeks sales and other months five.'

'Yes.'

'There's no point in combining statistics,' I said, 'it's like adding apples and pears.'

'What are you going to do about it?' asked Tim.

'I'll ask Bruce to take a lead and identify what statistics should be reported to the Board and the computer system to be used.'

This alarmed Helena, who said, 'Estate agency is a very uncertain business and it would be unwise to saddle it with high fixed costs.'

'That may be so but when you're part of a big company there is the need to have reliable and relevant information. Otherwise we will mislead our shareholders; that is a serious offence.'

Ruaridh said:

'All I would ask Bruce is to look at the system we use. No point re-inventing the wheel.'

Before we finished I asked the two other regional MDs why they'd kept quiet. It turned out that they used an ad hoc approach.

***

Leaving Nick to get on with buying agencies worked a treat. The next twelve months saw a spate of estate agencies selling out to Camelot. By the end of 1989 we had signed up one hundred agencies and had a total of four hundred branches. In the process we'd spent close to £200m in buying them. I had a persistent nightmare that success was not due to Nick's powers of persuasion but because he'd pitched our offer too high. There was no way of finding out.

Dealing with estate agents had exposed me to a completely different lifestyle. Monthly management meetings were held, on a rotational basis, in each of the four regional head offices, Bristol, Chelmsford, Birmingham and Leeds. The Royston brothers travelled in their own plane ('We're not extravagant, we've one plane between the three of us') and would often give me a lift back even though Bristol was not in the flightpath and the nearest airport was a long way away. Magnus Droitwich and Paul Postlethwaite came in their own Rolls Royces although Paul was thrifty and did not employ a chauffeur. Only Helena was frugal and drove a Sierra.

***

Bruce reported that the 3R's management information system, whilst not perfect, met practically all our requirements. He recommended that we implement it across the whole of Camelot Estates. An in-house system would require very little additional cost. I was supportive in principle as were Tim, Nick and the Royston brothers. Helena, Magnus and Paul appeared not to know how to react but it didn't matter as the vote was carried.

Helena then asked, 'Just how much is the little added cost and will someone train us in how to use it?'

Roland Royston, the techie amongst the Royston brothers said, 'The software is proprietary and is owned by us three brothers. We didn't sell it to Camelot.'

'So how come 3R's is using it?' I asked.

'It is leased out to them under a three year renewable agreement.'

'You learn something every day. How much does the lease cost?'

'£1000 per month.'

'We can afford that can't we?' I asked Bruce.

'£1,000 per month per branch, I should explain,' said Roland.

'What? We pay you £100,000 per month? Is that right, Bruce?'

'I knew there was a charge because it's in the budgets shown in the Operational Plan. But I thought it came back to us as I thought we now owned the software.'

'I can't recall signing an agreement?'

'It was done shortly before you bought us.'

'Why didn't you tell us that the software was not a part of the deal?' I asked.

'You didn't ask,' said Ruaridh trying to take the heat off the nerdish Roland.

'You must have hidden it. We'll sue you for non-disclosure.'

'You didn't object when Tracy waived due diligence.'

I went white, or as white as someone with brown skin can. Bruce then said, 'I don't want to comment on whether we've been misled or not but looking forward, it might still be cheaper to use the Royston software.'

'I'm not so sure,' said Helena. 'I'm not going to authorise the payment of £1,000 per branch in my region every month.'

'Nor me neither,' said both Magnus and Peter.

'Guys,' said Ruaridh, 'it won't be £1,000 per month. We had to recover our development costs, which we've now done and you guys are family anyway. For you all, we'll reduce it to £500/month.'

'Even that's too much,' said Helena, Magnus and Paul almost in unison.

'Please stop bickering. Let's just sleep on it.' It was a piece of advice I could preach but not practise. I tossed and turned all night. I kept thinking of a Shakespearean play at school when I had to wear an ass's head. What else had I missed by not carrying out due diligence? I'd passed the responsibility to Nick and that rogue Tracy. Is Camelot paying inflated prices for a bag of skeletons? The rate at which they were going they'd have a thousand branches by the end of 1990 and will have shelled out perhaps £300m. I remembered something Dad often said:

'Man is remembered by the last thing he's done.'

How I missed the dose of common sense Ellen provided. MI5 was a hard taskmaster. She had no spare time and when she did manage to snatch a spare moment to talk to me, she had little to say about her own life and concerns. The Civil Service code of confidentiality was all consuming. It's not as if she was involved in another relationship but the old spark had dulled. Perhaps career was taking precedence over companionship. They say that a near brush with death often causes you to re-evaluate your priorities. Perhaps I'd dropped down her pecking order.

***

A couple of months later, we were no nearer implementing 3R's management information system.

Indeed Ruaridh was having difficulty in his own South East region. Board meetings had become farcical. I would set out what I thought should be done and Tim would usually support it. There wasn't much debate although Ruaridh was never short of an opinion. A vote would be taken and usually the motion would be carried. Then, nothing. 'It is a bit like the French and the Common Market', I thought.

Then in the summer of 1990 there was a bust up. Roland complained that licences had been given to every subsidiary of Camelot Estates but no one had as yet paid anything.

'That's because it's worth nothing,' said Helena starting off a civil war. I called the meeting to order and asked why it was worth nothing.

'It's compiling information that's not needed,' said Helena.

'How can you say that?' I asked. 'Camelot is the owner and it needs it to monitor the progress on its investment.'

'But we managed without it and we must have managed successfully. Just look at the fancy prices you paid to buy our businesses.'

'That might be our foolishness.'

'Don't pile on more costs and paperwork,' said Helena.

'You just don't get it, do you?' said Magnus. 'Estate agents are entrepreneurs; they live by their wits. You Camelot people thrive on bureaucracy. We're not like that.'

'OK. We'll pick up the development cost and exclude the annual licence fee when computing the profit for the year.'

'That's eminently fair,' said Ruaridh.

'The profit target we set would be correspondingly higher of course.'

'So what you give with one hand you take away with the other.'

The following month Tim said that the next phase of development was to re-brand all the estate agencies as Camelot Estates. This was condemned by the Roystons, Helena, Magnus and Paul. 'These names have local identity; they're not faceless monoliths.'

Tim would not give in. He had invested too much of his personal prestige to back off. Sensing an impasse Ruaridh suggested a compromise retaining the local brand under the umbrella of a national brand. He gave the following example

Royston, Royston & Royston
Estate Agents
A Camelot Estates Company

Tim would have none of it. The motion was carried. Once again, nothing happened afterwards. No steps were taken to re-brand; the old signage remained everywhere.

I was in charge but not in control.

We carried on like this for another year. How do you control and motivate a bunch of street-smart and independent-minded rogues whom we had made rich beyond their dreams?

I was in charge but not in control.

***

Tim summoned me, early in March 1991 to discuss Camelot Estates. I took Nick and Bruce with me and resolved to go on the offensive if Tim tried to pin all the blame on me. It's ridiculous what they've asked me to do.

The three of us travelled on the same train to London. We were taken aback by a lengthy interview of Ruaridh Royston in the Daily Mail. Some choice phrases were attributed to Ruaridh. 'Tim's a buffoon and Majid's incredibly naïve. Selling out to them for over £50m was like stealing from an unguarded open safe', 'Majid operates from a run-down Edwardian house on one of the steepest roads in Bristol whilst we operate from plush state-of-the-art offices in leafy Essex.'

When we met him, Tim looked like a bundle of bones held together in saggy skin. Practically the only parts of his body unchanged were his lungs. His voice was as lusty as ever but he was slurring his words. A whisky decanter was on his desk and a glass of whisky in his hand.

'Why did you offer sky-high prices?' asked Tim.

Steeling myself against being influenced by Tim's pathetic condition, I replied:

'You know perfectly well that I expressed reservations about the unrealistic prices at which firms were being bought. You accused me of reverting to type.'

'That was a general comment not to take caution to extremes. I would have expected you and Bruce to be alert to the falsification of numbers. Call yourself an actuary? My mum would have smelt a rat.'

'Only one rat? I smelt a whole colony of them, but you didn't want to know; nor did Tracy Pitt, the guy you asked me to rely on.'

'Even if I did, which I didn't, you don't do things blindly. If the figures look suspect you should challenge them.'

'We did challenge their figures all the way. The problem was how we used it to value the business.'

'What did you do?'

'I was doing what you wanted. These guys will tell you how much I agonised over the folly of it all.'

Neither Nick nor Bruce responded.

'I never gave you any steer,' said Tim.

'You asked us to rely on Tracy and his stuff was straight out of Alice in Wonderland.'

'Don't pass the buck. Show me one piece of written evidence that I asked you to offer silly prices.'

I didn't respond so Tim carried on, 'This is not the first time you've tried to pass the blame on to me without being able to prove it. Remember the crooks who stole our monies in Australia?'

My self-control snapped:

'How can anyone trust you?'

The meeting ended there. On the way back to Bristol, I said to Nick and Bruce, 'I thought I could count on your support.'

'You can, you can. But he was so aggressive that I didn't have the guts to intervene. But I promise you, if he'd only asked me I'd have confirmed everything that you said,' said Bruce.

'Me too,' said Nick.

'You especially, Nick. You're the one who pressurised me to raise the offer.'

Who Runs Camelot Life?

The regulators issued a damning press release, after an audit of Monarch Life. 'Management seemed to be unaware of the principles underlying the new legislation, let alone its details.'

Tim and his management colleagues must have chuckled when they read it for they drew attention to it in internal mail. Not having been included in the initial rounds of audit, they had become a touch complacent.

Not for long, as the regulators told Tim of the imminence of their first audit of Camelot Life. The focus would be on selling practices and complaints handling.Tim asked Kate and I to organise a teach-in to avoid suffering the same fate as Monarch Life.

With the entire Board assembled as well as Nick, Bruce and Archie, Kate began with Rule 1 which she wrote out on a flip chart:

Rule No. 1: If the same product is available at more than one price, your own salesmen must offer the cheapest price to its customers.

'That means that the practice of selling more expensive, more profitable products through our own sales-force, must cease.'

I felt it necessary to stress the obvious.

'What are you trying to do? Destroy Merlin Life?' asked Tim

Archie looked at Tim through the gap above his glasses which had slipped to the tip of his nose, and shrugged his shoulders.

'Don't try to be tougher than the regulators, Majid. They err on the side of caution. They don't have a business to run,' said Sir Alfred.

'All I'm doing is interpreting their statements, not trying to outdo them,' I replied.

'Rule 1 is ridiculous,' said Tim.

'It may be but it's been around since April 1988.'

'Are you saying that Littlewoods and Marks and Spencer cannot co-exist?' said Nick.

'No they can, so long as they only sell their own products. If they sell own brand fish-fingers they can't sell Birds Eye fish fingers at a dearer price.'

'But they do and it's the customer's choice, there's no pressure,' said Tim.

'Yes, that's clearly the case for fish fingers but financial products are different.'

'But the whole point of setting up our own sales-force is so that we can charge the customers more,' said Tim.

'The regulators would say, "I rest my case",' I said.

'I'm not having it.'

'You'd better persuade them to reconsider 'best advice.''

'I'll do just that,' said Tim.

'What's your view, Sir Alfred?' I asked.

'I'm with Tim and Nick on this one. Common sense is bound to prevail, surely?'

'Where's the common sense in paying a higher price when you cut out the middle man? How can you win that argument in the Courts?'

'Well, let Tim slug it out with the regulators.'

'He'll have to demonstrate that it is against the customers' interests to have this rule. Simply saying, "I'm not having it" will not work,' I said.

'I'll be the judge of that,' said Tim.

'It's futile bringing this up now. You should have raised it three years ago, when the rules had not yet been set in stone.'

'I said I'll be the judge of that. What's the second rule?' asked Tim.

At this point Sir Alfred intervened and said to me:

'If you're right then we've overpaid when buying out Archie and his men.'

'Yes.'

'Why didn't you alert us before the transaction?'

'When I was asked last year to review the valuation, I came up with a figure of £15-20m as the value of Merlin Life. I wasn't involved in this year's process which valued Merlin Life at £150m.'

'There's a yawning gap between the two figures. Tim we rely on your being able to persuade the regulators that our approach is right. Otherwise someone will have to pay for overpaying Archie and his cronies.'

'I will.'

'You'll pay or you'll take it up with the regulators?'

'The latter. Let's get on to Rule 2.'

Kate put Rule 2 on the flipchart:

Rule No. 2: When selling to a customer, the product must be suitable to his requirements and affordable by him. A rule of thumb for affordability is that, in the case of a mortgage the total monthly cost outlay must not exceed 25% of take home pay.

I pointed out that the only part of Rule 2 that was mine was the limit of 25% of take home pay. That was my interpretation of affordability.

'I'd rather carry on as before and let the regulators set the limits,' said Nick.

'I agree,' said Tim.

The session came to a close as the allotted time had been used up. Afterwards Kate and I had a brief discussion. The conclusion was that we had a job on our hands keeping the company on the right side of the law.

***

We were in for a surprise. The regulators, possibly prodded by the trustees of the Black Gold Pension Scheme gave two weeks notice of change in the purpose of their visit. Instead of what they originally proposed, the audit would be of Camelot's personal pensions business.

Ingrid Stokes led the audit and she talked to Nick Knight about the sales process, Bruce Herrington about new business processing and complaints handling and me about the product development and training processes. They also talked to line managers. Kate attended all the interviews.

Three months later they presented a report. The lengthy delay for what was a relatively short and pithy report suggests that there were high level discussions within the regulator regarding the tone of the report and the severity of sanctions.

The findings were discussed with Tim, Nick, Bruce, Kate and me. Ingrid started by thanking the management team for the cooperative approach they took to the audit. There was no concealment or obfuscation.

'I wish our findings were as positive. Here is what we found:

'*Poor management:* The product was launched to an unrealistic timetable.

'*Poor controls:* Power to the People meant abdication of managerial responsibility. There were no procedures in place to ensure that the sale complied with such rules as there were. Staff in customer services were inadequately trained.

'*Poor training:* Superficial training given to salesmen with inadequate testing. Training given to Merlin Life sales-force was practically non-existent.

'*Poor selling practices:* Pretty widespread arising from poor training and controls.

'*Poor complaint handling:* Under resourced and there were some ad hoc practices.'

'This is a pretty bleak picture of incompetent management,' said Ingrid.

'You're talking of one aspect of our business out of context,' protested Tim. 'All you have to do is to look at it and criticise. We've been very busy the past three years. I have to constantly review priorities to see what is best for our shareholders. In an ideal world we'll do everything to perfection. Life is not like that.'

'I'm not interested in shareholders. You are soliciting business from uninformed customers and there are certain minimum standards you have to meet. That is not negotiable.'

'You've never done a real job have you?'

'I'll ignore that remark. I give you three months to bring your sales process under control. I expect you to halve the complaints backlog within three months and by a further half in another three months.'

'Are you asking us to eliminate the backlog entirely within six months? Which world are you living in? There'll always be a hard core of cases which will remain unresolved.'

'Tim they're not asking you to eliminate the backlog, only to reduce it to a quarter of the current level,' I said.

'How do you work that one out?'

'Halve it in three months; then halve it again in the next three months. So you're halving what is already half the original. So you're left with a quarter of the original.'

After the meeting ended Sir Alfred made it clear that the responsibility for delivery ultimately rested with Tim.

The Fall of Tim

'Hello, it's me, Ruaridh. Me and my brothers are resigning.'

I stopped what I was doing and asked, 'What? You're not? Why?'

'We've had enough. We'll support the software licences but they won't be renewed once the three years are up; in the case of the 3R's that'll be later this year.'

'What will you do?'

'You've been so generous to us that we'll never have to work again but we'll do something; something that we'll enjoy.'

'What do you mean, generous? Did we overpay?'

'Damn right, you did, £20m more than Holborn Bars offered.'

'Hang on; you said I had to double my offer to compete?'

'I did, and you fell for it; and you waived due diligence. How stupid can you get?'

'Don't rub it in.'

'We're going to set up a rival agency.'

'You can't do that. There's a non-compete clause in the agreement we signed.'

'Show me. I couldn't find any.'

I had no riposte for that. I rang off and got the sale and purchase agreement out of the filing cabinet and studied it. I felt very foolish. How could I miss the absence of such a vital clause? I had read the document carefully and picked up quite a few errors but not this one. Hang on, I'm not a lawyer. I can't be expected to spot what's not there. It's Kate's fault. She ought to have picked it up. I'll mention it to Tim but should he ask Kate first? That would be the decent thing to do. It must have been an oversight on her part. We can all make a mistake. But no, I'd better go straight to the top. This is a gross error.

Rather than telephone Tim I decided to see him. I phoned his secretary and fixed up an appointment straight after lunch. I only just caught the next train to Paddington.

Tim looked preoccupied when I entered his room.

'What can I do for you?' he asked.

'We've got a problem. The Royston brothers have resigned and set up a rival business. Apparently there was no non-compete clause in the sale and purchase agreement that we signed. This is a pretty fundamental omission. I thought I'd better bring it to your attention before speaking to Kate.'

'How can she not have such a clause?'

'I'll ask her next.'

'You signed the agreement didn't you?'

I nodded.

'How come you didn't spot it?'

'It's not easy to spot what's not there.'

Tim phoned Kate and asked her to come over.

'Sit down, Kate.'

She did.

'The Royston brothers have just resigned and set up a rival firm. Did the legal agreement we signed with them not have a non-compete clause?'

Kate looked at Tim and then looked at me but said nothing.

'You'd better give a straight answer. It is a sackable offence for a lawyer to miss that clause.'

'No, it didn't.'

'It didn't? OK, let me ask you another question. All the other estate agencies we've bought, did none of them have the clause either?'

'No, all the others did.'

'So what happened with the Royston's contract was not an omission but a deliberate act.'

'Yes.'

Kate avoided eye contact and said nothing.

'Speak up. Somebody's career's on the line. It might be yours.'

'I deleted it because I was asked to.'

'It had to be someone important for you to delete a fundamental clause like that. It wasn't me. Who was it?'

Again avoiding eye contact, Kate said nothing.

'Speak up. Was it Tim?'

'It was Majid.'

'What? Me?'

'The first draft contract was supplied by Ruaridh and did not contain a non-compete clause. I inserted it and sent it back to him.'

'Go on.'

'Ruaridh must have spoken to Majid because Nick came to me saying that he'd asked me to delete it. He said that, according to Majid, it amounted to entering into a transaction in bad faith, like having a pre-nuptial agreement.'

'But the other party might be doing just that, acting in bad faith. That's why we have these agreements. Did you ask Nick to put it in writing, or at least check with Majid yourself?'

'No, because Nick phoned him from my office to say that he'd asked me to make the deletion.'

Then, seeing the expression on my face, she added:

'But I did make a file note.'

'This is a libellous lie. Why would I do it?'

'Nick said that you were under pressure from Tim and badly wanted the deal.'

'But couldn't you at least have phoned me and checked the facts out. Anyway, its two years since the deal was signed, we've met hundreds of times since then, why didn't you ever ....?'

I struggled for words not knowing how to react and then said:

'Honestly, she's fabricating all this. She must be protecting her own backside. I can't see any other reason.'

'We need to get to the bottom of all this.'

He phoned Nick Knights on the conference call and said, 'Hello Nick, do you know that the Royston brothers have resigned and set up a rival firm?'

'No.'

'They have. Do you know why we didn't have a non-compete clause in the agreement we signed with them?'

'No. Oh, yes I do. Majid asked us to take it out as it was a stumbling block.'

I opened my mouth but shut it again as I thought the better of it.

Tim thanked Nick and Kate. Left alone with him, I said:

'Is this the end of the line for me?'

'Your career has peaked. But I'd like you to stay on at least until the next regulatory audit is over.'

***

I was in for a surprise. One day, the following month, March 1991, waiting in my in-box, was an urgent e-mail from Sir Alfred Lyttleton, the Chairman;

Dear colleague

With immediate effect Tim Fredricks has resigned as Chief Executive of Camelot Group and Chairman of Camelot Estates. I am taking over both roles on a temporary basis. I have instructed a firm of head-hunters to find a suitable replacement.

Tim has had a distinguished career but latterly we have faced a number of problems and attempts to overcome them have made matters worse. So we decided mutually that it was best for him to stop digging.

Sir Alfred called me over for a one-to-one chat, my first with him. The topic was the poor performance of Camelot Estates.

'I told Tim that competitors were pushing prices to hysterical levels. Nick and Bruce will confirm that. But Tim was determined to achieve his goal of a thousand branches whatever the cost.'

'OK you did as you were told but what would you rather have done?'

'Cut our losses and sell?'

'With the housing market in the state it is in now? Come on, we won't get anything for them.'

'You might even have to pay someone to take it off our hands; or you may have to sell the businesses without debt, keeping the debt ourselves.'

'Be sensible Majid, what would we get for them?'

'Nothing. Actually my girlfriend, who's a lawyer, says that you can't have a contract without consideration. So you may be able to get a token pound for Camelot Estates.'

'You're being funny.'

'No, I'm not. In fact you may have to fight really hard to get it up to a pound; they might only offer 50p.' Seeing the incredulous look on Sir Alfred's face, I quickly added, 'That *was* a joke.

'So your grand idea is to sell for a pound the businesses we paid £300 million for. You expect me to sell that to the stock-market and keep my job?'

'Management are taking decisions all the time. They can't expect them to get all of them right. What good management does is identify early which ones it's got wrong and get out of them as best as it can.'

'Cut out the Business School patter. This is the real world and you've not coped with it well. You put the blame on Tim but are you sure that's fair?'

'Nick will bear me out.'

'That's just it. Nick doesn't back your version of events.'

'You've asked him already?'

'Yes.'

'Which particular version of events?'

'About what made you pay silly prices.'

'How can he do that when he hasn't heard my version of events?'

'He didn't refute you but the version he gave contradicts what you said.'

I was stunned into speechlessness. After a while Sir Alfred asked:

'You didn't expect that did you?'

I didn't reply.

'He also said that he could turn the company round in two years.'

'Did he now? I doubt if anyone can do that without doing more dodgy things.'

'Sounds like sour grapes.'

'Not at all. If you want to test it out, by all means let him have a go. I'll step down.'

'What will you do instead?'

'Devote more time to my day-job, as Camelot Life's head of marketing.'

'I'm glad to hear that. That's exactly what I had in mind. I would promote you to director level and put you in charge of marketing. You'll be the Marketing Director of Camelot Life. Nick, in addition to being the Chief Executive of Camelot Estates would be the Sales Director of Camelot Life and Bruce Herrington its Operations Director. That's the plan but I won't do it until later this year, by which time I hope to have found Tim's long-term successor. Keep it to yourself until then.'

'I presume you've said the same to Nick and Bruce?'

'Yes.'

Taking Stock

So Tim has had his comeuppance but the rewards have gone to Nick. I couldn't complain. I was warned when offered the Camelot Estates job that if I couldn't make it work then I'd be out of the job. Let's see Nick make a success of it.

Interesting times lie ahead for him. I don't think he realises just how limited his powers are. Six months ago the regulators had given notice of another visit to audit Camelot's personal pensions business but had yet to give a date. Either they've been extremely busy or they were trying to lull Camelot into a false sense of comfort.

No point moping about, I looked at the positive side of things. My career might just possibly have been derailed but at least I now had the time and space to rebuild my relationship with Ellen. I had last seen her Christmas before last. I'd not even spoken to her for over a month. It irritated me that MI5 was coming between us although my commitment to Camelot was equally to blame. I phoned her to re-establish contact but again she was not in. I went back to my flat and for the first time slept in the sin bin, muttering to myself, 'It is as much my fault.'

That weekend I got up very early to beat the traffic and travelled up to London and went to her Knightsbridge flat unannounced. I let myself in using the spare key I held. As I entered I shouted, 'Are you there luv?'

A startled voice answered, 'Who's that?'

'Am I that forgettable?'

'Oh you, you startled me. Why didn't you phone first? How did you get in?'

'I let myself in. I've got the spare key remember?'

A bleary eyed Ellen walked through into the lounge. 'For a moment I thought you were a burglar.'

'The only thing worth stealing in this apartment is your heart but I hope that's mine already. Isn't it?'

'Don't talk nonsense.'

'Is it nonsense?'

'It's nonsense to ask that question,' replied Ellen, by now fully awake.

I've always thought that she looked better without make up. I recognised the night dress she was wearing. I was with her when she bought it. We used to be inseparable, even finishing each other's sentences. Why is there a chasm? Or is there a chasm? Is it just me?

'What are you thinking?' asked Ellen. 'You haven't come all this way to say nothing, have you?'

'I used to get an ache in the pit of my stomach if I hadn't seen you for a week.'

Ellen listened but did not respond so I continued:

'Last night, by way of penance for being pre-occupied with my job and ignoring you, I slept in the sin bin in my flat; for the first time.'

Again I paused for response but again I didn't get any so I continued:

'You too have been pre-occupied with your job. Do you have a sin bin in your flat by the way?'

'No, I don't actually. That was last year's idea, not even last year's, actually. I'd forgotten about it completely.'

We spent the entire weekend together, visited the Natural History Museum, saw Carmen at the Royal Opera House, strolled through Soho and Chinatown, made love a few times and generally caught up; she caught up on my life that is; she was as reticent as ever to talk about her work for MI5.

'I have to be frank. If you can trust me why can't MI5?'

'I don't make the rules. That reminds me, you'd better give me back the spare key. I'm not allowed to give it out to someone not living in the same abode.'

I handed it over.

The weekend was nearly over and I had to depart. Both of us said we'd communicate and meet more often. As I drove back, I reflected that whilst we'd re-established rapport, the old spark was missing. I'd have to work hard to retain the relationship. Perhaps I should visit Mold more often.

***

Six months after Tim's departure the regulators made a snap announcement of coming within a week to audit the administration of personal pensions business.

With so much at stake and time short, I suggested to Sir Alfred that it might be a good idea if a pre-audit audit was carried out to get advance warning of what might be levelled against them. He thought it was a splendid idea and Kate and I were delegated to carry it out. As time was short it was going to be a 'quick and dirty' review.

We concluded from it that a regulatory audit might find the following faults:

Poor controls: There were procedures in place to ensure that the sale complied with rules but these rules had not been updated since 1989.

Poor training: Only a superficial training was given to salesmen and there was no subsequent testing.

Poor complaint handling: This area was under resourced for the current level of complaints. If levels were to rise then backlogs will mount. The process was not streamlined. Training of customer services staff was inadequate.

These findings were discussed with Sir Alfred and Nick.

'You're simply regurgitating what they said at their first audit.'

'It seems that way but that's because nothing has changed,' I said.

'What can we do?' asked Sir Alfred. 'Are we on course for a severe fine?'

'Or even a ban. Tim's militant approach to the regulators did us no favours,' I said.

'OK, we've got to sort this out but in the short term, is there anything we can do about it?' asked Sir Alfred.

'The worst aspect from a regulator's point of view is that things have not got any better since Tim left. They may cite the lack of a full time replacement of Tim as a problem. I'm sorry, I'm not having a go at you, Sir Alfred.'

'Ah, that's where we can spring a rabbit out of the hat. Keep it to yourself, you Majid, Kate as Company Secretary already knows, the Board is about to appoint Nick as Tim's full time successor.'

'Most of our problems arise from the sales-force Archie Balaskas set up in Merlin Life. Closing it down is commercially justifiable and would go a long way to appease the regulators. Most of the pension misselling cases are theirs too.'

'Sir Alfred looked at me and then at Nick and said:

'But we've valued it at £150m less than two years ago and paid out nearly £40m to Archie and his cronies. We've got to recover some of it.'

'What's done is done Sir Alfred. The question is which is the best course of action looking to the future? Cutting your losses or throwing good money after bad?'

'That sounds like a biased set of alternatives.'

'No, that's the choice. We were taken for a ride.'

'So what do you suggest?'

'Use Tim as the lightning rod. Blame it all on him and paint Nick as the good guy that the Board has brought in to clean up the act.'

'Sounds a good approach,' said Sir Alfred.

'But Tim was right in one respect,' said Nick. 'The regulators shouldn't run a company. That is the job of its Board.'

'Of course it is, the regulators are the policemen. But, when law and order breaks down the police have to step in,' I said.

'Let's not debate semantics, we need to sort this out,' said Sir Alfred.

'Hang on. If Nick were to take the same militant attitude as Tim then you might as well forget it. I can't begin to think what punitive sanctions they would impose,' I said.

'What do you suggest we do?' asked Sir Alfred.

'Nick would need to be attentive and servile in front of the regulators, treat every pronouncement of theirs as an edict to be immediately complied with. I can go on but I need to know whether Nick is comfortable with that.'

Nick shuffled in his chair grimaced paused and eventually said, 'If that's what it takes to get them off our backs, then I will dissemble like that.'

'No, no, that's not good enough and could be counterproductive. For a start Kate has heard you say that and, as Compliance Officer, she cannot ignore that. You can't fake sincerity. Sir Alfred, it's down to you. Is it worth taking the risk? If not the regulators will either go for you or for Nick; quite possibly you as you were around when Tim was here.'

'You'd still have to explain why things haven't got any better since Tim left,' said Kate.

'All you can say is that the problems were deep rooted and a few people had to be got rid of,' I said.

'Have you?' Sir Alfred asked Nick.

'I don't think so, not for this reason.'

'Then you'd have to sack someone, anyone, or it's your job on the line,' said Sir Alfred.

'OK, I'll find a goat,' said Nick.

'Right,' said Majid. In that case we'll write up these findings in the form of a report and you should respond immediately saying that you accept the recommendations.'

'Is that all?'

'That's a start. The challenge is to progress it in a timely and efficient manner. You'll have to appoint someone with clout as a Project Manager.'

'That could be tricky, we've trimmed back resources.'

'That is not an acceptable excuse. You need to show commitment to meet the deadlines set by the regulators.'

'Management have to juggle priorities all the time. This is important but sometimes something else comes along that may be more urgent.'

'To a regulator, that's not an acceptable excuse.'

'But that's a fact in the real world.'

'OK, you've heard everything I've said. Ignore it and do it your way when the regulators come to visit you. See what happens.'

'No, he won't do that. Will you?' Sir Alfred said looking at Nick.

'I have half a mind to, bloody unelected boffins, trying to run my company. Hmmmm. Tell you what. I'll send Majid a letter accepting all recommendations, set up an implementation plan with budgets and timescale. I'll keep it in my drawer when the regulators come in but make no mention of it to them. Let's see what happens.'

'You should also have a credible resource plan. The volume of cases could double.'

'We'll have to recruit. I'll ask HR to get on with it.'

***

Sir Alfred was clearly stung by my comments regarding the inflated value placed upon Merlin Life. A quietly worded e-mail announced that Archie Balaskas and his management team had left by 'mutual consent'.

***

I no longer had any access to what was going on in Camelot Estates. I had no spies or moles within that organisation. I had to piece together a picture from snippets of information in the internal circulars and press releases issued by them.

The press release on the half yearly trading results compared three months under me with three months under Nick—-- that wasn't what the press release said but the sub-text was clear to all.

Camelot Estates had its best quarter to date, all performance indicators showing a marked improvement:
Number of estate agency branches; up from 1021 to 1100
Housing sales: up 20%
Endowment mortgages: up from 30% of mortgages to 56% (target 88%)
Accident, sickness and unemployment insurance: up from 0 to 25%
Building insurance: up from 25% to 50%
Expenses: down 25%
Loss before debt interest: down from £15m to £3m (forecast to break into profit in the next quarter).
Commenting on the result, Nick Knights the new Chief Executive, said, 'These are an exceptional set of results in a difficult market. Whilst it is difficult to forecast the recovery of the housing market, I am confident that we'll maintain our improvement in future quarters.'

The year-end results of Camelot Estates were even better than the third quarter's. The profit before debt interest was a profit not a loss, for the first time in Camelot Estate's history. In anticipation of this outcome it was announced, just before Christmas, that the search for Tim Fredricks' successor was over. 'We've searched far and wide using head hunters to find a Chief Executive for the Camelot Group. When we eventually found him, he was on our own door-step. Nick Knights, who had successfully turned round Camelot Estates will endeavour to do the same with Camelot.'

The press release announcing the year-end results also indicated that Camelot Estates were in an advance stage of implementing an agreement to outsource its administration to India having already outsourced its accounting

***

I received a call from Nick asking me over for a chat. He had appointed Helena Peel as the Deputy Chief Executive of Camelot Estates and moved out of Bristol into Tim's old office in London. He had relinquished the title of Sales Director of Camelot

Life but had not filled that position. I went up to London expecting clarification of his own role. He was greeted with a smile.

'I bet the news about my promotion came as a surprise to you,' said Nick.

'Not really.'

'Oh come on, it surprised me.'

'I knew that I was out of the reckoning and guessed that you and Bruce would be in the frame with you as the favourite.'

'It is ten years since the three of us were put on the fast-track programme but you always were the front runner.'

'But sometimes the front runner runs out of puff.'

'I'm sorry for you but now that I've been given the opportunity, I'll run Camelot my way.'

'Of course and you can count on my support.'

'Good. I don't want to be hindered by an over-zealous application of rules.'

'I always do what's best for Camelot. There's no other motive.'

'Good.'

'There is one thing though. I've been made the fall guy for the lack of a non-compete clause in the agreement with the Roystons. I'm one of two people who know that I'm a victim of cold blooded calumny. The other person who knows is the guilty person.'

'Why are you telling me this?'

'I want you to know that when the time comes he'll pay the price.'

I left Nick's office.

Rock Bottom: Incomplete Again

Dear Majid,
'Camelot Life is grateful to you for years of diligent service. Unfortunately two blemishes in
your conduct led to the firm losing hundreds of millions of pounds. Your contract is termi-
nated with immediate effect. Ted Leary will write separately to you regarding the terms of
the dismissal.'

So ran a letter from Nick Knights dated 15th January 1992. Moments later Ted Leary
popped in.

'You've received Nick's letter have you?'

'Yes.'

'He said I'll let you know the details of your redundancy package. They are set out
in this letter. It also gives the name and address of an outplacement consultant. I would
urge you to meet them.'

I took it all in but didn't respond.

'Before you leave you must hand in the keys to your car. Perhaps you can post the
spare key, unless you prefer to drop it in.'

'Can I buy the car off the company?'

'I'm afraid that's not possible. It's a leased car and not ours to give.'

'Can I liaise with the car company?'

'I'm afraid that's not possible.'

'That's that then?'

'Yes. No need to rush; you have until lunchtime to vacate the premises.'

Although not entirely unexpected, the news left me in shock. I asked my secretary
Louise not to put any calls through. Mechanically I cleared my desk. I pulled myself
together after a while when I realised that I was collecting rubbish in my briefcase and
discarding valuable stuff in the waste bin.

I then called Louise in and told her that I'd been sacked and would be leaving
shortly. She was stunned. I tried to send a round-robin good-bye e-mail but found that
my access to the office network had been blocked.

I then called all my staff together and bid them good bye and left at lunch time.
As I made my way to the office car park I thought I'd dump my stuff in the flat and go
to London for an unannounced visit to Ellen. With my mind in turmoil I thought it
safer not to drive and to go by train instead.

It was only when I'd reached the Mercedes that reality hit me. I had no choice, I had to use the train. The car was no longer mine to drive. I had surrendered the keys. I was redundant and that personal humiliation had been given visibility by the loss of the car. Worse, I had to go back to Ted, collect the key and come back to the basement car park to take out everything in it that was mine. My collection of cassettes, the road atlases, the box of Kleenex tissues, the jar of boiled sweets, the foot pump. Was the car radio mine? It wasn't the standard specification but a superior model that I'd paid for. Did that make it mine? I didn't want to be accused of theft if it wasn't mine and yet if it was mine I was damned if I was going to leave it behind. But it seemed too petty to ask. In the end I left it and, when leaving the key with Ted's secretary, left a note to the effect that if the radio was mine, I'd donate it to my charity, Oxfam; could they please let me know one way or the other.

I got out of the car park and waived down a cab to take me to the railway station but going via my flat. There I dumped everything apart from my briefcase. On the way to the station I resolved to buy a car soon.

I rang the door bell to Ellen's flat but there was no response. I hung around in the foyer for the best part of an hour, waiting for her return. Then I heard the sound of her apartment door being opened from the inside. I saw the back of a man who was kissing her and gradually emerging backwards from the apartment. When he finished kissing and waving good-bye the man turned round to walk towards the lift. Our eyes met. It was hard to tell who was more startled, I or Ishtak Brownstein, unless it was Ellen.

'Hi Majid, you should have come a little earlier. Lots to talk about but I've got to go now. Ellen will fill you in.

'What were you doing in my girlfriend's flat? How long have you been with her?'

'We were reliving the debate you set up. It's come to haunt me as I try to enter Israeli politics.'

'You didn't answer the question.'

'I've got to go. Good bye.'

With that he was gone. I walked up to the front door of the flat. I looked into Ellen's eyes and thought that she was trying to avoid eye-contact. Neither of us said anything as we went back into her flat. She went into the kitchen and returned with cups of coffee and then, rather like a long-married couple, the two of us drank it in silence. She gave no explanation as to why Ishtak had been there. Perhaps it was an MI5 assignment; perhaps Ishtak had links with Mossad. But the kiss was more than a continental salutation, it seemed to have warmth and passion. I pulled myself from the brink of despair by selecting a safe subject for discussion: myself.

'I got the sack today.'

'Oh no. Did you fall out with Sir Alfred?'

I explained that I'd been fitted up by Nick.

'You're going to challenge this aren't you?'

'I'll make him pay but not yet; I'll have to bide my time.'

'Can't Kate give evidence?'

'She can't prove that Nick lied. No, this happened today and I need to get my thoughts together.'

'My poor thing.' She moved to sit next to me and gave me a hug.

We went over my redundancy package.

'Your pension won't start until you're sixty.'

'Sixty-five not sixty.'

'Oh yes, I forgot that you're not a civil servant. Let me see now. You've worked for fifteen years so you'll get a pension of fifteen-sixtieth of your salary. I make that a quarter. Am I right?'

'You are but it is a quarter of today's pay. Inflation will reduce its value, perhaps to a quarter, so the pension would really be one-sixteenth.'

'How do you work that out?'

'A quarter of a quarter is a sixteenth.'

'You did that in your head? Show off.'

I ignored that with a shrug. 'The redundancy payment might last two years so I need to find work.'

We discussed my job prospects. There was no denying that in difficult times marketing budgets are the first to be cut.

'Perhaps I'd better swallow my pride and see the outplacement consultant.'

We were discussing everything as if we were a couple and I drew immense comfort from it.

Ellen came up to me and gave me a reassuring hug, holding me for a long while. Still holding me she swung back from her hips to have a long look at me. I could see tenderness in her eyes. She then gave me a long kiss. It was intoxicating stuff, like water to a Bedouin.

'Darling,' said Ellen, 'You know there was no man before you in my life and I'm pretty sure there'll be no one after you.'

I extricated myself from her embrace and, walking away from her but looking intently at her, asked:

'Am I past tense? Am I history now?'

'Don't be like a wounded bear, hear me out,' said Ellen moving closer to me.

'Why should I?' I asked moving a step back.

'Please. Ever since I joined MI5 I've not had time for relationships. It's quite unreasonable the demands they make but I love the job. I'll quite understand if you find another woman.'

Was this her way of dumping me? I decided to call her bluff and said:

'But I want you. Now that I've got the sack I can move to London.'

'I'd still be married to the job.'

'I'd just have to get used to it.'

'OK, then, let's give it an extended try.'

'One other thing, where does Ishtak fit into all this?'

'He doesn't. We bumped into each other by accident and have met a couple of times since. All he does, when not talking about himself and Israeli politics is, talk about you and the Cambridge Union debate.'

'A couple of times? Does that mean you've met him twice? Once, when I was with you and then now. Is that it?'

'I meant a couple of times as a figure of speech.'

'So you've met him more than twice?'

'Yes.'

'Three times?'

'No.'

'More than ten times?'

'No. What is this, an inquisition?'

'So more than three times but less than eleven times?'

'Where did eleven come from?'

'You've not met him more than ten times so you could have met him ten times; which is less than eleven.'

'You've not changed; still a fastidious actuary.'

'Did you sleep with him?

'Once, when a good night kiss got out of control. There's no chemistry between us.'

'That makes it worse. What a way to round off a pretty rotten day.'

With that I got up to leave.

'Oh, don't be like that. Stay,' she pleaded with tears in her eyes. 'I don't want to lose you. Please stay.'

'What, and sleep in the bed you've shared with another man?'

'Oh, come on. Everyone is allowed one mistake. Nobody's perfect not even you.'

I didn't respond. Instead, I picked up the debris of my shattered self-esteem and left for home.

My mind was in turmoil throughout the tube and train journeys. Passengers provided the odd bit of diversion. Such as the young man on the tube who pretended to be reading a newspaper but was really taking a top down view of a buxom lady's cleavage; what drew my attention to him was the fact that he was holding his newspaper upside down. Or the little boy on the train who was reading aloud every word he could see and pronounced Slough station as 'sludge' (very apt, I thought). The boy's error made me panic. I was on the wrong train. I quickly got off at Reading station and waited for the right train. It was a thirty minute wait so I had a quick drink in a drab cafeteria then went to the public toilet to relieve myself. The toilet was absolutely filthy but to my surprise had no bad odour. I had an awful thought that I'd lost my sense of smell again. More mundanely, I realised that I didn't have a car at the other end and there is no cab rank. I'd have to phone for one.

I nearly missed the next train so engrossed was I in my own thoughts. All through the journey I wondered what life would be like without Ellen. A couplet of Sahir Ludhianvi kept recurring to me:

'*Tum agar mujh ko na chaaho toa koi baat nahin If you don't love me, somehow I'll get by again*

'*Tum kisi aur ko chaahogi tho mushkil hoagie.' But if you love another, I couldn't bear the pain*'

I got home quite late and had a leisurely shower. I tried to smell the body perfume I normally use and couldn't detect any. When I couldn't smell it didn't worry me. What I didn't have I didn't miss. But for fifteen years or thereabouts my world had the added dimension of fragrance. Now that it had gone I felt diminished; just as bad as suddenly becoming deaf.

What was a gift from Ellen, she had inadvertently taken away. But I wasn't going to give up easily. I will see if I could cure my problem.

Feeling hungry, I then had toast and fried egg for dinner. Still wide awake I tried to decide which video to watch, *Shane* or *High Noon* but in the end opted for *The Gunfighter*. Gregory Peck's character, Jimmy Ringo always moves me no matter how often I watch it. It was just as well that I knew every scene, every frame, every line of dialogue as I wasn't concentrating. For all I knew I might have been watching the test-card. My mind kept going back to the twin loss I had suffered. Eventually, my alter ego, Percy came on the scene.

'It is strange that you're so pre-occupied with Ellen after you've lost her. If only you'd paid more attention in the past, you'd have read the danger signals.'

'Don't rub it in. The damn estate agency job has ruined my career and my love-life.'

'Why blame the job, it was your fault. All this wouldn't have happened if you'd not asked her to delay her return to London. She wouldn't have been car-jacked and wouldn't have ended working for MI5.'

'Actually she was offered the job before the accident, so don't blame that on me.'

'Yes, but she didn't become so obsessive before the bang on her head.'

'So you're a medic now are you?'

'OK, is all this self-flagellation and remorse necessary?'

'How do you mean?'

'Have you really lost her? Are you making a crisis out of nothing?'

'No, there's something definitely going on between them. She's had sex with him.'

'She says it was a solitary mistake,' said Percy.

'So that's alright then. You make her sound like the American running for President, what's his name, Clinton, saying, "I smoked marijuana once or twice when at college but I didn't inhale."'

'Nobody's perfect. You pride is blurring your vision.'

I wasn't listening. I said:

'Fancy being cuckolded by Ishtak of all people? The guy who owes his fame to the debate I organised.'

'Does that give you a lien on him?'

Again I wasn't listening and carried on with my own train of thought:

'Can I be cuckolded when I'm not married? What the heck, English is flexible.'

Fed up with not being listened to, Percy disappeared. I slept intermittently.

Bless him, Percy returned to the scene.

'If I were you I'd consult a specialist regarding your loss of smell.'

'What can he do?'

'For a start he'll establish whether you had really lost it and, if you have, whether you can regain it.'

With that he disappeared.

Somehow the night passed.

***

The following morning I telephoned Dad and told him I'd got the sack.

I explained what had happened. I said I'd not had the chance to think things through but one option was to set up a consultancy. Dad asked how Ellen had taken the news.

'She tried to console me. Actually we're no longer together. She's wedded to her job.'

'But don't give her up, son.'

'Right now I'm focussing on getting my career back on the rails.'

'Yes, but not at the expense of your personal life.'

'She's had an affair Dad.'

'Have you two split up?'

Suddenly I heard Mum's voice on the phone, 'What? She's left you for another man?'

'She's had an affair. These things happen, Mum.'

'Is the other man a Jew?'

'Actually he is but what's that got to do with anything?'

'I knew it; you can never trust a Jew. They stick to their own.'

'What nonsense you talk Mum.'

'Still, if you'd married a nice Pakistani girl.'

'Now who's sticking to her own kind? I don't have to put up with this nonsense.'

'Don't ring off son. I'll come to Bristol to console you.'

'Mum, if you come, I'll leave the country.'

The next voice I heard was Dad's. 'Don't take her words to heart son. She'll calm down. I told you she's not well. She's been losing a lot of weight. '

I had to get out of my flat before Mum sent me round the bend. I telephoned the outplacement consultant and set up a meeting. His office was in Cardiff. I found a kindly young man not much older than me. It was quite possible that he had not experienced redundancy so he must be counseling without personal experience.

'You must be very angry at what has happened to you,' he said.

'I was very upset at the treachery involved. But I've overcome it.'

'Redundancy is like bereavement, you must grieve to get it out of your system.'

'No, that is a negative approach. Revenge is best served cold.'

'No you should grieve. You should be angry with Nick. Hate him, absolutely hate him, wish him ill.'

'But I don't see it that way.'

'Then you'll never be able to put this behind you.'

'Oh yes I will. I've sublimated it.'

'That's what you think. It'll gnaw away at you.'

'Look, I came here to listen to tips on finding a job, not to learn to hate people.'

'Well, the first thing to do is to have an established routine, almost as if you're still at work. You can use our offices to type letters, make telephone calls etc. Prepare a CV, no more than two pages long, focussing on what you have achieved. Use action-oriented words; achieved this, delivered that etc. That could be used for a general mail shot. However the most useful approach is to focus on people you know well and who could give you a job. Don't ask for a job, ask them how to go about it.'

'All good stuff. I'll bear it in mind. Thanks.'

'Don't forget to grieve.'

'I'll do it my way, thanks.'

I'll have to sort this one out myself, I concluded as I went back to the flat. For several months I'd wanted to break free from the all-consuming nature of my commitment to Camelot. Leaving them was an option but once you've dedicated your soul to the fortunes of one commercial company, how could you switch your allegiance to another you hitherto regarded as a foe? I'd never understood the way footballers regularly switched clubs. Now that I'd forcibly been removed I was uncertain how to react. I felt like someone whose long-standing marriage to his childhood sweetheart had broken up and was out of practice on how to play the field. Monogamous in life, monogamous at work; let down in both.

Luckily, the cricket world cup provided a diversion. I started taking interest in cricket again. Graham Gooch and Mickey Stewart had introduced a work ethic that was missing when Gower and Botham ruled the roost. The World Cup in Australasia was coming up and it looked as if England were the best prepared side. They weren't the best collection of players but the whole might just be greater than the sum of its parts. I had to get Sky to watch it on television and I had to get up in the middle of the night to watch it.

Meanwhile, my old team, Pakistan, were on the brink of elimination and were saved only by results of matches they weren't playing in going their way, and rain causing their match with England to be abandoned.

Suddenly, to my chagrin, Pakistan gelled as a team in the semi-finals and got through to the final where they met an England team that had already peaked. Botham blamed it on over-training. Pakistan came out winners on merit. Gooch gutted, said, 'It's not the end of the world but it's pretty close'. Then Imran spoiled it all by making a crass speech.

When the world cup ended I realised that it was practically the end of March. More than two months had passed since I got the sack and I'd still done nothing to start a new career. I went to Bristol library for some peace and quiet, away from Mum's persistent phone calls. There I contemplated my next steps. It was a strange feeling, being made redundant. A damming word, meaning as it does, surplus to requirements. In HR-speak, it has a wider definition. Anyone who is not fired for incompetence or fraud is redundant. That includes people like me, people expelled because they knew that the emperor had no clothes. But most people would think you're surplus to requirements and losing your company car would reinforce that view.

The outplacement consultant's platitudes were a waste of time. Should I find another job in the industry or change careers? If I left the industry at this stage, at the first crisis in my career, then I would later in life wonder whether I would have been up to it. To misquote an old couplet,

He who fights and runs away
~~*Lives to fight another day*~~ *is a coward*

With my track record I was hopeful that I'd find another comparable job notwithstanding the pressures on marketing budgets.

I went back home, a lengthy walk, and spent the afternoon going through my files for the names of the three head-hunters who most frequently approached me in the past. All of them were sympathetic but none had any suitable openings just now. 'We will keep your CV on our file and when an opening comes up we'll let you know.' In other words, 'don't phone us, we'll phone you.'

Two further weeks of inactivity was my limit. Time for radical thinking. Should I be a coward and leave the insurance industry altogether? Perhaps research the relevance of Islam in a modern society? Or set up an Islamic insurance company or an Islamic bank? Or do a dissertation on 'Is monotheism superior to polytheism?' All these were of interest to me but I lacked credibility to attract funding. Indeed if they knew my views on Islamic banking and insurance I would get no funding at all.

The only option remaining was to set up a consultancy. But there again there was a problem. I'd have to steer clear of pure actuarial work as I'd been so long out of touch with it as to lack credibility. Suddenly, I had a frightful thought: 'Was I an Emperor without clothes?'

Is the price for being a high flyer that you're never on the ground long enough to build a detailed knowledge of the terrain? But dammit, I wasn't completely useless. What I can offer is an eagle's panoramic vision. So what if I didn't have the eye of an ant? I could set up a consultancy to offer an analytical and actuarial approach to management problems. I would give trenchant and fearless advice.

The following month, the Financial Adviser carried the news of Camelot Life being fined £2m for failing to meet deadlines in dealing with complaints, mainly but not exclusively, on personal pensions and for systemic failures in their sales process. They were given six months to address the issues or face a ban; so the grapevine said, although neither Camelot nor the regulator would be drawn on the matter.

***

By now it was pretty clear that I had lost the sense of smell and this was bugging me. I consulted a specialist in Harley Street. He talked at great length but the reality was that he didn't know. The advice he offered was informed speculation. Two *possible* causes, and that is all they were, were shock and depression.

Either could have caused me to lose it in my early years. The snag was that I can't recall any shocks. If I did have one it wasn't deep enough to stay in my memory. The specialist thought that it could be the death of my stillborn brother. What caused it to be overturned? A negative shock, i.e. elation? Plausible, but what does that prove?

Lahore Revisited

I kept getting calls from Mum, wanting to speak to me; from Dad, imploring me to speak with her. This happened practically on a daily basis. I ignored them all and was getting increasingly irritated.

Then I had an urgent e-mail from Dad.

Dear Son,
You are taking your anger to unreasonable extremes. Your mother speaks before she thinks but her heart is in the right place. You know she dotes on you. In the past few months she has been losing weight. Initially I thought the she was pining for you and starving in the process. Last week I took her to the hospital for tests. She has stomach cancer. Tomorrow they operate on her. I would urge you to come over straightaway. There is a chance that she may not survive the surgery.
PS Let Ellen, Gareth and Glynis know.
PPS By the way, I'll explain when we meet, Ellen is known here as Deena

The past few years had delivered a series of shocks but none as shocking as this news. They say that sons are always closer to their mother than to their father. In my case I'd felt that that was untrue but perhaps I was wrong. I couldn't imagine life without her. There were so many things I'd said or done that I shouldn't have; so much left unsaid. Would fate give me the chance to put them right?

She was not making things easy. Deena, eh? So she's told her friends that I'm married? I phoned Dad to establish facts. They were more complicated than I'd feared.

She had told everyone that I had married a Welsh girl who had converted to Islam and acquired a new name, Deena. Her Jewishness wasn't mentioned. Then, when she heard that the two of us had our differences, she jumped to the conclusion that the split was permanent and announced that 'It didn't work out and they were divorced.'

What a mess. If she got better, I'd give her a piece of my mind for having stolen the peace of it. But she was gravely ill and I must go and see her.

I decided to catch the first plane back to Lahore.

But first I had to let Ellen and her parents know. I forwarded Dad's e-mail to Ellen. I then phoned Gareth. Glynis answered, and I gave her the grim news and said that I was hoping to catch a plane later that day. Glynis was shocked to hear the news and asked if I'd told Ellen. She then said:

'I don't know how busy Gareth and Ellen are but I'd quite like all of us to go over and see her. We're unlikely to make it today but we'll catch the earliest possible flight.'

'Before you do that,' I said, 'there's something you must know.'

I told her Mum's fabrications and added:

'You must be prepared for overbearing interest in your family's background and why the marriage didn't work.'

'Oh hell. Still, I'll have to put up with it, I can't not go.'

'Thanks Mum. I'll keep you posted about my whereabouts.'

I checked with my normal travel agent and found a British Airways flight that evening from Heathrow to Lahore. I checked my e-mail one last time to see if Ellen had received my e-mail. She hadn't. I phoned Dad to let him know that I was coming and to give him the flight details. This was my first trip back to Pakistan for the best part of fifteen years.

***

I had to queue to go through customs and immigration at Lahore airport. I then caught a taxi home. The ageing cook was there to receive me. I said a quick hello, had a shower and set off for the hospital.

I asked Dad, who was waiting there, how Mum was.

'Don't know; she's not yet come round from the operation.'

She looked peaceful in her sleep. A tube had been inserted to feed her intravenously.

'This is all a bit sudden. Why didn't the doctor pick it up sooner?'

'This is Pakistan son, not England. Your mother had been losing weight for a few months and I took her twice for a check up. The doctor said he'd detected a dead ulcer in her stomach but it was harmless.'

'Dead ulcer? What's that?'

'I asked that and was told that it was an ulcer that was dead. Didn't understand it.'

'Me neither. Anyway, what happened next?'

'Well she continued to lose weight and then she got into a right state, when you refused to speak with her. I took her to another doctor and well, here we are.'

'How did the operation go?'

'It was successful, I'm told. They've removed something. She'll have to use a bag.'

I wanted to know more about Mum's health, Dad more about my job prospects. We exchanged information in a disjointed way, without shedding much light; Dad because he was never one to take a deep interest in medical matters, I because my future was in flux. We carried on for four hours before Mum regained consciousness. She was still not completely aware of where she was and did a double take when she saw me.

'Yes, Mum. It's me.'

Tears rolled down our cheeks as I stooped and gave her a hug but had to quickly stop when she grimaced in pain. We stayed with her for another two hours before we went home. She was going to stay in the hospital for the rest of the week.

When we returned to our house the cook soon served dinner. He had a good memory. Even though he had hardly any notice he had rustled up my favourite, lamb chop curry. I would have enjoyed it more if Mum had been there.

Then the phone rang. It was Ellen asking for me:

'How's Mum?'

'She's had her operation and is heavily sedated. She's OK.'

'Look, the three of us have managed to get visas and tickets. We're arriving on Saturday morning by British Airways. Could you arrange accommodation for us?'

'That's tomorrow isn't it?'

'Yes.'

'Mum'll be glad to see you all. Don't worry, there are enough rooms in our house.'

Next morning Dad went to the airport to receive them whilst I went to see Mum in the hospital. She was awake.

'Mum, guess who're coming to see you? Ellen and her parents.'

'You mean Deena and her parents?'

'Yes, we'll talk about that later.'

'You're back together?'

'We'll talk about that later.'

'They've come to Lahore?'

'Yes.'

'*Haye Allah,* I'm not properly dressed,' she said attempting to sit up but collapsing.

'Steady Mum, you've just come through a difficult operation. They don't expect you to be dressed up.'

'But I must at least have my make up on.'

'Don't worry. Dad's collecting them and will bring them here. You've got time.'

'What have they done to me, son?'

'They told me it was an operation but didn't tell me what it was. Did you not have to give consent?'

'My God, what did I give away?'

'Consent, permission. Didn't you give permission for the surgery?'

'Your father must have done that.'

'But it's your body Mum. He can't give permission for invasive surgery on your body.'

'You're scaring me. What invasion? What have they done to me, what have I got?'

'Haven't they told you?'

'No.'

'Hasn't Dad told you?'

'Oh come on, what have I got?'

'Dad'll be here in a moment or two, I'll ask him.'

A moment or two was in fact three hours during most of which Mum slept. When they arrived I woke her up. She was still groggy when one by one Ellen, Glynis and Gareth said:

'Hello.'

She acknowledged each greeting with a slight movement of her head. There was an uneasy silence, nobody knowing what to say although there were plenty of pressing questions needing answers. After a while, possibly to break the ice, Gareth said, 'It's amazing the power Daud has over the Customs and Immigration people. We sailed right through them in no time at all.'

'In Lahore it's not who you know but how you know them that counts.'

'That's a bit subtle. I don't understand,' said Gareth.

'Here everyone claims to know everyone else. If you'd come by taxi, the taxi driver would claim to know Benazir Bhutto, Imran Khan, Wasim Akram etc. So anyone can claim acquaintance. If you've done them a favour or, more important, if they need a favour from you, then it's different.'

'Or if you have a photograph of them coming out of a brothel, then that is pretty handy too,' I said.

Daud took a deep breath and said, 'I have told everyone here that you two had got married, then separated and divorced so people are bound to ask what is the position right now.'

'*You've* told everyone, Dad?'

'OK, Mum's done it, let's not split hairs.'

'All of that is untrue,' said Ellen. 'What do you want us to say if asked?'

'Your affair with a Jew is over?' asked Mum.

'There was no affair and don't forget I'm a Jew myself.'

'Keep your voice down,' said Mum agitatedly.

'Mum, the more you hide the truth, the bigger the problem you create for yourself.'

'I'm sorry my dear. I'm an old woman, suffering from something they won't tell me but is serious. Can you two pretend that you're married?'

Dad intervened to say:

'We're very sorry about the mess we've got ourselves in. Look at it this way, it'll be a lot worse for us than for you.'

'What do you want us to do?' I asked.

'Like I said, it would be a great help if you pretended that you're married.'

I looked in the direction of Ellen who nodded.

We returned to our house and had a late lunch. We were then left to have a siesta to deal with jet lag. Dad had arranged for Ellen and I to share a room but placed twin beds rather than a double bed.

In the evening I took them for a tour of Shalimar Gardens, the garden and water fountains laid out by the Mughuls three centuries ago. I wondered whether Brother Henderson of St Anthony's who taught me History and was a widely read person was still around. I wanted to introduce Gareth and Glynis to them.It was eighteen years since I'd left school, Henderson might have retired.

I made a few phone calls and established that he was still there. He lived in accommodation on the school premises and was glad to meet us, the following morning.

So the next day, after seeing Mum again I took the Evans' to St Anthony's. Dad stayed behind with Mum.

Brother Henderson was there and delighted, as always, to see an ex-student. He took us for a tour of the school and offered us lunch. He was very downbeat saying that there was a backlash against schools such as St Anthony's. They were accused of trying to convert children to Christianity. You must know, he said, that it wasn't true. The underlying concern was that it was elitist, a school for the rich. But the outcome was a dumbing down.

'Have you thought of returning to Scotland?'

'I've been here nearly forty years. I'm a Pakistani, whatever the locals might say.'

We bid good bye at the end of a pleasant evening and returned home. When they got back Dad greeted them at the gate.

'You should've told me,' he said to me, 'you should've told me that your mother wanted to know what the operation was about.'

'She has a right to know Dad, it's her body.'

'Of course it is but she is terrified of cancer. The surgeon said it was important that she approached the operation calmly. There was no alternative to the operation anyway.'

'When did you plan to tell her?'

'Yesterday but I couldn't get her on her own. Then I was going to tell her today after you'd gone but she was quite agitated.'

'How did she take the news?'

'She was devastated but once she'd come to terms with the situation she was in, she was glad that it was over.'

'Still, it's quite something losing your stomach.'

'It is, but if that is the price you have to pay to save your life, wouldn't you think it was worth paying?'

I didn't answer.

Mum was discharged from hospital the day after the Evans' arrived. The house began to resemble a transit lounge as one by one members of our extended family and close and distant friends came to visit Mum. To each of them Dad introduced Ellen as Deena. Some of them came twice, ostensibly because of their concern for Mum but actually to have another look at Ellen.

Mum was in a right state. A great believer in hospitality she wanted to have dinners every night and invite as many of her friends as possible. What she didn't have was the physical energy of even a year ago. She delegated all of the cookery to her cook with total freedom on menu management, He had enough experience of what she normally organised. On the first night my aunt Salma, Mum's sister, and her husband Idris were at the dinner table; as were Akbar, my closest friend at school and his wife Nina. With cloying sweetness Salma asked Ellen,

'Deena, my dear, why didn't you come with Majid?'

'I couldn't get time off. I have less clout than he does.'

'You still live in London and Majid in Bristol?'

'I still work in London and he in Bristol.'

'How often do you meet?'

'Often enough.'

'How often is that?' asked Nina.

'I guess it is a little easier for us than it is for you. Akbar works in the Gulf doesn't he whilst you're here?'

'That's different, he's earning a living.'

'We're doing the same.'

'No cross-examination please,' said Dad. 'This is not a law court and Deena is our guest.'

They turned their attention to the food. What a sumptuous fare was served and yet so different, Ellen found, from the stuff she ate regularly in Indian restaurants back home. No pappadam, no chicken tikka masala; and no naan or rice. Instead dry chapaatis were served and daal had no cream. On the whole Ellen found it more piquant than stuff back home.

When the dessert arrived, Idris tried another line of questioning:

'What do you think of Islam, Deena?'

'It is one of the three great monotheistic religions.'

'Three? Islam and Christianity, which is the third?'

'Judaism,' I said, quickly.

'But which is the best of the three?'

'I think all religions preach pretty much the same message,' said Ellen.

'But Islam is the best, don't you think?'

'It's certainly the most recent.'

'Idris, leave the girl in peace,' said Dad.

'But she must agree with me or she wouldn't have converted from Christianity to Islam.'

'British people don't have an obsession with religion. Certainly she doesn't,' I said. 'So she doesn't pray or fast?'

'Neither do I,' I said. 'If we don't stop this ridiculous questioning, we'll all go back tomorrow.'

'Oh please don't,' said Mum. 'Stop it you two.'

Gareth spoke for the first time. 'Don't be too severe on them Majid. They're just trying to know us a bit better. If they came to England we'd be asking them questions. Different questions but we'd still ask them.'

'What sort of questions would you ask?'

'We'd steer clear of politics and religions. I suppose we're not as nosey so we let it all emerge gradually.'

The next evening two more couples joined us for dinner and one of the ladies observed:

'I see that you're sharing a room so you must be married, Deena. Why aren't you wearing a ring?'

'Ellen never wears one as it irritates her skin,' responded Glynis quickly.

'Ellen, who's Ellen?'

'That's her birth name.'

'You prefer that to Deena?'

Before she could answer that Idris, who'd been itching to say something spoke:

'Deena, you're a lawyer aren't you?'

'Yes.'

'I can see that. I've been going over your answers, yesterday. You chose your words carefully and never answered the questions directly. What you said could still be true even if you were Christian and were not married.'

'I'm not Christian but you can believe whatever you want to.'

With that she retired to the lounge and her parents and I followed. There was a commotion and ten minutes later Dad and Mum returned, the guests having left.

The rest of the week soon passed and the Evan family had to leave. Dad and I saw them off. I stayed another two months helping Mum come to terms with the stomach-substitute, the bag. She had to find out by trial and error what she could eat and what she couldn't.

To her dismay onions were a no-no as the bag gave out a vile smell. She contemplated life without curries. Not worth living was her initial reaction, until she contemplated the alternative. Gradually, as she reconciled herself to her diminished lot, the old ebullience returned. She was even prepared to rehabilitate Ellen.

Eventually, both parents said it was time I went back and rebuilt my career.

Seeking Redemption

I returned to Bristol, relieved that Mum was better. Lovely Ellen, she'd been considerate enough to visit Mum in Lahore and shown great forbearance in the face of really rude and intrusive questioning. No wonder I loved the girl. Still, that doesn't condone her affair, her one night stand.

My inbox and my letter box were both relatively light. Out of sight out of mind, in the jobs market? Temperamentally allergic to sloth, I wanted a job. Norman Tebbit had criticised scroungers by saying that during the Great Depression his father just got on his bike and sought out a job. Although I had no intention of joining the dole queue, not having the modern bike (the car) was a handicap. A carless person wouldn't live in Downleaze, have a girlfriend in London and her family in North Wales.

As I settled into a life of monotony I was in danger of sliding down the slippery slope of self-pity. Realising this I pulled myself together. I needed guidance.

I showered, changed and took a train to Paddington and from there a tube to Chancery Lane station. It was half past six as I emerged from the underground station and walked a short distance until I came to an opening in the parade of Dickensian looking shops. I went through it into a quadrangle. This was Staple Inn. In the top right hand corner Staple Inn houses the Institute of Actuaries. I planned to spend the night in the quadrangle deep in meditation. There was only one snag, the gates, the one I walked through and the one at the back, are shut at seven. I resolved to hide in a nook to escape detection. For the moment the last few people were leaving the office of the Institute of Actuaries. I recognised Tony Ratcliff, who was the President the year I qualified as an actuary and who handed out my diploma. Tony did not recognise me however.

Once the gates were shut and the place deserted I sat down in one of the wooden chairs which surrounded the large circular flower pot. It was cold, very cold and it was dark. Although the sky was cloudless there was no moon and only a solitary star. I fell into deep meditation.

I was in that state for, I guess, an hour before I went into a trance. It was just as well that there was no one there as I started speaking in a loud voice:

'Oh Wise One. Give me some guidance.
'I am a Muslim, my girlfriend is a Jew
'I studied in a Catholic missionary school
'I beseech neither Allah nor Yahweh nor the Holy Trinity

'I seek not the certainties of their domain,
'Where black is black, white is white
'There are no shades of grey
'Instead I beseech thee
'The Great Big Actuary in the Sky
'I have led an honest and righteous life
'I have abided by the profession's Code of Conduct
'I have put the interests of my employer and its customers above mine
'I understand that the future is uncertain
'I understand the difference between the causal and the casual
'Between choice and chance
'Yet today I stand before you a broken man
'Victim of calumny, my career and love-life in tatters
'Should I abandon my principles?
'Should I stop turning the other cheek?
'And take instead an eye for an eye, a tooth for a tooth?'

I stood up at this point and started spinning round in the manner of a dervish and spun off the ground. I found myself on a steed with golden mane and held tight as it soared above and beyond the earth and into the sky. I lost track of time as I went into a vortex of darkness and emerged through it into bright light.

I saw cricket fields with David Gower batting against Andy Roberts and Michael Holding, Imtiaz Ahmad hooking Roy Gilchrist and Wesley Hall, Garry Sobers batting against Richie Benaud and Alan Davidson and, most amazing of all, Don Bradman batting against Harold Larwood. I saw Pavarotti, using a piano, not to accompany his voice, but as support for his immense frame, and a few hours later, Mohammed Rafi singing in his rich effortless way and Elvis Presley singing Heartbreak Hotel.

I strained to see and hear more but the steed was moving at too rapid a pace. I then went past another group of people all carrying rosaries, counting their beads and chanting debit, credit, debit, credit, debit, credit. 'Ah, the celestial accountants,' I said to myself.

I went beyond that and saw a large mansion with double gates which carried the picture of a man weighing up the odds:

'This must be the celestial Staple Inn,' I thought.

Waiting outside the gates were actuaries who were still alive, as far as I knew. I recognised Hugh Scurfield, the current President and Tony Ratcliff, who had seemed in a hurry leaving Staple Inn earlier that evening. Other Past Presidents I recognised included Roger Corley, Marshall Field, Stewart Lyon and Philip Moore. There were other famous actuaries I recognised, such as Monica Allanach, Dilip Chakraborty, Colin Coles, Brian Dawson, Chris Daykin, Derek Fellows, Tony Fine, David Graham, Sami Hasan, Geraldine Kaye, Colin Lever, Jeff Medlock, David Purchase, Bill Scanlan and Howard

Webb. When I entered inside there were many more. As I went into the central hall I saw a dozen, perhaps thirteen, men seated at the table and I saw Frank Redington, the most famous English actuary who died a decade back.

'I heard your pleas, Majid,' said Frank.

'Forgive me for my impertinence. I needed some guidance.'

'You were right to seek it but it wasn't necessary to come here. You could have consulted my agent on earth, Howard Webb.'

'I'm sorry.'

'No, don't apologise. Your conduct has been exemplary and you are right to consult before seeking retribution. I think it was Gandhi who said that if both parties seek an eye for an eye then they will both end up blind.'

'I understand.'

'You actuaries have tried to deify me since I retired. In fact in my business life I too had to make compromises. If you were to see some of my Board reports you'll find that they're less well argued than some of my professional publications.'

'I didn't know that.'

'In the real world, you can't win every battle, every argument. You've got to let the other side win some. Just make sure that you don't lose the ones that matter.'

'That's a pragmatic approach, not a principled one,' I said.

'Principles are for the guidance of the wise and enslavement of the foolish. Be sensible but don't compromise your core principles.'

'What are the core principles for an actuary?'

'To technical actuaries I say that it is better to be approximately right than precisely wrong. But you're on the commercial side; all I ask you is to respect the 3Ps.'

'What's that?'

'Can't you work it out? Probity, precision and prescience. One other thing. No matter how strong the evidence in support of a particular course of action, remember that the unexpected can happen. So always have a Plan B ready.'

'One other question. I noticed Christians, Jews, Muslims and Hindus inside the pearly gates. Do all actuaries get to heaven regardless of creed?'

'Oh those weren't the pearly gates you are thinking of. We're not in heaven.'

'You're not?'

'We're in purgatory.'

'Why?'

'You said it yourself in your supplication. Everything is black and white to God. We believe in uncertainty. He doesn't like that. He doesn't like us forever playing Devil's Advocate.'

'Has anyone been let out from purgatory into heaven?'

'None that I'm aware of. They're all still here. I saw Galileo the other day. He's our spiritual ancestor.'

I was woken up on Monday morning by the security man who opened the gates. I was shivering, haggard, confused and famished. I had no idea how I got there. Looking like a tramp, I went to the nearby McDonalds and had two Big Macs before setting off for home.

***

There were several issues to consider when setting up a consultancy. I called up Percy, for a discussion. Increasingly Percy was a substitute for Ellen, although they provided different perspectives.

.'Right,' said Percy. 'The first requirement is differentiation. What is it that you have to offer that others don't?'

'For that we have to first see what they offer.'

'OK, I'm listening.'

'Actuarial firms stick with facts. They steer clear of giving a commercial forecast. If pressed they'll hedge it with so many caveats as to make their opinion useless.'

'But you're not competing with them. Talk about strategy consultants.'

'That's a very wide universe,' I pleaded.

'OK, talk about the big ones.'

'They have a recognised brand name. Their calling card is that nobody will ever get sacked for adopting their recommendations.'

'You can't match them on that. What else?'

'They have the ability to engage at Board level. I can do that.'

'Can you?'

'Yes I can.'

Percy looked at me challengingly whereupon I added:

'Once I get in.'

'So getting a hearing without a brand name is the challenge. What else?'

'Their patter is good. They make the obvious seem thoughtful.'

'You can do that, faking erudition.'

'I'm afraid I can't.'

'I'm sure it's a matter of training. Anyway, what else?'

'The really skilled ones listen to what the client says, find out what they want to hear and give it back to them as advice.'

'You mean, even if that is the wrong advice to give?'

'Remember, the customer is always right. Isn't that a golden rule of marketing?'

'So, why don't you do it too?'

'I'm afraid I'm a compulsive teller of the truth.'

'What else do they do?'

'Recommend change. If your organisation is centralised, suggest decentralisation and vice versa.'

'You're being cynical. Why would they do that?'

'Because major change involves disruption. Implementation requires major external support; and generates lots of fees.'

'There's an opportunity for you.'

'How do you mean?'

'Make a virtue out of a necessity. There's only one of you in your firm so you cannot do a major implementation job. You can provide the strategic advice and let the client implement. A lot cheaper for the client.'

'There is a perception that cheap advice is cheap advice.'

'You don't expect everything on a plate do you? Go out and do the hunting.'

I was grateful for Percy's clinical analysis but frankly I'd had enough of it. I banished him and decided to start afresh next morning.

Overnight I decided that my firm would have three differentiators. I'd focus on giving strategic advice and let the client implement the blueprint. I'd come for a post implementation review. I would undercut the strategy consultants by at least half.

Secondly I wouldn't sit on the fence but give unequivocal advice. I'd give them a definite steer.

Finally, I'd give them best advice, no better not use that pejorative term; I'd give them the right advice rather than what the client wants to hear. That might make it harder to win assignments but I would try to point out the consequences of ignoring it.

It had taken me a while to get this far. Now for the name of the firm. I feared that it would take me longer to decide the name of the consultancy than to decide what it would do. The name had to reflect the type of values that the consultancy would espouse. In the event it came to me, out of nowhere, in a flash. I decided to call it Probity, Precision and Prescience, the 3Ps. I was quite proud of the strapline.

I checked its visual appeal using various layouts and fonts.and in the end settled on:

3Ps: Probity, Precision and Prescience

It had the right balance between formality and light heartedness. The logo would stand out and it would be difficult for them to knock it. Or could they? 'How would *he* criticise it if a competitor chose this logo for themselves?

Before I could answer that I had another thought: *3P's* did not cover an important differentiator, the fact that I won't sit on the fence but give unequivocal advice. So I decided to change it to *4Ps*

4Ps: Probity, Precision and Prescience, sans Piles

They can't corrupt that, I thought. I tested it out on Gareth.

'What's piles got to do with it?'

'Ah, if you don't sit on the fence, you won't get piles.'

'Aargh. That's not just obscure, it's in poor taste.'

I wavered and eventually decided to delete it; its alliterative irreverence appealed to me but it might not to my target clients.

The next issue was whether to rent office space and whether I needed a secretary. Rather than start incurring costs before there was fee income, I decided to operate from home and defer the recruitment of a secretary.

What I couldn't defer was professional indemnity insurance. There was always the risk of being sued and although the chances were low, if a successful lawsuit was awarded against me the cost could destroy the firm. I didn't want to ask Camelot for a quote so I approached three other insurers. With all of them I faced a problem. In order to get the lowest premium I had to hedge my opinions with as many caveats as I had criticised other actuarial firms for hiding behind. Yet my differentiator was that I wouldn't sit on the fence, I'd give unequivocal advice. I eventually had to agree a compromise; have the fence nearby, ready to sit on it.

Everything now in place, I placed an ad in the Times and Financial Times and sent a copy to the Chairmen and Chief Executives of all insurance companies and, banks.

Majid Khan MA FIA is please to announce the launch on 1st July 1993 of *3Ps*, a brand new consultancy to provide strategic advice. It's motto will be

Probity, Precision and Prescience

The past five years have shown the dangers in carrying on driving without pausing to see if we are making the right journey.

In order to create a presence in the market as well as an image, I decided to issue regular Newsletters. For the first of these, I refashioned the substance of the Marketing & Compliance Circulars I'd pioneered at Camelot.

These Newsletters took up a fair amount of time. Regular reading of actuarial journals and trade magazines was another way to occupy time.

***

I met the Chief Executives of practically all the companies, to identify the issues exercising their minds. Business volume or, rather, a lack of it, was a problem. I also sensed that misselling of personal pensions was an industry-wide problem and the underlying cause was the same and the approach of each company was similar.

Not having come to terms with the sea-change in business methods that was now required, they concentrated on winning individual skirmishes with the regulator rather than limiting the overall damage. They were therefore blind to the fact that the regulator's approach was hardening.

I don't blame them. My eyes were only opened after I'd left the industry. Perhaps companies should introduce sabbaticals for senior executives to spring clean their minds of unessential clutter. On second thoughts that's not a good idea. If someone takes a sabbatical his deputy would step up to the plate and possibly do more damage by trying too hard to impress.

***

The year was nearly done; a year with no income and rapidly depleted funds. Christmas beckoned. I looked forward to a week of tranquillity in Mold. Without a car getting there would be tricky. Proof that Ellen still cared came in the form of a phone call from her. It was the first time we had spoken to each other since the Lahore visit. She offered me a lift which I gratefully accepted.

The door bell rang and I thought, 'That can't be her, she's not due for another hour.' But it was her, having driven to my Downleaze flat all the way from Knightsbridge.

'Can I come in?' asked Ellen. As she moved forward with pursed lips, I offered my cheek.

'Oh, come on,' she said and then added, 'Can we at least make it a French kiss,' and gave me a peck on the other cheek too.

Salutations completed, she went into the lounge. The bookshelf and the desk were tidy but the rest of the lounge was in a mess. A dinner plate and cutlery were on the centre table and three used mugs were lying around. My coat and jacket had been slung on the double settee. Seeing her survey the mess, I said:

'I'm sorry, I thought I had another hour.'

'Oh, I'm early, am I? No dear, what you're missing is a good woman.'

'Do you know of one?'

'I mean a girlfriend not a cleaner.'

'Whose fault is that?'

'Let's not start that again. I gave you an explanation. You choose not to believe it. Let's at least have a civilised conversation.'

'I'm sorry. Its jolly decent of you to give me a lift. Christmas in Mold is what keeps me sane.'

'OK, then let's go. It'll take me ten minutes to tidy up here.'

Once on the motorway, Ellen began, 'You never phoned me even once since your return from Lahore.'

'You could've tried phoning me.'

'I've done a few times but you weren't in.'

'I've spent a lot of time in the library.'

'I want you but what more can I do?'

'Relationships are based upon trust.'

'I've told you everything about me worth knowing apart from my work. You know I can't talk about that.'

'Let's not talk about it, let's look to the future.'

'Is there a future for us?' asked Ellen.

'Let's get through this Christmas. One step at a time.'

'Just remember I'm not a chauffeur, I offered you a lift because I care about you.'

It was around nine and dark when we reached Gareth and Glynis's house. Our chilliness soon dissolved under the warmth of the greeting we received.

'It's good to see you two together again,' said Gareth and Glynis in unison.

'It's good to see you two too,' I said. 'Dad you look run down.'

'Too old to be a butcher. I'm packing it in.'

'You're serious?'

'I'm nearly sixty-five now. It'll take a couple of years but I've started the process. I've instructed an investment bank to look out for potential buyers.'

'Anyone I know?'

'He knows you. He's Tracy Pitt.'

'Oh no, not Tracy. Wouldn't touch him with a bargepole.'

'He gets paid a percentage of what I get. So long as he winkles out buyers willing to pay a good price, what do I care?'

'I suppose you're OK as you're selling. I pity the buyer. Anyway, when its all over, come and live near Bristol.'

'Better still, let's all live in Knightsbridge,' said Glynis.

Neither Ellen nor I responded.

'Come on you two must be tired. Have a quick dinner and then retire. We'll talk in the morning.'

I was beginning to realise what was about to happen. Ellen and I were going to share a bed. Was this wise, I wondered. If there was to be a rapprochement it had to emerge spontaneously, it must not be rushed. I decided to carry on talking with Gareth. Ellen was in the kitchen with Glynis. I would carry on as if I was unaware of what was planned.

'How's *3Ps* coming on?' asked Gareth.

That was just the opening I needed. I explained my frustration with potential clients and with the Association of British Insurers.

'It seems to me that the industry is hell bent on sleepwalking to destruction. There's nothing I can do about it.'

'Isn't there a business opportunity for you?' asked Gareth.

'What, as an undertaker to bury insurance companies?'

'From what you've said, every company is busy dealing with problems, all have trading problems and are cutting back staff numbers and all have problems with this pensions thing?'

'Yes.'

'All are likely to be set tight deadlines to sort out the problems with the pensions thing or face huge fines,?'

'Yes.'

'But they wouldn't have budgeted for it and wouldn't have the people to do it,?'

'Correct.'

'Money can't be a problem, they'll find it one way or another. The farming industry has a similar problem with mad cow disease. If it gets much worse the Government might order the wholesale slaughter of at risk cattle. Farmers will have no option but to comply.'

'Where's this getting us?'

'Money can't be a problem but resources can be. Why don't you set up in business to work out the amount of compensation from this pension thing? Companies can then use you and not have to divert resources from their main job, which is getting business and servicing customers.'

'It's boring number crunching.'

'But you can charge what you like and you'll be doing your industry a favour.'

I had stopped listening. I was thinking the idea through. The regulators specify the basis upon which the loss should be calculated. So it is an objective calculation, not based upon opinion. I could computerise the process and set up a dedicated team to do the calculation. I could get my first client to verify the accuracy of the calculations, on the pretext of asking them to be satisfied that the calculations are correct.

The first client could be Camelot Life.

***

As we drove back on New Year's Eve, Ellen said to me, 'You've shared my bed without sleeping with me; yet you acted in front of my parents and yours as if you did. You can't fool them you know.'

'I wasn't trying to fool them.'

'Whatever, are we finished, is this the end of the road for us?'

'You tell me?'

'I'm seeing a side of you that I was unaware of. You were gentle, tolerant, giving and even loving in your sort of way; not unbending and unforgiving.'

I didn't respond and we carried on in silence. There is nothing so bleak as two people driving in isolation for three hours in total silence; not the silence of long standing couples who communicate without saying anything; the silence born out of distrust. As we left at the Bristol exit and made for Downleaze, I said:

'We can get together again so long as you promise not to see Ishtak again.'

'I can't do that. I told you, you're the only man in my life ever and it will always remain that way. But I can't promise you that I'll never see Ishtak again. If that means you walking out on me, I'll have to live with that. I'll be a spinster.'

***

Kate telephoned me and wondered whether we could meet and have a chat.

'How's Camelot doing?' I asked.

'Same old story. Beating sales and profit records Continue to have problems with the regulator. Fines getting bigger, so are backlogs.'

Before getting down to the purpose of her call, Kate had a confession to make:

'I know you feel that I'm partly responsible for your fall from grace. You've been of great help to me and on the two occasions you needed me I was unable to help.'

'The 3R's contract I remember; what was the other one?'

'The Sword of Truth case. In both instances I didn't have the information that would have cleared you. I promise you I didn't say anything untruthful and if you were framed someone else was to blame.'

'Don't worry, I worked that out myself. Why did you want to meet?'

'I need your advice. Can I rely on your confidentiality?'

'If you tell me something I can use to nail Nick, I can't promise that I won't use it; but not in any way that'll compromise you.'

Kate didn't respond so I said, 'Look, I'm in London next week. Let's have a chat. I'll let you decide how much you wish to tell me.'

We met in the pub at Paddington Station. Kate was already there when I arrived. The barman greeted me with a 'long-time-no-see' to which I replied saying that I'd been busy. When Kate arrived, I went up to her and sat down. After exchanging a brief hello with her I returned to the bar to get a round of drinks. The barman winked at me.

'Oh, she's a colleague from work,' I said.

'That's what they all say, Sir.'

'No, its true.'

'I believe you.'

'I'm not sure that I care.'

I took the two glasses of wine and joined Kate.

'What really happened at the regulatory audit? Your public pronouncements were muted.'

'Well, Nick was unable to demonstrate that the change in leadership had brought increased commitment. We were fined £2m and asked to clear the backlog within six months.'

I decided to get to the point, 'What's bugging you, Kate?'

'Everything is going exceptionally well on the sales front, both in the insurance companies and the estate agencies. We're bucking industry trends. I can't put my finger on it but it doesn't seem right.'

'As Compliance Officer, you have a duty to follow up concerns. I don't think you can alert the regulators until you have something concrete to report but you need to alert management.'

Kate didn't say anything but there was a plaintive look in her eyes. Like many lawyers she was non-numerate. So I said:

'Let me give you a steer. Here's an old press release I found in my briefcase. It's the first quarter since Nick became Chief Executive.'

Camelot Estates had its best quarter to date, all performance indicators showing a marked improvement:

Number of estate agency branches; up from 1021 to 1100

Housing sales: up 20%

Endowment mortgages: up from 30% of mortgages to 56% (target 88%)

Accident, sickness and unemployment insurance: up from 0 to 25%

Building insurance: up from 25% to 50%

Expenses: down 25%

Loss before debt interest: down from £15m to £3m (forecast to break into profit in the next quarter).

Commenting on the result, Nick Knights the new Chief Executive, said, 'These are an exceptional set of results in a difficult market. Whilst it is difficult to forecast the recovery of the housing market, I am confident that we'll maintain our improvement in future quarters.'

'Let's analyse this. The housing market overall had not increased. The 20% increase in the number of houses sold can be partly explained by the 10% increase in the number of branches. The rest seems an impressive increase at the expense of other estate agencies.'

'Perhaps it is a reflection of Camelot being relatively underweight in the South East,' suggested Kate.

'Perhaps, but it still takes some believing bearing in mind that the Royston's new agency was bound to hit 3R's sales.'

'However comparing second quarter with the first is misleading. The housing market picks up in the spring so you'd expect more sales anyway.'

'Dead right. We should compare results with the corresponding quarter in the previous year or use seasonally adjusted figures. We don't know what was done here. But what concerns me most was how expenses could be slashed by as much as a quarter and that too without any one-off redundancy costs. Maybe they've cancelled the licence for 3R's MI system. That would save a fair amount of money but not 25%. '

I paused to see her reaction and then continued:

'It'll also mean that the statistics on housing sales etc are probably unreliable, certainly not produced on a consistent basis. Perhaps he's made a lot of staff redundant; perhaps the accounting basis has been changed so that the two quarters are not comparable.'

'This is too complicated, I need an actuary.'

'Or an accountant. Have a word with Bruce. He and I have long been concerned that statistics on sales volume comes from the Sales Department. It should come from the Finance or the Marketing Department.'

'Actually there is something else that concerns me. The high level of sales of insurance products might amount to overselling which will lead to higher cancellation and provoke the ire of the regulators.'

'There you are then. You can manage on your own.'

I bought another round and we sat drinking it. I then asked:

'We've talked about fraud. How about more routine things such as pensions misselling? Is that under control?'

'Good Lord, no. Even as we try to make headway the problem grows in size. We had another audit and the results are due shortly. I fear the worst.'

'Stay in touch. My consultancy can help reduce the backlog.'

'How would you do that?'

'We have the resources to calculate the amount of compensation someone is due. You can offload that work to us.'

'The man to talk to is Bruce. The pensions review team reports to him.'

***

A month later I had another call from Kate and we met again in the Paddington pub.

'We had feedback from the regulators on their last audit. We knew it was serious even though they gave no advance warning of their findings.'

'A Compliance Officer's sixth sense?'

'No. Ingrid Stokes came with Gary Edgar, the Director responsible for Enforcement.'

'That's a big clue.'

'That's not all. She didn't want the usual crowd of Tim, me and the head of Customer Services. a quorum of the Board had to be present, Sir Alfred, Nick, Ted MacAfee, Ernie Absolom and Bill Ashford.'

'Ingrid then said, "Normally I like to begin by giving all the good news, all the areas where you have met deadlines or shown improvements. But I have to make an exception this time."

'Ingrid continued, "Yours was not the worst company at the first regulatory audit. But it is the worst in the latest round of follow-up visits."

'Gary Edgar turned to Sir Alfred and said, "You put all the blame on the outgoing Chief Executive and promised a sea change under Knights. Frankly it's got worse. The backlog's actually increased, the sales training on compliance is perfunctory and you're still accepting cases you shouldn't."

'"Oh, is that so?" said Nick. "I'll make sure I get to the bottom of it and fire the responsible person."

'"One's got to ask who created such a lax and laissez faire atmosphere in the first place. Management must take the blame for such systemic failures," replied Gary.

'"Are you blaming the Customer Services Director or the Compliance Officer?" asked Nick, cheeky sod.

'"I have no quarrel with Kate. No, the buck has to stop with the Chairman or the Chief Executive," said Gary.

'"What are you suggesting?"

'"I'm banning Camelot Life from selling personal pensions and fining you £5m. If the backlog is not cleared by the year end the ban will be permanent and you two gentlemen will have to consider your positions"'

'Pretty damning,' I said. 'I'll see if I can help them.'

The following morning I phoned Bruce and asked him what he was up to.

'Life's hectic. I've taken over management of the pensions review team in addition to the day job of managing the finance function. No more resources but unlimited attention from the regulators. Enough of me; how are you doing?'

'I have a strategic management consultancy. Things are progressing. Actually we might be able to help each other.'

'How's that?'

'I can handle the calculations of compensation on any pensions misselling. Your customer services will continue to handle the case until it is established that there has been misselling. At that point they pass the electronic files over and we'd do all the complicated sums.'

'Can that work?'

'Absolutely.'

I had my first client.

We agreed a method of operation which then became the blueprint for other clients. I made sure that I didn't get involved in management decisions. By the time a case came through to *3Ps*, all that was required would be pure calculation. Any dispute on what the salesman said or didn't say would have been resolved. A detailed drill was established. Complex calculations were transformed into a well oiled production line. The calculations were performed from home by people with access to the *3Ps* computer network. I recruited a team of self-employed actuaries (either retired or laid-off) and paid them on a per case basis. Some care was required before signing off the calculations. A reasonableness test was required to stop silly answers being thrown up, for example if the decimal point was entered in the wrong place.

It wasn't long before I had the second and then the third client. After that, there was no stopping *3Ps*.

Two Years Later: 1996

Ellen phoned to ask if I was interested in a small assignment for MI5. It was our first contact for over two years. I responded cautiously saying:

'If it's within my skill range I would be delighted to assist. What is it?'

'We're having trouble breaking a particularly intractable numerical code. You don't need to know which country or what background; just to crack the code. You'll have to swear to secrecy.'

It was an opportunity to open lines of communication with Ellen. The assignment occupied me, on and off, for a month.

My new consultancy was the fastest growing business in the UK. From a standing start in mid-1993, I had built up fee income of £5m in 1995 and was on course to treble it this year. Of course salaries and other costs, have to come out of it but I still netted a profit of £2.5m last year, one-half of which I paid into a special purposes charity he had set up under the name of *Ecumenical Giving*. I appointed Gareth and Glynis as co-directors with myself to manage the charity.

Funny the life of a businessman. You do all the right analysis, identify a gap in the market that your own skill-set is capable of delivering to, design an attractive proposition and then; and then zilch business. Meanwhile your guardian angel, Gareth, hands an unexpected largesse on a plate. Luck does not guarantee success but don't try it without it.The success of the firm meant that I had to rent premises in Cribbs Causeway, a business park on the northern outpost of Bristol, close to the M5 exit. I used it as my Head Office and training room. It was more convenient than central Bristol for people to travel to for training. When the work expanded last year, I had recruited three senior people from Camelot: Bruce Herrington as the Operations Director with responsibility for delivery; Clive Grobbelar an actuary with pensions background with responsibility for the integrity of the calculation program and Ted Carty, IT specialist with knowledge of networks.

Bruce had been a casualty as Nick followed the policy of eliminating all potential competitors for his position. I gave each of them the right to a share of the profits; 12½% for Bruce, 10% for Clive and 7½% for Ted. They were entitled to take monthly drawings, which were deducted from their profit entitlement.

By the end of 1995 the workload had increased substantially. The regulators were getting irritated at the still slow rate at which disputes were being resolved by insurers. The insurers did not admit liability unless it could be demonstrated that their salesmen gave wrong advice. In many cases, notably with Black Gold, the initiative to switch to personal pensions came from the employee or ex-employee himself such was their loss of faith in their employer. Eventually the regulators issued a ruling that so long as loss was suffered there should be compensation regardless of whether the insurer was culpable or not. This certainly speeded up the process but increased the number of cases requiring compensation perhaps four-fold.

***

Early in 1996 it was announced that Sir Alfred Lyttleton and Nick Knights were stepping down from the board of Camelot and Ted MacAfee and Clem Hill taking over on an interim basis. Clem invited me to join the Camelot Group Board as a non-executive director warning me that a lot of irregularities had come to light, partly going back to Tim's days but more especially Nick's. He said that there will be an announcement shortly that Nick was facing criminal charges. He was accused of aiding and abetting money laundering.

I had to decline the offer as there was a conflict of interests. My consultancy had just taken off and a significant proportion of its income came from Camelot. The practice was too new to be able to withstand the loss of Camelot's business. If I was asked again in another couple of years I might be able to accept.

'Can we at least retain you as an adviser to the Board for six months? So much of what you warned us about has turned out to be prescient that we'd value your counsel.'

'I'd be delighted to help.'

'Right, the next Board is on the first of Feb.'

'I'd like to get up to speed on what's been going on in the last couple of years. Shall I get Kate to give me an update?'

'Yes, that'll be a good idea. I'd better phone her first to reassure her that it is OK to talk.'

Later that afternoon Kate phoned me, 'I gather you've been retained as an adviser and want an update from me?'

'Yes, Kate that would be nice. The sooner the better.'

I travelled up to London and met her in the pub in Paddington station. We exchanged pleasantries, ordered a round of drinks and a pie each and sat down in a quiet corner.

'You have a fair idea of what's been happening from our occasional meetings but now I can tell you everything and hold nothing back'

'I've been careful to make sure that I only give you tips on what to look for and let you do the finding. I didn't want to land either of us in trouble.'

'I know, I know. Let's start where I started. You showed me that press release of Camelot Estates and speculated as to why the figures were so good. One of the things you suggested was accounting irregularities.'

'What precisely were they doing wrong?'

'They were taking credit for estate agency commission as soon as an offer was made on a house, even though their stated accounting policy was not to do so until completion had taken place. Sometimes two offers are accepted on a house when there was competition for the property when obviously only one could complete. What's worse, when an offer was not completed they should at least have reversed or written off the commission they'd taken credit for. They didn't do that.'

'That's downright fraud but one that either Bruce's people or the auditors should have picked up.'

'They did last year, after I'd given them a steer. That's what led to Helena's departure.'

'How did they get suspicious?'

'The amount of commission owed to Camelot Estates had built up to several million whereas usually it is next to nothing. Commission is deducted from the sales proceeds before the transaction is completed. Bruce spotted this and brought it to Nick's attention. As you know Bruce was made redundant shortly afterwards as part of a cost-cutting exercise.'

'Of course that had nothing to do with his discovery of the fraud.'

'You mean accounting irregularities?'

'No, I mean fraud. Don't sanitise it and make it sound like a professional disagreement.'

'Anyway, Bruce now works for you so you can get chapter and verse from him.'

'He's been tight-lipped so far. What's this thing about money laundering?' I asked.

'But you must know about that surely?'

'No, you haven't told me about it yet.'

She gave me a puzzled look

'Don't look at me like that. I haven't a clue what you're talking about.'

'Oh come on, you must know that your girlfriend Ellen Evan is leading the investigation into money laundering by Nick.'

'Is she now? Well she's pretty tight-lipped about her work.'

'She needn't be any more as I will tell you. Do you remember ten years ago we turned down a billion dollar piece of business from a Henry Shilling one of Nick's brokers?' asked Kate.

'The Sultan of Brunei case?'

'That's the one. Can you remember the name of the client?'

'We never got that far. It foundered at the principles stage.'

'That's a shame. It came up again and against advice Nick accepted the business. I had to report it. They took their time but in the end they acted.'

'Did Camelot lose any money?'

'No, the money went in and out within a matter of a week and we were able to collect surrender charges which covered the broker's commission.'

'Was it the same idea?'

'No, it was a standard product, or rather a thousand of them each worth half a million. So it was only half a billion but no fancy footwork was needed. It went into and out of the cash fund.'

'Did he think he'd get away with it?'

'When we dug deeper we found that he'd been getting away with it for several years. The same Henry Shilling has been laundering money via Nick for several years but the amounts were just below the limits above which we carry out money laundering checks. But this time I've got him.'

'What did you do?'

'He'd obviously learnt from Tim Fredricks. Nothing implicating him was ever put in writing by him but I taped all his instructions.'

'That's underhand isn't it?'

'After your experience I wasn't going to let him get away with it.'

'What exactly did you tape?'

'I'll play it back to you one day. That's not all, the rest of the Board have thrown him to the wolves.'

'I suppose if they can't finger one person the entire Board is deemed guilty.'

'The prospect of prison certainly concentrates the mind.'

'Nick had the top job. What made him take such a risk?'

'I guess if you've got away with misdemeanours for over a decade you become a bit blasé. But as to why this one, I've got my theories.'

'Go on.'

'He got a large tranche of share options when he became Chief Executive and the share price was low. So he wanted to show improvement in sales to improve the share price.'

'I'm not sure where this is leading us to.'

'Well, when the misstatement of Camelot Estates was discovered the profits in that company dived into loss and the share price fell sharply. I suppose he was tempted to make up the loss.'

'So he fiddled the profits of Camelot Estates, wittingly or unwittingly got involved in money laundering.'

***

'So, you and Ellen are back together?' asked Gareth.

'Not exactly. She gave me a small MI5 assignment but that job is finished.'

'Still, that's a start. She still cares for you, only you, you know.'

'We'll see. That job's finished.'

'Look, I know you have a business to manage but Bruce runs the day-to-day operation. Your Cribbs Causeway offices are just off the motorway. Why don't you buy a bigger flat in London and ask her to move in with you?'

'What makes you think she'll want to?'

'I'm telling you she still cares for you. Anyway what have you got to lose?'

'OK. I'll think about it.'

I did think about it and decided that it was worth a try. I telephoned a couple of estate agents in the Knightsbridge area and asked them to send me details of flats for sale in that area. A whole sheaf of particulars landed on my doormat within a couple of days. I drew a short-list of three worthy of consideration, all in Rutland Gate.

Before I phoned Ellen, she phoned me on the *3Ps* number with another, highly confidential, code-breaking assignment. I had to go to London to meet a colleague of hers in her office.

I met him, a young man with the darting eyes commonly seen amongst the bright. He showed me two pages of coded text. Many of the characters were Roman, the odd ones Arabic and some that seemed to be Hebrew or Aramaic neither of which I knew. I was not sure that I could crack the code within the stipulated two weeks but had the innate self confidence that said 'no mathematical problem is beyond me.' Besides it was a chance to spend two weeks with Ellen and see if Gareth was right. So I accepted the assignment. For its duration I had to work from MI5's offices on a local computer not connected to any network. I booked into a hotel in Knightsbridge.

I met Ellen during the lunch break and then again in the evening. We went to her favourite Chinese restaurant in Brompton Road and spent three hours there each evening. Ellen was a little more open about her work. I had taken the secrecy oath prior to entering MI5 premises and seeing me there on a regular basis made her think of him more as 'one of us'.

I told her about my re-involvement with the Camelot Group.

'Yes, I know, Kate Spencer phoned to tell me.'

'I gather you're leading the investigation into money laundering which led to Nick Knights being charged.'

'Yes.' She spoke freely and with warmth. 'We've grown apart because I built a fortress round my work. There was a good reason for it. I was involved in city crimes and money laundering cases. Some of them involved your competitors; some your colleagues. I didn't investigate you but a colleague did.'

'Me?'

'Yes, but you were squeaky clean.'

'My colleagues?'

'The first of these was the 3R's.'

'The Royston brothers up to no good? I don't believe it. They maybe street-smart but they're not crooks.'

'Ruaridh Royston facilitated some large property transactions for Middle Eastern investors. These were cash transactions and we suspected that dirty money was being laundered. Ruaridh did not launder the money himself but the transaction facilitated it. There was one particularly large investor whose name was Omar Khayyam. We tapped his telephone to trap the investor but he was an elusive individual who used a pseudonym. But it led to other discoveries that will interest you.'

'What were they?'

'For example you said that Nick Knights overheard Ruaridh talking to his brother about another bid, which led to you raising your offer to ridiculous levels. Well, that never happened. Ruaridh was talking to his wife about her brother-in-law who was having an affair.'

'How can you be sure that that was the phone call he was overhearing?'

'We've bugged every call and you told me about it the same evening so we could pinpoint it. That's not the end of it. It was from Ruaridh's phone that Nick phoned Kate to say that you'd asked that the non-compete clause be deleted.'

'Why didn't you tell me this before? It could've saved my career?'

'I am sworn to secrecy. Besides phone tapping is illegal. All we can use it for is to force a confession.'

'I don't know whether to laugh or to cry.'

'But darling, you're a man of principles if ever there was one. What was I to do?'

'Principles are for the guidance of the wise and enslavement of the foolish,'

Ellen carried on, 'I can understand if you're angry with me or even if you never forgive me but don't do self pity. Look on the bright side. Now that it's out in the open we can work together to nail Nick. The other point concerns Ishtak. I'll break my oath and tell you something. You know he's entered Israeli politics. His opponents were dubbing him Jew-hater because of the stance he took in the Cambridge debate you organised. When it grew from irritation to a serious vote loser he started looking to counter attack the extreme right wing parties. He explored their links with right wing parties in the UK, some of whom are odd-bedfellows and that led to uncovering theft and money laundering. I'm leading the team assisting him.'

I was still in a daze so Ellen carried on, 'Two of the guys Ishtak was chasing were South Africans, Ben Shmeuli and Ariel Cohen. Do you remember them?'

'Yes,' I said, suddenly alert. 'Aren't they the Sword of Truth crooks?'

'Yes, they ran off to Venezuela with your Australian monies. In fact I went with Ishtak to Venezuela one Christmas to interrogate these guys. It was there where I slept one night with him; not in my flat on the day you saw the two of us together.'

I said, 'Look it's getting late and I've a full day tomorrow. Same time, same place?'

There was too much new information and my brain was scrambled. I tried to think things through in my own time, slowly. I could now understand why Ellen was trying to build a professional firewall round her. Who knows, she might even have had to investigate me. If now she felt more able to discuss some aspects of her work I ought to welcome her with open arms. Even her association with Ishtak made sense. But that doesn't mean she should sleep with him.

I agonised over it. As she said nobody's perfect. After all, although I'd been totally faithful to her, it is not as if I'd not fancied other girls. As Jimmy Carter said, 'I've been unfaithful in spirit if not in the flesh'. In the end I decided that Ellen was too precious and our bond too strong to be broken by a single episode. She'd made a peace offering and I'd better take it.

The following evening I raised my hand in a salute and said, 'Scouts honour, are we friends again?'

'Come here luv,' she said bringing me closer, 'I'm glad we've cleared the spurious gap between us. We've wasted six of the best years of our lives.'

'Through my bloody-mindedness.'

'And mine.'

As they went through their dinner, Ellen said, 'Do you want to hear more surprises?'

'Only if they're good ones.'

'They're not bad. You know the main character who was laundering money through Nick?'

'Kate didn't give me his name.'

'His name is Omar Khayyam.'

'Hang on, didn't you say that was pseudonym of a guy who purchased property in London through Ruaridh Royston?'

'Yes, the very same guy. Do you know who he is? He's Jalal Babar.'

'Well I'd never. Can't believe he's gone off the rails. How did you find out?'

'He's up to something with Ishtak. MI5 works with Mossad but Ishtak is not part of the Government. One wing of the MI5 is supplying him some information without MI5 proper, who deal with Mossad, knowing anything about it.'

'But how?'

'I can't tell you much more because it is supremely confidential. But you'll have an opportunity to meet both of them. They're planning a twentieth anniversary re-union of the debate in London. I was asked to check your availability.'

'I'd quite like to meet the pair of them. It's been ages.'

'The thing is, whilst they're very close in political outlook, they're quite different persons. Ishtak is squeaky clean and can't afford any hint of impropriety to survive in Israeli politics. He has no idea of Jalal's money laundering activities.'

'Someone will find out so he'd better watch out.'

'Do you want to hear more?'

'I'm not sure I can handle more surprises, but go on.'

'Nick wasn't helping Henry Shilling to launder money. It was the other way round.'

'You're making this up.'

'No, really. It seems that Nick had kept tabs on Jalal since Cambridge. When Jalal approached him for help with money laundering he used Henry as a tame broker.'

'But why would Jalal go to Nick for money laundering?'

'Banks used to be the vehicle for money laundering until they got their act together. Then these people targeted insurance companies as a soft touch.'

I didn't know whether to laugh or cry. I'd been put through the mincer by Nick, suffered professional humiliation, my private life put in disarray, and all the time the love of my life was sitting on evidence that could have exonerated me.

'Don't do self-pity, darling. I've agonised over it every night but I couldn't break my oath.'

'What hurts even more was that had it been the other way round I'd have done the same thing. Maybe we attach too much importance to duty and not enough to feelings.'

'Never again,' said Ellen.

'Me neither.'

At the end of the first week of my assignment, I said to her that I was thinking of moving to London and would like to move in with her. What did she think of the idea?

'I thought you said my flat was too pokey?'

'We'll buy a bigger flat. I've got enough money now; thanks to your Dad. Nineteen ninety six has been an exceptional year.'

'New flat, where?'

'Here in Knightsbridge. I've got details of three good ones in Rutland Gate.'

She took the documents from him saying, 'Rutland Gate's just round the corner.'

She perused the specifications. 'Hey they all look good.'

'My only concern was whether there was something wrong with the area. Why are three up for sale?'

'No it's a good area.'

'Shall we have a look this weekend?'

She concurred and I got in touch with the estate agent, a Camelot Estates branch, and asked them to set up the appointments. On Saturday we had a look at all three and made an offer on the first, which we liked best. The flat was unoccupied so completion within four weeks was feasible. Ellen's flat was put up for sale.

'Oh, there's one thing I forgot,' said Ellen.

'You'll need MI5's security clearance to move in with me but it ought to be a formality. You were vetted before you were offered the last assignment.'

'Was I? Nobody told me.'

'Oh they have ways of finding out. You'd better not ask. Orwell was right.'

There was the question of furnishing the flat. I left the selection to Ellen but finding the time for it was a problem. We had to wait until the second weekend to do that. As the second week was drawing to a close it looked as if the assignment would not be completed as the Eureka moment was not arriving. There was a real chance of failing to deliver. As often happens, the inspiration came in the early hours of the morning when in bed and by Friday it was clear that I had solved the problem but the task would not be complete for another two or three days. I agreed to carry on for another three days at no extra cost.

So that weekend I accompanied Ellen to select carpets curtains and furniture. After the assignment was over I returned to Bristol and did not return to London until the weekend following the completion of the purchase.

We moved in. As I was going to retain the Downleaze flat the only possessions I took with me were two suitcases of clothes and two boxes of files delivered by courier and the framed photograph of Ishtak, Ellen and Jalal Babar taken after the Cambridge debate, which used to hang in my study in Downleaze until I took it down recently. All of Ellen's possessions were transferred across from her flat.

The new flat was in a mess until the new furniture arrived, in stages over two months. But at least it had two easy chairs and a double bed. It was my first night of sex for, perhaps five years, I couldn't remember, certainly at least four years. It felt so good to be together again and, more important, see the joy in Ellen's face and demeanour that I wanted to propose to her. But an attack of nerves made me pull back at the last moment. 'What if she said, she preferred things as they were? It might fracture the bond we were recreating. No, it's better for the idea to come from her.

I appointed Bruce as the day-to-day-head, the managing partner of *3Ps*. That freed me to seek new clients rather than do the work. It also enabled me to spend most of my time in London; spending no more than a day and a half in Cribbs Causeway on average.

***

I invited Ellen to become a director of *Ecumenical Giving*. All of the paperwork and the investment of funds, I handled myself. I appointed an accountant to prepare the accounts and deal with tax. The directors collectively decided what cause to support.

I didn't want any publicity but without it progress was slow. As the funds had been generated out of financial consultancy, I was very keen to support any initiative designed to improve financial literacy in schools. We couldn't find a viable initiative to support.

A series of low key ads were placed in the national press. Perhaps I shouldn't have put it out under my name. I was inundated with request for support from Islamic chari- ties. The language in many cases was quite militant. I chose to ignore them all.

Instead, the trustees agreed to retain a quarter of million pounds as a reserve and distribute the remaining million equally between Oxfam, Princess Alice Hospice, Red Cross and Crisis.

***

'I've not had a decent holiday for a while,' said Ellen. 'Why don't we visit Lahore? I quite fancy a proper look.'

'Not sure. Mum'll want to make up for not looking after you the last time you were there. Two weeks of her introducing you to everyone under the sun and going out of her way to hide your Jewish background, frankly it'll be a punishment rather than a holiday.'

'But perhaps it is the necessary penance to win your hand.'

My eyes lit up.

'Are you proposing to me?'

'Yes.'

'We can't get married in Lahore, that'll be bigamy as Dad said…. I get it, its leap year, although leap-year-day is gone.'

'Should we wait four more years?' asked Ellen.

'Eight you mean? 2000 is not a leap year. No, forget Lahore, let's get married now. I'll phone the Registry Office.'

'Don't panic, I'm not going to change my mind. Let our parents enjoy it.'

'OK, let's have our holiday first. I'd leave Lahore for after we're married. Let's go to Kerala to visit Cochin your Mum and Dad grew up in.'

'I've a better idea. Let's get married and honeymoon in Cochin.'

That weekend we drove up to Mold and told Ellen's delighted parents. Glynis said she'd waited twenty years for this day. I then phoned my parents whilst Ellen and her parents waited anxiously. Dad answered the phone and the news went down well. He then handed over to Mum. Ellen was listening intently to my responses:

'Thanks Mum, her parents are delighted too.'

'No Mum it'll be a registry office wedding.'

'No, Mum we won't have an Islamic wedding afterwards.'

'If that means we'll not be married in the eyes of God, so be it.'

'No, Mum I'm not going to ask her to become a Muslim.'

'I'm sorry Mum, that's our position. We won't change our minds.'

I rang off and said to the others, 'She'll come round.'

Ellen mentioned that we were planning to honeymoon in Cochin and would like to visit her parents' old haunts. Gareth looked wistfully into the horizon,

'Those were the days, young and in love, peaceful surroundings, friendly neighbours, plenty of fish and plantains. I wonder what it's like now. Is Jewtown still there? And the synagogue I worshipped in?'

'We'll find out and let you know,' said Ellen.

I had a better idea.

'Why don't you come with us?'

'What, and spoil your honeymoon?'

'Come on, if you hadn't kick-started my consultancy, we would not be talking of a honeymoon. I'd be skint.'

Gareth was evasive so I pressed him further.

'Son, part of me wants to go back and re-live some idyllic days of my childhood but there are some bad memories that I don't want to rekindle.'

'What bad memories?'

'Something else I don't know about?' asked Ellen.

'Afraid so. darling. It's to do with our marriage,' said Glynis.

'You see we Jews got on well with others but not with each other. I a White Jew fell in love with Hannah a Black Jew. We secretly married, with a Hindu friend as witness. Life became hell and we had to emigrate. We left our parents behind and Mum died in disgrace and Dad emigrated to Israel but didn't survive long there.'

'What about Mum's parents?' asked Ellen.

'It was bad but not so bad for them. It's the White Jews that were the problem.'

'So what you told Dad when you first met him was a sanitised version?' I asked.

'I'm afraid so.'

'What about your wedding dress you asked me to wear at mine?'

'It was made for me but I couldn't wear it as we got wed in secret.'

'Why don't you come with us? Things may have changed.'

They decided that they would come, curiosity overcoming diffidence.

On the fourteenth October we got married in Mold Registry Office. Bruce Herrington who was the witness and the two sets of parents were the only ones present. Before the ceremony, the Registrar asked if there were any issues for either side with inter-faith marriage.

'None,' said Gareth, Glynis and Dad in turn.

'It is better to have loved and lost than ever to have lost at all,' said Mum.

'I beg your pardon?' asked the Registrar.

'What my wife is trying to say is that there are no issues,' said Dad.

'Oh, there are certainly no children,' said Mum.

'What are you talking about, woman,' said Dad.

'You're the one who said there are no issues. Issues, children. I was agreeing with you.'

'I see your point,' said the Registrar.

When we arrived at Cochin we took a cab to the Taj, a reasonable hotel. The cab wasn't air-conditioned and we had a most uncomfortable journey. Not only was it extremely hot, it was extremely humid too; the combination had Ellen gasping for breath.

'Is it particularly hot this year?' asked Gareth.

'It is always hot in Cochin,' said the driver.

'I don't remember it being this hot but I've been away for forty years.'

We stayed inside for the rest of the day to overcome jet lag and lack of sleep. The hotel was close to both the beach and a shopping centre. We went out for a stroll in the evening in search of a restaurant. Ellen couldn't believe the volume of traffic on the road. Neither Gareth nor Glynis could follow the spoken Malayalam, even written Malayalam was difficult as the type-face used for the script was slightly different.

The next day we hired a cab for the day and said to the driver, 'Take me to the Kadavumbagham synagogue. It used to be in Jewtown, I'm not sure what it's called now.'

'Jewtown is still there,' said the driver, 'but the synagogue's gone.'

'Gone?'

'Yes, maybe twenty years ago. They grow plants there.'

'What happened to the ancient scrolls?'

'You mean the Jewish bible? It went to another synagogue in Mattancherry, which is ten kilometres away.'

So, we went there. When we got there, the driver tried to park in a small gap between two parked cars. The space was insufficient so he bumped the car in front and switched off the engine. I put the handbrake on and got out.

The caretaker of the synagogue confused me. He had typical Semitic features and I instinctively expected him to converse in English or Hebrew. Instead he was speaking to a local visitor in fluent Indian language, presumably Malayalam. He then turned around to greet the tourists from England in fluent English.

'Hi, I am Abraham Ashkinazy and this is my wife Hannah. Our families had been in Cochin for several hundred years. We were kosher butchers. We migrated to England in 1952. It's a long time ago but I wondered if anyone from my generation is left. You don't look as if you were born before 1952.'

'No, I'm thirty-two. My father, Benjamin Aaron, was the rabbi then. I'm Isaac.'

'Ah I remember him well.'

'Is he still living?' I asked.

'No he died in 1979.'

They were shown giant Old Testament scrolls, copper plates, painted tiles, believed to be from China and magnificent chandeliers. Gareth bought some curios from the synagogue as a means of making a donation. He did not have enough local currency but they were prepared to accept traveller's cheques. When he furnished his passport, Isaac looked at it and said,

'Come on, what's your game?'

'What do you mean?'

'You're not Abraham Ashkinazy at all, you're Gareth Evan.'

'I'm sorry I didn't tell you. We changed our name when we migrated to England.'

'A likely story. Why would you want to do that?'

'In 1952, there was still some anti-Semitism in England.'

'Prove it?'

'What's your problem? If you don't want my money, I'll keep it. Good bye.'

With that we left the synagogue. We got back to the cab and asked the driver to take them to Glynis' parents' house. He started the engine only to find that it stalled. He looked reproachfully at me and said, 'Please leave the driving to me. Nobody engages the handbrake in Cochin.'

Glynis' parents had sold the family home for a knock down price when they emigrated to Israel. When the driver took them to the address, they found that the old house, which had tiled roof to keep the house cool had indeed been knocked down.

In its stead stood a garish concrete house. It must get very hot inside but perhaps it had air-conditioning.

They then went for a drive to see all the high points of the city. Seeing so many impressive church buildings dotted around the city I asked if there was a Christian majority in Cochin.

'Possibly. I seem to recall that there were more Christians and Muslims than Hindus and the Christians were wealthier. Do you know that their liturgy is in Aramaic which pre-dates Hebrew?'

'Well, you live and learn every day.'

As the evening came and the sun set the temperature became more bearable and there was a pleasant smell of jasmine acted as a counter to the smell of waste on the verges.

When we got back to the hotel, Gareth had visitors. First Isaac Aaron came with some questions:

'I've been checking my records. The last Ashkinazy, Daniel, emigrated in 1956. He was a widow.'

'That was my father.'

'The only other we have a record of was his son Abraham'

'That's me.'

'But he broke the taboo of not marrying a Black Jew. He left in disgrace and haste in 1952.'

'That's me.'

'You have the cheek to come back?'

'I can do what I like. We lead a very happy life in England, This is my daughter who's married this lovely young man. And look at you lot, where are you?'

There was a tiff as Isaac thought Gareth wasn't giving the respect a rabbi commanded, to which Gareth replied that he was being given as much respect as he deserved. Shortly after he left, two local policemen came to see Gareth. They spent an hour questioning his antecedents. Eventually Gareth gave him the name and address and phone number of another Keralan Jew who now lived in England. A call was made, the time difference being a help. Having obtained the corroboration the police left him in peace.

The next few days, we did the usual tourist journeys to the backwaters and to Cape Camorin although Kerala did not appear to cater for tourists. The people were unfailingly courteous and helpful but the facilities weren't there.

***

It was twenty years almost to the day since the famous Cambridge debate, when Ellen and I went to the Dorchester to meet Ishtak Brownstein. Jalal Babar was already there. He looked well settled and clearly had been there for a while and must have done all the catching up as, for the entire duration of our stay they, Ishtak and Jalal, said nothing of significance to each other. Instead we were the focus of their conversation.

Ishtak wished he hadn't taken part in the Cambridge debate.

'It has put me back perhaps ten years in Israeli politics.' .

'Would you have been Prime Minister by now?' I asked.

'No, I'm not known well enough in Israel. No, the real problem is that I've had to dissemble, pretend to be a hard-line right-winger opposed to any deal with the Arabs.'

'You still believe in peaceful coexistence with the Arabs do you?' I asked.

'Actually, at the moment hatred of the Arabs is what unites the Israelis. If that disappeared the world would see how disunited the citizens of Israel are. The indigenous Jews hate the European Jews, the Ashkenazi's hate the Yiddish Jews, etc etc.'

'Watch it,' said Ellen. 'I'm an Ashkinazy.'

'You mean you're just the same as the Arabs, the Pakistanis and the rest of the world?' I asked.

We rambled on without giving much away although I got the clear sense that the old fire still burned in both Ishtak and Jalal.

I don't know whether Jalal suspected that I knew but I certainly felt uncomfortable knowing that he was a serial money-launderer. I don't know how Ellen felt dealing with him. I asked her on our journey back.

'I've never had to deal with him. It's a question you should ask Ishtak not me but then again he's a politician.'

'I've been thinking,' I said. 'You know the safe deposit firm, *Mazboot Aur Mahfooz* was it, that got burgled. Was Jalal behind it?'

'He was certainly the owner and he almost certainly was the man behind the burglary. We've had trouble confirming that. A lot of the theft was of goods belonging to his own colleagues. So there were a lot of accusations flying around.

1997

I was now practically an absentee owner. My strategic consultancy was no more than a calculation engine not an actuarial or strategic consultancy. New clients were coming in on the strength of its reputation for the speed and accuracy of calculations for pensions misselling compensations. I was not actively seeking to widen the scope of services.

I was enjoying married life, rediscovering the charms of Ellen, something I had feared I'd lost for ever. I'd even got my sense of smell back. Oh what fragrance she has. One evening we were chewing cud and Ellen asked me

'Do you remember when you became an actuary; Tim put you in the claims department to get you to be less of a figures-freak?'

'Numbers-gnome, not figures-freak.'

'Whatever.'

'Any regrets?'

'None. It's been a rough ride but worthwhile. I've got money in the bank and a pipeline of business three years long. The business runs itself. I've got you back and am happy to be a house-husband for as long as you wish to carry on working.'

'Do you really mean it?'

'Yes, I do.'

'You certainly gave every impression of having discovered heaven on earth.'

'I have, I have. Wasn't it Milton who wrote Paradise Lost and Paradise Regained?'

'Yes, have you read them?'

'No, but the titles describe what I've lost and found.'

'What will you do with yourself, you're still too young to retire?'

'I could spend all day watching you, your long golden tresses, your twinkling eyes.'

'Stop it, you're gushing like a teenager.'

'Wasn't it Oscar Wilde who said "Youth is so precious it's a shame to waste it on the young"?'

'Is this another of your corny jokes?'

'When I was young I was accused of being autistic, avoiding touchy-feely things. Now in middle age I've become very tactile. My sense of smell has come back. I blame you for it.'

As usual, Ellen was right. I had to do something. I revived my interest in comparative religion. Islam has always fascinated me. The version that exists today has buried the original message under subsequent accretions. Like the concept of the Trinity with

Christianity, there were features that modern clerics purport to be intrinsic to Islam that are not.

'People forget that the core purpose of all religions is the same,' I said to Ellen.

'What's that?'

'Have a guess.'

'The righteous path.'

'That's true but I was thinking of helping the needy, a form of social function. Insurance does the same thing but that's lost its way too.'

The problem was having a sensible debate on these matters. I had no credentials in this sphere. It saddened me. Instead, I started taking an active interest in politics. The Tory party I felt was ungovernable and it was time for a change.

'You're up to your old tricks,' said Ellen.

'Meaning?'

'You're voting against a party rather than for one.'

'Yes and no. I'm quite taken in by New Labour. It might all be hype and spin but if they do some of the things they say, like taking the setting of the interest rates out of the political arena and improving the regulation of the city, that would be a good thing.'

'What about social reform?'

'They have better credentials than the Tories but whether they'll deliver remains to be seen.'

I was pleased when New Labour won. But other than that I took little active interest in political or financial affairs. I no longer read the Financial Times or actuarial journals. My only contact with the world I once lived in was the occasional phone call from Kate or Ted. Kate phoned whenever she needed a second opinion. Sometimes she phoned to update me on matters of interest to me; such as the prosecution of Nick Knights. Ted phoned me perhaps once a quarter, trying to entice me out of exile back into the fray. I kept declining.

Then JM, the analyst specialising in insurance company shares, started a campaign via the press saying that what Camelot needed was the guiding hand of Majid. JM had been an avid reader of the Newsletters issued by *3Ps*. In his own Newsletter he said,

'Clem Hill, who has been running the company since 1997 has proved a safe but uninspiring leader. The company had gone nowhere in the past two years. Admittedly tales of fraud have ceased but the company is still haemorrhaging funds as customers have lost faith in them. It is clear that investors have lost faith too as evidenced by the continuing fall in the share price.

Majid in his time with Camelot showed considerable flair and since he set up 3Ps great strategic insight. He's the man Camelot now needs.'

I discussed this with Ellen and said, 'It's best to quit when you're still wanted. I'll resist any pressure to return to Camelot.'

'It's your call luv but you're too young to be doing nothing.'

'I'll do something else. I've had enough of Camelot, enough of insurance. In fact I want to sell *3Ps* and let Bruce run the show.'

'That's your call but do something with your brain.'

'I'd still be available for anything MI5 care to throw at me.'

***

I had a letter from Ellen, marked Strictly Private and Confidential' and sent to my Cribbs Causeway office.

'*Dear Mr. Khan,*

'*The preliminary trial of Nick Knights, the former Chief Executive of Camelot Insurance group of companies is scheduled to take place in November. In similar trials we have been unable to secure convictions. In order to avoid tripping on technical detail, we would like to hold a mock trial in September and would welcome your participation.*'

I sent a short letter in reply confirming my attendance. The following evening, knowing that Ellen would have received his reply, I said to her:

'You haven't forgotten that we've booked a two week holiday in October?'

'That's why the mock trial is in September and the preliminary trial in November,'

'I can believe the first part but not the second. Surely you've fitted your holiday around the trial rather than the other way round?'

'You know what I mean, you pedant.'

Although she would not discuss the details she mentioned that night that she was having trouble getting hold of Nick. She had to make sure that he was available on the date set for the preliminary trial.

'I've tried his mobile, his land line, his cottage in Suffolk. I've even asked his old secretary. The only plausible explanation is that he's on holiday abroad.'

'Still there's nearly two months left, no need to panic.'

'If I can't reach him within the next fortnight the trial would have to be postponed. He would have reasonable grounds to request it.'

She added, 'I'd better alert Terry Leather of the Metropolitan Police, to the possibility that Nick is missing.'

'How will the mock trial work? Obviously Nick won't be there.'

'We will have a stand in. Dad has agreed to do it.'

'Gareth?'

'Yes, he's got a lot of swatting to do'

On the morning of the mock trial Ellen spoke with Paul Pritchard the head regulator. 'I'm increasingly convinced that we will fail to secure a conviction.'

'He's certainly a very slippery customer and one I would love to see justice be done to,' said Paul.

***

The mock trial took place at 10.30am on Monday 15th September 1997 in the head regulator's office in Canary Wharf. By the time the preliminary trial took place the regulator's role would pass to a new body, the Financial Services Authority. The mock trial would be conducted assuming that the transition had taken place.

It was my first visit to the Canary Wharf, the extension of the city into reclaimed dockland. As land cost so much less than in the city, the property developers could put up state-of-the-art buildings at much lower rent and still make a handsome profit. Two things struck me. The streets were much wider and much of the area was still a building site. As I was short of ready cash I looked for my bank and was surprised to find that it was operating out of what looked like a portakabin.

When I arrived at the regulator's offices I had to confront their security. A secretary had to come and fetch me and take me to the designated meeting room. A number of people each with a role to play were present. The list was as follows:

Character	Played by
Nick Knights	Gareth Evan
Judge	Ellen Evan
Ashley Dunmore-Bexley	Himself (Prosecuting barrister)
Defence lawyer (DL)	Kim Alabaster
Paul Pritchard	Himself
Sir Alfred Lyttleton	Himself
Bruce Herrington	Himself
Kate Spencer	Herself
Ted Macafee	Himself
Henry Shilling	Himself

Judge   Mr Knights, I have here a document with a profusion of charges. I'm going to concentrate on just two for the moment.

The first charge is that you facilitated the laundering of substantial sums of money by a man who was travelling under the name Omar Khayyam. How would you like to plead?

DL   Your Honour. My client pleads not guilty.

Judge   I'd like to hear what he has to say before forming a view

Ashley   Your Honour, I'd like to call my first witness, Henry Shilling

Mr. Shilling, what is your occupation and what is your relationship with the defendant?

Henry   I am an independent financial adviser based in Macclesfield. I've known the defendant for ten to twelve years, having first met him when he was the marketing manager for Camelot Life.

Ashley	When was your most recent involvement with the defendant.
Henry	That was several years ago. He moved into their estate agency business and I lost contact.
Ashley	Last year, on 14th of November you placed a substantial investment with Camelot Life on behalf of a non-UK resident client. Can you remember the amount and the name of the client?
Henry	I remember both. It was half a billion pound but I cannot reveal the name of the client.
Judge	If you withhold information, you will be guilty of contempt of court and will receive a custodial sentence.
Henry	OK but you must promise not to divulge it to anyone else.
Judge	I can promise you nothing except justice.
Henry	His name is Omar Khayyam
Ashley	How did Omar Khayyam come to know you?
Henry	He has used me before.
Ashley	Has he now. OK, tell me how he came to know you, the first time he came to you?
Henry	It was through Nick Knights
Ashley	You mean the defendant introduced you to him?
Henry	Yes
Ashley	How did that come about?
Henry	I understand that the two of them know each other from Cambridge. Omar Khayyam was looking for an investment vehicle and approached Mr Knights. As Camelot Life deal through brokers, he passed the lead on to me. That was the last time we met.
Ashley	I've finished with this witness, your Honour
DL	Did you not wonder why Omar Khayyam, a man living in the Middle East, would choose you to place a half billion investment when he could have chosen a London or offshore bank?
Henry	In my business sometimes you work very hard for no reward, sometimes riches land in your lap. I've learned not to question good fortune.
DL	Really? Are you not aware of the requirements of Money Laundering Act?
Henry	But I didn't handle any money. Payment was by cheque which was passed to Camelot. It was their duty to check.
DL	Which bank was the cheque drawn on?
Henry	Can't remember. It was a Pakistani bank.

DL	I put it to you that there was sufficient doubt about the source for you to alert the authorities. I put it to you that the duty of care, in the first instance, fell on you.
Henry	I don't agree. Anyway, it's not my trial.
DL	Have you been offered immunity from prosecution?
Judge	The Defence team is aware that Mr. Shilling has been given such immunity. However he's still under oath.
DL	I reserve the right to ask further questions at a later date but for the moment I have no more.
Ashley	Your Honour, I'd like to call my next witness, Kate Spencer Miss Spencer, what is your relationship with the defendant?
Kate	I was the Company Secretary, Compliance Officer and Money Laundering Officer of the Camelot group of companies. Mr. Knights was its Chief Executive from 1992 to the date of his resignation.
Ashley	Can you recall the circumstances surrounding the half billion pound investment Mr. Shilling tried to place with Camelot?
Kate	Yes, I do.
Ashley	Can you describe it to the court?
Kate	In accordance with our guidelines on money laundering, the new business processing manager placed us on alert and sought clearance to proceed with the application. In view of the size of the investment, the case was escalated to me.
Ashley	What happened?
Kate	It failed the basic smell test. The client
Ashley	(interrupting) You mean Omar Khayyam?
Kate	Yes. He was very evasive and declined to be interviewed, even on the telephone. Also, the cheque was drawn against the Daulat Bank of Pakistan which in itself fails the smell test.
Ashley	So what did you do?
Kate	I told Bristol branch to turn down the business and informed the police.
Ashley	Did you tell anyone that you'd informed the police?
Kate	I observed standard procedure which is not to tell anyone.
Ashley	Did the matter end there or was there any plea for reconsideration?
Kate	There was no such plea and I thought it had ended there. However, when the sales figures for that month were announced there was a spike in the sales from Macclesfield branch. I checked and found to my surprise that the investment had been accepted.
Ashley	Did you investigate why?
Kate	No, I asked Internal Audit to investigate

Ashley	The Internal Auditor will take the witness stand in due course. Can you tell me your version of events?
Kate	He established that Nick Knights had given an oral sanction to the Macclesfield branch manager.
Ashley	Only oral? Surely he would have insisted on confirmation in writing. After all, he'd be very vulnerable without it.
DL	He could have taken it upon himself to accept the business.
Kate	No, new business department would not process the business if neither I nor Nick had sanctioned it.
Ashley	So why did they?
Kate	The new business manager said that he had received oral sanction.
Ashley	Is it not strange that both the branch manager and the new business manager claim to have received oral instructions? Could they be colluding?
Kate	I can't comment on that but there have been past instances of oral instructions.
Ashley	Really, by whom?
Kate	By Nick Knights and by Tim Fredricks, his predecessor.
Ashley	I have no further questions, your Honour.
DL	All you have is two men's word with no corroborating evidence. Would you agree that there could conceivably be another explanation?
Kate	I can't think of one.
DL	Couldn't the two of them be in collusion?
Kate	They could be but they'd both know that it would be an offence that would lead to imprisonment.
DL	But they might be prepared to take that risk if they were well rewarded by Omar Khayyam
Kate	Have you any evidence of such rewards?
DL	I ask the questions, you answer them. Would you agree that you've not got a shred of corroborative evidence against my client?
Kate	I would submit that the two managers corroborate each other.
Ashley	I have no further witnesses
Judge	In that case the meeting is adjourned until 9am on Friday 19th, when we will consider the second charge.

All of them stayed on for a review of the proceedings.

'Why wasn't I cross-examined?' Gareth asked Ashley.

'That was deliberate; we didn't want to give Nick a soap box.'

Ellen asked him:

'Do you think the charge will be sustained?'

'I think so. Henry and Kate's evidences were pretty useful,' said Ashley.

'I found the whole exercise artificial,' I said.

'It was nevertheless useful,' said Paul. 'When we reconvene later in the week, shall we cut out the procedural formalities and stick to the facts and arguments?'

'What do you mean?' asked Ellen.

'Cut out references to Your Honour; stop asking questions about relationships.'

'Let's do that,' said everyone in unison.

'The tricky thing is defending Nick. We don't know everything that he knows. All we've made sure is that Kim knows everything we know. That's the best we can do.'

That evening Ellen had a phone call. I became concerned as he listened to her responses.

'Ellen speaking'

'Yes we did.'

'But it had all been set up. Cancelling it would have raised more questions.'

'I'm trying to ensure that a conviction does not fail on a technicality.'

'I really wish you wouldn't do that.'

'OK. I can't ignore an order.'

'Good bye.'

'Something fishy's going on,' said Ellen. 'I've been instructed to cancel Friday's meeting. No mock trials.'

'Why?'

'Apparently it's not the done thing.'

A week later Ellen returned home from work looking very grim-faced.

'Just as I feared. He's got away with it?'

'Who's got away with what?'

'Nick. Whilst we were away, the money laundering case against him was dropped.'

'You're the one who brought the charge against him. How can someone else drop it?'

'My superior can. That's why he's superior.'

'Does he think that you can't win?'

'I don't think so. It wasn't inability to prove his culpability but political pressure from the Foreign Office. I can't say much more.'

'Why, don't you trust me or do you not know all of the facts?'

'Both. I certainly don't know the full story but mainly because it is higy confidential; something to do with it being an inopportune moment to charge Jalal Babar.'

I tried to work out the significance of this development. Ellen, misreading my mind said,

'Don't worry. I got the news from Paul Pritchard not from my boss. Paul is taking steps to ban Nick from holding directorships for the foreseeable future. He will be deemed to be an unfit and improper person. He won't trouble you any more.'

'It's easy to say that. Goodness knows what damage he'd do. This changes everything. I'd better do something about it.'

The following day I got in touch with Tracy Pitt and asked him to seek out a buyer for my stake in *3Ps*. I told him that it was on track to generate profit this year of £22.5m on a turnover of £30m.'

'Its spectacular growth has been on the back of managing compensation calculations on missold personal pensions. That probably has another four years to run but we've demonstrated our capacity to react to opportunities.'

'Will you continue to be involved?'

'No. It means that some confidential work which I had personally done for MI5 will not be repeated but in terms of income that was not material. More important, it is Bruce Herrington who runs the consultancy on a day-to-day basis and he stays.'

'Do you own 100% of the equity?'

'No, the management team own 30%. They'd consider selling two-thirds of their stake if the price is right.'

'But they will stay?'

'Yes.'

'So in total 90% of the equity is up for sale with the management team in situ?'

'Yes.'

'Leave it with me. I'll make some preliminary soundings. I think we may find a buyer without doing a formal prospectus.'

***

Shortly after that I had a call from Ted MacAfee inviting me for a chat with the Board of Camelot. I went to the meeting out of curiosity.

'Majid, long time ago you said to my predecessor Sir Alfred McAlpine that we should cut our losses and sell off Camelot Estates. Well a few years and more losses later we've done that. You said we might get a pound for that. We've done better, we've got a hundred pound, but the debt mountain is bigger.'

'At least you've done it,' I said.

'Everyone seems to think that you are what Camelot needs. Would you be interested in returning as Chief Executive?'

'I'm not looking to return. Life is good as it is. I've nothing to prove by coming back.'

'You never made it to the top job. Surely you'd like to see whether you would have been a success had the opportunity come your way?'

'If I succeed now it won't prove that I'd have succeeded then. Besides I have no ego. Nor does it worry me that Nick is free.'

'Think about it. We'd like you to return to claim what many people thought was your crown.'

'Thanks but no thanks.'

'OK, I won't press you any further. However we would like to hear what plans you might have had if you did return.'

'That's a hypothetical question but without a clear cut answer. Everyone who was around at the time is aware that I had grave reservations about the strategy pursued by Tim Fredricks. A lot has happened in the last ten years not just at Camelot but in the wider commercial and social environment. Frankly I see no future for insurance. And even less for Camelot.'

'So are we doomed to fail?'

'Not doomed to fail but doomed to a lot of hard work with no guarantee of success. You have three options.'

'What are they?'

'The first option recognises the fact that there is no future for insurance. So we close Camelot down, cease trading and run off the existing book of business in an orderly fashion and in a way that maximises the returns to the various stakeholders. The first step would involve buying out the existing shareholders. As the share price has collapsed it would be a good time to do it.'

'Sounds like a controlled destruction of Camelot,' said Ted.

'That's a very apt description but one I'd prefer not to use as the term "destruction" suggests wilful extinction.'

'How long would the process take?'

'My guess is that within ten years the company would have got to a non-viably small size and would then merge with a bigger player.'

'So from the staff's point of view they'd have to look for new jobs within a decade.'

'Much sooner in many cases as our cost base would need to be shrunk. For a start we'd need fewer directors.'

'What's the second option?' asked Ted.

'To do a King Canute. Buck the trend and go back to the origins of insurance. In the future target only customers who believe that insurance is a social function. Perhaps they should be church or mosque or synagogue-goers.'

'What about other faiths?'

'Oh any faith, I'm just giving an example. But there's a point here. Under this option our customers would be the Chosen People; people who're part of a collective undertaking for mutual self-help. Although only Judaism talks of the Chosen People and with them it is a tribal thing, Christianity and Islam are similar.'

'So what's the third option?'

'We could try and back ourselves to make better decisions than our competitors, or at least some of our competitors and slowly haul ourselves from the second to the first and ultimately back to the Premier League.'

'That sounds like a typical ten year plan.'

'It'll be a long haul and investors and policyholders would have to be patient. Our communications will have to be excellent for them not to lose patience.'

'The shareholders won't wait; they have the attention span of a gnat,' said Clem.

'So the first thing we'd have to do is to buy them out and become a mutual.'

'You'd be bucking the trend. Most mutuals are going the other way,' said Clem.

'They expanded too fast.'

'OK, which of the three do you prefer?' asked Ted.

'I sit on the sidelines. Which does the Board prefer?'

'We'd like to hear your views first.'

'My preference is for the second option but I don't think it'll work. People will revert to type.'

'Why not the third?'

'We'd simply be aping our successful competitors without their advantages. It'll be like entering a Formula 1 race without a racing car.'

'Majid, you keep slipping into using "we" rather than "You". You obviously still care for us. I offer you the job on the basis that we do an in-depth study of options 2 and 3 before choosing one. We'd then have to sell the strategy to our shareholders,' said Ted.

'So we do a detailed study of options 2 and 3 and then we select option 1?'

'No, that would be silly; we select the better of options 2 & 3.'

'That makes sense subject to the caveat that if detailed study rules out both options 2 and 3 then you're left with only the first.'

'Agreed. You make the obvious sound profound.'

'Under option 2 you likened us to the Chosen People. You choose and lead us. I see you as our Moses,' said Ted.

'I don't get it.'

'You take us across the Red Sea to the Promised Land.'

'But there's a difference,' said Clem with a smile. 'Moses took his flock to the Promised Land. Majid is asking us to choose between turning left or turning right or even going straight on. He's not telling us which way the Promised Land is. '

'With the benefit of hindsight we know that Moses should have turned right,' said Ted.

'Why's that?' asked Clem.

'Because his people would now have all the oil reserves and the other lot would have to make do with avocados and jaffa oranges.'

'OK I accept it as an intellectual challenge. I'll do it for two years, or at the most three and then retire having sorted out Camelot's future. But there are two things I must do first. First and foremost, I must talk it over with my wife.'

'Are you married now? You've kept that quiet,' said Clem.

'Married for a while now, 14th October 1996 was the day I married Ellen.'

'Please accept congratulations from me and the rest of the Board,' said Ted. 'Of course you must talk to her. What's your other point?'

'I have to sell my consultancy to avoid conflict of interest. Give me a few months.'

'Assuming that Ellen is in favour, shall we say that you'll take over on 1st July?'

'OK.'

I had of course already decided to come out of retirement. Ellen was aware of it and delighted.

1998

Tracy let me know that he'd been able to find potential buyers for my consultancy. As it concerned the entire management team, a meeting was arranged in Tracy's office in London.

'Hello guys, I've got good news for you. You asked me to place 90% of *3Ps*' equity. I'm pleased to tell you that I've done that.'

He grinned whilst waiting for a reaction.

'Go on, don't keep us in suspense.'

'I've found a private equity firm prepared to buy 60% and four private investors who have made an offer for the remaining 30%. '

'At the right price?' asked Bruce.

'I think you'd like it. It values the firm at £90m.'

'Which private equity firm?' I asked.

'High Noon.'

'I've heard of them as being OK. Have they got the cash?'

'They do, although this transaction will cost them £54m and clean them out.'

'Who're the private investors?' asked Majid.

'One of them is Gareth Evan, your father-in-law. He's buying 10% for £9m.'

'Gareth? Gosh, he's a dark horse. He's got the cash from selling off his meat business.'

'The other three are a Middle Eastern gentleman called Omar Khayyam, who's also buying 10% for £9m and Nick Knights and Archie Balaskas, your ex-colleagues each of whom is buying 5% for £4.5m.'

'I can't sell to those three.'

'Why what's wrong with them?'

'I can't sell to them.'

'If you can't give a valid reason for rejecting their offer, you will be in trouble.'

'I don't like Archie and there are money laundering issues with the other two.'

'I'll have to tell them that.'

'They know. How did you get in touch with Nick?'

'I didn't. His lawyer got in touch with me.'

'Anyway, I won't sell to either of those two and I'd rather not sell to Archie. Does that mean that I'll be left holding 30% of the shares?'

'You really have no choice with Archie if you wish to avoid a lawsuit. With the other two, depends how you want to play it. The management team were intending to retain one third of their 30%. If that is still intended then you'd be left holding only 15%. However I need to get back to High Noon and Gareth to confirm that they stand by their offer?'

'Hang on a minute,' said Bruce. 'Our views should matter more than Majid's. We are the management and we'd have to live with the new owners.'

Tracy was caught off guard. He turned around and asked, 'Are you worried about Archie?'

'Yes, I won't work for him,' said Bruce and his colleagues nodded in assent.

'OK, I'll block Archie and see what happens.'

The meeting ended and we left. On our way back, Bruce again reiterated that he wouldn't work for Archie who was a 'conman'. I said I understood. Back in their Cribbs Causeway office, I alerted Ellen to the fact that Nick and Omar had tried to take a stake in *3Ps*. She thanked me for the tip off and promised Tracy a hard time. In fact Nick was easy to trace as he was back living in his home. Omar she was asked to stay clear of.

Tracy was back on the phone to me to say that both High Noon and Gareth were prepared to stick with their offer and Nick and Omar, whilst disappointed did not demur. Archie was a problem. Unless someone offered a better deal, he demanded justice.

A meeting was arranged, in Cribbs Causeway, between Archie, and the *3Ps'* directors. Archie arrived in his Porsche but he was not alone. He brought his side-kick Jeff Hamilton-Jones with him.

'I want to know,' began Jeff, 'why this meeting is necessary?'

'You, I mean Archie, asked for it,' I said.

'Jeff is right, the meeting is unnecessary. I matched the best price offered, so I should get the shares I asked for. It's not as if it was oversubscribed.'

'Yeah, what's wrong with his money? Isn't it good enough for you? Isn't it?' asked Jeff.

The normally restrained Bruce Herrington suddenly found his voice:

'I'll tell you what's wrong with it, it is ill-gotten. Archie is a thief and an imposter.' He then turned his wrath on to me and said, 'If you sell out to this Archie then I'd resign.'

'So would we,' said the other members of the management team.

'That'll suit me fine,' retorted Archie. 'I'd bring in my old management team.'

'Majid, don't let us down. We helped build this business, don't throw us to a wolf.'

'OK, instead of selling my entire holding, I'd retain 5% so that only 85% of the shares are available for sale. That has already been spoken for with the other investors. Sorry Archie.'

'Archie peered through his glasses and said, 'You dragged me all the way here to tell me that? I'll make you pay for this.'

He left in a huff, dragging Jeff as a mother would drag a recalcitrant child, and tore off in his Porche. I was thanked profusely for the stance I took. I still had a problem of conflict of interest if I was to take up the job of running Camelot. I got round it by rearranging my donation to *Ecumenical Giving*. Instead of donating it half his annual income, I'll gift them 20% of the shares of *3Ps* and Ellen and I would resign from the Board of the charity. A lot of paperwork, but eminently do-able.

***

On the first of July, I became the Chief Executive of Camelot Life. After making an appearance in the London office first thing in the morning, I spent the rest of the first day in the Bristol office. I called a meeting of all head office staff. Colleagues in the other cities were able to watch it by television monitor.

'It's great to be back in the Company I always regarded as home and among people I regard as my extended family.

'Camelot, once a strong company is now a weak company.

'Even when we realised that we were punching above our weight, we did not cease doing so.

'Our more canny competitors did go through a period of austerity and are now well placed to kick forward.

'It's our turn now.

'For a few years we have to live,

'not beyond our means,

'not within our means,

'but below our means.

'The directors are setting an example

'All of us are taking a 30% cut in salary

'First class rail travel is out

'The directors' flat in St James Square will be sold

'The Directors' Dining Room will be closed down

'There is a downside.

'You people will now have to eat with us.

'Many of you have subscribed to our SAYE scheme and have share options that are standing at a loss.

'I ask you to show patience. With your help, we'll turn the company around.

'We need your help, firstly in determining our future strategy. I plan a series of workshops, shortly. Then we need your help in implementing it.

There were quite a few questions. The principal one was:

'Why are the directors making so many sacrifices and what will they get in return?

'We have to show the way and hope that you will follow suit. What do we get in return? There will be a compensatory bonus if the chosen strategy is successful.'

***

The directors and senior management took part in a strategy weekend. To get the widest possible debate a dozen policyholders, staff and their families (three of whom were Gareth, Glynis and Ellen) and key opinion formers such as John Michael were invited. Two strategies were going to be debated. I would lead the discussion in favour of *Camelot, the Chosen Company for the Chosen People*, and Ted MacAfee in favour of *Camelot, the Fallen Star Rising*.

I began by saying:

'Ladies and gentlemen, Ted and I will argue different points in an attempt to put the case of each to you. Please do not vote on the basis of whether you like me or Ted more. Neither of us will be offended if you vote for the other point of view. We want to arrive at the best decision and you're here to help us.

'Right, I will begin.

'When life assurance began in its modern form two centuries ago, it had a social purpose and the management had a social conscience. The growth of the welfare state took some of the basic need away. More recently people have become more selfish. Everyone is in it for himself. This undermines the basic principle of insurance, the healthy subsidising the unhealthy, the affluent the less well off.

'We should create an environment where Camelot is the Chosen insurance company for a Chosen group of people who share a common view; that of mutual self-help. Financial self help would be provided by means of life insurance policies whilst emotional support will be provided by a network of mentors.

'Why do I recommend this? Because, it gives us a distinct identity. Because I believe that there is a need for it. The use of a mentor service plugs a gap created by the decline of vicars, bank managers and doctors as shoulders to cry on. In effect Camelot assumes the welfare bit of religion without the God bit.

'How do we vet new policyholders? I don't have an answer yet.

'What do we do with those existing policyholders who don't buy into this strategy? Again I don't have an answer yet.'

I invited questions from the floor.

'Have you researched how big a market there is?' asked John Michael. I said that needed to be ascertained.

Gareth Evan asked:

'Is it wise to call ourselves the Chosen People. It is clearly a powerful bonding slogan for those who're in it but it provokes animosity towards it from others. Think of what the Jewish people have been through. Think of the freemasons.'

'Are you against it?'

'No I'm not but just don't call them the Chosen People.'

'Can you cost justify having mentors?' asked John Michael again.

'We'll have to look at that.'

'Will there be restrictions in investment powers, for example by excluding socially undesirable investments?' asked John Michael again.

'That would have to be considered but my instinct says that that's going a step too far.'

'I sense that this meeting is premature as you don't have answers for many key questions,' said Phil Bunyon.

'If I had answers for all of them I'd be presenting you with a fait accompli. I thought it was better to have your input before then.'

'I can't argue with that.'

I said, that was enough for the moment. Let Ted speak his case.

'I put it to you that modern man is selfish and the Biblical exhortations to help thy neighbour fall on deaf ears. Just look at the decline in numbers attending church. Look how far right the left wing parties of most countries have shifted. We should not buck the trend but instead go with the flow.'

I propose therefore that we continue on our present strategy and set a goal of once again becoming a top-six company. It'll take us longer because past failures have depleted our resources but it's the right thing to do.'

John Michael asked, 'How long will it take and will you need more capital?'

'Too long, I'm afraid. Fifteen, possibly twenty years. Yes we may need more capital.'

'No chance.'

'If that's the case, we'd buy them out.'

At the end of the two days there was a show of hands which did not show a clear majority in favour of either, I won 52:48. It was decided that, as both options involved buying out the current shareholders, Camelot should proceed with that and at the same time seek answers to several issues that my option raised.

And, no they won't call themselves the Chosen People.

***

I called Tracy Pitt for advice regarding changes to Camelot. Clem Hill also attended the meeting.

'Tracy, we want to buy out the shareholders and make a couple of other changes.'

'Always ready to help, Majid, you know that.'

'Yes, but this time you are acting for me not against me.'

'No, we were on the same side as I recall.'

'You could've fooled me.'

'No, seriously, I was retained by Tim Fredricks and my brief was…'

'Yea, yea yea. Now listen just as carefully to the brief I now give you.' He then explained the new rationale for Camelot and that the shareholders would not have the patience to wait for the results. So he wanted to buy back the shares unless another way could be found to buy their consent.

'Understood.'

'Well, let's look at some figures now. Camelot's share price is currently £4.75. In the past twelve months it has traded in the range £4.75-£5.75. I think if we offered our shareholders £6.00/share they'd accept,' I said.

'If you offer £6.00 they'd push you up to £6.50 but you should get a deal.'

'I see.'

'At £4.25 a share the group is valued at £1,275m but if you offer £6.50 you're valuing the business at nearly £2bn,' said Tracy.

'Can we afford to pay that much? What's the business worth, Clem?'

'If you're talking about intrinsic worth, our latest figures suggest a value of £2.1bn. If you deduct the debt of £400m, that leaves a residual value of £1.7bn. That's what its worth but we can't generate that amount of cash internally to buy back the shares.'

'So we have a shortfall. What if we sold Camelot General, and our US life company?. That should fetch around £1.8bn in cash,' I said.

'But you'd have to pay tax on the profits.'

'Yes but thanks to Tracy, we're carrying massive tax losses on Camelot Estates which we sold not long ago. That should cover the taxable profits on the other two,' I said.

'After repaying the debt, that'll leave us £1.4bn cash and the worth of the group would rise to £2.1bn,' said Clem.

'Actually I don't see why we should buy back the shares. Let's give them back £1bn in cash as a special dividend, leaving us a buffer of £400m,' I said. 'We'll simplify our operation to a purely UK based life insurance company.'

The proposed changes to Camelot were implemented by the year end. I had used the opportunity to push the concept, not of the Chosen People but of the Caring Society. It aroused as much enthusiasm as Tony Blair's the Third Way. Gareth Evan had warned me that trying to find a catchphrase that appeals to all will end up in effect appealing to no one in particular.

Three Year Later: 2001

Whilst others were ushering the new millennium in on 31.12.1999, I was savouring the last year of the previous one. Ellen saw the logic of my argument but saw no advantage in marching out of step.

'If the whole world is wrong and you are right then the terms needed redefinition.'

I would have none of it, if there was a contest between truth and courting popularity, truth would always win, in my book. However these arguments were indulgences of the slothful. Before the year was out I had to grieve the loss of my parents. Mum died in her sleep and Dad, suffering from the grieving partner syndrome, followed her within six weeks. They were buried in the same plot

When Mum died, Ellen and I went to Lahore to console Dad and stayed with him four weeks and so missed his death as well. I had to go back to supervise the execution of his will.

***

As the year began, one issue exercised my mind and it wasn't Camelot's financial position. Financially it was very strong. In 1999 I had persuaded the Board to take a huge gamble and switch out of equities into bonds. The subsequent fall in long term interest rates vindicated that gamble and at the same time caught out our competitors. However another of my ideas had become my albatross. The concept of mentoring had become hugely successful but with unintended consequences.

There was no doubt that we had tapped into a latent need. The customers wanted it, the media lauded it, and even the Government stood up and took notice. Towards the end of 2000 I was unofficially asked:

'Hypothetically, if you were offered a knighthood would you accept it?'

I replied that I would decline it.

There were two problems with mentoring as it had evolved. People were treating it as another form of Citizen's Advice Bureau. So it wasn't leading to the sale of additional insurance policies. That was a serious problem as Camelot was an insurance company not the Salvation Army. Such customers as were coming to Camelot and buying policies were those who required care and attention and were therefore expensive to service. So Camelot's products were in danger of becoming bad value for money as compared to other companies that did not provide the same degree of service. Unwittingly, we had recreated the old home service sales force associated with the Prudential. The difference was that those products had expense margins of 30-40% whereas modern day products could not withstand more than 5% without incurring the wrath of consumer journalists. So Camelot was losing money on its sales.

More worrying was the finding that the mentoring service far from being socially cohesive was actually divisive. There were some conurbations of policyholders, around Luton, Birmingham, East London, Bradford, Manchester, Leeds and Glasgow where the mentors turned out to be preaching Islamic fundamentalism to willing audiences. I went incognito to attend one of the meetings. The preaching was muted and the sermon had me alarmed. Superficially didactic, I realised that it could be a coded call to arms against an unknown enemy.

I decided to quietly drop the mentor service but found myself trapped. The Government, keen to offload as much responsibility as possible to the private sector, lauded Camelot and its Chief Executive for its social concern. I was offered a position as Minister for Socially Responsible Business. It was very flattering and the advice of Ted MacAfee was to take it. I didn't want it and this was reinforced by strong pressure from Ellen to turn it down.

I turned down the cabinet role saying, 'I can do more good outside the cabinet.'

I then said that I'd roll out the mentoring service more widely to include giving wider financial advice but it was best done by spinning it off as a separate entity, possibly expanded to take over the current Citizen's Advice Bureau. This suggestion met with warm support from the Government until they read my rider; that the funding had to come from them. There the idea foundered. Early in June, my last month in office, I disbanded the mentoring service with immediate effect.

Ellen was relieved. She did not want me to be embroiled in it and be forced to carry on beyond my end date in June. She had handed in her notice so as to be free of MI5 by the end of June.

First of July arrived. I was relaxed but Ellen could not quite switch off. When asked what was bugging her, she said, 'Ishtak and Jalal are hatching something counter-intuitive and the Foreign Office is either being duped or playing a game of double bluff. I don't know which.'

'Not your problem any more.'

We took an extended holiday round the world. Australia, New Zealand, the Rockies, London, yes we were tourists in London and finally Europe. Early in September, having just returned from Cologne, we were unwinding in the lounge in the afternoon in front of the television. The BBC news channel was on but we weren't really watching it. Suddenly it appeared that the channel had switched spontaneously. The screen was showing images of planes crashing into a tower building, incandescent flames, debris and chaos. Both instinctively turned round and watched. I was expecting Arnold Schwarzenegger or Bruce Willis or Sylvester Stallone to make an appearance in the nick of time but no.

'Hell, this is real,' exclaimed an astonished Ellen. I watched transfixed by images of fact imitating fiction. Within a matter of hours Al Qaeda had claimed credit.

'So they've failed,' said Ellen.

'Who's failed? Hang on, did you know about this?'

'Of course I didn't. I doubt if anyone in MI5 did.'

'So, who's failed?'

Ellen looked at me, then made a movement with her hands and lips as if she was about to say something, but clearly thought the better of it, as she said nothing.

'So who's failed?' I asked again.

'It's classified. I'll let you know in due course. I'll publish my memoirs in 2014.'

'I can't wait.'

'I'll tell you one thing though. Ishtak and Jalal are blood relatives. Work that one out.'

Acknowledgments & Disclaimers

My daughter Deena encouraged me to stick to my normal writing style and son Zamin made some pithy but helpful comments on the first chapter. My wife Kadeeja's scepticism acted as motivation. Thank you, family.

I'd also like to thank Helen White's Creative Writing Group of Cobham, Surrey, Hilary Johnson's Authors Advisory Service, the Headless Chickens Writing Group of Cobham Surrey and several friends who have provided candid and constructive criticism of this and other works. To single out some might upset others but I must especially thank Jenny McNulty, David Holland, Alan Lewell, John Treneman, Steve Little and Ian Clark. Finally four friends, Brian Dawson, Jeff Medlock, David Purchase and Bill Scanlan, actuaries all, cast a professional eye on the storyline.

Practically all the case studies of claims are based upon real life examples but the names and places and other details are fictitious.

A couple of years ago there was a story circulating in the city that the Chief Executive of an unnamed FTSE-100 company had an improper relationship with his head of HR. Apparently it created alarm in many boardrooms. 'Has our gaffer been found out? Should we ask him to come clean?' The CEO of one major insurance company did come clean to his Chairman only to find that he was not the subject of the rumours. I should therefore point out that all the corporate activities post-1985 are imaginary and do not relate to any particular company; certainly not to the two companies in which I held senior positions at that time. Nor are any of the leading characters based upon any real individual. No insurance company in the UK, or any of its directors or employees, as far as I am aware, has ever been accused of money laundering. All the insurance company and estate agency characters are fictional, products of my unbridled imagination.

Finally, although I am an actuary from an Asian background, this is NOT an autobiography and Majid is NOT my alter ego. I chose to write in the first person as the narrative flowed better that way.

www.ingramcontent.com/pod-product-compliance
Lightning Source LLC
Chambersburg PA
CBHW081004280626
47160CB00017B/2823